KU-060-830

a deadly brew

Susanna Gregory

sphere

SPHERE

First published in Great Britain in 1998
by Little, Brown and Company

This edition published by Warner Books in 1999
Reprinted 2001
Reprinted by Time Warner Paperbacks in 2003
Reprinted 2003
Reprinted by Time Warner Books in 2006
Reprinted by Sphere in 2007, 2008, 2009, 2011, 2012

Copyright © Susanna Gregory 1998

The moral right of the author has been asserted.

*All characters and events in this publication, other than those
clearly in the public domain, are fictitious and any resemblance
to real persons, living or dead, is purely coincidental.*

All rights reserved.
No part of this publication may be reproduced, stored in a
retrieval system, or transmitted, in any form or by any means, without
the prior permission in writing of the publisher, nor be otherwise circulated
in any form of binding or cover other than that in which it is published
and without a similar condition including this condition being
imposed on the subsequent purchaser.

A CIP catalogue record for this book
is available from the British Library.

ISBN 978-0-7515-2007-1

Typeset in Baskerville and Omnia by
Palimpsest Book Production Limited, Polmont, Stirlingshire
Printed and bound in Great Britain by
Clays Ltd, St Ives plc

Papers used by Sphere are from well-managed forests
and other responsible sources.

MIX
Paper from
responsible sources
FSC® C104740
www.fsc.org

Sphere
An imprint of
Little, Brown Book Group
100 Victoria Embankment
London EC4Y 0DY

An Hachette UK Company
www.hachette.co.uk

www.littlebrown.co.uk

Susanna Gregory was a police officer in Leeds before taking up an academic career. She has served as an environmental consultant, doing fieldwork with whales, seals and walruses during seventeen field seasons in the polar regions, and has taught comparative anatomy and biological anthropology.

She is the creator of the Thomas Chaloner series of mysteries set in Restoration London as well as the Matthew Bartholomew books, and now lives in Wales with her husband, who is also a writer.

Also by Susanna Gregory

The Matthew Bartholomew Series

A PLAGUE ON BOTH YOUR HOUSES
AN UNHOLY ALLIANCE
A BONE OF CONTENTION
A WICKED DEED
A MASTERLY MURDER
AN ORDER FOR DEATH
A SUMMER OF DISCONTENT
A KILLER IN WINTER
THE HAND OF JUSTICE
THE MARK OF A MURDERER
THE TARNISHED CHALICE
TO KILL OR CURE
THE DEVIL'S DISCIPLES
A VEIN OF DECEIT
THE KILLER OF PILGRIMS
MYSTERY IN THE MINSTER

The Thomas Chaloner Series

CONSPIRACY OF VIOLENCE
BLOOD ON THE STRAND
THE BUTCHER OF SMITHFIELD
THE WESTMINSTER POISONER
A MURDER ON LONDON BRIDGE
THE BODY IN THE THAMES
THE PICCADILLY PLOT

To Angelyn and Ralph

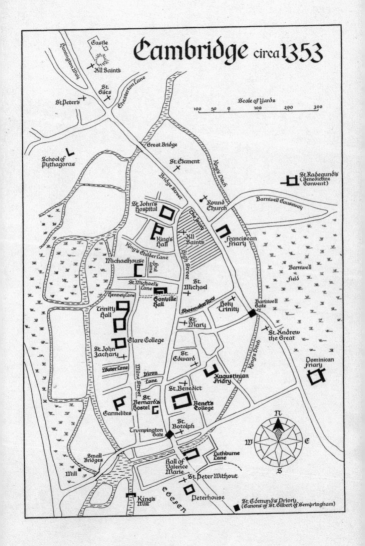

PROLOGUE

October 1352

THE AFTERNOON HAD BEEN GROWING GRADUALLY darker as storm clouds massed overhead. The scholar glanced up at them and realised he would not be able to reach the abbey at Ely, still some nine miles distant, without getting drenched. In his saddle bags, he carried several finely illustrated manuscripts that had been given to him by the grateful parents of successful students; if they became wet, the ink would run and they would be ruined. He cursed softly to himself. The summer and autumn had been unusually dry, so why did the heavens have to choose now, while he was forced to travel, to soak the parched earth with rain? With an irritated sigh, he urged his horse into a trot along the raised causeway that snaked through the desolate marshes. Since the storm would break long before he could hope to claim refuge with the monks at Ely, he resigned himself to the fact that he would have to take shelter at the Franciscan convent of Denny Abbey, the ramshackle rooftops of which he could already see poking above the scrubby Fenland vegetation.

From a dense tangle of bushes at the side of the road, three men watched the scholar's progress impatiently and heaved a sigh of relief when the sound of his horse's hooves finally faded into the distance. They had no wish to be caught unsheltered in the storm that was brewing either.

They clambered down the slippery bank of the causeway to the barge that was moored at the side of the canal, and seized the ropes by which it was drawn along. It was more usual for horses to be used for towing barges, but there was always a risk that the beasts might give away the presence of the boat to travellers on the road. And that would be unfortunate for everyone concerned.

The three men hauled on the ropes, and the barge was on the move, slipping soundlessly along the black, glassy waters of the channel that eventually meandered behind Denny Abbey's walled gardens. They heard voices as the scholar was admitted into the nuns' guesthouse, and then all was silent again except for the gurgle of water under the keel and the occasional sound of dead, dry reeds snapping under their feet as they walked. When the bargemen reached their destination, they coiled the tow ropes and began to unload their cargo – a number of roughly sewn sacks, the contents of which clanked together mysteriously as they were moved.

One of the men, younger than the others and curious, started to untie the cord that fastened the top of one particularly heavy sack. His friends, seeing what he was about to do, leapt forward to stop him.

'Fool! We were told to deliver the sacks without asking questions. They will kill us if they think we have been prying into their business!'

The young man scowled angrily. 'If the cargo is so valuable, why did you charge them so little to bring it here? And why did you agree to deliver it at all if you are so frightened of them?'

'Because it was impossible to refuse once asked,' said the other, lowering his voice, and glancing around him uneasily, 'but when we have finished here, we will lie low for a while to make sure we are not hired for this again.'

The younger man treated his friends to a look of scorn for their timidity and returned to the heavy labour of removing the sacks from the barge to their hiding place. After a moment, the other two followed suit, straining and sweating under the weight of the irregularly shaped bundles.

Their voices, however, had carried across the otherwise silent Fens. Had they looked behind them, they would have seen the veiled head of a nun observing them from one of the upper windows of the convent. She stood unmoving, watching them struggle with their bundles until, with evident relief and a few final furtive glances around them, they finished and slipped away as silently as they had arrived. Within moments, the first drops of rain began to fall, lightly at first, but then harder until the lonely marshes were enveloped in a misty white pall as far as the eye could see. The nun tapped a forefinger on the windowsill thoughtfully before going to pay her respects to the scholar waiting in the guesthouse.

December 1352

The thief pressed back into the shadows as the soldiers of the night watch passed so close he could have touched them. He grinned to himself, guessing that they were more interested in returning to the fire in the guardroom than in checking the dark streets and alleyways for furtive figures who were breaking the curfew. Once the guards' footsteps had echoed into silence, the thief continued his meticulous examination of the windows and doors of houses, hunting for a faulty lock that would let him inside. Just as he was beginning to despair, he discovered that a hatch leading to a cellar had been carelessly left open.

The thief looked both ways before easing himself through the hatch and pulling it closed behind him. The cellar was pitch black, but this did not deter the thief: he was used to working under difficult conditions. He groped his way around damp walls and a low ceiling with flaking plaster but, to his disappointment, found the cellar contained nothing he could steal to sell in the taverns. There were a few empty wooden boxes, all of them soft and rotten with mould, but the room smelt wet and stale and had evidently been disused and forgotten for decades. He flapped dispiritedly at a cobweb that brushed across his face and decided to try for richer pickings elsewhere.

As he began to make his way towards the door, his foot bumped against something hard. He crouched down, hands extended to assess whether it was something worth taking. A crate of wine! His fingers traced the smooth glass outline of bottles that the moist air of the cellar had rendered damp and cold. They had probably been there for years and their contents would doubtless be sour by now. But, reasoned the thief, whoever bought them from him in the Brazen George would not know that until they had paid, and by then he would be long gone. Deftly, he began packing the bottles into the sack he carried over his shoulder, wrapping each one in the rotting straw that littered the floor so they would not clank together and betray his whereabouts to the night watch.

Six bottles were wrapped and stowed away when the thief became aware that the hatch to the cellar was opening and someone else was entering. Frightened, he pulled the drawstrings of his bag tight and hefted it over his shoulder, abandoning the remaining half a dozen bottles. He stood up carefully and moved back among the crates, desperately hoping that the second intruder had not brought a lamp with him. The thief was small, quick and expert at gaining access to other people's property, but he abhorred fighting and violence, and avoided any kind of confrontation with his victims if he could. Thus, when the second man moved silently into the centre of the room, the thief nimbly side-stepped him in the inky darkness and was out into the night as fast as his legs could carry him.

He darted towards the river and disappeared into the fringe of reeds that choked the banks, breathing heavily. Moments passed and there was no sound of pursuit: he was safe. He heaved a shuddering sigh of relief and lowered the sack of bottles to the ground next to him while he considered his next move. He could sell the wine for enough to keep him in bread for a week if he told people it was finest claret and charged a penny a bottle. He raised an eyebrow and allowed himself a grin of satisfaction: perhaps it had not been such a bad night after all.

Back in the cellar, the other man had lit a candle and was staring down at the half-empty wine box with a mixture of horror and fury. A rat slithered across the floor behind him and he spun round, a knife appearing in his hand as though by magic. He relaxed when he saw the rodent's tail disappear behind the pile of crates, but did not sheath his dagger. He rubbed his chin with a hand that shook, and wondered who had stolen the wine and why. A glimmer of a smile flickered across the man's harsh features: whoever it was would be in for an unpleasant shock when the bottles were opened. The certain knowledge that the crime would not go unavenged helped to counterbalance the intense and impotent anger he felt towards the thief.

ChAPTER 1

Cambridge, late January 1353

RAIN SLANTED ACROSS MICHAELHOUSE'S YARD IN A steady hiss, drumming on the wooden roof of the stable and staining the College's honey-coloured stone walls a deep amber. The cat, its fur soaked into black spikes, sat morosely under the meagre shelter of a leafless tree and watched a scholar clad in the ceremonial red robes of a University doctor splash his way across the muddy yard. The scholar paused for a moment to glance up at the dull grey sky before disappearing through one of the doorways that led to the rooms where the students and their masters lived.

'We will be late,' he warned, looking round the door of Brother Michael's chamber and seeing that the monk was not yet ready to leave. Michael made no reply and stood in front of a strategically placed silver plate plastering his thin, light brown hair into place with dabs of water. This performed to his satisfaction, he turned his attention to his newly purchased Benedictine habit, brushing away imaginary dust with the head of a teasel.

Matthew Bartholomew sighed impatiently, striding across the room to lean out of the window. 'The bell has already stopped ringing.'

Michael waved a dismissive hand and continued with his primping. 'There is no point in attending these festivities if we do not look our best, Matt,' he said, taking up an ornate cross of gold and hanging it round his neck, careful not to disturb his immaculate hair.

'It is not you being installed as Master of the Hall of Valence Marie, Brother,' Bartholomew pointed out. He gazed across Michaelhouse's yard at the undergraduates hurrying from their lectures to the midday meal. 'In fact, I do not understand why we should be there at all. I still have not finished Galen's *Prognostica* with my third-year students, there is an outbreak of sickness among the river people, and I want to work on my treatise on fevers. This installation is a distraction I could do without.'

Michael gave an exasperated shake of his head. 'You think of nothing but your work these days,' he chided. 'This grand installation will be good for you. You can see all the great and powerful of the University gathered together under one roof and watch the games being played.'

'Over the past five years I have seen enough of the University's games to last me a lifetime,' said Bartholomew vehemently. 'I want only to teach my students and attend my patients.'

Michael's green eyes gleamed. He thrived on the intrigues and plots that were as much a part of University life as teaching, and loved nothing more than to attend an event like the installation of the new Master of the Hall of Valence Marie, where he could watch alliances being formed and plans being hatched to avenge ancient grievances. As well as being a Fellow of Michaelhouse, Michael was Senior Proctor, a position that meant he was well-placed to observe – and meddle in – the murky affairs of the University and its scheming scholars.

'Besides,' the monk said briskly, ignoring Bartholomew's grumbling and turning his head this way and that as he studied his reflection in the plate, 'all Fellows of Michaelhouse were personally invited by the Master-Elect. It would be ungracious to decline, especially if the reason is that you prefer teaching and seeing patients.'

He took a thick winter cloak from a hook on the wall and draped it over his shoulders, fiddling with it until he was sure the expensive cloth fell in even folds before carefully lifting the hood over his head. Then he stepped over to the plate once more and admired the finished product, adjusting a strand of hair here and a fold of his habit there. He glimpsed his friend's morose expression as he continued to stare out of the window and tapped him lightly on the shoulder.

'Forget your students, Matt. Forget your patients, too. Enjoy yourself for once!'

'With a group of men whose idea of fun is an all-night debate on the efficacy of Ockham's Razor?' asked Bartholomew gloomily. 'Or, worse still, with those of our colleagues who will drink the new Master's free wine until they are sick, violent or insensible?'

'You are in a miserable mood today,' said Michael, amused. 'But you will make us late by keeping me here chattering. Come on, hurry up. We do not want to arrive last.'

Glumly, Bartholomew followed Michael down the wooden stairs and out into the yard, a morass of churned mud from the rain that had fallen almost incessantly since Christmas. The cat, seeing the door had been left open, tried in vain to reach it without getting its feet wet. Despite his ill humour, the physician could not help smiling when he noted a similarity between the cat's dainty, careful footsteps and those of Michael, who held his habit clear of the ground with thumbs and forefingers. The monk cursed and swore at the brown slime that oozed over his carefully polished sandals in language that belied his contemplative vocation.

'I have never seen such rain,' he muttered. 'We are a cursed race. First came the pestilence that claimed so many lives; then there was the drought of last summer when we baked under a sun that turned the whole country brown; and now we have endless rain. The crops will rot in the fields and there will be an even greater shortage of bread than there is now. You mark my words.'

'Rain in winter should not be a problem,' said Bartholomew, splashing along beside Michael, oblivious to the mud. He had dressed in his best scarlet robe when he had finished teaching – around ten o'clock that Saturday morning – but had been called out to tend to a patient with a winter fever. His feet were already wet inside his boots and avoiding puddles would make little difference to him now. 'It is summer rain that rots the crops in the fields.'

Michael shot him a disbelieving glance and continued with his litany of complaints. 'This rain is worse than snow. The roof leaks in my room and I can barely sleep for the noise of drips falling into the bucket.'

Bartholomew recalled pulling the bed-covers over his ears the night before in a vain effort to muffle the sound of Michael's snores thundering from the room above his, and treated the monk's words with scepticism.

'And the dampness is unbearable. All my bones ache with it,' Michael added, looking resentfully up to a lead-grey sky that made the noon light seem like late afternoon.

Bartholomew turned to him in concern. 'Do they? Do you need a physic? I have a poultice that, if applied daily, can ease soreness in the joints.'

Michael sighed and gave a wry grin. 'I am not so bad that I need a physic. It is nothing a dry blanket and a doze by a fire would not cure. But this foul weather must be hard on your older patients.'

Bartholomew nodded. 'A number of them are complaining about painful joints. But it is this winter fever that worries me. I have never seen anything quite like it.'

'It is not like the Death, then?' asked Michael, picking his way cautiously around a gigantic puddle that shivered and rippled as the rain pattered into it.

Bartholomew shuddered. 'No, thank God!' Even after five years, Bartholomew had not forgotten his helplessness in the face of the plague that had defied all treatment and seemed to strike at random, carrying off at least a third of the population of Cambridge and completely annihilating the people who lived in the impoverished little settlement near the castle, where cramped and filthy conditions seemed to hasten the disease's relentless progress.

They reached Michaelhouse's great gates and unlatched the wicket door. Michael stepped into the lane and rinsed the mud off his feet in a puddle of cleanish water, wincing at its coldness. They walked up the lane and then along the High Street towards the Hall of Valence Marie. For a while, they were forced to abandon conversation and concentrate on avoiding the deep potholes that lurked unseen under the flooded surface of the road.

They passed St Michael's Church, short, squat and an even darker grey than usual with the rain blackening its walls, and then St Mary's with its creamy yellow stone and delicate traceried windows. The houses between them looked shabby in the wet, and the resin from their timbers leeched out to ooze in dirty brown trails down their whitewashed walls.

The Hall of Valence Marie, where Bartholomew and Michael were to attend the ceremonies for the installation of its new Master, stood just outside the town boundary near the Trumpington Gate. They were about to pass through it when a young man tore up to them, gasping for breath, his eyes wild and his clothes dishevelled.

'Brother Armel is dying! It was not what we intended! You must believe me!' He took a handful of Michael's best cloak and tried to haul him back towards the town. Michael disengaged himself firmly, resentful at being man-handled after he had taken so much trouble with his appearance.

'What are you shouting about?' he demanded crossly, trying to brush the creases out of his sleeve. 'Who is Brother Armel and what must I believe?'

The boy gulped for breath, clenching and unclenching

his hands and clearly forcing himself to resist the urge to grab at Michael again in his agitation.

'It will be quicker if you speak rationally,' said Bartholomew gently, taking pity on the frantic student. 'Tell us what has happened. Is someone ill? Do you need a physician?'

The young man nodded and then shook his head. He took a deep breath, screwed his eyes tightly shut and fought to gain control of himself. 'We – I and the other students – were drinking in the Brazen George,' he began, referring to a tavern near St Mary's Church. Michael gave him an admonishing stare. Students were not allowed in the town's taverns, chiefly because the University did not want bands of drunken undergraduates meeting gangs of equally intoxicated townspeople: the relationship between University and town was uneasy at best, violent at worst, and it took very little to spark off fights that resulted in bloodshed on both sides.

The young man continued. 'A man sold us wine. We took it home and Armel drank from the bottle. Then he fell into a swoon. He was poisoned! You must come!'

The lad's story was still far from clear, but Bartholomew guessed they would prise no more sense from him until one of them went to see Brother Armel. It occurred to him that not even the sensibilities of the Master-Elect of the Hall of Valence Marie could be offended if his excuse for being absent was that he was dealing with a medical emergency. He seized the opportunity with sudden enthusiasm.

'You go to the ceremony,' he said to Michael. 'I will see Brother Armel.'

'But he needs you both,' pleaded the student, his hands furiously twisting the buckle on his belt to avoid laying hands on the august personage of the University's Senior Proctor a second time. 'He needs last rites and a physician.' His self-control finally broke and he grasped Bartholomew's cloak to haul him back up the High Street, evidently assuming Michael would follow.

'Then you need a priest, not a monk,' called Michael, standing firm. 'One of the Gilbertines will oblige, or the Carmelites just across the road. I have pressing business to attend.'

'You can give last rites!' said the student accusingly, turning back to him without relinquishing his hold on Bartholomew. 'You did so during the Death – Father Yvo told us how you gave last rites to his predecessor. And you have heard my confessions before now!'

The student was right. While friars lived and worked among the people, monks led contemplative lives in the cloister and were not authorised to hear confessions or give last rites. But Michael had been granted special dispensation by his Bishop so that he might attend the needs of the small number of Benedictines enrolled at the University. During the plague, he had been tireless in his spiritual duties and had trudged around the town with Bartholomew tending the hopeless cases. These days, however, he seldom drew on his authority, preferring to advance the Benedictines' earthly interests rather than their spiritual ones.

'Please!' cried the student, desperation making his voice crack. 'We need the Senior Proctor *and* a physician. Armel has been murdered!'

How poor Armel had gone so suddenly from a swoon to being a murder victim was unclear, but Bartholomew allowed himself to be led back along the High Street by the frightened student. Michael followed reluctantly, muttering bitterly about missing the installation ceremony to which he had been so looking forward. Bartholomew did not for an instant imagine they would find Brother Armel murdered, nor even poisoned. The student who tugged and heaved at his cloak to make him hurry was very young – no more than fifteen years old at the most – and Bartholomew was sure he would not be able to tell a drunken stupor from an unconsciousness brought on by poison. He wondered how much of the installation he might legitimately escape, although a backward glance at Michael's black scowl suggested the answer would be very little if the monk had any say in the matter.

'Which hostel do you live in?' Bartholomew asked, more to soothe the student's increasing agitation than to solicit information.

'Bernard's,' said the student, hauling harder still as they drew closer to the dirty brown façade of St Bernard's Hostel. 'My name is Xavier.'

'Bernard's is a Franciscan institution,' said Bartholomew, puzzled, 'so why are you not wearing your friar's habit?'

Xavier gave him a look of disbelief. 'We could not go to the Brazen George wearing our habits! The landlord would know we were students and would refuse to serve us.'

Before Bartholomew could comment further, he was propelled into the building. A large room that opened directly off the street was occupied by six students, all arguing among themselves in apprehensive whispers. None of them wore either scholars' tabards or the robes of Franciscan novices, and Bartholomew imagined the entire hostel must have been involved in the illicit trip to the tavern.

As they entered, the students parted to reveal someone lying on the floor with his eyes closed. Bartholomew knelt to examine him while Michael snapped questions at the others.

'Where is Father Yvo? He is Principal here, is he not?'

Miserably the students nodded, some hanging their heads and none able to meet the stern visage Michael reserved for dealing with recalcitrant undergraduates.

'He is at the installation, but Brother Henry has gone to fetch him home,' said Xavier. 'I came to find you. I was lucky to catch you before you reached Valence Marie.'

Michael's grimace suggested he did not consider the encounter to be a fortuitous one. 'I suppose you took advantage of Father Yvo's absence to go visiting taverns?' he surmised, eyeing the students' odd assortment of secular clothes with proctorly disapproval.

They nodded again, exchanging guilty glances and shuffling their feet uncomfortably.

'Well, Brother Xavier,' said Michael, eyeing the sheepish undergraduates with weary reproach. 'Now you have me here, tell me what happened properly.'

Xavier took a deep breath, less anxious now that Michael had assumed control of the situation. 'We have all worked really hard this term and yesterday the last of us passed our disputations. It seemed as though we were being given a perfect opportunity to celebrate – with Father Yvo at the installation along with all the other Masters, Principals, and Fellows. And Proctors,' he added, giving Michael a sidelong glance. 'We meant no harm – just a tankard or two of ale and we would have been home. None of us intended to become drunk.' This statement was confirmed vehemently by a chorus of agreement from the others. 'Then a man offered to sell us some wine. He was asking a very reasonable price for claret from France and we thought we could bring it here and continue our celebrations more discreetly. We bought three bottles and came home.'

'What did this man look like?' asked Michael, reflecting with a distinct lack of enthusiasm on all the petty thieves he knew who might approach a gaggle of gullible undergraduates and sell them inferior wine under the pretence that it was fine quality stuff from abroad. He supposed the culprit would be well away by now, doubtless enjoying the congratulations of his cronies for having so easily cheated members of the University the townspeople so despised.

Xavier looked to his friends for help. 'Not tall. He had a brown beard.'

'He wore a blue tunic,' put in a student with freckles and red hair, who looked about fourteen.

'And his hose were undyed homespun,' put in another. 'Like these.' He plucked at the rough material of his leggings and looked expectantly at Michael, as if the monk should immediately know the identity of the wine-seller from his meagre scrap of information.

'He had brown eyes . . .' added the red-haired student uncertainly.

'No, he had blue eyes,' said Xavier, frowning as he tried to remember. 'Well, a sort of blue-grey. And there was something wrong with the skin on his hands.'

'And what happened after you brought your ill-gotten gains back here?' the monk asked, looking from one to the other with eyebrows raised in disapprobation.

'Brother Armel was carrying one of the bottles. When we arrived . . .'

Xavier faltered, gazing down at his feet, and the red-haired student took up the story. 'Brother Armel opened his bottle, took a great swig and . . .'

'And what?' prompted Michael.

As one, the novice Franciscans looked to where Armel lay on the floor. Xavier gave a sudden sob, loud in the otherwise silent room.

'He staggered for a moment,' continued the red-haired student unsteadily. 'Then he grabbed at his throat and fell to the floor. We thought he was playing the fool, so we ignored him at first. Then we tried to rouse him, but it did no good.' He swallowed hard. 'Brother Henry said he would fetch Father Yvo, but Xavier said we needed the Proctors because Armel had been . . .'

'Poisoned,' finished Xavier in a whisper, as the red-haired student failed to utter the dreaded word. One or two of the novices crossed themselves and all eyes were, once again, fixed on the prone figure on the floor. Xavier choked back another sob and continued with his tale. 'I ran to fetch Father Philius, the Master of Medicine at Gonville Hall, but he is sick himself and could not come. Then I went to look for you.'

Michael pursed his lips at the sorry tale and looked down to where Bartholomew still knelt next to Armel. 'Well? Is

Armel's sudden fainting a case of too much ale and too few wits, like the rest of these silly boys?'

Bartholomew shook his head, and met his friend's gaze sombrely. 'Not at all, Brother. Xavier's suspicions seem to have been correct: Armel has been poisoned.'

Michael's jaw dropped. 'You mean he is dead?' he asked in a whisper. The students hurriedly crossed themselves again and one or two dropped to their knees to begin intoning prayers for the dying in uncertain voices.

Bartholomew nodded helplessly and stood. There was nothing more he could do for Armel. The young man needed a priest to give him last rites to ensure the safety of his soul for whatever journey it was about to take.

Michael pulled himself together, dispatched Xavier to fetch the chrism he was sure Father Yvo would have and began to recite the office for the dead. Bartholomew withdrew to the far side of the room and watched. When Xavier returned with the little bottle of holy oil, Michael used it to trace a cross on Armel's forehead, mouth, hands and feet. Bartholomew had seen Michael perform last rites many times when the plague had ravaged the town, and the monk's ministrations had been of far more comfort to the victims than Bartholomew's desperate, hopeless treatments. Watching Michael kneeling next to a dead youngster brought back memories that made Bartholomew's blood run cold. He looked away.

As Michael finished and clambered inelegantly to his feet, Father Yvo, dragged from the celebrations at Valence Marie, entered the room at a run. He gazed at Armel in horror and his eyes widened in shock as he heard Michael's brief summary of what had happened.

He swung round to Bartholomew. 'You are a physician! Can you do nothing to help him? Perhaps we can make him drink water to wash the poisons out. Perhaps if we stood him up and made him walk—'

Bartholomew spread his hands helplessly. 'He was beyond all earthly help when I arrived, Father. The poison had settled too far into his body for me to do anything to save him. I am sorry.'

'Where is this wine he drank?' asked Michael of the watching novices. Xavier presented a slender, smoked-glass bottle, which the monk took from him warily. He inspected it minutely, lifting it to the light to see if he could detect any residues, and then sniffed cautiously at it. Bartholomew moved towards him quickly, afraid that he might inhale noxious fumes, but Michael shook his head to indicate that he could detect nothing. Meanwhile, Yvo had gathered his novices around him and had them kneeling in a circle around the dead Armel.

'There is nothing more we can do here,' Michael whispered to Bartholomew, watching them pray. 'I will return tomorrow when they are less shocked and try to gain a better description of this wine-seller. Meanwhile, I am sure my beadles will be delighted with the task of visiting the taverns to see if they can find a man hawking illicit claret.'

Bartholomew took the bottle from him and wrapped it in his hat. 'From what the students say, Armel took only a single mouthful of this and yet it affected him immediately. The poison must be very strong.' He beckoned Xavier away from his prayers, collected the two unopened bottles and instructed the tearful student to tell everyone to wash their hands lest some dangerous residue remain. This done, Bartholomew and Michael took their leave.

Michael stepped outside with evident relief and began to head back along the High Street towards the Hall of Valence Marie. The rain still fell and the day seemed more dismal than ever. 'What a ghastly business,' he said with a shudder. 'Poor Father Yvo! He runs a respectable hostel – unlike some of the establishments I could mention around here – and he is still not immune to foul play.'

'Foul play,' echoed Bartholomew thoughtfully. 'I hope

this does not herald the beginning of another sour period between University and town. There are still ill-feelings over those riots of last summer and I would not like to see all that started again.'

'Lord, Matt!' sighed Michael, his baggy, green eyes anxious. 'This could have a devastating impact on town and gown relations. The University will be suspicious of trading with the merchants, and the townspeople will be anticipating a revenge attack at every turn.' He stopped walking and stood still, his mind working quickly. 'You are right in that the atmosphere is still uneasy between the students and the townspeople. It would take very little before we are back to the riots and lootings of August.'

'But we might be jumping to the wrong conclusion,' said Bartholomew, taking Michael's arm to make him continue walking. The rain was blowing straight into the physician's face and he felt chilled to the bone. 'There is always the possibility that this wine-seller did not know his wares were poisoned, or even that he was unaware Xavier and his friends were students – they were not wearing their habits, after all.'

'Come on, Matt,' said Michael tiredly. 'Of course he knew! You recognised Xavier immediately as a student, even in secular clothes, and so would any intelligent person. And what kind of man does not know that the wine he sold to a handful of credulous lads – in a tavern, mind you, under the very nose of the man whose trade he is stealing – is poisoned?'

'One who perhaps bought the wine from someone else?' mused Bartholomew.

Michael considered for a moment and then dismissed the idea. 'No, that is too contrived. Why would someone provide an innocent man with poisoned wine to sell? No, Matt. You were right with your first guess – that someone is aiming to foul the relationship between University and town. But what about this poison in the wine? Can you tell me anything about it, other than that it was horribly powerful?'

Bartholomew shook his head. 'All I can say is that it did not kill Armel instantly, but rendered him unconscious and blistered his lips.'

They walked towards the Hall of Valence Marie, each lost in his own thoughts. Michael fretted over the possibility that his beloved University was once more to be the victim of the townspeople's ire, while Bartholomew tried to fight away the feelings of helpless inadequacy he always experienced when he lost a patient.

Despite the rain, the High Street thronged with people. Liveried apprentices scampered this way and that as they ran their masters' errands, while carts with heavy wooden wheels ferried goods to and from the Market Square and the river barges moored at the wharves. Here and there, strangers to the town gawked at the sumptuous buildings that lined the town's main thoroughfare – such as the wealthy new College of Corpus Christi and the Blessed Virgin, founded just the previous year, with its mullioned windows and carved pediments; the sumptuous guildhouses with their coats of arms emblazoned over their doors; and the homes of the merchants with their stained-glass windows and decorative plaster. Few of them paid much attention to the untidy houses of Cambridge's less wealthy inhabitants that were crammed in the spaces between them, noticeable only because their badly built walls and sagging roofs seemed to defy gravity.

Street vendors proclaimed the virtues of their wares in ringing voices, vying with each other and with the constant clatter of horses' hooves and the thunder of wagons rumbling past. A small white dog, showing patches of black and pink skin through its filthy coat, yapped and worried at a small herd of sheep that was being driven to the slaughterhouse, so that frightened bleats added another tenor to the general cacophony.

They reached the Trumpington Gate, and elbowed their

way through the crowd, squeezing past an indignant pardoner who was being denied access to the town for some spurious reason known only to the sergeant in charge of the guards. The sergeant waved cheerfully at Bartholomew, who had once set his broken leg, and then rearranged his face into a black scowl as he turned his attention back to the trader who was being refused admittance. Michael nodded approvingly as the sergeant sent the man packing: he did not like pardoners.

Once outside the gate, it grew quieter. The buildings gradually petered out to give way to narrow strips of fields tilled by the villagers who lived on the manor of Sir Roger de Panton. Opposite, water meadows rolled down to the River Cam, a peaceful swath of grass lined with trees, where people grazed their cattle – or did before it had become swamped and boggy from the rain.

Bartholomew stopped walking and looked up at the Hall of Valence Marie looming in front of him. 'The last thing I feel like doing now is celebrating an installation.'

'Me too,' said Michael, pulling the hood of his black cloak further over his head against the chill. 'I was looking forward to this, but giving last rites to a child has blunted my desire to enjoy myself.'

They stood in silence for a moment as they looked up at the powerful walls of the young College. It was a splendid building, comprising four ranges around a central courtyard, protected by powerful walls and a squat gatehouse tower. Founded only six years before, it enjoyed the patronage of the wealthy Countess of Pembroke, who ensured her College had the best architects and building materials money could buy.

'So why did you decide not to accept the position of Master of Valence Marie when it was offered to you last year?' asked Bartholomew, changing the subject from the poisoned wine but still making no move to enter. 'You would have made them a fine Master.'

Michael looked sly. 'I felt I was too young for such a position,' he replied, bending down to brush at the mud on his habit.

'Nonsense, Brother,' said Bartholomew mildly. 'What was your real reason?'

Michael gave a short bark of laughter and slapped his friend on the back. 'You know me too well. Perhaps far too well for a man destined for great things.'

'I assume you mean you, not me?' asked Bartholomew, smiling an absent greeting to one of his patients, who waved before disappearing down one of the alleyways that led to the huddle of shacks near the King's Mill.

Michael drew himself up to his full height. He had grown fatter during the last few months, despite his endless complaints about the paucity and poor quality of food since the plague, and his bulk and height made him a formidable size. 'I spoke at length with my Lord the Bishop about that,' he said, referring to Thomas de Lisle, the churchman who had jurisdiction over the See of Ely and the University of Cambridge within it. 'He intimated my career would be better served by my remaining Senior Proctor.'

'And how might chasing errant students in taverns in the dead of night help your career, rather than being Master of a new and wealthy College?' asked Bartholomew with raised eyebrows. He was being unfair, he knew. There was more to Michael's duties than policing the undergraduates, although keeping the rowdy, undisciplined students out of fights with the townspeople was vital to the smooth running of the town. Michael had amassed considerable power as the University's Senior Proctor, and recently had started to undertake duties usually performed by the Chancellor himself – much to the offended disapproval of the Vice-Chancellor, who considered such duties should have been delegated to him.

'I will be of more use to the Bishop while my attentions are not divided between his interests and those of a College,' said Michael, favouring Bartholomew with a superior look. 'He promised to look to my advancement when the time is right.'

'And you trust him?' asked Bartholomew dubiously. Bartholomew's own experiences with the Bishop had taught him that although the Bishop was the spiritual leader of a large part of East Anglia, he had not attained his exalted position by being pleasant, honest and reliable. Bartholomew would not have trusted any promise made by the Bishop any more than he would one made by the Chancellor.

'I do,' said Michael firmly. 'He needs me every bit as much as I need him. Since the Death, when he lost half his monks, he has been desperately short of intelligent, able men he can trust with his business. He cannot afford to lose someone like me.'

'Modestly put, Brother,' said Bartholomew drily. 'Has he promised to make you Chancellor one day? Or is it his own position you crave?'

'Either would do nicely, Matt,' said Michael comfortably. He looked again at the clean yellow-white stone of Valence Marie. 'This is a fine building,' he said, almost wistfully.

Bartholomew agreed. 'I heard that the election of Thomas Bingham as its new Master – after you declined the honour – was hotly contested,' he said. 'It all but tore the College in half.'

Michael's eyes glittered as he recalled the intrigues and rumours that had abounded during the race to elect Valence Marie's new Master. The previous incumbent had been sent to York in disgrace after some unsavoury business involving a fraudulent relic the previous year, and his unexpected departure – as much a shock to him as to his College – had thrown the Fellowship into disarray.

'I heard that considerable sums of money changed hands before Bingham finally secured the majority of votes,' said Michael somewhat gleefully. 'Rumour has it that James Grene, his rival, is bitterly resentful.'

'It will not be easy for Bingham to rule Valence Marie if it is so divided,' said Bartholomew, wondering whether such a feat would be even remotely possible given the plotting and intrigues that festered and bubbled, even when a College or hostel was in a state of relative harmony, let alone when there was a serious division among members.

'Quite,' said Michael smugly. 'Another reason for declining the Chancellor's generous offer to have Valence Marie handed to me on a plate – neither Grene nor Bingham would have allowed me to run the College without fighting me at every turn, because they would have deeply resented my appointment. And on top of their ambitions, Valence Marie remains in turmoil over the bones Thorpe found last year. Some of the Fellows still think that the hand he dredged from the King's Ditch was that of a saint.'

'Thorpe is in no position to benefit from their loyalty,' said Bartholomew, thinking of how the aloof Master had been transferred to a post at an obscure grammar school to punish him for his foolish belief in the bones' authenticity. The new post had been 'offered' by the King himself, leaving Thorpe no choice but to pack up his belongings and go.

They stood for a moment longer, thinking about Thorpe and his relic, and then entered Valence Marie through its handsome front gate – Bartholomew with reluctance, Michael with a growing enthusiasm, fired by the discussion of the uncertain, insalubrious world of University politics.

The physician had just handed his soggy cloak and the three bottles of poisoned wine – he could hardly take them with him to the festivities in the hall and then the church, and there was no time to take them to Michaelhouse first – to a curious porter, when a messenger arrived, leaning breathlessly against the doorjamb. He was one of a family of tinkers who lived near the river and whose family Bartholomew had recently treated for winter fever. The tinker's sharp eyes darted everywhere, taking in the elegant tapestries that hung on the walls in the entrance hall and the highly polished brass handles on the doors. Bartholomew wondered if he were sizing it up for a future burglary. Apparently, the porter thought the same, for he bundled the tinker out of the door and demanded to know his business.

'Doctor Bartholomew,' said the tinker, ignoring the porter and addressing the physician. 'You are needed urgently at Master Constantine Mortimer's house. He has been struck down with pains in the stomach and asks that you attend him immediately.'

'But he is not my patient,' said Bartholomew. 'He is in the care of Father Philius. Do you know Philius? He is Master of Medicine at Gonville Hall. You need to contact him, not me.'

'You are far too honest,' said Michael reprovingly. 'Go to Mortimer, man! He is one of the wealthiest merchants in the town and a burgess, too. He will pay you handsomely for making you miss the installation. To the Devil with Philius!'

'I know Philius,' said the tinker. 'But he is unwell himself, and Mistress Mortimer told me to fetch you instead. You had better hurry, because she told me she thought he might be dying.'

'It seems you are destined not to see Master Bingham take his oath of allegiance to Valence Marie, Matt,' said Michael, trying to rub away the spatters of mud that clung around the hem of his fine new habit. He straightened and gave Bartholomew a wink, leaning forward to whisper conspiratorially. 'You can always just come for the food later. That will be the best part anyway. I have been told there will be roast boar!'

Bartholomew did not much mind the summons that took him from the tedious Latin investiture ceremony to attend a patient, grateful for the excuse to escape yet more of what was going to be a lengthy occasion. He retrieved his cloak from the porter, and followed the tinker to Milne Street, where many of the wealthy town burgesses had their homes. Most of them would have been invited to the installation, and Bartholomew was sure that Master Mortimer must be ill indeed to pass up the opportunity of rubbing shoulders with some of the most influential men in the town.

Activity in Milne Street was, as usual, frenetic. Raised voices yelled the prices of this and that, and goods were being carried from the barges moored at the wharves on the river to the great storerooms in the merchants' yards. Bartholomew saw wooden crates filled with clanking bottles from France, while Mortimer's own cellars were being loaded with bulging sacks of flour brought from the arable lands around Lincoln to the north. Among it all, gulls screamed and squabbled for the rubbish along the river banks, and a dog barked furiously at a teetering pile of cloth bales behind which a rat had fled. The rain seemed to have had little effect on trade, and bargemen and apprentices alike seemed oblivious to their dripping hoods and sodden clothes.

When Bartholomew looked behind him for the tinker, he had disappeared, and the physician wondered with irritation whether one of his students was playing some kind of practical joke – Master Mortimer the baker was a far cry from the town's poor that Bartholomew usually treated. But as he pondered, glancing around to see if he could detect any watching undergraduates, a woman darted out of Mortimer's house and seized his arm.

'Thank you for coming,' she said. 'My husband says he is dying and Father Philius cannot attend because he has an ague. If you had not come, we might have had to ask Robin of Grantchester!'

Her horrified expression, and the hush in her voice as she uttered the name, bespoke the trepidation many people felt for Cambridge's only surgeon. Unlike physicians, who were University educated, surgeons were mere craftsmen. Robin of Grantchester was an insanitary individual, whose habit of demanding payment before treatment, to avoid the trouble of suing bereaved next of kin in the event of sudden death, did little to inspire confidence in his skills. While the duties of physicians and surgeons overlapped, their techniques and expertise seldom did. Unusually for a physician, Bartholomew regularly performed a number of basic surgical operations, which led him into bitter confrontations, both with his fellow physicians who deplored the use of surgery and with Robin who felt his trade was being poached.

Katherine Mortimer gabbled at him as she led the way through the bakery and up a wide flight of stairs to the living quarters on the upper floor. She was a pleasant woman with a kindly face and sad blue eyes, whom Bartholomew had known for years and liked. In fact, he liked her a good deal more than her husband, whose short temper and brutish behaviour made him generally unpopular with townsfolk and scholars alike.

'All the apprentices are busy unloading the flour,' said Katherine, 'so I had to pay that tinker to act as messenger when Constantine told me he was dying and that I should summon help. I told the tinker not to go to Michaelhouse, but straight to Valence Marie, since all the Fellows of the University will be there today for the celebrations . . . well, not you now, I suppose—'

'How long has your husband been ill?' asked Bartholomew, as soon as he could slip a few words into her almost continuous nervous babble.

'Since mid-morning,' she replied, leading him along an attractive corridor with a floor of polished wood and colourful paintings on the walls. At the end was a large, masculine room containing a massive bed surrounded by curtains of a deep red velvet and several damp, smelly dogs. The room was quiet, yet was filled with people, like that of a dying statesman. Bartholomew looked about him uneasily, uncomfortable at the notion of treating a patient in front of such a large audience. He saw the nursemaid with Mortimer's younger children gathered about her, all regarding him with frightened faces; the household priest knelt in a corner, his lips moving as he spoke soundless prayers; and a huddle of men, clearly Mortimer's foremen and chief bakers, stood near the glazed window holding their hats awkwardly in their hands.

Since no one did anything other than gaze at him expectantly, Bartholomew took the initiative and strode across the room to the curtained bed, wondering whether he had already been called too late and the baker was already dead. His footsteps clattered on the wooden floor, sounding even louder in the silent room. He drew the thick material back, and peered inside.

Master Constantine Mortimer lay on the bed in a tangle of covers, his face unhealthily white and his balding pate covered with a sheen of sweat. Both hands were pressed firmly to his stomach. As he heard the curtains open, he looked up and glowered, but his expression softened when he saw Bartholomew. Weakly, he flapped a hand to indicate that the physician should come closer.

Bartholomew fought his way through the hangings, and sat on the edge of the bed. The ailing baker looked at him helplessly, the aggressive demeanour, which filled his family, his apprentices and a good many of his colleagues with fear, absent. Bartholomew leaned over and felt his forehead. It was cold and clammy. Then he felt the lifebeat in Mortimer's wrist, assessing its strength and speed. It was steady, but rather faster than it should have been for a man of Mortimer's age and size according to the guidelines established by the great Greek physician Galen. But, even so, Mortimer was not dying as everyone seemed to think.

'The messenger said you had pains?' whispered Bartholomew, not liking to speak too loudly in the reverently hushed chamber.

'Terrible pains, Bartholomew,' replied Mortimer hoarsely. 'I am not long for this world.'

He hauled up the front of his expensive linen shirt, revealing a considerable expanse of white, jelly-like flesh for Bartholomew to inspect. Bartholomew rubbed his cold hands together in a vain attempt to warm them, and then gently palpated the baker's abdomen, assuming his icy fingers rather than discomfort were responsible for the sharp intakes of breath on his patient's part.

'What have you eaten over the last day?' Bartholomew asked, sitting back and replacing the shirt over the vast abdomen.

'Why?' whispered Mortimer, his face pale. 'Was it the last meal I will have on Earth?'

'You are not dying, Master Mortimer. You have just eaten something that has disagreed with you. What have you had since yesterday?'

In Bartholomew's experience, patients stricken with stomach aches caused by over-indulgence usually required a moment to recall precisely what they had consumed, and then they often lied about it, embarrassed to admit to their gluttony. But Mortimer answered immediately and with great precision, suggesting that food was something he took very seriously.

'Dinner last night was light – just a hare pie, venison cooked with cream, a loaf of barley bread and some egg custard to follow. I broke my fast with wine, a bowl of oatmeal, some bacon, a mess of eggs and fresh bread. Then, before I became ill, I had some fruit and a few of the cinnamon cakes my wife makes.'

Bartholomew gaped at him. 'Do you always eat so heartily?'

Mortimer shot him a sharp look. 'I told you, dinner was light last night. I have been saving myself for the installation feast today.'

Bartholomew sat back and considered. The man was clearly an habitual glutton and so his stomach cramps were unlikely to be caused by simple greed if his constitution was used to such vast quantities of food.

'Have you eaten anything different over the last day – something you do not usually have?'

'Only the fruit,' said Mortimer. 'And the sugared almonds.'

'Do you usually avoid fruit?'

'No,' replied Mortimer. 'I will eat most things.' This Bartholomew could well believe. 'But these fruits were special. Lemons from Spain.'

'Lemons?' queried Bartholomew, surprised. 'At this time of year? In Cambridge?'

The Master Baker gave a superior smile. 'They are very expensive so I would not expect a man of your meagre means to know. Thomas Deschalers, the grocer, sold some to me. I ate them quartered and dipped in fine white sugar.'

Bartholomew winced at the mere concept. 'You ate raw lemons?'

Mortimer nodded, unaware of or indifferent to Bartholomew's revulsion. 'With sugar. I am told they are an acquired taste and should not be given to women or children lest they disturb the humours. I bought ten. I gave one to Edward, my eldest son, and I ate the rest myself.'

Bartholomew shuddered, his teeth on edge. 'I have been to Spain and the people there cook lemons or use the juice for drinking with water. I have never seen anyone eat one raw – sugar or not – and certainly not nine at once. Their juice is sour and has probably upset the balance in your stomach.'

'But Thomas Deschalers said nothing of this,' protested Mortimer. 'He said the King has lemons at his table – and what is good enough for the King is good enough for me. I named my first son after the King, you know.' He gave Bartholomew an ingratiating smile that vanished as he was racked with a spasm of his gripes. Bartholomew poked his head through the curtains and asked Katherine to fetch warm milk from the kitchen.

She glanced towards the bed, as if trying to see through the thick hangings to where her husband lay like a beached whale. 'Will he live?'

Bartholomew smiled reassuringly. 'He is not dying.'

She regarded him uncertainly. 'Are you sure? He told me he was breathing his last.'

'It is just indigestion from the lemons. It can be very painful,' he added when he saw her uncertainty change to anger.

'Indigestion?' she repeated in disbelief. 'He said he was on his deathbed and had me summon all these people. Now you tell me it was his greed with those wretched lemons? I told him to peel them first but he would insist that he knew best!'

With some difficulty, Bartholomew managed to interrupt her tirade and send her for the milk. When it arrived, he added a small amount of finely ground chalk powder and some laudanum. After the potion had been swallowed to the last drop, he untangled the bedclothes and made his patient comfortable for the deep sleep he knew would soon come.

'I feel better already,' murmured Mortimer gratefully. 'The terrible burning has eased. I will have words with Deschalers about those lemons. I wonder how the King's constitution deals with such sour foods. He must be a strong man indeed.'

'I am sure his constitution is nothing compared to yours,' said Bartholomew ambiguously, helping Mortimer to ease further down the bed.

Mortimer closed his eyes drowsily, but then opened them again and fixed the physician with a hard stare. 'Your reputation belies your abilities, Bartholomew. It is said you indulge in surgery and I was expecting to be sliced open like a pig in order to be cured of my pains, but you have been as gentle with me as a mother with a new-born babe. My only complaint is that your hands are as cold as those of a corpse. Buy some gloves, man!'

Bartholomew nodded vaguely and began to buckle his bag as he prepared to leave. Mortimer reached out and rested a moist, flabby hand on his wrist.

'I am quite serious, Bartholomew,' the baker insisted. 'You will kill someone with shock one day if you continue to place them on bare flesh in so reckless a manner. I have some gloves you can buy. Katherine!'

'No, please, I—' began Bartholomew. But it was too late. Katherine was dispatched for the gloves and Bartholomew's protestations that he did not want any were overridden.

'Look on them as a tool of your trade,' preached Mortimer condescendingly. 'A physician with cold hands is about as desirable as a baker who dribbles in his dough. Ah, here is Katherine with the gloves. Choose a pair, Bartholomew. I will make you a good deal.'

'Yes, choose,' said Katherine. She smiled nervously at her husband and then addressed Bartholomew. 'But you will not pay for them; they will be a gift to compensate you for the fact that you have missed the installation in order to attend Constantine.'

'What?' gasped Mortimer in shock, attempting to raise himself from his pillow. Bartholomew opened his mouth to object, but Katherine was not interested in interruptions. It was unusual to see the shy, diffident woman cross her husband and Bartholomew wondered whether his claim to have been brushed by death had rendered him suddenly more human and fallible in her eyes.

'Doctor Bartholomew could have declined to come to you, Constantine,' she reasoned. 'You are not his patient and he will be the only Fellow in the University to miss the grand installation that the town has been discussing for weeks.'

'Except for Father Philius,' grunted Mortimer. 'You told me he is ill, too.'

'And you should remember that Father Philius would not have answered your summons until the festivities were over,' said Katherine. 'Now, try these green gloves, Doctor. They are the best ones here and suitably fine for a man of your profession.'

'They make his hands look leprous,' said Mortimer, eyeing them critically. 'Give him the black pair. Black goes with anything and you would not want him to don green gloves with that red robe.'

'True enough,' admitted Katherine. 'And the black ones are harder wearing than the green. Your sister tells me you are careless with clothes and so you should probably take a more durable pair. Do they fit?'

'They fit perfectly,' announced Mortimer, as though Bartholomew was incapable of answering, leaning forward to tug at one of the fingers experimentally. 'Now, if you will excuse me, I feel terribly sleepy. Next time you come to me, Bartholomew, I shall expect to be examined with hands as soft and warm as a baby's, not rough, red and frozen like a peasant's.'

Bartholomew smiled and made his farewells to the baker. He ushered the assembled people – and dogs – out of the bedchamber, assuring them that their master needed only rest to make a full recovery, although not all of them seemed overjoyed by the news that death had been cheated of its prey.

Katherine saw him to the door and handed him two silver pennies. 'It was kind of you to come when you should be at the installation.'

'So should you,' said Bartholomew, certain that Valence Marie would not risk offending one of the most powerful merchants in the town and his wife by not issuing them an invitation.

Katherine gave a long-suffering sigh. 'I am tempted to go now since it seems the reason I am to be denied is my husband's greed. But I am sure word has gone out that Constantine is gravely ill, and I do not want to appear uncaring. When he wakes in the morning, he will be telling folk how you snatched him from the jaws of death. My son Edward is the same. While the rest of us suffer simple rheums, he has a terrible fever; a tiny cut is a life-threatening wound with him.'

'Not everyone bears discomfort stoically,' said Bartholomew carefully, not wanting to tell her that he considered Mortimer's summons a complete waste of his time, because the baker would have recovered perfectly well after a good night of sleep and a day of careful eating anyway.

Katherine sighed again, but then became businesslike. She took Bartholomew's elegantly clad hand and smiled. 'I am keeping you from the celebrations while I run on. Thank you again, and enjoy the festivities.'

For the third time that day, Bartholomew turned towards the Hall of Valence Marie. He glanced down at his best gown and saw that it was liberally splattered with mud, while water dripped from the hem. His boots were filthy, and kneeling on the rush-strewn floor of St Bernard's Hostel to tend Armel had caused fragments of the dried plants to adhere to them. In short, he looked scruffy, impoverished and disreputable. He wondered if the Valence Marie porter would even let him in, or whether he should obey his strong inclination to head home, perhaps to sit by the fire in the kitchen and watch the rain teem past the window. He hesitated, seriously considering returning to Michaelhouse.

But, like it or not, he was committed to attending at least part of the installation ceremony, and he could not, in all conscience, use Mortimer's ailment as an excuse to stay away for much longer. He would be missed, if not by the Fellows and Master-Elect of Valence Marie, then by his own colleagues at Michaelhouse, some of whom would claim that his absence was a dereliction of duty and that he had done disservice to Michaelhouse's good relations with another College.

Stamping his feet to try to dislodge some of the mud from his boots, he stepped through the sturdy front gates of Valence Marie and prepared to be admonished by the condescending porter for his bedraggled appearance on such an auspicious day. The porter, however, seemed to have gone off duty and a student was performing the role of doorman. He was considerably more polite than the porter had been, and cheerfully helped Bartholomew to brush the worst of the mud from his clothes.

By the time the physician had been conducted to Valence Marie's splendid hall, the ceremony was virtually over. He stood at the back, leaning against the wall, and remembered the events of the previous summer when, had it not been for the timely intervention of Michael, he would have lost his life in that very room. Since then, the hall had been redecorated on the orders of its incoming Master, and new tapestries in brightly coloured wools adorned the walls. Above his head, the wooden musicians' gallery had been rebuilt and boasted some of the finest carvings in Cambridge. A group of students was there now, singing to occupy the guests while the Fellows of the Hall of Valence Marie lined up to sign the writ that would make legal the installation of Thomas Bingham as Master.

When the last Fellow had shuffled his way forward and added his name to the official parchment, the singing stopped and Bingham began to make his speech. In Bingham's position, Bartholomew would have been brief. The election had not been unanimous and ill-feelings might be resurrected if Bingham spoke at too great a length about his victory over his rival and his plans for the College. The new Master, however, had a good deal to say on a wide range of matters and, in the body of the hall, the assembly became restless. The language of the University was Latin, and while Bartholomew and the other scholars were fluent, few of the guests from the town would understand all of Bingham's words. Despite the chilly weather, the hall, filled to overflowing with people, began to grow stuffy and soon became uncomfortable.

Bartholomew edged nearer the door, where a welcome

draught wafted in from outside, and thought about the events of the day. He wondered about the three bottles of wine, still wrapped in his hat and left in the porter's lodge for safety. Had a townsperson deliberately sold the students poisoned claret? Michael clearly thought so, but Bartholomew had his doubts. He was certain the Franciscan novices would not have been behaving sufficiently rowdily to warrant someone wanting them dead – none of them had been drunk when he and Michael had arrived and they seemed a tame group to him, particularly compared to his own students. The Franciscans seemed the kind of young men whose idea of wild behaviour was three goblets of ale and staying up past midnight – a stark contrast to some Michaelhouse scholars, whose ways of merrymaking sometimes verged on the criminal.

And the business of the lemons was odd, too. Bartholomew could not recall ever having seen lemons in Cambridge in February before. Mortimer must have paid dearly for such a luxury – from his purse as well as his innards. Bartholomew smiled to himself as he imagined the merchant sitting at his table eating the sour fruits one after the other. Regardless of the amount of fine white sugar he had added, it would not have been a pleasant repast. Bartholomew recalled that Mortimer was the son of a ditcher, and had worked hard to haul himself from his lowly beginnings to his present status. Whatever Mortimer had heard, Bartholomew was certain the King did not devour raw lemons on a regular basis, and it was ironic that, even as Mortimer tried to show the world he was wealthy and accomplished, he betrayed his simple origins by revealing he did not know how to prepare the luxury foods he was able to buy.

At the dais to the front of the hall, Bingham looked up from his sheaf of notes and paused for breath. Immediately, someone began to clap. Bartholomew saw it was Thomas Kenyngham, the gentle Master of Michaelhouse, beaming his customary seraphic smile and nodding in a congratulatory

manner to Bingham. Seizing the opportunity for an early end
to the tedious speech, everyone else hastened to join in the
applause, while the Fellows of Valence Marie prepared to lead
the procession out to the church. The students began to sing,
while the people in the hall stretched stiff limbs in evident
relief. Bingham's mouth dropped open in dismay, but his
Fellows clustered about him to offer their felicitations, and
then the procession was on the move. Bingham had to
scamper to take his place of honour behind them, or run
the risk of being left behind.

Amused by Bingham's discomfiture, Bartholomew waited for
the Fellows from his own College as the other guests filed past
him. Master Kenyngham led the Michaelhouse deputation,
a guileless smile still playing about his lips, his eyes raised
heavenward and his lips moving in prayer. Bartholomew had
no doubt that Kenyngham's timely interruption of Bingham's
speech was wholly innocent: of all the scholars in the University,
the honest, kindly Gilbertine friar would be the least likely to
do something purposely malicious.

Behind Kenyngham scurried Roger Alcote, a small,
vindictive man whose ambitious eyes were already on the
Mastership currently occupied by Kenyngham. Blind Father
Paul leaned on the arm of Father William, both Franciscan
friars who taught theology and the Trivium – grammar,
logic, and rhetoric. Michael brought up the rear with
Michaelhouse's newest Fellows – John Runham, who taught
law, and Ralph de Langelee, who lectured in philosophy.

Runham was the cousin of a previous, highly unpopular
Master of Michaelhouse who had died during the plague, and
seemed to have inherited some of his detested kinsman's less
loveable traits: he was arrogant, smug and condescending. But
he was easily one of the best teachers of law Michaelhouse
had ever seen. His lectures were eloquent, precise and
logically flawless, and his reputation meant that the College
was inundated with applications from students who wanted
him to teach them. Because the numbers of new would-be

scholars were low following the plague, a popular master like Runham was a valuable commodity, and Bartholomew tried hard to maintain a cordial relationship with him for the College's sake.

Meanwhile, Runham's room-mate, Ralph de Langelee, did not look at all like a philosopher: he was a hulking figure with brawny arms so heavily muscled that they jutted from his body at an angle. As he passed, Langelee shot Bartholomew an unpleasant look for being late, which Bartholomew ignored. Although Langelee had only been a Fellow for a few weeks, he had already made himself unpopular with the students and staff. He bullied the servants, belittled his undergraduates, and tried to thwart every attempt Bartholomew made to improve living conditions at Michaelhouse.

Unlike Runham, Langelee was not a good teacher. His lectures were confused and filled with contradictions, and he did not seem to enjoy them any more than did his bewildered students. He compensated for his lack of skills by making it known around the University that he was available for any other kind of work, and was making a fortune by acting as scribe and writing letters for the rich and illiterate in his ugly, laboured roundhand. Bartholomew did not like Langelee, a feeling he was sure was fully reciprocated, and avoided his company whenever possible. The physician worked hard at his teaching and his ever-growing practice of patients, and did not want to waste the little free time he had in the company of an arrogant, opinionated man like Langelee.

Michael dropped behind the two new Fellows so that he could walk with Bartholomew.

'I have had a complaint from the porter with whom we left that wine,' he said, speaking in a low voice so that he would not be overheard. 'According to him, he was moving the bottles to a safer place – although I imagine what really happened was that he was wondering whether they were worth stealing, or perhaps siphoning and diluting.'

'What happened?' asked Bartholomew anxiously. 'I hope to God he did not drink any.'

'Fortunately for him, no,' said Michael. 'But he touched the bottle, as you specifically instructed him not to do. He has a burn on his hand the size of an egg.' He shuddered. 'Lord help us, Matt! What is that stuff?'

CHAPTER 2

BARTHOLOMEW TOLD MICHAEL ABOUT MORTIMER lemons as they walked to St Botolph's Churc where prayers would be offered for the new Maste and his College. As if to compensate for the long ceremor at Valence Marie, the College priests rattled through th mass at a speed that left the congregation bewildere after which everyone trooped back to Valence Marie fo the feast. Evidently, the servants had anticipated more tim to prepare, for the hall was in disarray and students had be commandeered into helping set up trestle tables and la out trenchers, while the guests milled about in the courtyar in growing ill humour. By the time the steward announce that the feast would begin, most people were cold, wet an irritable.

The feast itself, however, was impressive and Bartholome imagined that Mortimer would be sorely disappointed t learn what he had missed. As Michael had predicted, th highlight of the meal was roast boar, each animal carrie on a huge platter by two servants. Bartholomew, used t simple Michaelhouse fare, ate sparingly, and did not nee the example of Mortimer to warn him of the dange of over-indulgence. Next to him, Michael ate as thoug it were his last meal on Earth, while, on his other sid Langelee provided impressive competition. Wine flowe freely and, as the feast progressed, the hall became hot, noi and stuffy. The final course, produced with a flourish b

Valence-Marie's steward, was lemons stewed with cinnamon and black pepper, which once again reminded Bartholomew of Mortimer. Thomas Deschalers the grocer must have made a good deal of money from his shipment of lemons, Bartholomew thought, declining the dish as it was offered. Michael helped himself to a generous portion, but left most of it, puckering his lips and screwing his eyes tightly closed at the sourness.

As the daylight faded, braziers around the wall were lit, making the room hotter than ever. Michaelhouse possessed no such braziers and Bartholomew was envious, for the light was ample by which to read and even one such lamp would have eased the boredom of long, winter nights when darkness came early. Valence Marie possessed fine silver, too, and huge jewelled chalices were placed at regular intervals along the tables, filled with almonds and raisins – expensive commodities that were just one indication of the feast's extravagance.

When the meal was over and the tables vaguely cleared of spilled grease, animal bones and bread trenchers, Master Bingham rose to his feet, an intimidating sheaf of parchments clutched in his hands. He cleared his throat importantly, and looked haughtily around the hall at the assembled guests who were about to be treated to that part of his painstakingly prepared discourse he had been deprived of giving earlier. Michael groaned loudly and Bartholomew felt his heart sink. But Bingham had done no more than make a preparatory rap for silence on the table with his spoon before the student minstrels in the gallery increased the volume of their singing dramatically and the Fellows on either side of their new Master reached up to pull him back into his seat. Thorpe, the previous Master of Valence Marie, would never have countenanced such an affront to his authority, thought Bartholomew, amused by Bingham's ineffectual outrage at his colleagues' presumption.

'Bingham will have a hard task controlling this new

College of his,' yelled Michael, putting his sweaty face near Bartholomew's to make himself heard over the racket. Bartholomew nodded vigorously. 'I wonder what those two are plotting.' Michael pointed to where the Sheriff and the Mayor sat, their heads bent together confidentially as they conversed in what seemed to be furtive whispers.

Bartholomew liked Sheriff Tulyet, a small, wiry man with a wispy fair beard and a tolerance towards the University usually absent in town officials. Tulyet saw them looking at him and raised a hand in affable acknowledgement. Even from a distance, the Sheriff looked tired and strained, and there were rings of exhaustion under his pale blue eyes. Tulyet's position was not an easy one to hold. His garrison had been sadly depleted by the plague and it was difficult to recruit replacements when crime was by far more lucrative. Since Christmas, a band of outlaws had settled in the area, using little-known causeways and canals in the Fens to make their escape after robbing travellers on the roads, disappearing as completely and cleanly as the marsh mists in sunlight long before Tulyet's men could catch them.

Bartholomew smiled a greeting to him, and looked around the hall. Sheriff Tulyet and the Mayor were not the only ones to be taking advantage of the installation festivities to conduct a little business. Bartholomew's brother-in-law, Sir Oswald Stanmore, was engaged in an animated discussion with the Master of Gonville Hall, while Bartholomew's sister was abandoned to entertain the morose Prior of Barnwell on her other side. The University was one of the Stanmore's biggest customers, and he was clearly embarking on some deal or other with the Master of one of its most powerful Colleges.

At the high table at the far end of the hall, Vice-Chancellor Harling, the University's second in command, sat between the Countess of Pembroke and a handsome woman in her middle years whom Michael had identified as the Abbess of nearby Denny Abbey, a rich community of Franciscan nuns.

Harling's jet-black hair glistened greasily in the candlelight as he inclined his head politely towards the Countess, giving every appearance of listening with rapt attention to what she was saying.

'Why is Harling in the seat of honour?' asked Bartholomew of Runham, who sat opposite him, speaking loudly to make himself heard over the discordant singing from the gallery and the roar of drunken voices. 'Where is the Chancellor?'

Runham pursed his lips to indicate his disapproval. 'With the Bishop in Ely. It is a mere seventeen miles so I do not know why Chancellor Tynkell could not have made the effort to be here. An installation is, after all, an important University occasion.'

'Perhaps his business at Ely is more urgent than gossiping with the Countess of Pembroke and the Abbess of Denny,' said Bartholomew.

A servant slapped a dish of sugared almonds so hard in front of him, that some of them bounced across the table to be claimed by Michael. When Bartholomew glanced up at him, the man gave a cheerful wink, and his red cheeks suggested that the guests were not the only ones to have availed themselves of Valence Marie's endless supplies of wine.

'Tynkell is probably too afraid to come back,' said Runham uncharitably. 'He knows he is not up to the task of being Chancellor and is hiding away in Ely behind the Bishop's skirts.'

The post of Chancellor was not a position Bartholomew would have willingly held. While it granted the holder a degree of authority over the University and the town, it was also fraught with political pitfalls. The previous incumbent had held office for four years, but the constant intrigues and crafty plotting had finally worn him down, and he had retreated to his family home in the Fens in poor health.

Harling, his Vice-Chancellor, had expected to step into his shoes as was the usual practice, but in an election that had astonished many scholars almost as much as Harling, a timid nonentity called William Tynkell – who had only agreed to stand for election because he thought it might raise the profile of his hostel in the University community – had won the majority of votes. Bartholomew might have questioned the honesty of the vote-counters, had it not been for the expression of abject horror on Tynkell's face when he was declared the winner. Harling had accepted his defeat with dignity, and had volunteered to continue as Vice-Chancellor, an offer that Tynkell had accepted gratefully, openly acknowledging his inexperience in the treacherous world of University politics.

'Tynkell!' muttered Runham in disgust. 'What a dreadful choice to be the leader of our University! All I can say is that *I* did not vote for him.' He gazed speculatively at Bartholomew.

'Neither did I,' said Bartholomew, not wanting to be blamed for the Chancellor's absence.

Runham nodded, satisfied, and went on. 'I am not a man to risk my good health by bathing, but I am always careful to scent my clothes with lavender, and leave my clean linen on the shelf in the latrine to kill the lice. But Tynkell does neither, and there is an odour about him I find most unpleasant.'

'I always feel itchy after an audience with him,' boomed Father William, whose Franciscan habit was one of the filthiest garments in Christendom, and who paid scant attention to his own personal cleanliness. To prove his point, he began to scratch, and Bartholomew was amused to see Runham and then Michael follow suit. A few moments later, Alcote started, and then Master Kenyngham. It continued until Kenyngham – somewhat out of the blue – changed the subject by asking if anyone had ever debated the question 'Let us consider whether the edge of the universe can be touched' and, as the discussion grew more heated, the itches were forgotten.

Listening to his colleagues with half an ear, Bartholomew watched Harling and the Countess, who, judging from the flapping of her hands, seemed to be telling him how to fly. The Vice-Chancellor reached out a beringed hand, took up his wine goblet, and drained it without taking his eyes off the Countess's face. Immediately, a servant hurried to refill it, and a few moments later the entire process was repeated. Bartholomew had heard that, despite her generosity – and resulting popularity – the Countess was not a lady renowned for conversational sparkle. He suspected Harling knew he had a long night ahead of him, and was preparing himself by dulling his mind with as much of Valence Marie's wine as he could stow away without losing consciousness. Perhaps Chancellor Tynkell had been wiser than all of them, with his timely absence from the town.

Harling was given a brief respite from the Countess's monologue as Sheriff Tulyet stepped forward to make his excuses for leaving early to the august occupants at the high table. Under his cloak, he already wore a mail tunic and boiled leather leggings, in anticipation of a nocturnal foray in search of the elusive outlaws.

'Poor Harling,' said Michael, watching as the Countess homed in on the Vice-Chancellor again as Tulyet left. 'I am reliably informed that the noble Marie de Valence is about as interesting a companion as stagnant ditchwater.'

'At least stagnant ditchwater does not hog the conversation,' bawled Runham, who had won the debate about the edge of the universe simply because he had a good deal more to say about it than anyone else. He leaned towards the monk, the flowing sleeve of his fine ceremonial gown knocking over Bartholomew's wine, and lowered his voice a fraction. 'She has but two interests: breeding dogs and gardening.'

'She is a very generous woman,' Bartholomew pointed out.

'She founded this College and the abbey at Denny, and she gives alms to the poor.'

'But gardening, Matt,' said Michael in distaste. 'That is for peasants!'

'Edward the Second liked gardening and look what happened to him,' said Runham ominously.

'I hardly think King Edward was executed because of his love of horticulture,' said Bartholomew drily. 'I imagine his murder had more to do with the fact that he was an abysmal ruler.'

'Please!' whispered Michael, glancing around him furtively. 'Edward the Second founded King's Hall and their Warden is looking right at us! If we are to indulge ourselves in treasonous talk, at least wait until I am too drunk to care!'

'Gardening is a vile pastime,' continued Runham, undeterred. 'All that dirt and dreadful creatures like worms and slugs creeping about. Try some of this candied mint, Matthew. It is quite delicious.'

'People who eat that sort of thing die young,' said Michael knowledgeably, eyeing the dish of sticky leaves disdainfully. 'It is a well-known medical fact.'

'I see,' said Bartholomew, laughing. 'And is this well-known medical fact from the same source as "green vegetables cause leprosy" and "a diet of nothing but meat and bread prevents baldness" that you mentioned to me last week?'

Michael favoured him with a withering look. 'You read too much, Matt. You refuse to believe anything unless it has been written by one of your dull Greek or Arab physicians. The facts to which I refer stem from simple common sense. Look at Harling – there is a man who declines his vegetables and he has a magnificent thick, black mane. The fact that cunning cooks have slipped the occasional bit of cabbage or carrot into my meals accounts entirely for my thinning hair.'

There was little point in arguing with Michael over matters of diet – or pointing out that a tonsure, such as the one

Michael sported, should obviate his own concern about baldness. Bartholomew let the matter drop and gazed at the hour candle, willing it to burn down to a point where it would not be deemed rude to leave. He sighed and rested his chin on one fist as he looked around the crowded, noisy, humid hall.

After a while, Deschalers the grocer and Cheney the spice merchant came towards Bartholomew with Constantine Mortimer's eldest son, Edward. Deschalers and Cheney had donned their finest clothes in honour of the occasion – Cheney wore a tunic of a rich amber with matching leggings, while Deschalers was dressed in a short red cloak with rust-coloured shirt and scarlet hose. Bartholomew was immediately reminded of two of the four humours: Cheney was known for his short temper and aggression and his gold-coloured clothes reminded Bartholomew of the yellow bile that caused choleric behaviour; meanwhile, Deschalers was aloof and laconic, usually moods considered to be caused by an excess of blood. Bartholomew wished his students were with him, because he was sure such a visual example would burn the characters of the humours into their minds for the rest of their lives. By contrast, young Edward Mortimer might have been a scholar himself in his sober brown tunic and plain hose.

'We heard Mortimer is dying,' began Cheney without preamble. 'When might the end come?'

'Not for some years yet, with God's grace,' said Bartholomew, aware of Edward's horrified intake of breath.

'My father is dying? I was told it was nothing more serious than stomach pains!'

'Get a grip on yourself, Edward,' said Cheney coldly. 'Your presence at your father's bedside would have been quite wasted. Had you been needed, he would have sent for you. You have other duties to perform – such as representing the family business here tonight.'

'Your father will make a full recovery,' said Bartholomew,

feeling sorry for Edward. 'His malady was a simple case of too many lemons.'

'Lemons?' queried Deschalers, perching on the edge of the table and tossing back his cloak to reveal the elegant cut of his clothes. 'The lemons I sold him?'

Bartholomew nodded. 'They are a bitter fruit unless properly prepared.'

'Ah,' said Deschalers as a faint smile touched his handsome features. He needed to say no more because the implication was clear: anyone of gentle birth would have known how to prepare the costly fruits and Mortimer had inadvertently exposed his humble origins by his ignorance. He exchanged a superior glance with Cheney.

'We thought it might be a case of this winter fever that has struck at the river people,' he said, addressing Bartholomew again. 'One of my servants was stricken yesterday.'

Bartholomew shook his head. 'I feel sure this fever has something to do with the well in Water Lane. Master Mortimer's house has its own well.'

Deschalers was patently uninterested in issues of health. 'Then can we expect Mortimer at the meeting of the town council next week, when we discuss our building plans for the town?' he asked.

Bartholomew nodded. 'I do not see why not.'

'Good,' said Cheney. 'We need him to help us finance the continuing construction of Bene't's.'

'The College of Corpus Christi and the Blessed Virgin Mary,' corrected Deschalers, giving Cambridge's newest College its full and official title. Most people referred to it simply as Bene't's because it was attached to St Bene't's Church by a slender corridor, like a cloister. 'The only University College to be founded by townspeople and paid for with town money,' the grocer added with an odd mixture of pride and smugness.

'It is a fine building,' said Bartholomew politely.

'It will be the best College in Cambridge given time,'

claimed Deschalers, 'and will be a noble memorial to the men of the Guild of Corpus Christi and the Guild of St Mary who endowed it.'

As they had been speaking, Deschalers's eyes had been roving around the hall, and Bartholomew had the distinct impression that the grocer was looking for someone more influential with whom to talk. Bartholomew watched as Deschalers suddenly became aware of the intense conversation between Oswald Stanmore and the Master of Gonville Hall. The grocer's eyes narrowed. He nodded a brusque farewell to Bartholomew and was away towards them, weaving his way between the revellers and expertly avoiding slopping, wine-filled goblets and hurled pieces of food. Cheney hastened after him, but lacked his colleague's agility, and his progress was marked by a profusion of apologies and spillages. Edward escaped from them with relief and went to talk to some of Valence Marie's students.

'Look at James Grene!' exclaimed Langelee, suddenly grabbing Bartholomew's arm with a hot, heavy hand and pointing at the high table. 'Now there is the face of a man who believes he has been cheated out of his rightful position as Master of Valence Marie!'

Bartholomew looked to where Langelee indicated and saw what he meant. While all around him his colleagues threw themselves into the spirit of the occasion with laughter and good humour, Grene leaned back moodily in his chair on the dais. Bartholomew saw him take a hefty gulp of wine, noted the redness of his face and drew the conclusion that while Grene might not be enjoying the festivities, he was certainly availing himself of the refreshments provided by his victorious rival.

Michael roared with laughter. 'I made a wise decision to stay away from Valence Marie, my friends!' he shouted, raising his cup in a slopping toast. 'Here is to Michaelhouse!'

'Michaelhouse!' yelled Langelee in reply, standing to crash his own brimming goblet into Brother Michael's.

'Have a care!' warned Bartholomew, looking to where several other guests were eyeing them with disapproval. 'We should not risk offending members of Valence Marie in their own hall.'

'Where lies the risk?' bellowed the belligerent Langelee, slamming his cup down on the table. 'Are you so lily-livered that you will not fight for your College?'

Bartholomew regarded him coldly. 'I should not want to set that kind of example to my students and I suggest you should not either.'

'Example!' sneered Langelee, leaning towards Bartholomew and wafting alcoholic fumes into his face. 'The example you set them is one of foolishness! All this washing of hands and clean rushes on the floor.' He spat viciously. 'What do you think we are, mewling babes?'

Bartholomew turned to Michael. 'This feast will end in violence soon. I am leaving.' He stood, but Langelee grabbed the front of his gown and jolted him back down. Bartholomew felt a surge of anger, but before he could react Michael had intervened.

'Fight him and you fight me,' said the monk, knocking Langelee's hand from Bartholomew's robe. 'And fight me, Master Langelee, and I will see you spend the next three nights in the Proctors' gaol.'

Langelee opened his mouth to reply, but was silent when Michael's unsmiling expression penetrated his befuddled mind. He glowered at Bartholomew briefly, before turning his back on them and beginning a discussion with Roger Alcote to his left. Fortunately, Alcote had the foolish grin on his face that told Bartholomew, familiar with the Senior Fellow's habits, that he was drunk to the verge of insensibility and could take no offence at anything Langelee might say to him.

Bartholomew flashed Michael a grateful smile and prepared to leave. At last, other guests were beginning to depart, drifting out in twos and threes as they made their farewells to the new Master of Valence Marie. As Bartholomew stepped forward to offer his congratulations to Bingham, there was a commotion further along the high table – shouts of alarm and the sound of chairs falling as people leapt to their feet. Imagining it to be another skirmish between Fellows made argumentative with too much wine, Bartholomew ignored it and hastened towards the door. Reluctantly, he stopped as he heard people calling his name.

Turning, he saw Grene lying across the table, his face a chalky white, while his hands scrabbled at his throat. Before Bartholomew could so much as take a step towards him, Grene gave a great groan and went limp. Bartholomew elbowed his way through the scholars who surrounded him, but could already see that there was little he could do. As he reached Grene and fumbled to loosen the clothes around his neck, he recalled how the scholar's face had been flushed deep red with drink earlier, whereas now his complexion was bloodless. Bartholomew searched for a lifebeat in the great veins of the neck and felt it pulsing weakly. As he heaved Grene on to the floor and tried in vain to restore him to consciousness, Bartholomew glanced furtively at the table. There, lying on its side, was a thin, smoked-glass bottle, its contents flooding out across the table and dribbling onto the floor.

Michael shoved himself to the front of the ring of spectators, ordering them back to give Bartholomew room to work, aided by an officious young servant wearing a blue tunic.

'Is it a seizure?' Michael asked, leaning over to look at the dying scholar, his voice barely audible over the excited hubbub. 'Was the strain of watching his rival installed too much for him?'

'I cannot be certain,' said Bartholomew, meeting Michael's eyes steadily, 'but I think Master Grene may have had an aversion to the wine.'

*   *   *

It was not long before the feeble pulse in Grene's neck fluttered to nothing, and Bartholomew commandeered the servant in blue to help him carry the body to St Botolph's Church. Michael accompanied them, all traces of his earlier intoxication vanished, while behind, the Fellows of Valence Marie clustered around their new Master and waited for him to tell them what to do next. Vice-Chancellor Harling had followed them and watched with his restless black eyes.

'Well?' Bingham demanded of Bartholomew, his uncertainty of how to deal with the situation making him uncharacteristically abrupt. 'I assume it was the excitement of the day that killed him?'

'I need to conduct a more thorough investigation of the body,' said Bartholomew cautiously. Although the symptoms of Grene's sudden demise and Armel's had been virtually identical, he wanted to be absolutely certain before he made his suspicions public.

Bingham appeared flustered by his reply. 'It was a seizure, surely? You said the wine had caused it. What will be gained from a more thorough investigation of the corpse now?'

Behind him, Bingham's Fellows were silent, but Bartholomew saw their rapidly exchanged speculative glances. He suppressed a sigh of resignation, aware that in that moment rumours had been given life: Bingham's surly rival for the Mastership had just died most conveniently and there would be few wagging tongues in the University community that would not gain some mileage from that fact.

Harling watched the exchange with cool interest, clearly unimpressed by Bingham's poor handling of the first crisis of his incumbency. It was no secret that Grene had been one of Harling's most ardent supporters during his campaign to be Chancellor. Bingham had immediately announced his vote would go to Tynkell, not because he considered Tynkell a better candidate – he, like virtually every other scholar in the University, knew nothing about Tynkell – but simply because the two contenders for the Mastership of Valence

Marie seemed to feel obliged to oppose everything the other said or did. It must be gratifying, Bartholomew thought, for Harling to see the man who had campaigned against him to be placed in such an awkward and delicate position.

'Doctor Bartholomew, as the University's most senior physician, will conduct an examination of Grene's body,' said Harling smoothly, smiling at the new Master with what seemed to be more vindication than reassurance. 'Just to establish beyond all doubt what we know to be true – that Master Grene died of a simple seizure brought on by disappointment.'

The uncertainty evident in his voice did more to fan the flames of mystery about the cause of Grene's death than anything Bartholomew could have said. The Fellows looked at each other with renewed suspicions.

'But what if it should be found that Grene's death was not brought on by disappointment?' asked one of the Fellows, a tall Dominican friar whom Bartholomew recognised as Father Eligius, Valence Marie's most celebrated scholar. There was a murmur of consternation from the others.

'And why should such a thing be found?' asked Harling softly, addressing Father Eligius but then shifting his eyes to Bingham, who shuffled his feet uncomfortably. Far from suppressing the rumours that would soon begin to circulate, Harling's meaningful look and Bingham's response seemed to suggest that the Fellows had good cause to speculate.

'That will be for the Senior Proctor to determine,' said Eligius. Behind him, the other Fellows muttered and gazed worriedly at Michael, concerned, no doubt, that having the Senior Proctor investigate the death of one of their number would do their College's reputation no good, thought Bartholomew uncharitably.

'Indeed,' said Harling politely. 'And Brother Michael will do a thorough job, you can be certain.' He regarded Bingham suspiciously again, before looking at Grene's sheeted body.

The loaded conversation, thick with inner meanings and

positively dripping innuendo, was becoming too much even for Michael. He took control.

'Go back to your guests, Master Bingham,' he said firmly, taking the new Master's arm and leading him away. 'Assure them that all is well and then arrange for a vigil to be mounted over Grene.'

Bingham hesitated, but then complied, evidently grateful to be given an escape route from a situation that was becoming increasingly uncomfortable. Vice-Chancellor Harling and the Valence Marie Fellows followed him out of the church, leaving Bartholomew and Michael alone. Michael closed the door as the last scholar left and came to stand near Bartholomew as he stared down at the corpse. Grene's body lay on a trestle table in the chancel, draped with a darkly stained sheet that had evidently been used to cover the victims of violent death before. At his head and feet, the servant in blue had lit thick wax candles that cast long shadows around the chapel.

'Well?' asked Michael, his voice echoing in the silence. 'Was he poisoned?'

Bartholomew took one of the candles and held it close to Grene's face, inspecting it with a care he had been unable to exercise while watched by the dead man's colleagues. Sure enough, Grene's lips were blemished with small blisters, like the ones Bartholomew had noticed on Brother Armel. Giving the candle to Michael, he prised Grene's mouth open and looked inside.

'Good God! Look at this!'

Grene's mouth was a mass of tiny white blisters that bled and oozed even after death. Michael glanced down and moved back quickly with an exclamation of disgust. Bartholomew forced Grene's mouth open further and tried to inspect the back of his throat.

'I cannot see,' he complained. 'Hold the candle nearer.'

'What more do you need to see?' protested Michael, keeping his eyes averted. 'It is clear that he has been poisoned. And we both saw that the bottle was of the same kind as the one from which Armel drank.'

Bartholomew snatched the candle from Michael impatiently and resumed his examination. 'No wonder death was instant!' he exclaimed after a moment. 'This poison has burned the skin at the back of the throat and the resulting swelling has closed it completely. Even if I had been able to force something into his throat to keep it open for air, he probably would have died when the poison reached his stomach. What a foul substance!'

'Was it the same with Armel?' asked Michael, noting with relief that Bartholomew had finished his repellent investigation and had closed the unfortunate Grene's mouth.

'I did not look,' said Bartholomew. 'I could not with all his friends watching me – you know how people react over such things. But I can look now.'

'Not now,' said Michael, nodding towards the unglazed windows. 'It is dark and the curfew bell will sound soon. I take it Armel's condition will not change overnight?' Bartholomew shook his head. 'Then tomorrow will be soon enough, when you have the daylight to help you.'

'I saw small blisters on Armel's lips, however,' said Bartholomew. 'Just like the ones on Grene. I have little doubt that we will also find the same damage to Armel's mouth and throat, and that the poison that killed one also killed the other.'

Michael heaved a great sigh and leaned heavily against one of the pillars. 'This is terrible, Matt! Two members of the University have been murdered most vilely by townspeople.'

'You do not know that is true of Grene,' reasoned Bartholomew. 'Bingham might have killed him. There is no question that Grene would have made ruling Valence Marie very difficult for Bingham. You heard what he said – that the excitement of the day killed his rival. How convenient for him!'

'Convenient indeed!' came a soft voice from the darkness

of the aisle. Bartholomew and Michael jumped in shock. They had believed themselves to be alone and that Bingham had taken all his scholars with him when he had left. Out of the deep shadows, Father Eligius emerged, his pallid features startlingly white above his black gown.

'Eligius!' exclaimed Michael, peering at the Dominican in the gloom. 'I thought you had returned to Valence Marie with the others.'

'I thought as much,' said Eligius coolly, 'or you would not have been discussing the murder of poor Grene so candidly. So, Matthew, you believe our new Master dispatched his hated rival with poison?'

'He does not,' intervened Michael quickly, before Bartholomew could respond. 'He has no evidence to justify such an accusation. A student seems to have been killed with a similar potion – as you no doubt overheard – and since Master Bingham is unlikely to have a motive for murdering a Franciscan novice, it seems he is also unlikely to have killed Grene. Regardless of what Matt might speculate.'

'Indeed,' said Eligius, moving closer to look at the sheeted body. He lifted a corner of the cloth and gazed down at Grene's face, eyes half open despite Bartholomew's attempts to force them closed. An expression of remorse flickered over Eligius's own features so quickly that Bartholomew thought he might have imagined it, before the sheet fell and Grene was covered once more.

'I do not find Master Bingham's guilt such an unlikely proposition,' said the Dominican, looking at Michael.

Michael spread his hands. 'How could Master Bingham have killed Grene at the feast?' he reasoned. 'There were dozens of guests present. The matter of the contest between him and Grene was public knowledge, and I am sure I was not the only person watching Grene closely to see how he was taking his defeat. Grene and Bingham did not so much as utter a word to each other all evening, let alone one give the other poison. And anyway, imagine how difficult

Bingham's position will be if there is so much as a whiff of rumour that he has harmed his rival. He would find making a success of his Mastership impossible.'

Eligius considered, watching Michael with unfathomable eyes, and tapping his pursed lips with a long forefinger. He was one of Cambridge's leading logicians and had taken part in debates in universities all over Europe. Bartholomew had always thought the Dominican philosopher looked every bit a man of learning: he had a head that was too big for his body, an impression accentuated by the way his dark brown hair was chopped short at the forehead and sides but straggled long at the back. He was a tall man, topping Bartholomew by the length of a hand, but was unnaturally thin.

'Master Bingham will find his Mastership difficult regardless,' Eligius said finally. 'Grene alive would have opposed anything he tried to do; there are still those loyal to the previous Master – Robert Thorpe – who consider his dismissal a grave miscarriage of justice; and now Grene conveniently dead will arouse suspicions regarding whether Bingham had a hand in it or not. Had Bingham used the few brains he was born with, he would have foreseen the impossible situation in which he was placing himself and declined the Mastership. Or, if he was wholly unable to resist the lure of power, he should have devised a more discreet way of dispensing with Grene's presence.'

Michael eyed him speculatively. 'And which of the two men did you vote for?'

Eligius's thin lips curved into a humourless smile. 'I was an avid supporter of neither candidate because I was impressed with the qualities of neither. But Grene had an edge over Bingham and I declined Bingham's offer of a rise in salary to shift my allegiance.'

'He bribed you to vote for him?' asked Bartholomew with distaste.

'The word "bribe" implies that he offered me something

and that I took it,' said Eligius reproachfully. 'He might have offered, but I can assure you I took nothing. But while I was content to watch Bingham struggle to rule with Grene alive, I am certainly not prepared to see him in power with Grene murdered. You see, Grene confided to me only last night that he was in fear of his life from Bingham. Naturally, I dismissed his claim as the bitter rambling of a thwarted man. Now I am not so sure.'

'What?' exclaimed Bartholomew, aghast. 'Grene claimed that Bingham might kill him? Are you certain? Could you have mistaken his meaning?'

Eligius shook his head slowly. 'Poor Grene made his point most clearly. There is no possibility that I could have mis-understood what he was saying. And then, of course, there is the Valence Marie relic.' He crossed himself reverently.

'Not that again, Eligius,' said Michael wearily. 'The Valence Marie bones were a hoax perpetrated by an evil man. It was *not* the hand of a saint.'

'Not everyone believes that to be true,' remonstrated Eligius. 'I saw that relic and I felt the holiness emanating from it like heat from a fire. Chancellor Tynkell has promised to reinstate it to us so that we can revere it as it deserves.'

'Has he?' asked Bartholomew, startled. 'I thought it had been destroyed.'

'It is in the University chest in St Mary's Church,' explained Michael. 'It cannot be destroyed until the question of its legal ownership has been resolved. Wretched thing!'

'It is a gift from God,' said Eligius, his eyes gleaming with the same fanaticism Bartholomew had seen in Father William's from time to time. 'And I am not the only Fellow of Valence Marie to be convinced of its authenticity – Grene believed it, too, although Bingham does not.'

'I hope you are not suggesting Bingham murdered Grene because of the relic,' said Michael.

Eligius said nothing.

'But do you honestly see Bingham poisoning Grene in

front of all the guests at the feast?' asked Bartholomew, simultaneously bewildered and unconvinced by the Dominican's suppositions. 'You know him better than I, but it seems to me that he does not possess such presence of mind.'

Eligius sighed. 'You are probably right,' he said, his tone of voice making it perfectly clear he did not believe so for an instant. 'But if Bingham did not kill Grene, who did?'

Michael and Bartholomew had no answer, and all three scholars looked down at the body lying under its dirty sheet on the table. A breath of wind gusted suddenly, making the candle flames flutter and lunge and splattering heavy drops of rain onto the stone floor to echo eerily around the otherwise silent church.

'There is something about Father Eligius I find disconcerting,' said Bartholomew, shivering as he watched Michael try to poke some life into the dull embers of the kitchen fire.

Michaelhouse, despite its fine buildings and formidable gateway, was not wealthy, and firewood had been expensive since the plague. Usually, Master Kenyngham allowed a fire in the hall during winter so that the scholars had some warmth for lectures, but the wet weather was mild and, at a meeting of the Fellows in December, it was mooted that a fire was an unnecessary extravagance. Bartholomew had argued that dampness was as chilling as winter snow, and that the students needed somewhere to dry their clothes. Kenyngham had wavered, since he took Bartholomew's concerns about health seriously, but Langelee, backed by Alcote – who was sufficiently affluent to afford a fire in his own chambers anyway – argued that such luxuries were needless, and that was that. The only fire in Michaelhouse was in the kitchen; Kenyngham had been forced to declare that out of bounds when Agatha, the College laundress, had claimed so many students were vying to sit near it, that the servants could not reach it to do the cooking.

By the time Bartholomew and Michael had returned from

the feast, Michaelhouse was silent. Here and there, lights flickered in windows, suggesting that there were a few scholars who could afford a candle to render the long winter nights more endurable with reading or illicit games of cards, but most were asleep, rolled up in their blankets in a vain attempt to keep the iciness of the stone-built rooms at bay. The kitchen, too, was deserted, the cook and his assistants having retired to their own quarters above the laundry for the night. Agatha often sat in her great wooden chair by the fire in the evenings, straining her eyes to sew, or holding forth about all manner of subjects to anyone who would listen. But it was late, and the barely glowing embers suggested that Agatha had long since gone to her bed.

On the table, wrapped in a piece of old blanket from the laundry, were the bottles of poisoned wine – three from the novices at St Bernard's Hostel and the one that had killed Grene. All four were identical, so that it was clear they had come from the same source. The Valence Marie porter, back at his post with his hand swathed in a huge and inexpertly tied bandage that bore the hallmarks of Robin of Grantchester's work, had regarded the containers fearfully, as though he imagined their contents might leap out and pour themselves down his throat. Bartholomew had tried to question him about his burned hand, but the porter declined to incriminate himself, and continued to insist that he had merely been moving them to a safer place. Exasperated, Bartholomew recommended that the wine Grene had spilled in his death throes was treated with appropriate caution, and had carried the other bottles back to Michaelhouse.

'This is a waste of time,' snapped Michael, glaring at the feeble glow of the fire. 'I am the University's Senior Proctor and one of the finest theologians in the country – do not look like that, Matt, it is true – and here I am reduced to blowing on ashes to warm my frozen feet. I have had enough of this!'

He stormed from the kitchen, leaving the startled physician

alone in the chilly kitchen wondering whether he was coming back. A few moments later, Michael returned, his arms full of logs.

'There,' he said, setting them in the hearth and watching the flames take hold. 'That is better. Now, all that aggravation has given me an appetite. Fetch some ale to mull, Matt, and I will see what can be salvaged from that miserable hole Agatha sees fit to call her pantry.'

He returned with several slices of fat bacon, some cheese and half a venison pie that Bartholomew knew was the personal property of Roger Alcote. The physician set the ale to mull over the now merry fire and watched Michael eat, wondering how he could, given the quantity of food he had put away at the installation feast.

'You were giving me your impressions of Father Eligius,' said Michael, barely understandable through a mouthful of pie. His eyes watered, and he began to cough as crumbs caught at the back of his throat from trying to eat and talk at the same time.

'Only that I find him disconcerting,' said Bartholomew, giving him a hefty thump on the back.

'Father Eligius is a fine scholar,' said Michael, swallowing the pie and jamming a sizeable chunk of bacon in his mouth. 'He has disconcerted some of the finest minds in the western world with his logic and theories.'

'I was not referring to his intellect,' said Bartholomew, pulling his stool as close to the fire as possible and holding his frozen hands near the dancing flames. 'I find his attitude to Grene's death unsettling.'

'Why?' asked Michael, surprised. 'His reaction seemed perfectly reasonable to me, given what Grene had confided the day before.'

Bartholomew pondered as he watched Michael sit in Agatha's chair, accompanied by a medley of grunts and sighs as he settled himself comfortably. 'I suppose it was the casual way he revealed that Grene was in fear of his life. Had you confided to me that you were afraid someone would kill you, and you were poisoned within a day, I would be a little more vocal about it.'

'With Bingham there?' asked Michael, stretching his sandalled feet towards the fire. 'That probably would have caused exactly the kind of confrontation Valence Marie needs to avoid. Bingham would have denied the accusation vehemently – perhaps even violently.'

Bartholomew was silent, thinking. 'The same kind of poisoned wine was used to kill both Armel and Grene. We know Armel bought his from a man in a tavern, but how could Bingham have acquired some – today of all days, when his every moment would have been filled with preparations for the installation? Surely Eligius, as a logician, can see that is unlikely.'

'Your own logic is failing you, my friend,' said Michael. 'It is entirely possible that this wine-seller sold claret to both Bingham and Armel. Perhaps not today, but maybe yesterday or last week. Bingham might have had no idea that the stuff was poisoned and it might be mere coincidence that Grene was the victim.'

'Do you honestly believe that Bingham bought a bottle of wine – just the one, mind you, since your own search revealed that there was not another like it in the hall – and it just happened to be poisoned and just happened to end up being consumed by his arch-enemy, Grene?' asked Bartholomew incredulously.

Michael rubbed the rough whiskers on his chin and answered with a question of his own. 'Do you think Bingham murdered Grene? You told Eligius you did not think he had the presence of mind, despite the fact that it was your observation of the convenience of Grene's death to Bingham that brought Eligius from the shadows in the first place.'

Bartholomew raised his hands in a gesture of defeat. 'All I think at the moment is that we have insufficient evidence to say whether Bingham is guilty or not. To be honest, I would not imagine he would have the audacity to kill his rival in full view of most of the town, but desire for power leads men to desperate acts, as we both know from past experience.'

'Eligius was right when he said the taint of murder will hang about Bingham regardless of whether he is guilty or innocent,' mused Michael. 'Even if he is acquitted, he will be hard pushed to rule Valence Marie as Master. Quite aside from the bitter division between supporters of Grene and supporters of Bingham, there is the fact that half the scholars are convinced that horrible hand Thorpe found last year is a sacred relic, while half have the sense to see that it is a fake.'

'I thought any faith in the relic's authenticity would have been destroyed when we proved that the man to whom the hand was said to belong was in possession of a full complement of limbs,' said Bartholomew tiredly. 'Eligius must be out of his mind to continue to think the thing is genuine!'

Michael shrugged. 'I agree. But you know how people are once they believe in something – all the evidence in the world will not shake their faith. You must have seen that gleam of fanaticism in Eligius's eyes when he spoke about the bones.'

'But if Bingham killed Grene because Grene believed in the authenticity of the relic, that would make Bingham a fanatic, too, and he is scarcely that. He is stuffy and pedantic, but not a zealot.'

Michael was about to reply when the door opened and a chill blast of rain-laden wind gusted into the kitchen, making the fire glow and roar. Cynric, Bartholomew's Welsh book-bearer, entered with the nightporter behind him.

'There you are, boy,' said Cynric to Bartholomew. 'Walter here has been looking for you.'

The porter pushed Cynric out of the way and strode into the kitchen. Walter's perpetual bad temper was legendary and, during the nine years Bartholomew had been a Fellow of Michaelhouse, he had never seen Walter smile except at someone else's misfortune.

'You are not supposed to be in here!' accused Walter. 'The Master said scholars are not allowed in the kitchens any more.'

'When Walter saw you were not in your room, he came to wake me, thinking you had gone out again,' explained Cynric. He looked sly. 'Although how he thought you could have left the College without being seen, I cannot imagine.' The porter glowered. Besides his reputation for surliness, Walter was also known for sleeping on duty, and most scholars knew that they could break the curfew and slip in and out of College at will when Walter was guarding the main gates.

His morose gaze fastened on the cheerful fire. 'Where did you get those logs?' he demanded. He turned to Michael and pointed an accusatory finger. 'You stole them! You stole them from Master Alcote's personal supply in the stables!'

'I am a man of the cloth,' said Michael, rising to his feet in indignant outrage. 'I do not steal!'

'It was him, then!' shouted Walter, spinning round to indicate Bartholomew. 'He pinched poor Master Alcote's logs – he is always complaining about how cold the College is, and so he decided to build himself a blaze in the middle of the night when there was no one else around to witness his crime. Master Alcote paid me a penny to protect those logs, and now he will want it back!'

'Give it to him, then,' said Michael unsympathetically. 'Matt told me you were nowhere to be seen when he borrowed the firewood from the stable. You do not deserve Alcote's penny.'

'What do you want, Walter?' asked Bartholomew, standing and stretching his back. 'It has been a long day and I am tired.'

'You will not be enjoying your warm bed for a while yet,' said Walter spitefully. 'A messenger just came from Gonville

Hall. Father Philius is sick and has sent for you.' He gestured towards the door where the rain could be seen falling heavily. 'You will get soaked,' he added smugly.

'Philius?' said Bartholomew, startled. Father Philius was a physician who deplored the use of surgery and was one of Bartholomew's most rabid critics over his unorthodox methods. The Franciscan must be ill indeed to resort to requesting Bartholomew's help.

'The messenger said you were to hurry,' said Walter, putting his hand out of the door to test the strength of the rain with an expression as near to a smile as he ever came.

'I will come with you,' said Cynric, standing and reaching for the cloak that hung on a hook in the fireplace.

'No,' said Bartholomew, picking up his own cloak and hunting about for his new gloves. 'There is no need for us both to get wet. Go back to bed.'

Cynric swung the woollen garment round his shoulders. 'The streets are far from safe for a single man. You will do better with me along.'

There was no disputing that. Since the plague, the price of food had risen dramatically and was beyond the means of many people. Bands of men simply defied the law, realising they could fare better by theft and robbery than by honest labour. Added to these were veterans from King Edward's temporarily suspended wars with France, heroes who expected more from their country than a return to virtual slavery in the fields. Travelling had always been dangerous, but since the onset of winter the outlaws had become bolder and had started to attack the town itself, darting in from the Fens to take what they wanted and disappearing again before the Sheriff's men could catch them. Cynric spoke the truth when he said the streets were unsafe for a single man and, although he was too tactful to say so, especially one with Bartholomew's inferior fighting skills.

Bartholomew set off across the muddy yard with Cynric

and Michael behind him. He made a brief detour to lock
the four bottles of wine in the little storeroom where he
kept his medicines, after which he secured the door carefully
and tied the key onto his belt. As he left, he saw Michael
give the door a surreptitious rattle to satisfy himself that it
was firmly locked. They exchanged a glance: Michael was
right to be cautious with the deadly brew and, once again,
Bartholomew wondered who could have a reason to unleash
such a hideous potion on the University's scholars.

Outside, the rain was falling in great sheets, and Walter
grumbled and cursed as he hauled the bar from the wicket
gate to let them out. Fortunately, Philius's room at Gonville
Hall was a mere stone's throw from Michaelhouse, but even
as they walked the short distance, Bartholomew thought he
saw a shadow move in the bushes to the side of the road. He
drew one of the surgical knives he carried in his medicine
bag and saw that Cynric already held his dagger.

'They thought better of it when they saw we were armed,'
said Cynric after a moment, glancing behind him.

'They?' queried Bartholomew. 'I only saw one.'

'There were three of them,' said Cynric confidently. 'They
must be desperate because they will be lucky to catch anyone
abroad on such a foul night, except the Sheriff's men.'

Cynric had been born and bred in the mountains of
north Wales, and prided himself on his clandestine skills
– especially prowling undetected in the dark. Indeed, he
had saved Bartholomew's life on more than one occasion,
and the physician sensed Cynric was enjoying the nocturnal
expedition, in spite of the rain.

He hammered on the gates of Gonville, and was admitted
almost immediately by a servant who was clearly expecting
him. Bartholomew had visited Father Philius in his room
on several occasions – physicians in Cambridge were not
so abundant that they could afford to shun each other's
company completely, even when they were as diametrically

opposed as were Bartholomew and Philius. He declined the porter's offer to guide him, and made his own way to the chamber on the ground floor in which Philius lived.

Unlike Bartholomew with his spartan room, Philius resided in considerable comfort. There was a fire crackling merrily in the hearth and the stone-flagged floor was littered with thick woollen rugs. The bed stood against the wall farthest from the window – well away from the night airs Philius considered so dangerous – while another wall boasted a line of hooks on which hung the physician's impressive array of robes and a selection of elegant crucifixes. A lamp had pride of place on the table in the middle of the room, a luxury virtually unknown at Michaelhouse, except in the sumptuous quarters occupied by Alcote.

Bartholomew left Cynric to close the door while he went to Philius. The Franciscan was lying on his side, curled up like a child, while his own book-bearer, Isaac, fluttered about him helplessly. Philius's breathing was not laboured, but it was strained, and sounded loud in the quiet room. Bartholomew led Isaac away from the bed.

'How long has he been ill?'

'All day,' Isaac whispered back. 'He is growing worse, and the purges he has prescribed for himself seem to be doing no good at all. He cannot even speak now.'

'Has he eaten anything today?' asked Bartholomew. 'Lemons, perhaps?'

Isaac looked at him askance. 'Not that I know of. He had a goblet of watered wine this morning before mass, as is his wont, but nothing since.'

'Where is this wine?'

Isaac gave him another curious look, but fetched the bottle obligingly. It was of dark green glass and was virtually empty, suggesting that, unless Philius's goblet was astonishingly large, most of the wine had been consumed earlier with no ill-effects. Bartholomew heaved a sigh of relief. Two cases of poisoning had led him to be overly suspicious.

He knelt next to the bed and gently eased Philius onto his back so that he could examine him properly. Philius's eyes flickered open as he was moved, but he said nothing as Bartholomew's hands moved across his stomach. As he worked, Bartholomew glanced at Philius's face, and saw a thin tendril of blood oozing from the corner of his mouth. Isaac hastened to wipe it away, but Bartholomew stopped him and motioned for Cynric to bring the lamp closer.

Philius winced as the light came nearer and closed his eyes. On his lips were small white blisters – not as many as Bartholomew had observed on Armel and Grene, but similar in appearance. Bartholomew told Philius to open his mouth and looked inside. It was bleeding and more of the blisters were on his tongue and gums – again, not to the same extent as those he had seen in Armel and Grene, but enough to tell Bartholomew the cause of Philius's discomfort.

By now, Philius was alert and watching him intently, fear and pain written clearly on his face.

'What else has he swallowed today?' Bartholomew asked of Isaac.

'Nothing else. Just the wine.'

'But you said he had taken purges,' said Bartholomew.

'Nothing other than the medicines,' said Isaac with exaggerated tolerance. 'Look, can you tell what is wrong with him or not? If you cannot, I think he might be better left to rest.'

'What purges has he taken?' snapped Bartholomew, irritated by the man's presumption. If Bartholomew's diagnosis was correct, leaving Philius as he was might mean leaving him to die. 'Do you have them here?'

'Obviously not, since he has swallowed them,' said Isaac insolently. 'It is not the purges that are making him ill—'

'When did he take these purges exactly?'

Isaac sighed heavily. 'He takes a purge every Saturday to cleanse his body from impurities. He drank the potion after he returned from mass – around dawn.'

'And he became ill after he took it?'

Isaac thought. 'Well, I suppose he did. He woke hale and hearty enough. He took the purge and complained that it tasted strong. He became ill shortly afterwards and has been growing steadily worse all day.'

'Who made these purges? Jonas the Apothecary?'

'I made them,' said Isaac. 'I make all of Father Philius's medicines when I can. It is cheaper.'

'But you are not qualified,' said Bartholomew in horror. 'You are not an apothecary!'

'I do not need to be an apothecary,' said Isaac, growing angry. 'I only need to follow Father Philius's instructions about quantities and—'

'I suppose one of these purges contained wine,' interrupted Bartholomew sharply, not wishing to embark on a discussion of the ethics of Isaac's actions while there was a chance of saving Philius if he acted quickly.

'Well, yes. The wine helps to take away the unpleasant taste of the herbs.'

'And did you use this wine to make the purges that Philius drank?' asked Bartholomew, holding up the green bottle.

'Of course not! I do not put best Italian wine in medicines. It would be wasteful. I used some cheap stuff.'

'Where is it?' asked Bartholomew, his patience beginning to fray. He glanced at Philius, who was listening intently to the exchange, his face white with fright.

'In the medicine room. I—'

'Fetch it, please. But use a cloth to pick it up. Do not touch it with your hands.'

Isaac made as if to demur, but Bartholomew turned his attention back to Philius again, and the book-bearer left reluctantly.

'Can you hear me?' Bartholomew asked gently, kneeling next to the Franciscan.

Philius nodded that he could.

'Today, a student drank from a bottle of wine that contained poison. He died almost immediately. Then, at Bingham's installation feast, James Grene died from swallowing a similar poison. I have not seen anything quite like it before. It seems to work by burning – I think it causes the throat to blister and swell and so kill the victim by asphyxiation. I think you might have swallowed some of this poison, although a very mild dose or you would not still be alive. Have you heard of any other such cases before?'

Philius's eyes widened in horror and he nodded vehemently. Bartholomew strained to hear what he was trying to say, but speech was impossible for Philius and his breathing became ragged. Bartholomew poured some of the wine from the green bottle into a cup and helped him drink it. Eventually, the friar grew calmer, but his eyes pleaded with Bartholomew that he wanted to speak.

'If I ask you questions, can you nod or shake your head?'

Philius nodded quickly.

'You have seen a case like the ones I described?'

A nod.

'Yesterday?'

A shake of the head.

'A week ago?'

Another shake of the head.

'A month ago?'

A vigorous nod.

'How many cases have you seen? One?'

A nod.

'More than one?'

Philius shook his head.

'Do you know what poison caused this?'

A shake of the head. Philius was beginning to tire.

'Were you able to treat it? Did you save the patient?'

Philius shook his head again and closed his eyes tightly. Bartholomew patted his shoulder.

'Believe me, Philius, I saw Grene stricken and he died almost instantly. You must have taken a very small dose of this poison since you are alive several hours after swallowing it, and there is every chance you will recover.' Bartholomew looked away as he spoke. Lying to his patients was not something he did well but he did not want to frighten Philius into losing hope.

He wondered what the best way to proceed would be. He considered administering an emetic to force Philius to vomit the poison out of his system, but Philius had swallowed the poison hours ago and Bartholomew was sure it was too far into his innards to be brought out. He rummaged around in his bag.

'Since this poison seems to burn, I think the best way to balance its effects is by absorbing the acid. I prescribed something for Master Mortimer much the same. He had been eating raw lemons.'

Bartholomew talked to reassure and saw the ghost of a smile play over Philius's blistered lips as he listened to the story about Mortimer's lemons. Bartholomew dispatched Cynric for milk, mixed as much of the fine, white chalk powder with it as he dared, and added a small amount of laudanum and some charcoal dust. Supporting Philius in the crook of his arm, he helped him swallow the potion sip by sip, a process which took so long that by the time it was finished Bartholomew's arms ached. Philius lay back exhausted and Bartholomew watched him anxiously. He was far from certain whether his cure would work. And even if Philius did not die soon, Bartholomew wondered whether his innards would be able to heal themselves of the poison's lesions.

Eventually, Philius slept and Bartholomew went to sit near the fire to wait with Cynric. Neither spoke, but sat in companionable silence, staring into the flames.

'Isaac is taking a long time,' said Cynric eventually, in a whisper so as not to waken the sleeping Franciscan. 'I will slip out and have a look for him.'

Bartholomew left the fire and went to check on Philius.

It might have been his imagination, but he thought the Franciscan's breathing seemed easier. Round his lips, the blisters seemed less raw where the chalky-grey milk had stained them, and Bartholomew felt his hopes rising.

Within moments, Cynric was back, his expression anxious. 'You had better come and see this for yourself,' he said unsteadily.

Mystified, Bartholomew followed Cynric across the yard to the cellar-like room where Philius kept his medicines. Judging from the bundles of herbs that hung from the roof and the neatly stacked sacks of flour at the far end, it seemed Philius shared his medicine room with the cook. At first, Bartholomew could not see why Cynric had dragged him away from the warm fire. And then he became aware of a regular creaking sound. Bartholomew looked upwards to the rafters where the bunches of herbs were hanging – along with the lifeless body of Isaac.

chapter 3

EVEN AS THEY CUT THE BODY DOWN, BARTHOLOMEW could see that help had come too late for Isaac. His hands had been tied behind his back and a gag fastened around his mouth to stop him from crying out. Bartholomew was curious as to why the room did not show signs of a struggle, but an examination of Isaac's body revealed that he had been dealt a vicious blow to the head. In fact, the blow had been so hard that Bartholomew wondered if that, and not the strangulation, had been what had killed him. His murderer, evidently, was taking no chances.

While Cynric went to fetch Michael – whose duty as Senior Proctor it would be to investigate a murder on University property – Bartholomew sat back on his heels next to the body and considered. Was Isaac a random victim of violence? Had he disturbed a burglar when he entered the storeroom to fetch the wine he had used in the purges at Bartholomew's request? Or was his death connected somehow to the wine itself? Bartholomew stood, and looked around for the bottle.

Isaac seemed to have used one particular bench for making his purges. Bartholomew inspected it, and then bent to peer underneath. The slender, smoked-glass bottle lay smashed, the wine pooling on the floor. As Bartholomew considered it, a ginger cat reeled out from behind one of the flour bags and swayed towards him unsteadily. Before he could stop it, it had bent to the wine and had lapped several

mouthfuls from a small amount that remained cupped in the
bottle's base. He watched curiously as it wove its way from
under the bench and rubbed around his legs. He picked it
up and inspected it closely. It was certainly drunk, and the
few gulps it had swallowed as he had watched were evidently
not all it had consumed that night, yet it showed no signs
of poisoning. He carried it to the candle Cynric had lit and
prised open its mouth. There was no blistering.

He released it and watched it wobble out of the door.
He frowned, puzzled, and then leaned forward to retrieve
the fragments of bottle. As his fingers groped around for
the glass, they touched something warm and furry and he
quickly withdrew his hand in disgust. A rat! He looked
closer and saw it was lying very still. He reached under
the bench and took a cautious hold of the rodent by its
long bony tail. A brief inspection showed him that it was
quite dead, and a bubble of blood oozing from its mouth
suggested that it, unlike the cat, had been poisoned. Now
Bartholomew was truly bewildered. He had seen the cat
drink the wine with no ill effects other than intoxication,
whereas the rat – that obviously had not been drinking
while the cat was under the bench and so could only
have had time for the merest sip – had been killed in an
instant.

As he pondered, an unpleasant thought occurred to him
that had him up on his feet and racing towards Philius's
room. If Isaac's killer had come for the bottle, and if
he had not found it because it had been smashed under
the bench, he might consider looking for it in Philius's
chamber!

He entered the Franciscan's quarters at a run, and heaved
a sigh of relief when he saw Philius move restlessly on the
bed. He was about to walk towards him when something
struck him heavily on the back, sending him sprawling
forwards onto his hands and knees. He tried to scramble
to his feet, but a blanket was hurled over his head. He

struggled violently, desperately trying to free his hands from the clinging material. Someone's arms wrapped round him, trying to hold him still. He struggled more frantically than ever, lashing out with his feet, and then threw himself backwards with all his might and heard a heavy grunt as he crushed his attacker against the wall.

There was a loud crash and his attacker's hold suddenly loosened.

'Leave him!'

Bartholomew was swung round so that he lost his balance and toppled over, and then heard running footsteps. He fought himself free of the blanket and was about to follow when he saw the fire at the far end of the room. The crash had been the lamp being hurled against the wall: it lay on its side and flames were already licking at the woollen carpets on the floor. There was a crackle as they ignited and fire inched towards the bed. Bartholomew saw two figures race past the window: Isaac's killers, and one was, perhaps, the man who had sold poisoned wine to young Armel, too. He stood immobile for an instant, itching to give chase. But the edges of Philius's blankets were beginning to smoulder and the room was filling with a thick, choking smoke.

He swept up the blanket that had been flung over his head and beat the flames away from the bed. Philius shifted slightly, but did not wake. Bartholomew swiped again, but the dry rugs were like tinder and the fire was already touching the tapestries on the walls. With horror, he wondered whether he would be able to douse it before it took a good hold. Fire was something everyone feared in settlements where most buildings were made of timber: if Gonville burned, the flames would spread to the adjoining houses in St Michael's Lane and the entire town might be engulfed. He redoubled his efforts, yelling at the top of his voice for help. In desperation, he hauled the bedclothes away from Philius, tumbling him to the floor, and hurled them over the burning rugs. He was looking around for something else to use when Cynric arrived with help in the form of a handful of students, Michael and John Colton of Terrington, the Master of Gonville.

Cynric and Bartholomew beat at the now blazing rugs, Michael yelled at the students to fetch water, and it was not long before the fire was under control. Leaving Cynric to ensure it did not ignite again, Bartholomew turned his attention to his misused patient. Philius stared around him in a daze as Bartholomew lifted him back onto the bed. Colton tucked him in, while Michael sent the porter with a message to his beadles to be on the lookout for the three people who had knocked him to the ground as they came hurtling out of Gonville's main gate.

'Three?' queried Bartholomew, looking round at him. 'I saw only two.'

'There were three,' said Michael. 'Cynric would have been after them had he not heard your shouts for help.'

'Has Father Philius come to any harm?' asked Colton anxiously, peering at the Franciscan in the room that was almost pitch black now the flames had been doused. 'He does not seem to be himself.'

Colton was a small, neat man with a well-trimmed grey beard and a dark complexion, almost like an Arab. He was the first Master the College had ever had, and had been elected at the height of the plague when no one was sure who, if anyone, would survive.

Bartholomew knelt next to the bed. 'The opiate is making him dazed. We should let him rest.'

He tried to stand, but Philius grabbed his wrist.

'What happened?' he croaked.

'You can speak!' exclaimed Bartholomew, pleased. 'That is a good sign!'

'Isaac.'

Bartholomew's heart sank, thinking of the lifeless body of

Philius's book-bearer in the storeroom, but, before he was forced to lie, Colton intervened.

'Isaac is resting, Philius. As should you.'

Philius shook his head. 'Isaac,' he croaked, his voice little more than a rustle. 'Isaac steals.' He swallowed painfully and tried again. 'He stole wine from Stanmore.'

'Oswald Stanmore?' asked Bartholomew, startled. 'My brother-in-law?'

Philius nodded. 'His apprentice drank the wine and died.'

His eyes began to close, and Bartholomew knew they would get nothing further from him that night. The dose of laudanum he had used had been a powerful one: Bartholomew had intended that Philius should rest until the morning, so that sleep could allow the body to heal itself.

'Did that mean anything to you?' asked Michael, leaning over Bartholomew's shoulder, and looking down at the sleeping friar. Bartholomew shrugged, his expression troubled, and stood up. He ordered that the shutters be opened to allow the smoke out, and closed again when the room was clear. Meanwhile, the nightporter set about building up the fire in the hearth, and restoring order to Philius's room. Bartholomew promised to return to visit the ailing physician the following morning, and took his leave. In a few words, he told Michael what had happened as they walked across Gonville's yard together. Colton hurried after them and waylaid them by the gate.

'What is happening?' he demanded of Bartholomew. 'The porter woke me to say Isaac was dead, and then I find someone has tried to ignite Philius in his room.'

'Some wine made him ill,' explained Bartholomew tiredly, not wanting to go into details. 'Isaac was fetching it for me to examine when he seems to have been struck down.'

'Isaac was struck down for wine?' asked Colton, confused.

'I expect he disturbed a burglar,' said Michael, rubbing his chin. 'The Sheriff was telling me only yesterday that the wolves-heads, who have been busy on the highways since

Christmas, attacked three houses inside the town itself last week. They are growing bolder all the time.'

'How secure is Gonville?' asked Bartholomew of Colton. 'How easy would it be to break in?'

Colton raised his hands, palms upwards, and gestured around him. Bartholomew saw he was shaking. 'There is a porter on the front door, but if he is called away, I suppose it would be easy enough for a determined person to gain access. Do you think that is what happened?'

'The alternative is that Isaac was killed by someone already inside,' Bartholomew pointed out.

Colton shook his head. 'No one in Gonville would attack Isaac. And certainly no one would harm Philius. How was Isaac killed? Come with me to see. He is in the storeroom, you say?'

Reluctantly, Bartholomew followed him across the courtyard, Michael in tow, and into Philius's medicine room. Colton bent to look at Isaac's corpse. 'Poor man. He has been Philius's book-bearer for many years.'

'Where is this bottle?' asked Michael in a low voice, as Colton began to pray over Isaac's body. 'We should retrieve it before anyone else comes to harm.'

'It is broken, under the bench,' said Bartholomew, pointing. While Michael went to look, Bartholomew sank down onto a stool, and rested his head in his hands. He wondered what time it was. It must be almost time for lauds. He looked up as Michael began to sigh in agitation.

'Where is it exactly?' he hissed irritably. 'I cannot find it.'

Wearily, Bartholomew hauled himself up from the stool, and crouched to point out the bottle. His jaw dropped in astonishment. A dark stain on the wooden floor indicated where the wine had spilled, but every shard of the broken bottle itself had gone. He exchanged a mystified glance with Michael, and looked again to ensure his eyes were not deceiving him.

He stood slowly and rubbed a hand through his hair. 'It was there,' was all he could think to say. He saw a furry body nearby and pushed it with his foot. 'And there is the rat that drank it.'

Michael knelt to examine the rodent. 'Are you sure?' he asked doubtfully.

Bartholomew nodded. 'I did not see it drink the wine, but the cat . . .' He looked around him. 'Is there a cat in the College?' he called to Colton. 'A big ginger one?'

Colton paused in his prayers, and treated him to a suspicious look. 'Yes. Why?'

'Have you seen it recently?'

Colton looked angry. 'Isaac is murdered, Philius's room set alight and there are robbers at large, and you enquire after the cat?'

As if on cue, the cat entered, still staggering uneasily on its feet.

Colton gave it an unfriendly look. 'It drinks. It haunts the storerooms and kitchens in search of ale and wine, and needs to be carefully watched or it smashes things.'

'We have one or two Fellows who are the same,' said Michael drolly. Bartholomew picked up the cat, and inspected it a second time. It looked back at him through contentedly half-closed eyes and began to purr loudly. It struggled when he looked inside its mouth, but purred again when he rubbed its fur absently. He had been right the first time: the cat showed no signs of poisoning.

He shrugged at Michael, who sighed, and gestured to Isaac's body.

'What can you tell us about his death?'

Bartholomew put the cat down, and knelt to re-examine Isaac. 'He was hit on the head first, and I think the blow was sufficient to kill him. Can you see how I am able to move the bones of his skull in my hands? The brain underneath must have been seriously damaged.'

The small room filled with unpleasant grating sounds.

Colton turned white and Michael looked away in revulsion. 'Please, Matt!' he said. 'We do not need to know every gruesome detail.'

Bartholomew grinned at him behind Colton's back. 'I think his hands were bound behind him and he was hauled up to the rafters by the neck after he was struck. There are no marks on his wrists, so he did not struggle as he would have done had he been alive and conscious. Whoever did this wanted to make certain he was dead.'

'They did a good job,' said Michael soberly. 'Could they not tell the blow to the head had killed him? Was it really necessary to hang him too?'

Bartholomew looked at Isaac's head. 'It was probably dark, and, although the bones of the skull are smashed, the skin is barely broken. Perhaps they thought they had only stunned him. Leaving someone to hang is a reliable way of ensuring death if you are in a hurry and cannot afford to wait.'

'But so is stabbing,' pointed out Colton. 'And a quick thrust with a knife would be considerably easier than heaving an inert body up by its neck.'

'True,' said Michael. 'But perhaps they had no weapons. They might have stabbed Matt, rather than engage in all that pointless struggling if they had.' He gestured around the room. 'And there are no knives here that could have been used, although there is plenty of rope.'

Bartholomew looked into the corner where Michael pointed and saw several lengths of rope discarded there that had been used to tie the sacks of flour. He was about to stand when a patch on one of Isaac's hands caught his eye. He looked more closely, and saw the left palm was blistered and the surrounding skin was inflamed. Bartholomew racked his brains, trying to recall whether the injury had been present before Isaac had gone to the storeroom, but the memory eluded him. The porter at Valence Marie had complained of a burned hand after he had touched the bottles from St Bernard's Hostel that Bartholomew had left in his care, and now it seemed as though Isaac might have sustained a similar wound after using the wine to prepare Philius's purge.

Bartholomew and Michael took their leave of Colton, collected Cynric and walked the short distance back to Michaelhouse.

'I was wrong about the outlaws,' said Michael. 'A band of thieves intent on robbery would not come without knives or swords with which to protect themselves. It must all relate to this vile wine. I will talk to Harling at first light, but I am sure he will want us to keep it quiet. There will be all manner of trouble if the scholars believe the town is trying to kill them with poisoned goods.'

'There will be all manner of trouble if they succeed because we have not issued a warning,' objected Bartholomew. 'Our priority must be to save lives. We will not do that by staying silent.'

'Oh, but we will, Matt,' said Michael. 'If we allow rumours to escape that three members of the University – Armel, Grene and now Isaac – have been murdered with or because of poisoned wine, the scholars will riot for certain. And then who knows what the death toll will be? We will talk with Harling and the Sheriff tomorrow, and decide what to do then.'

'You talk to them,' said Bartholomew. 'I will test the wine from Valence Marie and Bernard's. You need to be absolutely certain that the poison is the same before you start your inquiries. Then I will check Armel's body and tell you whether the blisters are the same as the ones on Grene.'

'What do you mean by *my* inquiries?' asked Michael suspiciously. 'Will you not help me solve this foul business? These are *your* colleagues who are being so callously dispatched.'

Bartholomew sighed. 'Not this time, Brother. I have my teaching, my patients and my treatise on fevers, and I cannot spare the time to help you delve into the sordid world of murder. I have told you what I will do to help. The rest is for you and your beadles to investigate.'

Michael said nothing and Bartholomew suspected his clever mind was already devising some plot to ensure his co-operation. But it was late, he had had a long day and he was disinclined to discuss the matter any further that night. He waited in silence while Cynric rapped on the great gate for Walter to let them in.

'You said you heard one of your attackers speak,' said Michael, after a while. 'Did you recognise the voice?'

Bartholomew considered and then shook his head. 'It could have been anyone. It might even have been Colton.'

'Really?' said Michael, startled. 'You think he might have set the fire in Philius's room?'

'That is not what I meant,' said Bartholomew wearily, closing his eyes and rubbing them hard. Cynric banged on the door again. 'I meant only that I did not hear the attacker speak long enough to be able to identify his voice.'

Michael pursed his lips. 'Damn! I have a feeling this will not be easy to resolve. Especially if you refuse to help me.' He shot the physician a resentful glance. 'These killers have left little behind in the way of clues.'

'You will not keep this wine affair quiet for long, you know,' said Bartholomew, stepping forward to pound on the gate himself. Where was Walter? 'The students at Bernard's will talk and Grene died in front of a large audience.'

'But they do not know Grene and Armel drank from similar bottles,' said Michael. 'And only you and I have surmised that there may be a plot afoot more damaging than the deaths of a couple of dispensable scholars – that someone is masterminding an attack on the University itself.'

'I doubt Grene and Armel would regard themselves as dispensable,' said Bartholomew drily. He hammered again, but the gates remained firmly closed.

Michael shuffled and tutted impatiently. 'Wretched Walter!' he grumbled. 'It is one thing dozing all night, but it is another being so soundly asleep that he cannot hear us knocking.'

'Perhaps he is out on his rounds,' said Bartholomew, leaning back against the wicket-gate.

He staggered as it gave way beneath him; it swung open under his weight and almost deposited him in the mud of the yard.

'So now, as well as sleeping, the lazy tyke cannot even ensure the College is secure!' said Michael indignantly, elbowing past Bartholomew and heading for the porter's lodge. 'I will have words with Master Kenyngham about this!'

Bartholomew exchanged an uneasy glance with Cynric, and a chilling sense that all was not as it should be gripped at him as he followed Michael inside.

The porter's lodge was in darkness, and Michael's mutterings and irritable sighs as he fumbled with a tinder were loud in the still room. As Michael's candle finally flared into light, Bartholomew braced himself for the unpleasant sight he was sure would greet them.

Walter lay on the floor, swathed in a blanket and bound with ropes at the feet, waist and elbows. The porter's own hood had been rolled lengthways and tied firmly around his head to prevent him from raising the alarm. Michael stared in horror and Bartholomew had to push him out of the way so that he could begin sawing through the ropes to set Walter free.

He was relieved when the porter started to whimper. At least he was alive. The ropes had been tied securely, and it was some time before Bartholomew was able to loosen them all sufficiently to pull the blanket away.

Terrified eyes greeted him. Walter gazed at Bartholomew for a moment and then began to look about him wildly.

'Are they still here? They said they would kill me if I moved before dawn!'

'Who?' asked Bartholomew, helping Walter to a stool. He went into the small adjoining chamber in search of the jug of stolen ale he knew he would find there. He poured some into a grimy clay goblet and handed it to Walter. The porter gulped it noisily and held out the cup for more.

'The men who came,' he said. 'They asked me which was your room and which was Brother Michael's, and then they trussed me up like a Michaelmas goose! They said if I tried to go for help or made a sound before dawn, they would kill me!'

'Who were these men? Did you recognise them?' asked Michael.

Predictably, Walter shook his head. 'I was asleep ...' he faltered, and gazed up at the scholars, aghast at his unintentional admission of guilt.

Michael gave a snort of disgust. 'Tell us what we do not know, not what we do.'

'I was resting my eyes in the dark, and the next thing I knew was that there was a blanket over my head. I started to yell and struggle, but a man's voice said that if I did not shut up, he would strangle me. He asked which rooms were yours and then tied me up.' He took another hearty gulp of ale and looked about him fearfully. 'This town is becoming too dangerous for law-abiding folk.'

'And I suppose you told him where our rooms were,' said Michael, looking down at him disdainfully, his large arms folded across his chest.

'Too right I did!' exploded Walter, puffing himself up with righteous indignation. 'They would have killed me if I had been difficult with them. And what does it matter, anyway? Neither of you owns anything worth stealing.'

'But there are potent medicines in my storeroom,' objected Bartholomew. 'They might be used to injure or even kill.'

'And I have a great many belongings that are of considerable value,' said Michael, offended. 'Besides my priceless illustrated books, I have a fine collection of gold crucifixes and a pair of silver candlesticks from the Holy City.'

'Do you?' asked Bartholomew, surprised. 'You have never shown them to me.'

'You are not supposed to own that kind of thing!' retorted Walter belligerently. 'You are a monk who has taken a vow of poverty.'

'You are confusing Benedictines with Franciscans,' said Michael contemptuously. 'I have taken no such vow. And anyway, what I own is none of your affair. What is, however, is that you have failed miserably in your duty—'

He was interrupted by Cynric, who appeared breathlessly in the doorway. 'When Walter said the robbers asked about your rooms, I slipped off to see if they were still there,' he began.

'And were they?' demanded Michael, angry at himself that time had been wasted with Walter when he might have caught the thieves.

Cynric shook his head. 'Your room is untouched,' he said to Michael. He turned to Bartholomew. 'But the chest in your room has been turned inside out and the lock on the medicine room forced. As far as a glance can tell, nothing has been stolen. Except the poisoned wine.'

Michael's eyes narrowed. 'All of it?' he asked. 'All four bottles?'

Cynric nodded. 'Every last one of them. They must have searched his bedchamber first and then forced the lock on the medicine store. The bottles were not hidden and so they would have been easy to steal once the thieves had gained access to it.'

'Damn!' muttered Bartholomew. 'Now we cannot prove that Armel and Grene were killed with the same substance.'

'You can always compare the lesions on the corpses,' said Michael. 'Those little blisters you were inspecting so keenly should be proof enough. Anyway, we both had a good look at all four bottles, and they appeared to be the same. I would say that is evidence enough – our testimonies should stand in a court of law.'

'This is the second time I have been attacked because of you,' said Walter in an accusatory tone. 'It was only a couple of years back that some other villain almost killed me in order to get to one of you two.'

'And this is the second time you have failed me,' retorted Michael, unmoved. 'You did not protect me from the scoundrel who wanted to break into my chamber to deliver that satanic regalia two years ago, and tonight you have allowed intruders to make off with vital evidence that might help me unmask a murderer.'

'But you just told Bartholomew that your spoken testimony would do, since the bottles have been stolen,' objected Walter. 'Do not try to browbeat me into feeling guilty!'

'He is *Doctor* Bartholomew to you!' barked Michael. 'And how did these intruders enter the College anyway? The gate should have been barred from the inside.'

Walter opened his mouth to answer, exchanged a glance with Cynric, and snapped it shut again.

'It is better to be honest, Walter,' said Cynric unsympathetically. 'You will be found out eventually anyway.'

'Thank you, Cynric,' said Walter heavily, favouring the Welshman with a venomous glare. 'Do I look like I need your advice?'

'You did not bar the wicket-gate after we left earlier,' said Bartholomew, frowning as he tried to remember. 'I think I would have heard you. You left it undone, so that you would not have to get up to unlock it again when we returned.'

Walter refused to look at him, and sat stiffly, chin jutting out and arms folded.

'Well?' demanded Michael of Cynric. 'Was the door barred when you came back to fetch me after you found Isaac dead?'

Cynric shook his head.

'The intruders left it open after they escaped with your wine,' said Walter with sudden inspiration. 'You three are out to get me into trouble with the Master. It was not me who left the gate open when Cynric found it; it was the men who stole your wine!'

'Lies!' snapped Michael. 'The intruders must have arrived *after* Cynric summoned me to Gonville. I am a light sleeper and would have heard someone ransacking Matt's room – or mine. You left the wicket door open all night – from the time Matt was summoned to attend Philius, in fact!'

'Oh, Walter!' exclaimed Bartholomew, disgusted at the porter's feeble attempts to vindicate himself. 'You know these are dangerous times. How could you jeopardise the College and the scholars you are paid to protect when you know very well there are outlaws at large, just to avoid a few moments out in the rain.'

'I do not even have a decent cloak,' whined Walter, trying to shift the blame. 'How can I be expected to go out on so foul a night with no proper clothing?'

'Would you care to exchange yours for mine?' asked Bartholomew sweetly, knowing that Walter had recently bought a very fine cloak that was far better than anything Bartholomew had ever owned.

Walter leaned forward acquisitively and felt the material of Bartholomew's cloak between thumb and forefinger. 'No,' he said firmly, after the most superficial of examinations. 'I will keep mine, thank you very much.'

'All this is totally unacceptable,' said Michael, watching the exchange in disdain. 'You are a coward and a lazy, good-for-nothing wastrel! However, in view of your unpleasant experience, I will not recommend that the Master dismiss you. But this is your last chance, Walter. One more incident like this and I will ensure you never set foot in another College for the rest of your life. Not even in Oxford!'

Walter glowered and did not appear in the least bit grateful for Michael's leniency. Michael favoured him with a scowl of his own and swept out, Bartholomew and Cynric at his heels.

'Lord, Matt,' said the monk, raising his face to let the rain patter down on it. 'What a mess! Where in heaven's name do we go from here?'

Michael wanted to discuss the case there and then, but Bartholomew was too tired. Ignoring the fact that his few possessions were strewn across his room, he took off his sodden cloak and best gown – now sadly stained and crumpled – and climbed wearily under the blankets clad in shirt and hose. The stone-built rooms in Michaelhouse could be miserable in winter: the constant rain had caused the roof to leak and great patches of moisture blotched the walls. Bartholomew had mould growing on some of his clothes and, worse still, he had noticed the College's few and highly treasured books had developed water stains from the damp. Even the blankets on his bed had a chill, wet feel to them. He pulled them over his head and lay shivering until he fell into an uneasy doze.

What seemed like moments later, he was awoken by Michael vigorously shaking his shoulder and looming over him in the darkness like a great bird of prey.

'What is the matter?' he asked, sitting up and rubbing the sleep from his eyes. He glanced to the ill-fitting window shutters, through which he could see the night sky was beginning to lighten, although dawn was still some way off.

'It is Sunday, Matt,' whispered Michael. 'It is our turn to prepare the church for mass.'

Bartholomew groaned and flopped back onto the bed. 'It is still the middle of the night!'

'It is almost dawn and well after the time we usually rise. You know Sunday services are later than in the rest of the week.' He gave Bartholomew an unsympathetic prod. 'Hurry up, or we will be fined again for failing to carry out our duties.'

Most scholars in the University – Bartholomew among them – had taken minor orders with the Church. This meant that they came under the lenient jurisdiction of Canon, rather than secular, law. Others, like Brother Michael, had taken major orders with their accompanying vow of chastity. In return, the scholars were obliged to perform a certain number of religious duties, which included officiating at masses and giving the occasional sermon. Before the plague, these duties had been light, but the Death had had a devastating impact on the friars and monks of England and it was said that almost half their number had perished. Clergy were thus in short supply and each Fellow of Michaelhouse was obliged to take services at least twice a week.

By the time Bartholomew had dragged himself out of bed, Michael had slipped away to the kitchen for an illicit breakfast. Bartholomew washed and shaved – unevenly and inadequately, but so did most scholars whose Colleges declined to provide them with candles, but still expected them to appear neat and tidy before dawn in church – in the cold water that always stood in a jug on the floor and pulled on some clean leggings with hands that shook from the cold. He groped around in the dark until he found his best shirt and hunted down a woollen jerkin that his sister had given him for Christmas. Finally, he pulled his black scholar's tabard over his head, ran his fingers through his hair to pull it into some kind of order, grabbed his cloak, gloves and medicine bag, and left.

Michael was waiting for him at the gate, his mouth still full of the oatcakes he had stolen from the kitchen. They usually had to wait for Walter to wake up and open the gate for them, but the porter had apparently not slept again after Michael's threat, because he appeared in an instant to let them out. Bartholomew asked him how he was feeling, but received only a sullen sneer for his concern.

Clean air wafted in from the Fens, smelling of the salt sea that lapped a few miles to the north. Bartholomew

inhaled deeply. Despite his reluctance to rise, he liked
early mornings when the streets were quiet and the breeze
was fresh. The rain had stopped too, although the lane was
still a treacherous snare of potholes, patches of slick mud
and ankle-wrenching irregularities concealed under a brown
film of water. He walked next to Michael in companionable
silence, content to save any discussion of the events of the
previous day until later.

St Michael's Church was a square, black mass against the
dark sky, its low tower dwarfed by the more elegant St Mary's
further down the High Street. Michael unlocked the doors
and waited while Bartholomew began the delicate operation
of kindling the church's single, temperamental lamp.

'Hurry up!' said Michael impatiently, after a while. 'The
others will think we overslept if the church is not ready when
they arrive.'

'The wick is damp,' said Bartholomew. 'We should have
brought a new one. Ah – there we are!'

He stood back in satisfaction as the lamp spluttered into
life, shedding a golden light around the porch. Michael
picked it up and walked to the sanctuary, his sandalled
feet slapping on the newly laid tiles. Bartholomew followed,
checking the level of holy water in the stoop and emptying
the buckets strategically placed to catch the drips from the
leaking roof. While Michael muttered lauds, Bartholomew
trimmed the altar candles and found the appropriate reading
for the day in the great Bible that sat on the lectern.

As Michael finished his prayers and laid out the sacred
vessels for mass, Bartholomew scraped some of the spilled
candle wax from the altar with a knife and hummed to
himself.

'There is a dreadful stench in here,' said Michael, wrinkling
his nose in distaste and looking around him. 'It is worse than
the King's Ditch.'

'It is Master Wilson's tomb again,' said Bartholomew,
sweeping the pared wax off the altar and onto the floor

with his hand. 'Or rather the flowers John Runham insists on leaving on it every week. He just jams the fresh ones into the vase without bothering to change the water or throw the dead ones away.'

Michael strolled to the side of the chancel that housed the late Master Wilson's neat black tomb, laid a hand on it and grinned. 'Runham was complaining yet again about this at the installation feast. He said you have done his noble cousin a terrible dishonour by providing him with such a plain grave, and claims Master Wilson was a great man who deserves a finer memorial than a crude slab of marble devoid of all decoration.'

'It is decorated!' protested Bartholomew, who had been responsible for having Wilson's tomb built, and for transferring the mouldering bones from their temporary home in the graveyard to their final resting place near St Michael's altar. He came to stand next to Michael, and leaned against the black stone as he trimmed the wick of a candle with his knife. 'It has knots carved on it. And Wilson was not a great man! He was a smug and arrogant—'

'At least have the decency not to sit on his grave while you malign him!' admonished Michael, amused. 'But last night, Runham announced his intention to rectify your insult to the saintly Wilson: he plans to mount your inadequate efforts with a gilded life-sized effigy.'

'A gold statue of Wilson in our chancel?' asked Bartholomew, aghast. He gazed at the simple, but beautiful lines of the arches and windows, and tried to imagine the dead Master's smug features presiding over them through a mask of precious metal. It was not a pleasant vision. 'How could he inflict such a vile thing on this lovely building!'

'With a good deal of money and a total lack of taste,' said Michael. He patted his friend on the shoulder. 'Do not fret, Matt. I will do all in my power to prevent this crime against architecture – even if it means buying all the gold leaf in Cambridge myself to thwart him. We must protect our town from men like him, or before we know it, some Colleges will take advantage of our tolerance, and will do something totally dreadful – like raising imitation Greek temples all along the river.'

Bartholomew laughed, and went to empty the stinking water from the heavy pewter vase that always sat on Wilson's grave. He tossed the rotting flowers out of the door, and scrubbed the green slime from the vessel with a handful of wet grass.

'At least the rain has stopped,' said Michael conversationally when he walked back inside, carefully laying a tiny piece of bread on the silver paten. 'All this wet must be the cause of the winter fever among your patients who live near the river. Living near the Cam and being deluged with constant rain must have over-saturated them, and destroyed the balance of their humours.'

Bartholomew leaned his elbows on the altar, his duties forgotten at the prospect of a discussion about medicine. 'I think the swollen river has somehow invaded their drinking water. The people using the well in the Market Square seem unaffected, but those using the one in Water Lane are falling victim to this intestinal sickness.'

'Then tell them to use the market well instead,' said Michael with a shrug.

Bartholomew grimaced. 'I have, Brother. But they do not see why something as simple as water should make them so ill. They show me a cup of clear river, and ask me to show them the contagion in it. When I tell them the contagion might be too small for us to see, they cross themselves like a gaggle of frightened nuns and call me a heretic.'

'I do not understand why you waste your time with ingrates,' said Michael, pouring wine into the chalice, downing it in a gulp and pouring a second measure. 'You could be making a fortune with the wealthy merchants in the town and, instead, you choose to frequent the hovels.'

It was not the first time he had been told this. But

Bartholomew did not want to spend his days examining the urine of healthy people or working out complex astrological charts for treatments they did not need. He wanted to cure genuine diseases and treat victims with wounds who might otherwise die. He had learned his medicine from an Arab physician at the University of Paris, an unusual choice of master, which was reflected in his unorthodox treatments and diagnoses.

The present Master of Michaelhouse had been quick to see the advantage of having a physician in his College who was prepared to treat the poor. The University was unpopular in the town, and Bartholomew's services to the sick went a long way in improving the uneasy relationship between Michaelhouse and its neighbours. His rate of success was unquestionably better than the other physicians in the town, a fact made even more remarkable because he dealt mainly with people who were unable to afford expensive medicines and palliatives. So Bartholomew was allowed to attend his patients without interference from the University – with the exception of occasional queries from scholars curious as to why he was contented with his small salary as a Fellow of Michaelhouse when he could have supplemented his income by treating the wealthy.

The door creaked as the first of the scholars arrived for the morning service. Bartholomew hastily brushed the remaining wax onto the floor and joined Michael at the altar rail. Master Kenyngham knelt next to him, followed as ever by the fawning Alcote. Singly, and in pairs, the other scholars joined them, the Fellows in a row to the right and the students ranged behind them.

'I hope you were pleasantly warm last night,' whispered Alcote to Bartholomew. 'Walter tells me you stole three of my logs to make a fire.'

'Not here, gentlemen,' said Kenyngham softly. 'There is a time and a place for a discussion of logs, and at the altar during mass is not one of them.'

'Theft is theft, Master,' said Alcote sulkily. 'I would not wish Matthew to begin the day with a crime on his conscience.'

'Then I absolve him,' whispered Kenyngham, waving a vague benediction in Bartholomew's direction. 'And now we will never mention the matter again.'

Alcote's bitter indignation was lost on the other-worldly Kenyngham, whose head was already bowed as he began to pray. Next to Bartholomew, Michael's shoulders quaked with mirth and even the dour Franciscan Father William seemed amused at Alcote's discomfiture.

Another clatter of the door heralded the arrival of the scholars of Physwick Hostel, who were obliged to use St Michael's Church for their offices – and to pay Michaelhouse handsomely for the privilege. At their head was Harling, who was their Principal as well as the University's Vice-Chancellor. He was immaculately dressed and his greased hair shone in the candlelight. As a physician, however, Bartholomew detected a darkness under Harling's eyes and noted that he looked grey and tired. He wondered whether the weight of responsibility thrust on him in the Chancellor's prolonged absence at Ely was too much for him when combined with running his hostel.

While Bartholomew intoned the reading of the day in his precise Latin, Michael rounded up his choir. The choir was something Michael regarded with a good deal of ambiguity. It was by far the largest in Cambridge, comprising men and children from the parish as well as scholars from the College, and was considered, by gentle souls such as Kenyngham, as proof that not all townsfolk wanted to kill scholars and vice versa – although the fact that choir practices usually ended with bread and ale explained why the parishioners were prepared to overlook a good many insults hurled at them by the student-choristers. However, Michael's choir was also one of the least musically inclined, making up in volume for what it lacked in tone.

Among the membership were several small children, and it was Michael's hope that one or two of them might have some hitherto undiscovered talent that he could hone and encourage. Bartholomew was always surprised that the fat monk had the patience to deal with children, but he was remarkably good with them, and they certainly did not hold him in fear, as did the unfortunate undergraduates who came within reach of his proctorial arm.

The anthem for the day was a difficult *Gloria* by Gherardello da Firenze, which, sung by them, bore more resemblance to the bawdy songs bellowed by students on illicit visits to taverns than a religious piece. It gradually increased in speed, too, despite Michael's frantic arm-waving to slow it down. The piece ended somewhat abruptly, although two elderly tenors in the back row had been left behind and found themselves singing a duet after everyone else had finished. As always, their Sunday morning efforts were greeted by a stunned silence, and it took several moments for Kenyngham to collect himself sufficiently to continue.

Eventually, the long service was over and the scholars lined up to process back to Michaelhouse for breakfast. Bartholomew saw Vice-Chancellor Harling reach out and grab Michael's arm, whispering something in his ear to which Michael nodded. Then both men turned and regarded Bartholomew speculatively. The physician felt his heart sink. He could decline Michael's request for help – the monk understood his reluctance to become involved, even if he did not approve – but if the demand came from the Vice-Chancellor he would have no alternative but to comply. As Harling nodded coolly in his direction, Bartholomew knew he was going to be dragged into the affair of the poisoned wine whether he liked it or not.

Kenyngham led the way down St Michael's Lane – at a healthy pace, for the rain had started again – and the scholars hurried across the yard, eager for their breakfast.

Bartholomew took his place at the high table, with Michael on one side and Father Paul on the other. As usual, he reached out to grab some of the best bread for Paul, who could not see, before Michael could take it all.

'What did Harling want?' said Bartholomew in a low voice, scraping egg-mash onto Paul's trencher before taking some himself. Sunday's breakfast, being later than during the week, was always better and Agatha's egg-mash flavoured with bacon fat was the highlight of a day in which much was forbidden. To escape the College and its dull restrictions, Bartholomew often walked to the nearby village of Trumpington on Sundays to visit his sister.

'He wants me to appraise him of Grene's death,' muttered Michael, smiling sweetly at Alcote, who was glowering at him for breaking the rule of silence at mealtimes.

'Is he enjoying all this unexpected power?' whispered Bartholomew. 'I thought he looked ill this morning. When is Chancellor Tynkell back from Ely?'

'He was due back yesterday for the installation, apparently,' Michael replied, holding a lump of bread near his mouth in a vain attempt to fool Alcote into believing he was not talking. 'Harling thinks he decided not to make the journey because of the bad weather.'

'Then Harling might enjoy his power for a good while yet,' said Bartholomew. 'This rain shows no sign of relenting.'

'You do Harling an injustice,' remonstrated Michael. 'Any other man who lost the post that should have been his would have been bitter. Harling accepted his defeat with a graciousness I find honourable, and he has continued to serve the University with the utmost integrity. Anyway, he clearly thinks highly of you, because he said your duties in treating the poor are more important than helping me solve the affair of the poisoned wine.'

'Really?' asked Bartholomew, startled into speaking loudly. Several heads turned towards him, and Michael pretended to be absorbed in eating his eggs.

Master Kenyngham looked at them with raised eyebrows. 'Since you two clearly have something to discuss, perhaps I should allow conversation at meals today,' he said wryly. 'Then you will not set a poor example to the students.'

'That would be a mistake, Master,' said the dour Father William promptly. 'It is only a small step from ill-discipline to heresy.'

'I hardly think erudite disputation at breakfast will lead to heresy, William,' said gentle Father Paul with a smile. 'And the students are restless because the rain is keeping them in. I think the time has come to make concessions before we really do have a discipline problem.'

'Nonsense!' said William. 'You are far too soft with them. If anything, they need a reduction of concessions, not an easier life. If I were appointed Junior Proctor, I would show the University how to keep order among the students.'

He shot Michael a baleful look that Michael pretended not to notice. Father William had put himself forward for the post of Junior Proctor when the previous incumbent had left to serve the King. Not surprisingly, given the Franciscan friar's uncompromising and inflexible views of the world and everyone in it, his application had not been successful. Bartholomew did not know whether Michael had played a role in William's rejection or whether the friar's reputation had spoken for itself, but Michael was, nevertheless, invariably uncomfortable when the issue was raised.

'Have some eggs,' said Bartholomew, before William could begin a tirade on how he would personally reform the University by burning half its scholars in the Market Square for heresy.

'Eggs!' said William in disgust, gesturing at the bowl Bartholomew held out to him. 'I was never so coddled when I was an undergraduate!'

'But you have eaten them, nevertheless,' Alcote observed, eyeing William's empty trencher. 'Anyway,' he continued hastily when he saw William preparing himself for a row, 'I see no harm in conversation, so long as it is kept to religious matters and is in Latin.'

While Father William shook his head in fervent disapproval, Kenyngham announced that conversation would be permitted during meals that day, provided the topic were theological and the language Latin. There was an immediate buzz of chatter from the students, although the little core of Franciscans followed William's example and maintained their silence.

'Good,' said Michael. 'Now we can discuss last night's events before I meet Harling.'

'Hardly a religious matter, Brother,' said Bartholomew, turning his attention back to his breakfast.

'But we are speaking Latin,' said Michael comfortably, 'so we are half-way there.'

'I do not want to become involved in this,' said Bartholomew. 'I am sick of murder.'

'So are we all, Matt,' replied Michael. 'I told Harling as much this morning, and that was when he said you need not assist me in this if you feel you do not want to, and that your work among the people with winter fever was more valuable to the University than assisting me.'

'Harling said that?'

Michael nodded, genuinely puzzled. 'I admit I was surprised. I thought he would have commandeered anyone's assistance in order to solve this as quickly as possible. He said you should not be forced to do anything that would interfere with your other duties.'

Bartholomew's opinion of Harling rose several degrees. It was certainly unexpected – the University's officials seldom considered people's preferences when their beloved institution was at risk – and Harling's sympathetic response came as a pleasant change from orders and demands.

'There is a curious thing about Tynkell's election as Chancellor,' mused Bartholomew, his mind wandering back to the ballot that Harling lost. 'I have never met anyone who voted for him. Everyone I know says they voted for Harling, but Harling still did not win.'

Michael shrugged. 'That is because Tynkell is an unknown quantity. No one would be foolish enough to admit voting for him when he might prove . . . inappropriate.'

'Not everyone I know is so dishonest,' objected Bartholomew. 'I voted for Harling myself.'

'So did I,' said Michael fervently. 'Although you know that – you took my voting slip to St Mary's Church because I was ill.'

'You had indigestion because you ate three apple pies one after the other and shared them with no one,' corrected Bartholomew.

'So?' asked Michael. 'Indigestion is being ill. I was confined to my bed, was I not? Anyway, by eating those pies myself, I saved you from a similar fate.'

'Most thoughtful of you, Brother.'

'But let us go back to Harling. He has his faults, but better the Devil you know. He works well with the Proctors, has the respect of the beadles and is a cunning negotiator.'

'I had never heard William Tynkell's name before the election,' reflected Bartholomew. 'Yet everyone knew Harling, and he is not unpopular. I do not understand why so many masters voted for such a nonentity as Tynkell.'

Michael stared at him. 'Are you suggesting the election was falsified?'

Bartholomew shrugged. 'I confess the notion has crossed my mind. Who counted the votes?'

Michael grabbed the egg bowl and began to dig out the bits left at the bottom with his knife. 'Each master signs his own name and that of his favoured candidate on a slip of parchment, and hands it to the Senior Proctor. The Senior Proctor and the Vice-Chancellor then count the votes.'

'Yes, yes,' said Bartholomew impatiently. 'I know what is supposed to happen. But when Tynkell was elected that procedure was not followed: Harling, as Vice-Chancellor, could not count the votes of an election in which he was a candidate; and you did not count them, as Senior Proctor, because you were brought low by three apple pies.'

Michael crammed a loaded knife of egg scraps into his mouth. 'In our absence, two men were selected whose integrity was beyond question.' He ignored Bartholomew's snort of derision and continued. 'Namely Father Eligius from Valence Marie and our own Master Kenyngham.'

Bartholomew reconsidered. He did not know Eligius particularly well, but Kenyngham's honesty was beyond question. He watched Michael's face grow sweaty with the exertion of reclaiming the last of the egg from the bowl and tried to put the matter from his mind. Michael was doubtless right, and most scholars would be waiting to see what kind of chancellor Tynkell made before admitting that they had helped him into power.

'We digress,' said Michael, pushing the empty bowl away from him and leaning back in his seat. 'I know you do not want to become involved – and that you have Harling's sanction to let me struggle against evil killers alone – but you will not refuse me a discussion of the facts, will you?'

Bartholomew shook his head, although his instinct was to decline. Michael steepled his fingers and rested his elbows on the table.

'Then let us review the events leading to these deaths. Yesterday morning, a man in the Brazen George sells three bottles of poisoned wine to a group of students, one of whom later dies. At some point, a similar bottle of wine found its way to James Grene, who perished horribly, but highly conveniently, before a goodly part of the town. Valence Marie's most eminent scholar, Father Eligius, believes Grene's rival, the newly installed Master Bingham, murdered him.'

'And Bingham's motive is either that Grene was proving to be a bad loser, or Grene's misguided, but fanatical, belief that a handful of boiled bones was a sacred relic was proving awkward,' said Bartholomew.

'Meanwhile,' continued Michael, 'we can surmise, from what Philius told us, that a fifth bottle came into the possession of your brother-in-law a month ago and killed one of his apprentices, after which it was appropriated by the light-fingered Isaac. Isaac eventually used the stolen wine to make Philius's weekly purge – obviously not knowing it was poisoned – whereby he brought Philius to death's door and burned his own hand in the process. Isaac was murdered as he went to fetch the bottle for you to inspect, probably by the three people who knocked me over in their haste to leave Gonville Hall. We have already established that they were unarmed – they hanged, not stabbed, Isaac and did no real harm to you or Philius – and I conclude that they came only to steal the bottle before we could inspect it properly.'

'No, not steal,' said Bartholomew, thinking. 'Retrieve.'

Michael looked blankly at him and waited for an explanation.

'This is a strange poison – I have never seen anything quite like it before. Isaac's killers seem to be going to some lengths to find the bottles, which suggests to me that they know exactly what is in them, and that, in turn, means that they must have had them in their possession at some point – so they came to retrieve, not steal them.'

'I see,' said Michael, nodding.

Bartholomew continued. 'At some point between the time Isaac used the wine to make Philius's purge and Isaac's death, the bottle rolled under the bench and was smashed: Isaac's killer could not find it. When Cynric called me to look at Isaac's body, the killers then slipped across the yard into Philius's room to look for the bottle there. I came back sooner than they anticipated and we struggled in the dark. They threw the lamp against the wall to start a fire to distract me long enough to allow them to return to the storeroom for a second search.'

Michael shook his head. 'Too risky. I agree that they started the fire to distract you, but it was to prevent you from chasing them not to give them time to search again.' He pulled at the straggling whiskers on his chin. 'You said you saw two people running away from Philius's room, whereas Cynric and I encountered three. I suspect one person was left in the storeroom to continue the search there, while the other two went to Philius's room. There were enough sacks and barrels in the room to make hiding easy.'

'You mean one of the people who killed Isaac watched me while I examined his body?' said Bartholomew in horror.

Michael nodded. 'There is no other rational explanation. You said you saw the bottle under the bench – thus revealing its whereabouts to the watching person who later removed all traces of it. But I think you were in no danger.'

'Isaac was!' said Bartholomew, unconvinced.

'I have no explanation for Isaac's demise,' said Michael pompously, 'but that third person could have killed you in the storeroom when you found the bottle: he did not. The other two might have killed you when you struggled with them in Philius's room: again, they did not. And they could have killed Walter when they came to "retrieve" the bottles from your room: but they did not. I think your theory is correct, and that the sole intention of these people was to regain possession of the bottles. We had five of them – three from Bernard's, one from Valence Marie and the smashed one from Gonville – and now we have none. In the bottles, and thus in the nature of this strange poison, lies the answer to this mystery.'

'So, have you abandoned the notion that this is a dire plot by the town to kill scholars?' asked Bartholomew, putting a wizened apple into Paul's hand before passing the bowl to Michael, who took three.

'Not at all,' said Michael, his mouth full. 'Such a plot is still the most plausible explanation for all this.'

'I suppose you think these bottles have been retrieved so that they can be used again?' asked Bartholomew flippantly.

'So all we need to do next time is to lay a trap for whoever comes to get them back.'

Michael gave him a withering glance. 'At least I have a theory,' he said irritably. 'You have nothing more than a collection of conflicting ideas – you think Grene's death is too convenient to be coincidence and suspect Bingham in playing a role, yet at the same time, you do not believe Bingham is competent to carry out such an attack. You say the wine in the bottle at Gonville brought Philius to the brink of death, burned Isaac's hand and killed a rat, yet you say you saw that sot of a cat drink its fill with no ill effects at all.'

'The cat!' exclaimed Bartholomew, ignoring Michael's peevishness. 'Colton said it prowls the College looking for wine and ale and smashes things. The cat must have smashed the bottle! It can scarcely uncork them for itself, and has probably learned that the best way into a bottle is to break it.'

'That would explain why the killers could not find it,' said Michael thoughtfully. 'It lay smashed under the bench. Perhaps they asked Isaac for it, and killed him when he could not tell them. Since in talking to them they had revealed their identities, Isaac was murdered to ensure he could not tell us who was so interested in obtaining poisoned wine.'

It was possible, Bartholomew supposed. They had certainly threatened Walter with death if he tried to escape from his bonds before dawn, even if they had not harmed Bartholomew when the opportunity presented itself.

The discussion was cut short when Ralph de Langelee slammed his goblet down on the table in a sudden display of temper. Bartholomew almost jumped out of his skin, and the babble of conversation in the hall died away abruptly.

'That is the most ridiculous thing I have ever heard!' Langelee exclaimed furiously. 'Of course the Earth is not irregularly shaped: it is a perfect sphere!'

'It is not!' shouted Alcote, equally angry. 'So there!' he added, as if that clinched the debate.

'Gentlemen, gentlemen,' admonished Kenyngham soothingly. 'There is no need for such rage while debating philosophical questions.'

'The shape in which God created the Earth is a religious question, not a philosophical one,' put in William quickly, determined not to lose the opportunity to utter a little dogma.

'Religion and philosophy reach a point where they become one and the same,' said Alcote.

There was a brief silence as the others digested this bit of profundity from such an unexpected quarter.

'Heretic!' yelled William after a moment, stabbing a finger at Alcote's puny chest. 'Theology is the noblest of all subjects and should never be mistaken for any of the lesser disciplines.'

'You are trying to sidetrack me,' snapped Langelee accusingly. 'I was just telling Alcote that the Earth was a perfect sphere and—'

'One does not "tell" another scholar something like that,' said Michael pompously. 'One raises the matter as a question, and there follows a stimulating and mutually beneficial exchange of views, during which each listens to the other, offering evidence for support or refute as appropriate.'

'Not if the other's point of view is the intellectual equivalent of horse dung,' retorted Langelee. 'I do not have time to listen to drivel!'

'I would stay out of this, if I were you, Brother,' cautioned Bartholomew in an undertone. 'You will not make them accept the validity of your statements, and Langelee looks as if he might resort to physical persuasion to me.'

'How can the Earth be a perfect sphere?' asked Runham with affected weariness. 'There would be nothing to prevent the sea invading the land, and there would be water everywhere.'

'And what about mountains?' asked Bartholomew, aware

of Michael's grin of amusement that he was unable to follow his own advice.

'And where, pray, do you see mountains?' demanded Langelee icily. He gestured out of the window. 'Show me a mountain and I will concede your point.'

'Obviously there are none in East Anglia,' said Bartholomew, wondering, not for the first time, how Langelee had inveigled an appointment at Michaelhouse. 'But there are hills in the north of England and mountains in Italy, France and Spain.'

'You are lying,' said Langelee dismissively. 'There are no mountains in York.'

In the body of the hall, the students were enjoying the dissension between the Fellows with unconcealed delight, much of their gleeful amusement directed against the unpopular Langelee.

'I visited York once,' said Kenyngham, smiling wistfully. 'What a charming place! The Minster is a fabulous thing, all delicate tracery and soaring windows.'

'But did you see mountains?' asked Alcote, reluctant to allow the Master to change the subject to something less contentious.

'Castle Hill is a mountain,' said Runham. 'Or it is mountain enough to prove Matthew's point. If the Earth were a perfect sphere, Castle Hill would not exist.'

'That is a foolish argument!' spat Langelee. 'If Castle Hill did not exist, there would be nowhere to put the castle!'

The others regarded him uncertainly, none of them sure how he had arrived at such a conclusion or how to refute it. Before the debate could begin anew, Kenyngham wisely took advantage of the momentary silence to stand to say grace. The others scrambled to their feet and bowed their heads as the Gilbertine's words echoed around the hall. As soon as he had finished, the students clattered noisily down the stairs and across the courtyard, some to read in their rooms, others to escape the College and indulge in something better than enduring Michaelhouse's petty restrictions on the one day they were free from their studies.

Michael and Bartholomew made a hasty exit, too, neither wanting to become embroiled in a debate with the others, particularly Langelee. Bartholomew shook his head in disbelief as he overheard the philosopher informing William that the Earth was a perfect sphere because it was created by God, and God could create nothing imperfect. Langelee, however, was preaching to the converted, and William agreed with him that all mountains and hills were therefore an abomination and should be levelled. Raising his eyes heavenwards, Michael went to the kitchens to scavenge leftovers, while Bartholomew escorted Father Paul to the room he shared with William.

'When a man loses a sense, such as sight, the body compensates,' announced Paul, somewhat out of the blue.

'I have heard that,' said Bartholomew, steering him around a puddle. 'I knew a deaf man once who was able to tell from shadows and smell when there was someone behind him.'

'I hear exceptionally well,' continued Paul, 'and although you and Michael took care to keep your voices low before that silly debate started, I heard what was said. I also have an excellent sense of smell. Should you recover these bottles, I would be happy to see if I can detect similarities or differences in this poison for you.'

'Thank you,' said Bartholomew. 'But this substance is foul, and I would not like anyone to smell it, in case they inhale noxious fumes. Presumably, the stuff is odourless anyway, or Armel and Grene would not have drunk it.'

'True,' said Paul. 'Although my offer remains should you need it. But, regardless, take care, Matthew. Brother Michael is an ambitious man, and little will stop him attaining the power and influence he craves. He will not hesitate to enlist your help to gain it.'

Bartholomew stared at him. It was true that Michael, as Senior Proctor, regularly called on his medical knowledge to help him solve mysteries concerning violent deaths. But would Michael involve him in something dangerous to secure his own advancement? Bartholomew would like to believe not, but he knew Paul's observation held more than a grain of truth. Michael's ambition must be strong indeed for him to forgo the opportunity to be Master of a wealthy institution like Valence Marie on the strength of some unspecified promise for the future made by a Bishop whose own empire might crumble in the shifting grounds of political alliances at any moment.

Although Bartholomew could attest that Michael really had been unwell on the day of the Chancellor's election, he had put up little resistance when Bartholomew had advised him to stay in bed. Bartholomew also knew the monk well enough to see that he had not been surprised in the slightest at the suggestion that the voting process might not have been honestly conducted. Was his illness that day a coincidence and, if so, did he know more about it than he was admitting? But it was surely in Michael's interests to have Harling as Chancellor – rather than the unknown quantity represented by Tynkell – and Bartholomew did not believe that the fat monk would keep silent if he had tangible evidence that the election had been fixed.

He was about to reply in Michael's defence, when Paul thrust something into his hand. Bartholomew stared down at the gold coins in astonishment.

'I hear there is fever among the town's poor,' said Paul. 'Perhaps this might go some way to providing medicines they might need.'

Bartholomew was startled. 'It would, indeed. But you cannot give me all this!'

He tried to make Paul take the coins back, but the friar pushed his hand away. 'I have recently come into a little money,' he said enigmatically. 'I would sooner it went to the poor than sat in my room. I plan to give the remainder to the leper hospital.'

'Then, thank you,' said Bartholomew. 'I will send Gray this morning to buy medicines, and Bulbeck can arrange for deliveries of eggs and bread to those that need them. The reason why many take so long to regain their strength is because they cannot afford the proper food.'

'So I have heard,' said Paul. 'You believe the well in Water Lane is responsible?'

Bartholomew nodded, forgetting Paul could not see. 'I have never encountered a fever quite like this – except once in Greece when a brook was fouled because a goat had died in it further upstream. But the Water Lane well is protected by a wall and a cover, and it is impossible for an animal to fall in. The only explanation I can think of is that the raised level of the river has invaded the well – the river became flooded around the same time that the fever claimed its first victim.'

They turned as a messenger was allowed through the gate and came racing across the yard towards them.

'Brother Michael?' he asked of Paul, and stopped dead as Paul's opaque blue eyes turned towards him. 'Where can I find Brother Michael?'

'In the kitchens,' said Bartholomew. 'Do you have a message for him from the Bishop?'

The messenger nodded vigorously. 'And then I must deliver the same message to the Vice-Chancellor. There was an attack yesterday on a party travelling from Ely to Cambridge for the installation. Three clerks lie dead. And among the injured is Chancellor Tynkell.'

ChAPTER 4

BARTHOLOMEW STARED AT THE MESSENGER IN HORROR. While the road from Cambridge to London was dangerous, the one between Cambridge and Ely had always been comparatively safe from outlaws. The Bishop of Ely was a powerful man, and usually ensured the routes between his Abbey and the towns and villages with which he needed to communicate were well patrolled.

'How many have been injured? How badly hurt?' he asked.

The messenger shrugged. He was a young man and, judging from his rough clothes and casual manner, not someone regularly employed by the Bishop – the Bishop set great store by appearances and his staff usually wore liveries.

'I was told only that three were dead and several injured, including the Chancellor,' he said impatiently. 'But I must find Brother Michael.'

Bartholomew hailed Cynric, watching curiously from where he was feeding the chickens outside the hall, and sent him to find Michael. Cynric knew exactly where Michael would be, and within moments the fat monk was puffing across the yard to greet the messenger. He received the news with the same shock as had Bartholomew.

'But the Bishop keeps a regular patrol on the Ely to Cambridge road. How could such a thing happen?'

The messenger shrugged again. 'I am telling you only

what I know. The Bishop said that you are to go to Ely immediately, and that you are to bring Doctor Bartholomew for the injured.'

'But Brother Peter at Ely is a fine physician,' said Bartholomew, puzzled. 'Why does the Bishop want me?'

The messenger was becoming exasperated at their questions. 'I do not know! Perhaps the Chancellor asked for you specifically.'

'I doubt it,' said Michael. 'The Chancellor is highly suspicious of Matt's dedication to cleanliness. Given his own aversion to bathing, I suppose that is not surprising.'

'We should not waste time,' said the messenger, squinting up at the sky. 'We do not want to be caught on the open road tonight, and the riding is hard after all this rain. The Bishop has provided an escort for you – I left them taking refreshments at the Brazen George. By your leave, I will give the Bishop's message to Master Harling and wait for you in the tavern.'

Michael waved him away and turned to Bartholomew. 'This is a bad business, but if the Bishop has commanded us to go, we have little choice in the matter. We will miss teaching for a few days. I will inform Master Kenyngham.

'A few days?' exclaimed Bartholomew in horror. 'I cannot leave my students that long! I am already behind with the third years and Gray looks set to fail his disputation—'

'Then they will just need to work harder when you get back,' said Michael unsympathetically. 'Your students are a worthless rabble anyway. None of them will make decent physicians, despite all the attention you have lavished on them.'

'Bulbeck will,' said Bartholomew, stung, but Michael was already striding away. Cynric, eyes alight with excitement, offered to pack what they would need and Bartholomew saw that the Welshman intended to accompany them, invited or not.

As he turned to hunt down Gray and Bulbeck, who would

need to supervise the other students while he was away, Father Paul stopped him.

'This has an odd ring to it,' he said. 'How could a large party – for the Chancellor never travels without his clerkly retinue – be attacked on the Ely road? And three dead? It sounds excessive!'

Bartholomew regarded him uncertainly. 'Do you think the messenger is lying?'

Paul pushed out his lower lip. 'I could not say,' he said, after a moment's thought. 'But I think he is not telling you the whole truth. And why would the Chancellor suddenly ask for you when he has never requested that you attend him before?'

Bartholomew watched Cynric disappear through the door to his room to collect what they would require for the journey. 'Are you suggesting we should not go?'

Paul shook his head. 'I am only reiterating what I said to you earlier. Be careful.' He sketched a benediction in the air above Bartholomew's head, and took his leave. Bartholomew watched him walk away and then thrust the warning from his mind. He knew from long experience that men brought low by sickness and injury often did or said things out of character, so perhaps Tynkell's request was not so curious after all. Perhaps he simply wanted a physician from his own University over the Benedictine infirmarian at Ely Abbey.

He found Gray and Bulbeck, his two senior students, playing dice in the room of one of his younger pupils, Rob Deynman. The substantial payments Deynman's wealthy father made for the training of his barely literate son kept Michaelhouse in bread for at least half the year, and so Bartholomew was stuck with him, despite the fact that Deynman would never pass his disputations. In time, bribes would have to be made, but, in the interim Bartholomew intended to shield the unsuspecting public from the lad's dubious medical skills for as long as possible.

He told the three students that he had been summoned

to Ely and that they would need to supervise the other students' classes until he returned. He handed Paul's gold coins to Bulbeck, and issued instructions about the food and medicines for the poor.

'Are you going to answer the charges of heresy brought against you for your theories about river water?' asked Deynman, his eyes wide with interest. Gray was unable to prevent a muffled explosion of mirth at Deynman's bluntness.

'No,' said Bartholomew tartly. 'It is about another matter.'

'Not the business of Armel and the poison?' asked Gray.

'What do you know about that?' asked Bartholomew, startled.

Gray glanced furtively at his friends. 'Nothing much. We heard that Xavier dragged you away from the feast and that Armel was poisoned. The story was all over the Brazen George last night.'

'Was it now?' said Bartholomew, eyebrows raised. 'And how do you know? Surely you did not break College rules and slip out to visit a tavern while all the Fellows were at the installation?'

Gray flushed red and Bulbeck shuffled his feet around in the rushes.

'Oh no!' said Deynman, grinning cheerfully. 'We went out long before that.' The others gave him crushing looks. 'What?' Deynman demanded of them, oblivious of the implications of his reply. He turned back to Bartholomew. 'We saw old Sacks selling Armel the wine, though.'

'What?' said Bartholomew, looking from one student to the other, confused. 'Old Sacks?'

'Sacks claims to be a Crécy veteran,' said Gray reluctantly, still glaring at Deynman. 'He is called Sacks because that is what he does – he makes sacks for flour and suchlike. He is often in the George, selling bits and pieces.'

'Often?' enquired Bartholomew casually.

Gray winced, caught out a second time.

Bulbeck gave Gray a withering glance and continued. 'Sometimes he sells ribbons and laces, such as a chapman might have. Sometimes pots and pans. But recently he has had wine.'

'My brother once bought a lute from him,' said Deynman, eager to take part in the conversation, 'but another student told him it had been stolen from Master Colton of Gonville Hall. We took it round to Gonville and the Master identified it as his, although all he did to reward us for our honesty was threaten to tell you that we had been drinking in the town's taverns. So we never buy anything from Sacks because whatever he sells is bound to be stolen.'

'Of course, Armel and his friends were not to know that,' said Gray in a superior tone. 'That bunch of nuns never break the University rules. They came to the George yesterday for the first time ever – can you believe it when the tavern is only next door to their hostel? – and fell for Sacks's patter.'

'Then why did you not warn them?' asked Bartholomew. 'Surely it was uncharitable to allow them to buy potentially stolen goods?'

'They are from Bernard's,' said Deynman with high indignation. 'A hostel! Had they been Michaelhouse students, it would have been different.'

'And it was only wine,' said Gray, grinning at Deynman. He sobered suddenly as he thought about it. 'Except it was not, was it?'

'No,' said Bartholomew shortly. 'It was not. What of Sacks? Has he a grudge against students?'

The three looked at each other, mystified. 'I would say not,' said Gray. 'Students provide him with much of his trade. He has been operating in the George for years.'

So, it would seem that Armel had not been sold the poisoned wine intentionally – at least not by Sacks. But there was always the possibility that someone had given it to Sacks to peddle knowing exactly what was in it.

'Where does Sacks live?' asked Bartholomew.

Gray shrugged. 'No one really knows. He has cheated so many people that it is safer for him to keep his lodgings secret. I think he has some kind of dwelling to the north, up in the Fens. He certainly does not live in Cambridge.'

'Two more questions,' said Bartholomew, 'and then we will say no more about these illicit visits to taverns. First, how many bottles did Sacks have yesterday?'

'Four,' said Gray promptly. 'And they looked like the same ones he had tried to sell last month – thin bottles of a smoky-brown colour.'

'And second, to whom did he sell the other bottle?' asked Bartholomew. 'We know Armel bought three.'

The students looked at each other, frowning in concentration.

Deynman suddenly brightened. 'One of fat old Stanmore's apprentices bought one when Sacks first tried to sell the stuff a month or so ago. I do not know his name.'

'One of Oswald Stanmore's lads?' asked Bartholomew.

Deynman blushed, embarrassed. He had forgotten Stanmore was his teacher's brother-in-law.

'That was ... four weeks last Saturday,' said Bulbeck hurriedly, before Deynman could dig himself into a deeper trench of indiscretion. 'Perhaps Sacks still has the last bottle. He said he had half a dozen when he first tried to sell them, and he had four last night. So, if he had only sold two bottles in a month, he could not have been doing too well with them.'

Gray and Deynman agreed and looked at Bartholomew warily, not certain what he would do with the knowledge that they had been regularly and flagrantly flouting the University's rules about inns.

'We only went out because Sam has been depressed,' said Deynman. He looked at Gray, who gnawed anxiously at his lower lip. 'He has been sad since Eleanor Tyler left town last year. He was fond of her and we only wanted to cheer him up.'

Bartholomew was unmoved. 'That was months ago and you had not known her for long.'

'But it was love at first sight,' protested Deynman, rallying to his friend's defence. 'They adored each other and he misses her terribly.'

Bartholomew sighed. Unconvinced as he was by Gray's lovesick state – he seriously doubted that anyone could penetrate the thick skin of self-interest that was one of the less attractive aspects of Gray's personality – he often felt the University's regulations were too restrictive for young men with high spirits. Trying to ban them from taverns was as hopeless as emptying a well with a sieve. But he was fond of these three students nevertheless, and the thought that one of them might go the same way as Armel filled him with horror.

'While I am gone, and until this business is over, I want you to promise me you will stay away from taverns and eat only in Michaelhouse. Do I have your word?' He looked at them one by one.

'But you might be gone for ages,' protested Gray. 'We will starve if we eat only Michaelhouse food.' He looked sly. 'And I need to build myself up for my disputation.'

Bartholomew could not help smiling. 'Then you must attempt to ingratiate yourself with Agatha. She feeds Michael well enough.'

Gray could not argue that the obese Michael was anything but well fed. He nodded with ill grace. 'I suppose, since you seem so concerned for our welfare, that we will humour you and suffer on Michaelhouse fare until you return.'

'I am more concerned that years of my hard work should not be brought to an untimely end by a single sip of wine,' said Bartholomew. He was gratified to see Gray look indignant. Gray had twice saved Bartholomew's life and both times had claimed his sole motive was that if he lost his teacher it would interfere with his plans to become a wealthy and successful physician. Bartholomew felt somewhat avenged.

When he had wrung similar promises from the other two, he took his leave. Cynric was waiting for him, holding Bartholomew's cloak over his arm and with spare shirt and hose packed in a bag. Michael joined them.

'I need to talk to Harling before we leave for Ely. I must tell him what we have reasoned about Grene's death.'

'We should also speak to Oswald about the apprentice that Philius said he visited a month ago,' said Bartholomew. 'The one who died of symptoms similar to those suffered by Armel and Grene.'

'Should we?' asked Michael, raising his eyebrows. 'And here was I under the impression that you wanted to have nothing to do with my investigation. Silly me!'

'I do not,' protested Bartholomew. 'I only want to ensure the safety of Oswald and his apprentices. And I promised to check on Philius this morning. It will not take long.'

Michael glanced up at the sky. 'We must leave enough time to reach Ely by nightfall and we will need longer than usual if the riding is rough. Especially with you along,' he added rudely, referring to Bartholomew's notorious lack of skill on horseback.

Leaving Cynric to take their bags to the Brazen George, Bartholomew and Michael went first to Gonville Hall. Michael talked with Master Colton while Bartholomew went to see his patient.

Philius was sitting up in his bed eating oatmeal cooked with milk. He was pale and ate carefully so as not to hurt his burned mouth, but at least he was well enough to eat at all.

'I hear I need to thank you twice – once for delivering me from the poison that was eating away at my innards, and once for quenching a fire that would have burned me to a cinder.'

He gestured for Bartholomew to sit on one of the stools near the bed. 'Now, as to the matter of payment . . .'

Bartholomew shook his head. 'Who knows? I might need your services one day.'

Philius smiled. 'So be it. Although I was always under the impression that you regard my traditional approach to medicine with more than a degree of scepticism.'

'That is not true,' said Bartholomew. He shrugged. 'I just experiment more than you do.'

'So I have heard,' said Philius. 'Isaac told me . . .' He trailed off and the events of the previous night hung in the air uncomfortably between them. Philius swallowed hard and continued. 'Isaac told me that you had treated a case of the bloody flux with nothing more than boiled water.'

'It worked,' said Bartholomew defensively. 'And I used infusions of cumin and anise as well, not to mention a specially devised diet for afterwards—'

'I know, I know,' said Philius, raising one hand to quiet him. 'I was not criticising you, merely repeating what I had been told. I was going to suggest we might learn something if we could be a little more patient with each other's ideas. I hear you are writing a treatise on fevers. I have always been interested in fevers and would very much like to read it when it is completed.'

'That will not be for some time,' said Bartholomew gloomily. 'There are too many distractions – teaching, my patients and now this summons to Ely.'

He told Philius about the attack on the Chancellor. The Franciscan shook his head. 'Cambridge is becoming a dangerous place. I am seriously thinking of leaving and returning to Italy. There are brigands there, too, of course, but at least it does not rain all the time.'

He toyed with his food and then looked at Bartholomew, his eyes anxious. 'It is a bad business with Isaac. I was uncertain whether you understood what I was trying to say. Isaac was always looking to make money, although I usually turned a blind eye. Anyway, I attended Stanmore's house late on a Saturday night – more than a month ago now – where one of the apprentices had been struck down with some kind of seizure. He was already dead when I arrived and, since there was nothing I could do, I left almost immediately. But I noticed the symptoms you mentioned last night – blistering of the lips and signs of suffocation.'

He paused, gazing at the logs crackling merrily in the hearth. The charred rugs had already been replaced with newer, finer ones, and large bowls of dried flowers added their pungent scent to the underlying acrid stench of burning. Philius continued.

'Out of the corner of my eye, I saw Isaac slip something into his bag, although I was not certain what it was. When I heard you question him about the wine he used in my purge, I realised exactly what had happened. I take a purge each Saturday morning to maintain the balance of my humours and Isaac makes it up for me once a month. The poisoned bottle must have sat harmlessly for four weeks before Isaac used it. I was lucky you guessed the cause of my ailment or I might be dead.'

'Probably not,' said Bartholomew. 'You might have recovered on your own.'

'Perhaps. But I would have taken the purge again next week – not knowing it was the cause of my illness – and then I would have died for certain. It is due to you that I am alive today and I thank you for it most sincerely.'

Bartholomew rose to leave, embarrassed by the Franciscan's profuse gratitude. 'I am glad the treatment worked, Philius. I admit I was uncertain that it would.'

'So was I, given that you had not consulted any astrological charts to see what my stars suggested, or even bled me.'

Bartholomew raised his hands, not wishing to become embroiled in a debate over the efficacy of the methods Philius employed while Michael waited for him. 'I imagine you had bled all too much as a result of the burning nature of the poison.'

Philius held out his hand to Bartholomew. 'Perhaps you are right. Meanwhile, when I am well I will make some inquiries among some of my brethren who have experience with poisons, and if I discover the nature of the potion that struck me down, I will let you know.'

Bartholomew thanked him politely, declining to ask how Philius's Franciscan brethren had acquired their 'experience with poisons'. Philius had completed his medical training at the University of Salerno in Italy, and Bartholomew had been told that Italians were very skilled in the uses of toxic substances. Philius probably knew far more about them than did Bartholomew.

'You said Grene died from drinking this poison, as well as the young student from Bernard's?' asked Philius as Bartholomew reached the door. 'Perhaps it was as well. Poor man.'

Bartholomew gazed at him uncertainly, the hand that had been stretching out to the handle arrested in mid-air.

'Around Christmas I diagnosed a wasting sickness in Grene,' Philius continued. 'You and I have seen many such cases before – there is no cure and the demise is long and painful. I estimated that he had a few months to live at most. At least he was spared a lingering death.'

Bartholomew nodded slowly and took his leave of Philius. Grene must have been told of his illness after he had lost the election to Bingham. No wonder he was bitter. Bartholomew considered Eligius's story – that Grene had claimed to be in fear of his life. Were they the ramblings of a man already fatally ill and perhaps weak in his wits? Or was there some truth to his fears? Or was the whole thing a fabrication and had Eligius's disregard for both Grene and Bingham driven him to use the death of one to rid Valence Marie of the other?

He told Michael what Philius had said as they walked the

short distance from Gonville Hall to Stanmore's house on Milne Street, but the monk had no answers either. Engrossed in thoughts of Eligius and Grene, he was almost crushed by a brewer's wagon as it thundered down the lane at a speed that was far from safe, and was saved only by a timely shove from the more alert Michael. The brewer was not in the least apologetic, announcing in a ringing voice that scholars had no right to wander all over the roads with total disregard for other users.

Several onlookers exchanged amused grins, gratified to see a townsman berating members of the detested University. Immediately, two friars and three undergraduates in black tabards came to stand next to Bartholomew, clearly itching to punish the brewer's impudence with a show of violence. Michael ordered them about their business, nodded curtly to the brewer, and the unpleasant atmosphere dissipated. Bartholomew glanced around him uneasily, sensing it would take very little to spark off a fight between scholars and townsmen; and a rumour that poisoned wine sold by a town thief to a young student would be more than enough.

The house of Bartholomew's brother-in-law, Oswald Stanmore, was one of the grandest on Milne Street, although Stanmore himself elected to live on his manor at the nearby village of Trumpington, away from the noise and the noxious smell of the river. Stanmore's business was cloth and, as Bartholomew strode through the gates into the cobbled yard with Michael, he saw evidence of it wherever he looked. The doors to the storehouses stood open, revealing bales of wool that were stacked to the ceiling, while piles of the wooden cones on which the cloth was wound occupied one corner, ready to be re-used. Scraps of material left from cutting were strewn across the yard in a kaleidoscope of colours, and fluttered here and there where they were caught on doors or timbers.

Because it was Sunday, Bartholomew had expected Stanmore to be in Trumpington and had intended to speak with his steward. He was pleased to find that not only was Stanmore in Cambridge, but that Edith was with him. She ran forward to greet her brother in delight.

'Matt! What a lovely surprise! I saw you at that dull installation yesterday, but every time I tried to make my way over to you, that boring Prior of Barnwell would start yet another tedious tale to keep me at his side. And after that dreadful scene with Grene, Oswald decided it was time to leave.'

Bartholomew hugged her, swinging her off her feet. She was ten years older than him, but she had retained the youthful exuberance he remembered from his earliest days. Her hair, like his, was black, although wisps of silver were beginning to appear here and there, and her dark eyes sparkled with humour. Stanmore placed an affectionate arm across Bartholomew's shoulder, and invited him and Michael for breakfast. Bartholomew shook his head, although Michael was clearly tempted.

'We cannot stay. We have been summoned to Ely by the Bishop.'

The laughter in Edith's face was gone in an instant. 'Why? What does he want with you?' She looked at Michael anxiously, wondering in what murky subterfuge the fat monk was embroiling her brother this time.

Bartholomew put a reassuring hand on her arm. 'Nothing to concern you. The Chancellor and a group of scholars attending the installation were attacked on the Cambridge to Ely road. I have been asked to tend to the injured.'

'How can you say such a thing does not concern me?' said Edith, knocking his hand away angrily. 'If the Chancellor was attacked, how can the Bishop be sure you will be safe?'

'He has sent an escort,' said Michael. 'And Cynric is going with us.'

'Cynric will look after you,' said Edith grudgingly. 'But I

am not happy about this. Tell the Bishop you cannot go. Tell him you are needed here. What will your patients do while you are gone – poor Mistress Pike took a turn for the worse last night.'

'Edith is right,' said Stanmore when she paused for breath. He stroked his beard thoughtfully. 'The Bishop's summons is unreasonable. He has his own physicians at Ely.' He called to his steward, who lounged against a wall watching two apprentices racing woodlice. 'Hugh! You travelled the Ely road yesterday. Did you see any signs of trouble?'

Hugh shrugged laconically. 'A cart had broken down near Stretham, but that was all.'

'Any signs of outlaws on the roads?'

Hugh shook his head, his eyes not moving from the apprentices' game. 'Quiet as the grave. Sinister place, the Fens.'

'Oh, Matt, please do not go,' begged Edith. 'The Sheriff told Oswald at the installation last night that three houses actually inside the town have been attacked by robbers. It is safe nowhere!'

'If the robbers have turned their attention to the town itself, then I am probably safer away from it,' said Bartholomew. He raised his hands to quell her angry objections. 'I cannot refuse a summons from the Bishop – you know that. He has a good deal of influence over the Chancellor and I have no wish to lose my Fellowship.'

'Take a couple of my men, then,' said Stanmore. 'Egil is from the Fens and Jurnet has a wife in Ely. They can go with you.'

'That is not necessary,' protested Bartholomew, but Stanmore had already moved away and was shouting instructions to Hugh. He turned to Edith. 'I might be away a week and Oswald will need them before then.'

'He will manage,' she said. 'And Egil and Jurnet will enjoy a few days away. Now. Why did you come? You know we are usually in Trumpington on Sundays, so you cannot have expected to see us here. Did you need something? To borrow a horse or a better cloak? Those are nice gloves you are wearing. They look new, although I see you have already torn the thumb. How long have you had them?'

Bartholomew smiled at her and evaded her question, not wanting her to know that he had managed to rip them in less than a day. 'I came to ask about the apprentice that died here a month last Saturday. The one Father Philius was called to attend.'

Edith looked at him blankly. 'What apprentice?'

'The one that died a month ago,' repeated Bartholomew. He wondered whether Stanmore might have kept it from her. He was apt to be over-protective of his family at times, as his insistence that Bartholomew took extra henchmen indicated. But Edith was probably more robust than her husband, and had no need of such coddling.

'But none of our apprentices has died,' said Edith, bewildered. She grabbed her husband's arm as he walked past. 'Tell him, Oswald.'

'Philius said he had attended one of your apprentices four weeks ago on a Saturday night,' explained Bartholomew again, trying to curb his impatience. 'He arrived too late and the apprentice died.'

'Not one of mine,' said Stanmore. 'They are all alive and kicking, believe me.'

'Then perhaps Philius was mistaken in thinking it was an apprentice,' said Bartholomew. 'But he said he came here to tend a young lad who had been stricken with some kind of seizure.'

'I repeat,' said Stanmore, 'not one of mine. I usually work late on Saturdays and Philius definitely did not come. And why would I call him? If one of my lads were sick, I would call you.'

Bartholomew had wondered about that at the time. Stanmore was well aware that Bartholomew and Philius did not see eye to eye on medical matters, and Bartholomew had been surprised to learn that Philius had been summoned to Stanmore's house in his place.

'But Philius seemed certain,' said Bartholomew. 'His book-bearer, Isaac, stole a bottle of wine from you – the wine that probably killed the apprentice although Isaac did not know that – and then it nearly killed poor Philius, too. Isaac was murdered last night—'

'Just a moment!' protested Stanmore, raising a hand to slow Bartholomew down. 'What are you involved in this time? I would have thought you had seen enough murder and mayhem to last you a lifetime! Now you say this man Isaac, who was supposed to have stolen from me, was murdered?'

Bartholomew saw the horror in his family's faces and regretted his decision to try to find out about the apprentice. Now they would worry about him until he returned, and he had learned nothing new from his questions. He knew that Stanmore discouraged drinking among his apprentices and discharged frequent offenders from his service. Perhaps they had kept the incident secret from Stanmore, so as not to incur his wrath. He suggested as much to the merchant, who dismissed the notion disdainfully.

'How could that be possible? Do you imagine I would not miss an apprentice if he disappeared?'

Bartholomew could think of no answer to the problem and was nonplussed. Philius had no reason to lie about a visit to Stanmore's house, and his own students – Gray, Bulbeck and Deynman – had said that they had seen one of Stanmore's apprentices buying the same kind of wine from Sacks in the Brazen George that had killed Armel. But Stanmore had no reason to lie either, and yet they all could not be right.

A nudge from Michael brought his attention back to the present. Time was passing and he had no desire to be out on the road after dark. With two heavily built labourers – clearly delighted by the unexpected excursion – in tow, he made his farewells, and he and Michael made their way back along Milne Street. Michael sighed in exasperation as

Katherine Mortimer hurried from her house to waylay them. Behind her were the merchants Cheney and Deschalers, and her son Edward.

'Doctor!' she said breathlessly. 'Edward and I wanted to thank you once again for coming to Constantine yesterday, especially since it meant missing part of Master Bingham's installation.'

Edward nodded his agreement. He still wore his sober brown tunic, looking like a drab little wren when compared to the colourful spectacle presented by the two older merchants.

'How is Master Mortimer?' asked Bartholomew, ignoring Michael's impatient huffing at his elbow. 'I hope he is feeling better.'

She smiled. 'He must be: he is sitting in the solar demanding his breakfast. Masters Cheney and Deschalers came to visit him.'

Bartholomew nodded a greeting to the two merchants and then turned back to Katherine. 'You must not let him overeat,' he warned. 'His stomach will not yet take kindly to the kind of repast your husband seems to enjoy.'

Katherine laughed. 'That is why I am so grateful to Masters Cheney and Deschalers – they took his mind off his food for a while at least. Constantine is not an easy man to advise – especially in matters concerning his stomach.'

There was a brief silence as Bartholomew, Michael and the merchants reflected that Mortimer was not an easy man in any sense of the word. He was unpleasant when he was fit and well, but being deprived of what seemed to be his main love in life would render him unbearable.

'We were telling him about that dreadful affair with Grene last night,' said Cheney, changing the subject and leaning forward conspiratorially. 'That should be a warning to us all. Grene was so sour and bitter during the celebrations that God struck him down for the deadly sin of envy.'

He looked unpleasantly smug, and Bartholomew was tempted to point out that malice and pride were just as likely to catch God's attention as envy.

'There are stories that he died in the service of Valence Marie's relic,' said Deschalers, regarding them questioningly. 'The one that some scholars tried to discredit last year.'

'That is arrant nonsense!' said Michael brusquely. 'Poor Grene's death had nothing to do with that hand – and I can assure you, Master Deschalers, that those damned bones are no more saintly relics than is that dead dog I can see on the top of that pile of rubbish!'

'But his demise was a shocking incident, nevertheless,' said Deschalers, looking anything but shocked. 'Perhaps he should have taken some lemon juice to soothe his choleric humour.'

'Those lemons of yours are an unusual sight in Cambridge in winter,' said Bartholomew, more to prevent them speculating about the Valence Marie relic than to learn about groceries.

Deschalers nodded proudly. 'Indeed they are. But I have developed a system for keeping them in the cool of my basement. They do not perish there as they do in the warmer storerooms above ground. Thus I can provide my customers with goods not normally seen in wintertime, and they pay most handsomely for the service. It is a pity you cannot do the same with bread, eh, Edward?' He gave the young man a poke in the ribs with his elbow.

Edward's attention had clearly been elsewhere. 'Of course not,' he said hastily, and smiled nervously. Deschalers looked piqued.

'Pay attention, Edward,' he said testily. 'You will never be a good merchant if you do not listen.'

Bartholomew had the distinct impression that a good merchant was the last thing Edward wanted to be. But he was the eldest son of one of the most powerful traders in the town and his fate was already sealed: Edward would inherit the business whether he liked it or not.

Michael tugged impatiently at Bartholomew's sleeve. They bade the Mortimers, Cheney and Deschalers farewell, and hastened to St Mary's Church on the High Street, where the Chancellor, Vice-Chancellor and their clerks administrated the University's complicated business dealings.

Harling was waiting for them, sitting behind the desk in his small office behind the church. He wore a neat, black gown and his short hair was, as usual, neatly slicked into a smooth cap with generous dabs of scented animal grease.

'There you are,' he said when they knocked at his door. 'You have heard what has happened?'

Michael nodded. 'Three dead and a number of people injured, including the Chancellor.'

'This is dreadful,' said Harling, his face pale and his hands unsteady. Bartholomew was surprised, imagining that Harling would relish the prospect of a little longer in his position of power. But, almost as soon as the thought had entered his head, he saw it was a foolish one: why would Harling wish to continue as Tynkell's representative when the University was facing such dire difficulties – Grene's death at a public occasion; the murders of Isaac and Armel on University property; and now a violent assault on the Chancellor himself?

'There has not been trouble on the Cambridge to Ely road for years,' Harling continued, gnawing on his lower lip. 'It is outrageous – a direct attack on the University! And so is this affair concerning Grene and the Bernard's novice!'

'The ambush of the Chancellor may have been random,' reasoned Bartholomew, to calm him. 'Tulyet said raids are becoming more frequent, and even houses inside the town have been burgled.'

'But this is the Ely causeway!' insisted Harling. 'Hitherto one of the safest highways in the kingdom.' He shook his head in despair. 'I profess I am uncertain how to proceed –

while I am keen for you to discover all you can about this foul affair, I am loathe to allow you to travel on the same road.'

'The Bishop has sent an escort,' said Michael soothingly. 'We will be safe enough.'

Harling looked doubtful. 'Brother Michael, you have provided – are providing – a vital service to the University. I have come to respect your opinions and judgement, and so I am considering sending a Junior Proctor in your place. You are, quite simply, too valuable to risk. Perhaps we can appoint that Father William from Michaelhouse – he has been pestering me to make him Junior Proctor for weeks. He can go to Ely with Bartholomew.'

'I am touched,' said Michael, his face expressionless. 'But it is unlikely these outlaws will strike twice in the same place. I will be perfectly safe, and anyway I cannot refuse a summons from the Bishop. As a humble Benedictine monk, I am duty-bound to obey my spiritual master.'

Bartholomew thought Michael looked anything but humble, basking smugly in the urgency of the summons from the Bishop, and the praise and open admiration of the Vice-Chancellor.

Harling raised a hand in a submissive gesture and regarded Michael sombrely. 'I suppose you are right,' he said, clearly reluctant. 'But I have already given my word that Bartholomew should be allowed to tend his patients without being hampered by University matters, and now he has been ordered to Ely!'

'He cannot refuse a summons from the Bishop, any more than I can,' said Michael.

'Although I appreciate the fact that you tried to keep me out of it,' Bartholomew added.

Harling gave the ghost of a smile. 'I suppose going to Ely will mean that at least you are free from this vile business of the poisoned wine. And speaking of that, have you made any headway?'

Briefly, Michael outlined Bartholomew's findings on the

deaths of Grene and Armel, and related what had passed in Gonville Hall the previous night. Harling paled and put his head in his hands with a groan.

'I will investigate all this as soon as I have returned from Ely,' said Michael comfortingly.

'Have you uncovered any clues the beadles might follow up in your absence?' asked Harling, lifting his haggard face from his arms.

Michael nodded vaguely. 'There is a man named Sacks they are trying to hunt down. He might be able to shed some light on the matter.'

Harling closed his eyes and slumped back in his chair. Bartholomew felt sorry for him. His few days of power while Tynkell was away had turned into a nightmare and he looked ill from worry.

Harling's eyes snapped open. 'Do you think he did it?' he asked.

'Who did what?' asked Michael, startled.

Harling sighed impatiently and patted his greased hair in an agitated gesture. 'Do you think Bingham murdered Grene? Father Eligius came to tell me of his suspicions this morning.'

'I have reservations about that,' said Michael, rubbing the whiskers on his chin and filling the room with a scraping sound. 'To kill a rival in full view of so many people would be very rash.'

'Bingham is a man given to rashness,' said Harling. 'Perhaps someone gave him this poisoned wine and he decided to use it on the spur of the moment.'

'But why would someone provide him with such a thing?' said Michael. 'It is not the kind of gift one usually presents at an installation.'

Harling gave him a curious look and Bartholomew wondered whether he, like the former Chancellor, de Wetherset, had been involved in University politics too long and had become paranoid in his suspicions. The University might be full of rumour and intrigue, but its scholars did not usually resort to killing their rivals. The students fought with the townspeople and with each other – hostel against hostel and hostel against College – but the masters usually managed to steer clear of physical violence, and generally employed more intellectual forms of vengeance.

Harling sighed and gazed out of the window. 'What a mess,' he whispered. 'My poor University, assailed from all sides by evil men.'

'Hardly that, Master Harling,' said Michael briskly. 'Just one or two minor mysteries that will easily be unravelled and eliminated. Do not fear. Matt and I will sort all this out before you know it.'

Bartholomew gazed at him aghast, uncertain whether he was more horrified at Michael's overconfident bragging, or the fact that he was being dragged into the murky world of University plotting and scheming.

'Just a moment—' he began.

Michael overrode his protestation with a wave of a flabby hand. 'If your help is needed to solve this mystery, Matt, then I know you will give it freely and without question to express your loyalty to the University. But time is passing and we should go. We should not be on the road after dark.'

'Very well,' said Harling wearily. 'Go if you must. But please return as soon as you can. We cannot be having scholars murdered with poisoned wine. And whatever you do, be cautious – both of you. I wish you God's speed.'

'Poor Harling,' said Michael, as they walked towards the Brazen George to meet Cynric and the Bishop's escort. 'He is beginning to crack under the strain. It is just as well he was not elected Chancellor.'

Bartholomew sighed, still angry at the way the monk had volunteered his services in such a cavalier manner. But by the time they had returned from Ely, the mystery surrounding the wine might well have been solved by Michael's beadles and he did not want to begin an argument over something that might transpire to be irrelevant. He thought about the state of the Vice-Chancellor. 'I would have expected Harling to be more poised. I did not imagine him to be a man given to panic.'

'He is always far more suave in the afternoons and evenings,' said Michael. 'I suspect he drinks, and is less controlled in the mornings before the alcohol has taken effect.'

It was an interesting concept, especially when Bartholomew recalled that Harling was well known for making all his appointments in the afternoons, maintaining that he liked to leave the mornings free for clerical duties. The Vice-Chancellor had been well in control of the situation with the Fellows in St Botolph's Church the day before, but that had been at night and the wine had been plentiful. During mass, at dawn, he had been pale and his hands had been shaking.

'I am sceptical of his concern, though,' said Bartholomew. 'He has never expressed any particular fondness for either of us before.'

'You do the man an injustice,' said Michael reproachfully. 'He is wholly loyal to the University and knows we serve it well. He is probably reluctant to let us leave Cambridge when he knows he will need our brains to solve the affair of the poisoned wine. If Tynkell dies of his injuries, Harling will need to find Grene's murderer if he is to prove to the voting masters that he is competent to accede as Chancellor. He will stand no chance of winning an election if that remains a mystery.'

They made their way quickly along the High Street to the Brazen George, where Cynric and the messenger waited. The messenger paced back and forth, glancing up at the sky as if he imagined dusk might settle at any moment, despite the fact that it was barely mid-morning.

'You are late,' he said irritably. He looked at Stanmore's

men who walked behind them, holding the reins of sturdy nags with eager anticipation of the expedition through the Fens. They were large men, both with dark, almost swarthy, complexions. Cynric stood with them, holding the bridle of a fat pony from Stanmore's stables that he liked to ride. Its saddlebags were already packed and Cynric, basically a man of action who chafed at the sedentary life of a book-bearer, was as keen to take part in the unexpected journey as were the two Fenmen.

'The Bishop seems to have done us proud,' said Michael, motioning to where their escort waited: six men wearing the boiled leather tunics and helmets of the mercenary.

'Who are they?' demanded the messenger, regarding Cynric, Egil and Jurnet with suspicion when he realised they were to form part of the group.

'Men whom I trust,' replied Bartholomew, resenting the hostility in the messenger's voice.

'They cannot come with us,' said the messenger, turning away. 'Send them home.'

'What is your name?' Bartholomew asked. Surprised, the messenger turned to face him.

'Alan of Norwich,' he answered. 'Why?'

'Well, Alan of Norwich, your career as a messenger will be short-lived if you dictate to your customers so,' said Bartholomew mildly. 'Now, you have two choices. Either these men come with us, or you return to the Bishop without me. Which is it to be?'

Alan eyed Bartholomew with dislike, but before he could reply, one of the mercenaries intervened, laying a callused hand on Alan's leather-clad shoulder.

'They will be no trouble,' he said in the rough accent of a northerner. 'Let them come.'

Alan pursed his lips but said no more. Michael and Cynric were already mounted, and Egil and Jurnet sprung lightly into the saddles of their small ponies. With a malicious glower, Alan handed Bartholomew the reins of a great snorting stallion that Bartholomew regarded with trepidation.

'I cannot ride this,' he called to Michael nervously.

Michael's horse, however, seemed even more skittish than Bartholomew's, and he reconsidered asking if they could change. With difficulty, and watched with undisguised amusement by Alan and the mercenaries, Bartholomew managed to clamber onto the beast's back. It immediately began to buck, and by the time he had gained some measure of control over it, the others had already set off and he had to force it into a canter to catch them up.

The distance to the Isle of Ely from Cambridge was about seventeen miles. In places the road wound tortuously, while in others it ran as straight as an arrow, and was said to have been built hundreds of years before. Almost as soon as they left Cambridge via the Barnwell Gate, the rain that had been threatening all day began to fall, at first just a haze of drizzle, but then in earnest. Bartholomew's threadbare woollen cloak had been treated with some kind of grease to repel water, but it was old and the wet found its way through the parts where the oil had rubbed away. Soon it was sodden and heavy, while drips trickled through his hood and down the back of his neck. It was not long before the only dry parts of him were his hands in his fine new gloves.

The rain, however, was the least of his problems. More immediate was the high-spirited black horse. It was still rearing sporadically, and showed no sign of settling into an easy pace as he imagined it would do once they started the journey. By the time they were through the little village of Chesterton, only two miles on, he was exhausted from fighting to control it, and even welcomed the rain to cool him from his exertions. He considered asking Egil or Jurnet if they would like to switch, but they rode almost as badly as he did, and would not have been any better able to manage the thing. He edged his way up the track until he was level with Michael, battling with the horse every inch of the way as it pranced and cavorted.

'I cannot control this wretched thing,' he gasped.

The fat monk shot him a sideways glance. 'Mine is no better – it is an undisciplined brute. A few months in the Bishop's stables would calm its spirits.'

'I thought these were the Bishop's horses,' said Bartholomew, hauling on the reins as the horse danced off to one side of the track.

'You need to keep the reins tighter,' said Michael, observing him critically. 'And hold your hands lower. The Bishop must have ordered Alan to hire fresh mounts for us in Cambridge.'

The advice rendered handling the horse a little easier and the animal slowed to a walk, enabling Bartholomew to talk to Michael.

'I find these contradictions over the allegedly dead apprentice very curious,' said the monk, still watching Bartholomew's handling of the horse in a way that suggested he was far from impressed. 'Philius has no reason to lie, and Gray and his cronies claim they saw one of Oswald's apprentices buying wine from Sacks.'

'Oswald would not be untruthful with me,' said Bartholomew.

'He is a powerful merchant, Matt,' said Michael. 'Business is not what it was before the Death, and many, just like him, are forced to use devious means to maintain their profit levels. You are well aware of the network of spies he has all over the town.' He jerked his head towards Egil and Jurnet, who were riding ahead with the mercenaries. 'For all we know, one of those two has been sent with us specifically to learn what he can from an opportune visit to the Bishop's Palace.'

Bartholomew drew breath to deny Michael's accusations but he knew them to be at least partly true. Stanmore did have an extensive organisation of spies, and he was always well-informed of all manner of occurrences in Cambridge, ranging from the world of trade to the University and even the Church. Yet Bartholomew was reluctant to believe his brother-in-law was deceiving him. They had been through an episode of mistrust once before, and it had proved an unpleasant experience for both of them. Bartholomew could not believe that Stanmore would risk offending Edith by lying to the brother on whom she still doted.

'Perhaps Oswald's apprentices have some agenda of their own,' said Bartholomew. 'Perhaps they have not been entirely honest with him.'

Michael puffed out his cheeks. 'It would be a brave apprentice who would attempt to best your brother-in-law, Matt. Although it is possible an exceptionally stupid one might try.' He paused as his horse leapt about on the track. Bartholomew's mount sensed the excitement of the other horse and began to buck so that it was some time before they were able to talk again.

'This is impossible!' grumbled Bartholomew, out of breath from his efforts to control the animal. 'It would be easier to walk!'

Michael, an excellent horseman who loathed any kind of exercise, regarded him askance. Bartholomew ignored his reaction and continued with their discussion.

'I meant to take a closer look at Armel's body today,' he said. 'He will be buried by the time we return, and I wanted to look at his mouth.'

Michael gave a grimace of disgust. 'You would have been too late anyway. I saw Father Yvo and the Franciscan novices from Bernard's while you were messing about on your horse as we left the town. They were just returning from burying Armel in St Botolph's churchyard.'

'On a Sunday?' queried Bartholomew. 'Does that not seem rather hasty to you, Brother?'

Michael nodded. 'My thoughts precisely. But you saw Bernard's – it is tiny with only one chamber other than the kitchen. You would be the first to disapprove of living in the same room as a corpse. Harling heard of Father Yvo's plight, and gave Bernard's special dispensation to bury Armel this morning. Apparently, his friends demurred, saying that they wanted more time to pray over the body, but Harling and Yvo cited you as saying corpses carry diseases, and both insisted that Armel be buried immediately in the interests of the students' health.'

'I do not recall ever making such a grossly general statement,' said Bartholomew, startled. 'In the summer a corpse might be problematic, but Armel's funeral could have waited until tomorrow. Or perhaps his body might have been moved to lie in the church.'

Michael shook his head. 'Bernard's is in the parish of St Botolph's, and Grene's corpse is already there. Apparently, there are a number of people who want to pay their last respects – undoubtedly a lot more than if he had died quietly in his sleep, as opposed to horribly and publicly at his rival's installation feast. The rector of St Botolph's said he could not take Armel as well, and so it is an act of great kindness on the part of Harling to go to the trouble of granting a dispensation for Armel's early burial.'

'I suspect Harling's motive for granting the dispensation was so that Armel's corpse could not become the focus of student unrest,' said Bartholomew, cautiously relinquishing his iron grip on the horse's reins to wipe away the rain that dripped into his eyes from his sodden hood.

Michael raised his eyebrows. 'Really, Matt! You have become horribly sceptical of late. But you probably have a point. In which case, Harling is showing a good deal of common sense. I would not like to see the students rioting, as they did last summer, because they believe one of them has been murdered by a townsperson.'

Bartholomew nodded, hastily clutching at the reins again as the horse, detecting a degree of freedom, swung its head round and tried to bite his leg. 'Damned brute,' he muttered, ignoring Cynric's soft laughter behind him.

'Anyway, there is no suspicion that Armel and his friends

were anything other than foolish for buying goods from a man they did not know in a tavern,' said Michael, leaning across to position Bartholomew's hands correctly. 'We do not know for certain that Sacks intended Armel's death to be a deliberate attack against the University.'

Their conversation was interrupted again, this time by a narrowing of the path. The route between Cambridge and Ely was called a road, but it was, in reality, little more than a trackway. In the summer it was pleasant – grassy and peaceful. In the winter the grass disintegrated into rutted mud and deep puddles and, after periods of extended rain, became a veritable morass. In parts some of the ditches that ran along the roadside were flooded, and water covered the path and surrounding land in an unbroken sheet. They were fortunate to have Jurnet with them, who knew the country well, and seemed to sense where the path went when all Bartholomew could see was bog.

The land on either side of the road comprised dense undergrowth that thrived on the dark, peaty soil, patches of which had been cleared for farming. At points, the road rose above the land, and Bartholomew could see the marshland rolling off in all directions, as flat and featureless as the face of the ocean. Isolated hamlets were dotted here and there, their few houses standing proud on the jungle of Fen that surrounded them.

Gradually, the small clearings grew scarcer, giving way more frequently to expanses of water. Here were the true Fens, an impenetrable tangle of reed and sedge, interspersed with tiny islands bearing alder and willow trees. The ancient track that had been built across them was more causeway than road, and constant repairs were required to prevent it from sinking below sea level. In places the causeway was well maintained, and stood proud of the surrounding bogs. In other areas neglect and the winter's heavy rains had caused it to collapse, and Bartholomew was certain that, without the expert guidance of Jurnet, they would have wandered off the path and been lost forever in the marshes. Years before, when Bartholomew had been a child living with his sister, Stanmore had told him stories about the Fens to while away the long winter evenings. They were said to be haunted with the souls of men who had strayed from the causeway never to be seen again.

He leapt almost as violently as his horse, as a flock of ducks flapped noisily into the air, startled by the proximity of the riders. Then it was quiet again, soundless except for the squish of the horses' hooves in the mud and the occasional clink of metal. Bartholomew began to shiver, despite his exertions to keep his horse under control. The silence of the Fens was total: no birds sang, there were no cracks or rustles in the undergrowth to betray the presence of animals, and not even the wind disturbed the bare twigs of stunted trees. Bartholomew stole a glance behind him, unnerved at the quiet and isolation, and recalled Stanmore's man calling the Fens 'sinister'.

The sound of Jurnet arguing with Alan came as a welcome respite to the stillness.

'It is safer to keep to the main path,' Jurnet was saying.

'Not when only yesterday three men were killed on it,' insisted Alan. 'If you do not like it, you can go home.'

'What is the problem?' asked Michael, edging his horse forward.

'I propose we avoid the section of the road on which the Chancellor's party was attacked yesterday,' said Alan. 'We kept away from it on our outward journey.'

'But it is dangerous to leave the causeway,' protested Jurnet. 'Other men have taken such routes and have never been seen again. I have lived in the Fens all my life, and I tell you it is not safe to leave the main road.'

'But I know this other route,' said Alan angrily. 'And I knew the men who were killed trying to defend the Chancellor. Believe me, we are safer cutting to the east.'

Egil and Jurnet exchanged pained glances, but offered no

further protest. They followed Alan wordlessly off the main
path and along a smaller track. Bartholomew was next, with
the mercenaries behind, and Michael and Cynric bringing
up the rear.

At first, the track seemed no different from the main
road, and cut through the Fens in a reasonably straight
line. Then Alan began to lead them in a series of twists and
turns that had Bartholomew totally disoriented. The path
became so narrow that the shrubs brushed past him on either
side, showering his already saturated cloak with droplets of
water from their leafless branches. Bartholomew's horse was
unnerved at the proximity of the trees, and began cavorting
again, so that he was forced to concentrate all his attention
on preventing the animal from rearing and thrashing around
with its forelegs.

The track then widened, but degenerated into a morass.
The riders could do little more than guide the mounts
around the edge of it, and hope that the sloppy mud was
not deeper than it appeared. One of Stanmore's stories
had been about bogs that could swallow a man and his
horse without trace, and Bartholomew had often heard
Fenland farmers complaining that they had lost sheep,
goats and even cattle to the black, suffocating mud of the
marshes. He began to doubt the sagacity of Alan's decision
to cut east.

Once round the morass, they were faced with a brackish
waterway that was too wide to jump, and looked too deep
to wade across. Bartholomew leaned forward in his saddle,
and saw the swathe of water disappear as far as he could see
in either direction. It was fringed with reeds, and was as still
as glass.

'You are lost!' said Jurnet accusingly. 'I told you—'

What happened next was a blur. Jurnet toppled from his
saddle, and Bartholomew saw the tip of Alan's sword stained
red. The injured man gave a high-pitched screech that rent
the air like a whistle. Alan ignored it, and spurred his mount

towards Bartholomew. Bartholomew's horse, however, startled by the sudden howl of pain and terror, went wild. Bartholomew hauled desperately at the reins in an attempt to control it, but, with a piercing scream of its own, it was off, bolting wildly and blindly through the undergrowth to the left of the track. Bartholomew caught a glimpse of glittering steel, and saw Cynric engaged in a furious battle with one of the mercenaries, and that was all.

'After him!' came Alan's enraged yell.

But Bartholomew had no time to assess what was happening behind him as the flailing branches ripped and tore at his face. He pulled on the reins as hard as he could, but the horse seemed oblivious to him. He could hear nothing except the thud of its hooves and the sound of branches cracking and tearing as it smashed through them. He imagined that at least one of the mercenaries was following him, an easy task given the trail of destruction the animal must have been leaving behind it.

Then the undergrowth gave way to another span of water, similar to the one that had caused Jurnet to accuse Alan of being lost. Bartholomew closed his eyes as the horse decided it could jump to the other side, but at the last moment realised it could not and faltered. The result was that horse and rider landed squarely in the middle with a great splash that drove spray high into the air. For a moment, Bartholomew was aware of nothing but a searing cold and gurgling water in his ears, and then he came to his senses.

He struggled to free himself of the thrashing horse, but his foot was entangled in the stirrup. He tried to reach down to release it, but his fingers were clumsy with shock, and the task proved impossible with water surging and frothing all around him. The horse kicked and tried to swim its way to the other side, but its flailing legs became hopelessly entangled in the weeds and sucking mud that choked the bottom of the waterway. It began to sink. Panic-stricken it reared its head and kicked even harder, but it was fighting a losing battle. Bartholomew watched the water rise up its neck, and then cover its head, although for an instant he could see its terrified, rolling eyes under the surface. And then the water began to creep up his own chest towards his shoulders. He struggled and squirmed as hard as he could, but the stirrup held fast. Then the brown water was up to his chin and the horse underneath him was still sinking. And then it closed over his own head, plunging him into a world of dirty brown bubbles and the roar of water.

chapter 5

OR PETRIFYING MOMENTS, BARTHOLOMEW WAS PARA-
LYSED with fright. He could see nothing, and the
sound of water thundering in his ears dominated
his senses. Beneath him, the horse continued to struggle, but
increasingly feebly. Then Bartholomew panicked, thrashing
around in a hopeless attempt to tear himself free. But the
stirrup leather held firm, dragging him deeper down into
the black water.

He felt himself growing dizzy from lack of air and his lungs
burned with the agony of suffocation. Knife! he thought. Use
a knife! He forced his numb fingers to the belt at his waist
where the dagger he wore for travelling was buckled. He
tugged at the hilt, but he was growing weak, and for a
moment he thought he would be unable to draw it. It came
out in a rush and he gripped it hard, terrified lest he should
drop it. He twisted down and began, laboriously, to hack at
the strap, fighting the increasingly desperate urge to give
way to panic and try to claw his way up to the air above.

As he sawed, he saw something white flash past his eyes,
and thought it was the effects of slowly losing consciousness.
But there was another and then a dull pain in his leg. Dimly,
a part of his mind registered that the mercenaries must have
followed him and were firing crossbows at the water where
he had disappeared.

But it was almost to the point where it did not matter.
Bartholomew's movements were becoming slower and slower

and he began to experience a strange light-headedness. The black water around him began to turn bright colours – reds and greens and blues – all swirling together. He made a final chop at the stirrup and felt the dagger slip from his nerveless hand.

And then he was floating upwards. The water turned from black to brown and he exploded from it into the air with a great gasp that hurt his throat. Instinctively, he kicked away from the deep water in the centre of the lode toward the shallows near the bank. His frozen fingers felt something solid and he grasped at it as he fought to regain his breath, caring nothing for the mercenaries who had been trying to kill him, and only for dragging in great lungfuls of air. Gradually, he came to his senses and began to take in his surroundings.

He was clinging for dear life to a tree that had partly fallen across the lode and that was shielded from sight by a line of the reeds that grew in the shallower parts of the marshes. As long as he had not made too much noise surfacing, it was possible the mercenaries had not seen him.

Soon he became aware of voices. Taking care not to relinquish his hold on the tree, he edged forward and peered through the fringe of sedge. The camouflage it offered turned out to be too scanty for comfort, and the soldiers were nearer than Bartholomew had imagined they would be. He tried to control his still ragged breathing.

'He is dead,' one was saying. 'I saw him go down with the horse.'

'But I heard something,' insisted the mercenary with the northern accent. 'I think he surfaced.'

'I saw him go down and I did not see him come up,' insisted the first soldier irritably. 'I tell you, he has drowned.'

'It takes longer than this for a man to drown,' said the northerner. 'Go and check over there.'

Footsteps came closer, dead reeds and undergrowth crack-ing noisily as the soldier made his way around the edge of the water. Bartholomew fought to quieten his gasping, certain they would hear him in the silent Fens. He sank further down into the water, so that only his head was above the surface. The mercenary began slashing at the reeds with his sword, his sweeps coming ever nearer. Bartholomew looked around him in despair. What should he do? He could not outrun them, and in the water he was a sitting duck for their crossbows. The reeds near to his head quivered as the sword hissed past them, and Bartholomew thought he could see the dark, wet leather of a boot.

A great bubble of water suddenly billowed out onto the surface of the water as the horse, presumably, breathed its last. The northerner gave a sigh of relief.

'*Now* he is dead,' he called. 'We can go back to the others.'

Their voices receded into the undergrowth as they left, but Bartholomew made no move to leave the water. Shock and cold were eating away at his reactions, and it seemed easier to stay where he was in case the soldiers returned. The rational part of his brain urged him to climb out, because if he stayed where he was he would die. With a supreme effort of will he dragged his body towards the bank, and struggled to stand upright. Immediately, black mud began to suck at his feet and he felt himself sinking. He grabbed the tree again, and crawled along it until he was able to roll off onto solid ground. For a while, all he could do was lie on his back and gaze up at the slowly moving slate-grey clouds above him. Then he realised that, far from his strength returning, it was ebbing from him, leached away by the cold. He forced himself to sit up, and then stand.

A dull ache above his knee caused him look down, and he saw a rent in the rough, loose material of his hose where the crossbow bolt had ripped it. He leaned against a tree, inspected his leg, but saw there was nothing more than a shallow graze. He had been fortunate, for a serious leg injury in the Fens, so far from the road, might have meant his death simply because he would have been unable to walk away. He looked at the tear in his leggings, noting that it was too large for Agatha to mend without a patch. He felt a sudden, irrational surge of fury towards Alan and his men: clothes had been expensive since the plague and a replacement pair would cost him most of the money he had been saving to purchase a scroll he wanted. His anger did a good deal to restore him to his senses.

He removed his clothes, wrung them out as best he could and then put them back on again. He almost abandoned his cloak, but suspected that, even though it was wet, it would help to protect him from the chilling effect of the wind. Reluctantly, he donned it. Contrary to common sense, his medicine bag was still looped over his shoulder. It was heavy, and he realised he was lucky it had not drowned him. He sorted through it, abandoning soggy bandages and ruined packets of powders, and keeping those bottles and phials he considered to be watertight. And then he was ready.

But ready for what? For the first time, the full implications of his predicament dawned on him. He was alone, wet and cold in some remote part of the Fens. Michael and Cynric were almost certainly dead, and the only people he would be likely to encounter would be those who wanted to murder him. He leaned against the tree as a wave of hopelessness washed over him. Why had Alan wanted to kill them? Was he from the Bishop as he claimed? Was this something to do with Michael's declining of the post of Master at Valence Marie? He thought about Father Paul's warning, and Stanmore's and Edith's misgivings about the unexpected summons, all of which he had blithely ignored. Hugh, Stanmore's man, had come from Ely and had heard no rumours of an attack against the Chancellor – and news of that kind usually travelled fast.

With a sudden, horrible clarity, he was certain that the attack on the Chancellor, quite simply, had never happened. Tynkell must have decided not to make the long journey in the rain to attend an installation ceremony that would be tedious and lengthy, and was probably even now sitting in front of a roaring fire in the Bishop's sumptuous palace. And Alan of Norwich had been remarkably cocky for a simple messenger – not the kind of man the Bishop would hire at all. Bartholomew cursed himself for a fool for having ignored the warnings of his friends and his own common sense.

He found he was shivering uncontrollably and fought to pull himself together. He had two choices: either he could stay and perish in the marshes, or he could attempt to find his way to the main road and then to Ely or Cambridge, whichever was closer. He remembered the blundering path his poor horse had taken from the first river. It should be easy to follow that. And he had watched Cynric tracking often enough, so that he might be able to retrace the route Alan had taken when he had left the causeway – if he were lucky.

Slowly, and with infinite caution, he began to make his way up the trail forged by his horse. Every two or three steps, he stopped to listen, but there was nothing. The silence was as absolute now as it had been before they had ventured off the road, when he had been so unnerved by the sudden flapping of ducks. The only sounds were those of his own laboured progress along the path.

Contrary to his reasoning, it was not easy to follow the route back to the first lode. Branches had swung back into place, water covered any hoof-prints that might have been left and the horse's long legs had made lighter going of the journey than could Bartholomew. The effort of walking, however, brought a degree of warmth back into his body, and the dead chill began to recede. He glanced up at the sky and saw that it was already late afternoon, which meant that there was little chance that he would reach the causeway that night. Tracking would be difficult anyway, but it would be impossible in anything other than full daylight; he would have to spend the night in the Fens.

He forced that unpleasant prospect from his mind and concentrated on walking. He was beginning to think he must have made a mistake and followed the wrong path, when he glimpsed Alan's river lying parallel to his path. Within moments, he had reached the place from which the horse had bolted.

He stood still, hidden by the undergrowth, and listened intently. It would be ironic to have survived the manic ride, the near drowning and the crossbow bolts only to die because he had blundered into Alan. But there was nothing to hear and nothing to see. After a while, the silence became so oppressive that Bartholomew coughed just to prove to himself that he was not deaf.

Cautiously, he inched his way forward, alert for any sign of Alan and his men, but the small clearing was devoid of life. Jurnet was there, a great ragged slash across his chest, and his eyes gazing sightlessly at the sky. With trepidation, Bartholomew wondered about Michael, Cynric and Egil, and his steps faltered with the knowledge of what he might find ahead.

A search of the area, however, revealed nothing to tell him what had happened to the others. There were signs of a violent skirmish, where the ground had been churned underfoot by horses' hooves, but there were no bodies. Bartholomew wondered whether Alan had taken them to the Bishop in order to claim they had been murdered by outlaws on the dangerous Cambridge to Ely road – perhaps he imagined the Bishop might reward him for bringing the slain corpse of a monk home to the abbey.

The daylight was beginning to fade and dusk was early because of the low clouds. The last place Bartholomew wanted to spend the night was in the very spot where two of his dearest friends had been slaughtered, but it would be foolish to attempt to find his way through the Fens in the dark. He looked around him helplessly.

Lighting a fire was out of the question. He did not have

a flint, and even if he had, he would be unlikely to coax a flame out of any of the sodden undergrowth that surrounded him. And anyway, he would not want smoke or flames to attract the attention of Alan and his mercenaries, although, he thought disconsolately, by now they would be on the road home, and would be spending the night in a tavern somewhere with a blazing fire and hot food. With the onset of dusk, a light drizzle began to fall, and he knew he had a long night ahead of him.

He forced himself to concentrate on finding a place to spend the night that would be out of the wind and not too wet. He settled for the rotten bole of an old oak tree. Although its crumbling sides oozed dampness, it faced away from the wind, and, wedged into it and wrapped in his dark cloak, he felt as though he was more or less invisible to the casual observer should Alan return. This gave him a measure of comfort – although not much.

He did not think he would sleep, but he was exhausted and dozed almost immediately. When he woke several hours later, he was freezing and the inside of the tree was dripping with the heavy rain that pattered down on the dead leaves that littered the ground. He peered out of the bole. It was pitch black, and all he could see were the faint silhouettes of trees waving in the wind against the sky. He tried to sleep again, but he was far too cold and his grazed leg throbbed. He considered taking a draught of the opium syrup he carried in his medicines bag, but was afraid that if he slept too deeply he might never wake. He leaned back in the tree, shivering and listening to the gentle hiss of rain on the ground, and waited for dawn.

Bartholomew was awoken from yet another restless, dream-filled drowse by a sharp crack. He lifted his head from his knees, and listened intently. Dawn had arrived, but the clouds allowed no streaks of colour to seep through them from the sun: the sky had merely changed from dark grey to a lighter grey. Bartholomew thought he must have imagined the sound – it would not have been the first time he had done so through the seemingly endless night. He lowered his head onto his knees again and closed his eyes. Although it was growing light, it was still far too dark to try to find his way out of the Fens. Cynric might have managed, but Bartholomew knew he certainly could not.

His head snapped up again as he heard a rustle among the dead leaves. Someone or something was moving around nearby! He felt his heart begin to pound. It might be a wolf – he had heard they had been seen in the Fens since the plague. Or a wild boar. Either animal might prove dangerous, and Bartholomew knew bare hands would fare poorly against fangs or tusks. But perhaps it was only a person. He considered: that might be even worse! All he could hope was that his hiding-place was adequate to keep him concealed. He was far too cold and stiff to run, and he had no weapon with which to fight – not that it would have done him much good against a mercenary anyway. He pulled his dark cloak further over his head, and looked out, scarcely daring to breathe.

A man swathed in an over-large tunic was systematically searching the clearing by the river. Bartholomew felt his heart sink – the man was being very thorough, and it would only be a matter of time before Bartholomew was discovered. The physician closed his eyes and listened hard, trying to detect whether the man was the only one, or whether others aided him in his search. After a few moments, he decided the man was probably alone. He reviewed his options carefully and decided the most sensible course of action was to try to slip away into the tangle of undergrowth. It might even be possible for him to double back, and eventually follow the man to the main road when he had finished his rooting about.

With infinite care Bartholomew stood, forcing his numb legs to bear his weight. He swayed unsteadily, and for a moment thought he might be unable to move at all, let alone disappear silently into the undergrowth. He gritted his teeth against the ache of cramped muscles, and took a step forward. His knees wobbled dangerously and he had to hold the tree for support. The man in the cloak was near the lode, doing something to Jurnet's body – probably stripping it of clothes and belongings. Bartholomew took another step, and then another. And then he trod on a rotten branch that gave way under his weight with a soggy crunch.

Bartholomew saw the man spin round in a crouch and face him. Without waiting to see what he would do, Bartholomew was off, stumbling through the undergrowth as blindly as the horse had done the previous day. Branches of leafless trees scratched and tore at him as he ran, and the blood pounded in his ears at the sudden exertion. A yell from behind told him that the man was following. Bartholomew ran harder, but it was like the nightmare he had occasionally where he was being chased, but could move only in slow motion. His legs simply would not obey him and move faster. The man behind was catching up!

The breath went out of him as he went sprawling over the exposed root of a tree. Desperately he scrambled to his feet and stumbled on. The man behind him was gaining ground, and Bartholomew could hear him coming closer and closer. Breath coming in ragged gasps, he forced himself forward, raising his hands to protect his face from the clawing branches. But then he fell a second time, tumbling into a morass of thick, sticky mud.

The man was on him in an instant, pinning him to the ground. Bartholomew fought back with every ounce of his failing strength, but the man was too strong for him. Eventually, seeing the situation was hopeless, he stopped struggling and looked up into the face of his captor.

'Cynric!'

Bartholomew awoke to warmth, and a gentle crackling

sound and moving yellow lights on the ceiling told him there was a fire in the room. He raised himself on one elbow and looked around. He recalled little of the journey back through the Fens that morning, only trudging behind Cynric along a tortuous path that meandered past the dank pools and endless reed and sedge beds that characterised this mysterious, forbidding part of the country. Cynric had explained what had happened when they had been attacked, but Bartholomew remembered none of it, except that the wily Welshman had escaped and had later found Michael.

Nearby was the convent at Denny, an ancient building that had once belonged to the secretive Knights Templar. Now it was in the hands of a community of Franciscan nuns, endowed by the wealthy Countess of Pembroke, who had also founded the Hall of Valence Marie. Bartholomew had vague memories of being given hot broth and shedding his wet clothes, but was asleep as soon as he lay on the bed provided for him in the guesthall.

He sat up and peered into the darkness. The shutters were drawn and the room was unlit except for the flickering fire. It was night, and he had evidently slept away the entire day. A gust of wind hurled splatters of rain against the windows, and Bartholomew hauled the blanket round his shoulders gratefully as he recalled the bitter chill of the previous day in the Fens. On the bed next to him was the unmistakable bulk of Michael, stomach rising majestically ceilingward. Cynric slept near the door, fully clothed, and with his long Welsh hunting dagger unsheathed near his hand.

The guesthall was a long, spacious room on the upper floor over what had been the Templars' church. There was a garde-robe set in the thickness of the wall at one end, and a great fireplace at the other. A table stood under one of the windows, laden with blankets, a bowl of water and some bread covered with a cloth, while a pile of straw mattresses lay heaped in a corner in readiness for more visitors. Bartholomew was impressed at the degree of luxury for a foundation located in the inhospitable Fens, but recalled that the Countess of Pembroke was said to spend a considerable amount of time in the convent, and had even had her own set of apartments built. When she came, her household would also need to be accommodated, hence the sumptuous guesthall.

Bartholomew's throat was dry and he needed a drink. As he eased himself out of bed, Michael woke immediately and sat up.

'What is wrong?' he demanded loudly. 'Where are you going?'

On the other side of the room, Cynric's eyes glittered in the firelight as he watched.

'Thirsty,' said Bartholomew. He padded across the hall in his bare feet to the water jug, filled a cup and took it back to bed with him. As he sipped it, he looked at the fat monk. 'Tell me again what happened to you,' he said.

'What now?' asked Michael irritably. 'It is the middle of the night; Cynric and I have already told you all there is to tell.'

'I cannot remember what you said,' replied Bartholomew sheepishly. He took another sip of the water. It tasted peaty and brackish, like the stuff in the lode in which he had almost drowned, and he put it aside with distaste.

'You have not told us your story yet,' said Michael. 'Cynric heard the mercenaries tell Alan they had seen you drown. How did you come to rise from the dead?'

Briefly Bartholomew told them, sparing much of the detail, not because he thought they would not be interested, but because it was a memory that would need to fade before he would feel comfortable recounting it for others. 'What about you?' he asked when he had finished.

Cynric left his bed and came to sit near the fire. His face took on a dreamy expression, and Bartholomew was reminded of the times that Cynric had entertained him by reciting ancient tales of Welsh heroes and great battles when he had been an undergraduate at Oxford – before he had gone to Paris to study with the Arab Ibn Ibrahim – and Cynric had first become his book-bearer.

'I was riding last in the line, and the path was narrow,' Cynric began. 'I had my suspicions about the expedition from the start – there were things that did not seem right, but mainly the timing. If the Chancellor had been attacked on Saturday on his way to the installation, then there would not have been time for the news to have been carried back to the Bishop and the Bishop to dispatch messengers to arrive in Cambridge so early on Sunday morning. And others used the Cambridge to Ely road to attend the installation, but none reported the attack on the Chancellor.'

'Why did that not occur to me?' asked Michael, putting his large arms behind his head and staring up at the ceiling. 'It is obvious now that you mention it.'

'When I heard Jurnet scream,' continued Cynric, 'I guessed exactly what was happening. Fortunately, I was able to engage one man in a fight, which blocked the way for the others.'

'Cynric is too modest to tell you, so I will,' interrupted Michael. 'He knew I was unarmed, and so he engaged this soldier long enough to allow me to escape. He saved my life.'

Cynric flushed with embarrassment and resumed his tale. 'When I thought I had allowed Michael sufficient time to flee, I killed the mercenary and ran away myself. There were another five soldiers and Alan, and I knew I would not be able to fight them all. I set my horse to lay a false trail and doubled back to see what I could do for you. That was when I heard the northerner tell Alan you had drowned. It was a terrible moment, boy,' he added, falling silent.

'For me too,' said Bartholomew, his eyes straying to the peaty water in the cup.

'By the time I judged it safe to stop running, I was hopelessly lost,' said Michael, taking up the story. 'I took

the saddle off the poor horse and discovered that someone
had put burrs under it. Yours was probably the same, which
accounts for their unruly behaviour. It was probably a ploy
intended to exhaust us so that we would be less able to fight
them when the time came. Anyway, I wandered aimlessly
for the rest of the day until Cynric found me just before
dusk. He brought us to the causeway and I suggested we
claim sanctuary here at Denny. I knew the nuns would not
refuse a monk in distress, even though they are usually wary
of accepting unknown men inside their walls.'

'At first light yesterday, I set off to look for Egil,' continued
Cynric. 'I have no idea what happened to him. I was searching for clues when I found you.'

'You were lucky, Matt,' said Michael, stating the obvious.
'You would not have survived much longer out there.' He
shuddered and drew the blankets up under his chin. 'The
Fens are a foul place to be in the winter. It is the one thing
about my abbey at Ely that I do not miss.'

'I wondered why Alan was so averse to having Cynric, Egil
and Jurnet accompany us,' said Bartholomew. 'He knew it
would be more difficult to murder five people than the two
he had originally envisaged.'

'Yes,' said Michael thoughtfully. 'Yet even so, I would have
expected experienced mercenaries to have put up a better
show. It was seven against five. I was unarmed, you are useless
in armed combat, yet they allowed three to escape.'

'Two – they thought they saw him drown,' said Cynric,
indicating Bartholomew. 'And I am sure they believed you
and I would go the same way, lost and alone in the marshes.'

'That is beside the point,' said Michael. 'The soldiers
Oswald Stanmore employs to guard his cloth carts would
not have been so incompetent.'

Cynric mused for a moment and then nodded slowly. 'You
are right – they were poor fighters. Perhaps they were not
soldiers at all.'

'I wonder if they were the outlaws the Sheriff has been

chasing this winter,' suggested Michael. 'They could be, you know. He told me they use the Fens like a stronghold, disappearing down little-known pathways when his men close in on them. And Alan did seem to know his way around when he took that short cut.'

'Perhaps they are, but what do we do now?' asked Bartholomew, standing and beginning to pace as he did when he was restless.

Michael watched him. 'Nothing. It is late, and while you may have slept all day, we did not. I have been hearing the nuns' confessions – and that was an eye-opener I can tell you; I should come here more often! – and Cynric has been searching for Egil. Go to sleep, Matt. We will talk again in the morning.'

He heaved his bulk onto its side and huddled down under the blankets as the wind rattled the shutters. Cynric did likewise, while Bartholomew lay back on his bed and stared up at the ceiling. He wondered what had happened to Egil, and dreaded telling Stanmore that his two men had been lost. Edith said that Egil was a Fenman. If by some remote chance he had not been killed by the mercenaries, he was one of the few people who might escape the treacherous marshes alive. There was thus a glimmer of hope, although Bartholomew suspected it was not a realistic one.

He listened to the patter of rain against the windows, watched the firelight flickering on the walls and felt a chill settle in his stomach. Stanmore's men were murdered, Grene and Armel were dead from poisoned wine, Isaac was hanged and someone had been to some trouble to ensure he, Michael and Cynric died in the marshes. What vile plot was being hatched this time?

By the following day, the rain had abated and there were patches of blue sky among the grey clouds. Bartholomew rose at dawn, woken by the sound of the nuns' chanting in the church. Michael opened a bleary eye, but grunted irritably and pulled the blankets up over his head to try to block out the noise. Bartholomew washed and shaved near the hearth, relishing the luxury of hot water and a warm room, and dressed in the clothes that Cynric had cleaned the day before. They were bone dry and crisp from being near the fire, something he had never experienced in Michaelhouse, even in the summer. He inspected the tear in his leggings, surprised, and not entirely pleased, to see that someone had repaired it using a patch of brilliant red.

'I did that,' said Cynric, not without pride. 'One of those nuns wanted to do it, but I did not like to think of your clothes in *their* hands.' He gave Bartholomew a meaningful look that the physician did not understand at all.

'Why not?' he asked, convinced that the nuns would have done a better job than Cynric, and most certainly would not have used a scarlet patch to mend the brown garment.

Cynric pursed his lips and would be drawn no further. Michael was listening from his bed and gave a sudden roar of laughter.

'You are right to be cautious, Cynric my friend,' he said, green eyes glittering with amusement. 'And if you had heard their confessions, Matt, you would understand why!'

'Michael, this is a convent,' said Bartholomew, suspecting that the monk was simply trying to unnerve his prudish book-bearer. 'What could nuns possibly do to pique your lecherous interests out here in the Fens?'

Michael laughed again, but whatever reply he had been about to make was forgotten at a knock on the door. He hauled the blankets around his chin primly, as Bartholomew admitted a lay sister who carried a tray bearing barley bread, some slivers of cheese and a jug of ale, and told them the Abbess wished to see them later that morning. When she had gone, Michael hauled himself reluctantly from his bed, and donned his habit, nodding approvingly at Cynric's efforts to remove the black, clinging mud from it.

Bartholomew fretted while they waited for the Abbess's

summons. 'I need to return to Michaelhouse,' he said, pacing in front of the window. 'We have wasted two days already with this miserable business, and I am worried about Gray's disputation. We should go home.'

'What do you plan to do?' Cynric asked of Michael. Bartholomew's steps faltered: it had not occurred to him that Michael would want to do anything other than return to College.

Michael mused. 'I am undecided. It is tempting to continue to enjoy the Abbess's hospitality, and a few days would give us the opportunity to think and to recover from our ordeal. But I would like to speak to the Bishop, and so am inclined to travel to Ely. Yet I also believe that the answer to this riddle we seem to have stumbled upon lies in Cambridge, and the sooner we return, the quicker we will have it resolved.'

'I see no reason to go to Ely,' objected Bartholomew nervously. 'We know the Bishop's summons was false.' He hesitated. 'At least, I suppose we can assume it was.'

Michael's eyes narrowed. 'What are you suggesting?'

Bartholomew regarded him sombrely. 'Perhaps the Bishop really did summon you on Sunday – for reasons of his own.'

Michael met his gaze with unreadable eyes. 'You suspect it has something to do with my rejecting the offer to be Master of Valence Marie?' he asked eventually. He did not wait for an answer. 'Believe me, Matt, the Bishop has his own perfectly good reasons for wishing me to refuse the Mastership. He would hardly encourage me to decline, and then arrange my demise. The reason he persuaded me to not to accept in the first place was so that I would be free to continue to act as his agent.'

Bartholomew supposed he was right, although sometimes the convoluted logic of the power-brokers in University, town and Church eluded him completely.

'So who do you think is responsible for luring us out here?' he asked.

Michael sat on his bed and stretched his long legs out in front of him, ankles incongruously white next to his black habit. 'It is someone with resources. It would not be cheap to hire six soldiers and Alan. Mercenaries are likely to demand a high price for premeditated murder.'

'Who has such resources?' demanded Bartholomew. 'Other than the Bishop?'

'Alan and his men were not mercenaries,' Cynric pointed out. 'We decided last night that they were too incompetent to be real soldiers.'

Michael ignored both of them. 'The Chancellor could probably lay his hands on sufficient funds, and doubtless has the contacts to organise such an incident. But he has no motive and he is not even in Cambridge.'

'De Wetherset lives near here,' said Bartholomew suddenly, thinking of the previous holder of the Chancellorship, who had retired into the Fens when University politics became too much for him.

'No, Matt,' said Michael firmly. 'By all accounts, de Wetherset is enjoying his seclusion and has no wish to re-enter University affairs.'

'But he has never liked us,' persisted Bartholomew. 'He used us to do his dirty work, but he never really trusted us and he lied constantly.'

'Who in the University does not lie?' asked Michael glibly. 'But you are on the wrong track altogether. De Wetherset has nothing to do with the University these days, and he certainly does not have the resources to hire Alan and his cronies. We need to look to Cambridge for our answer. Besides the Chancellor, there are a host of townspeople who could afford to have people killed – your brother-in-law to name but one.'

'That is ridiculous!' protested Bartholomew. 'Oswald is not a murderer! And he has no reason to wish harm on us.'

'Perhaps,' said Michael. 'But there is the mystery involving his apprentice and this bottle of wine. Father Philius has no reason to tell us untruths.'

'And neither does Oswald!' insisted Bartholomew. 'There must be some misunderstanding. I will see Philius when we get back, and we will probably find out that it was Cheney's apprentice he saw, or Deschalers's or Mortimer's. All four live next to each other on Milne Street and he may have mistaken one house for another.'

Michael regarded him sceptically. 'Philius is not stupid, Matt, regardless of what you might think about his medical abilities. And, anyway, your students said they saw Oswald's apprentice buy poisoned wine from Sacks in the Brazen George. Or were they mistaken, too?'

Bartholomew was racking his brain for an answer when the lay sister returned and said the Abbess awaited them in her solar. Still unsettled by Michael's accusations, Bartholomew followed her down the stairs, Michael and Cynric in tow. Bartholomew glanced behind him, and saw Michael patting his hair into place and making haste to brush a few crumples out of his habit. When the monk rubbed surreptitiously at his teeth with a corner of his sleeve, Bartholomew's suspicions were aroused regarding Michael's motives for tarrying at the convent.

There was only one entrance to the guesthall and that was through a small door to one side of the main gate. In this way, visitors were kept entirely apart from the nuns; a person wishing to enter the convent from the guesthall was forced to do so through the main gate like everyone else: men staying there could not inadvertently stray into the nuns' living quarters, while the nuns themselves would see no one for whom they might be tempted to break their vows. It was doubtless only Michael's vocation as a monk that prompted the Abbess to relax the rules and allow three men inside her hallowed walls.

As they walked across the cobbled yard towards the Abbess's quarters, Bartholomew was aware of being watched with intense interest. He glanced upwards and saw several veiled heads eyeing him with undisguised curiosity from the unglazed windows of the dormitory, while others looked from the cloister that surrounded the yard. Voices whispered and giggled and, from the lewdness of the laughter, Bartholomew strongly suspected that the nuns were not discussing matters spiritual. He began to feel uncomfortable, although Michael did not appear to mind greatly. Cynric muttered that he would wait in the guesthall, and, before Bartholomew could stop him, he had scuttled back across the yard and was out through the main gate. Hoots of laughter followed him and Bartholomew was tempted to follow, unsettled by the nuns' behaviour.

Finally, they were across the yard and were being led up the wide wooden staircase that led to the Abbess's solar. The Countess of Pembroke's money had provided the residents of Denny with sumptuous surroundings, despite the fact that Franciscan nuns were commonly called 'Poor Clares'. Thick woollen rugs covered the floor and the walls were painted with vivid murals depicting scenes from classical mythology and local folklore. By comparison, the decorations in Constantine Mortimer's elegant house appeared crass and tasteless. The rugs had been chosen to complement the dominant hues of the wall paintings, while even the bowls on the low table near the fire had been carefully selected to match the solar's colour scheme.

The Abbess was waiting for them, her hands hidden demurely in the wide sleeves of her gown, and was flanked by two of her nuns. Bartholomew had last seen her at the high table next to Vice-Chancellor Harling at the installation at Valence Marie, and knew her reputation for learning and saintliness. She was tall for a woman, and her movements had a fluid elegance born of a grace that was innate. Her eyes were an arresting turquoise, accentuated by the plain grey of her habit, and her face was not yet blemished with the wrinkles of middle age.

The nuns at her side were chalk and cheese. One was an elderly lady whose hooked nose swooped down towards her prominent chin and whose skin was as wrinkled and brown as an old nut; the second was apparently a relative of the Abbess, for her eyes were a similar, although less vivid, blue-green colour.

The Abbess stepped forward, and Michael elbowed Bartholomew out of the way to take her hand and effect an elegant bow.

'Brother Michael!' said the Abbess courteously. 'I am pleased to see you well again. And your companion.' She looked at Bartholomew, who hastened to follow Michael's example and bow.

'My Lady Abbess, may I present to you my friend and colleague Doctor Bartholomew,' said Michael, holding her hand for rather longer than was necessary. She looked uncomfortable and tried to free it, but Michael appeared not to notice and did not slacken his grip. 'He is also a Fellow of Michaelhouse. We would like to thank you for your gracious hospitality.'

The Abbess finally succeeded in retrieving her hand and inclined her head politely. She indicated the nuns who stood at her side. 'May I introduce Dame Pelagia, my cellarer, and my niece Julianna.' The nuns curtseyed demurely, although Bartholomew was discomfited by Julianna's somewhat brazen stare. This did not seem to bother Michael, who met her eyes boldly as he took her hand and bowed almost as deeply as he had done to the Abbess.

'Are you quite recovered from your ordeal?' enquired the Abbess, indicating that they should sit in the chairs that were arranged around the fireside, and selecting the one that was farthest from Michael for herself.

'Almost,' said Michael, before Bartholomew could reply, 'although you will notice that my colleague still limps from the near-fatal wound in his leg.'

The three nuns made sympathetic faces and Bartholomew

shot Michael a look of embarrassment. By no stretch of the imagination could a graze be called 'near-fatal' and Bartholomew was certain he had not limped.

'Then you should remain here until you are fully well,' said the Abbess while, next to her, Julianna gave Bartholomew a smile that verged on being a leer.

'We have imposed on your generosity quite long enough,' he said firmly, before Michael could agree to a lengthy sojourn. 'We will leave today and trouble you no further.'

'But you are no trouble at all,' said Julianna, smiling coquettishly at Bartholomew from under her thick eyelashes. 'We would be honoured if you would stay longer.' Her eyes travelled down his body to the patch on his leggings. 'And perhaps there are little services we might perform for you.'

Bartholomew was unable to look at Michael, whose eyebrows shot up into his hair. Instead he gazed at Julianna, uncertain how to respond to her ambiguous suggestion.

'Your servant clearly cannot count the mending of garments among his undoubted talents,' said the Abbess, indicating the scarlet patch and smiling sweetly to relieve Bartholomew's discomfiture.

'He cannot, but I can,' interposed Julianna eagerly. 'And if you agree to stay longer, I will re-mend that hole for you. I could do it now, as we talk.'

'No!' said Bartholomew, more vehemently than he intended, but determined not to be divested in the Abbess's private apartments. 'It is perfectly functional as it is.'

'And our Abbess is a far neater needlewoman than you anyway, Julianna,' said Dame Pelagia, in the blunt manner of old ladies. 'If the doctor's leggings require attention, then she should do the honours if he is to receive the best the Abbey can offer.'

'All this is quite unnecessary,' said Michael impatiently. 'The leggings look perfectly good as they are. After all, us monastics should not be encouraging vanity among the laity.' He folded his hands in his sleeves and assumed a saintly expression. Bartholomew eyed him in disbelief, recalling the amount of primping that had taken place as the monk had prepared himself for the installation ceremony.

'But regardless of whether the leggings should be mended properly, you must both stay until you are fully recovered,' said Julianna firmly, 'however long that might take.'

'Well . . .' said Michael.

'You would be most welcome,' said the Abbess sincerely. 'And with all these outlaws prowling the roads, it will be good for us to have the security of three men within our walls.'

'But we are not fighters,' said Bartholomew, alarmed. 'I do not even have a weapon!'

'That can be arranged,' said Julianna comfortably. 'I have a dagger you can borrow.'

Bartholomew regarded her with dismay. What kind of nun offered to lend people her dagger? He looked at the Abbess, who seemed as startled by Julianna's offer as Bartholomew had been. Dame Pelagia merely sat back in her chair and raised her eyes heavenward, although a smile of amusement played about the corners of her lips.

Bartholomew had always known Michael was a man of culture and breeding – he was the younger son of an influential knight of King Edward's court – but he had seldom been in a position to observe him in action. The monk skilfully manipulated the conversation to topics he sensed would interest and entertain the three nuns, ranging from issues of philosophy that had the Abbess eagerly inviting him to tell her more, to humorous anecdotes from the Bishop's Palace that had Julianna enthralled and even the dry old Dame Pelagia chuckling in amusement. The physician marvelled at the transition from Michael the Senior Proctor to Michael the Courtier, and wondered whether he would ever know the monk well enough never to be surprised by his hidden talents and abilities.

After a while, as Julianna was wiping tears of laughter

from her eyes at a story about the Bishop's mother, and Bartholomew and the Abbess were kneeling solicitously at the side of Dame Pelagia – who had cackled so hard she had started to choke – the lay sister tapped on the door, and entered with a dish of small cakes and a jug of wine. Michael, apparently hungry after his display of courtliness, reached for the food almost before it had been set on the table.

'What a splendid object,' he said, taking the plate and inspecting it minutely. Several cakes slid from it into his lap and were suavely transferred to his mouth.

'It is gold,' said the Abbess, somewhat unnecessarily, given the way it gleamed in the pale light of the winter morning.

Dame Pelagia regarded it with interest, leaning forward to see more clearly. Even the Abbess's cellarer, it seemed, was not privy to the full extent of the convent's wealth.

'It is very fine gold,' said Michael, running his soft, white fingers across the delicately etched surface. 'It is almost too fine for mere cakes.'

The Abbess reached out and removed the plate from Michael's hands, firmly replacing it on the table. 'It is the only serving plate we own. We do not often entertain in our humble home.'

Bartholomew and Michael looked around at the luxurious surroundings simultaneously. Perhaps they had been too long in the squalor of Michaelhouse, Bartholomew thought.

'I understand the Countess of Pembroke stays here from time to time,' he said, desperately trying to think of something to say in the silence that followed. Now that there was food to hand, Michael seemed to have passed the burden of conversation to Bartholomew, while he concentrated on fortifying himself for his next performance.

The Abbess smiled. 'You understand correctly, Doctor,' she replied. 'But the Countess has her own apartments. She does not need to debase herself by using our plain rooms.'

Bartholomew's already sumptuous vision of the Countess's

apartments escalated to the realms of the impossible. He wondered what the Abbess would make of Michaelhouse's austere halls and stained pewter tableware.

'When might the Countess next visit?' asked Michael, licking sugar from his fingers. The cake plate, Bartholomew noticed, was empty, allowing Dame Pelagia to inspect it even more minutely.

'She will be with us in a matter of days,' said the Abbess. 'King's Hall celebrates its Foundation Day soon, and the Countess will visit us after she has attended the festivities there.'

Julianna suddenly started to cough in a way that, to Bartholomew, was clearly contrived, although it had her aunt jumping up to press a cup of wine into her hand. The Abbess hesitated, looking uncertainly at Bartholomew, but then seemed to make up her mind.

'Since you are here, I wonder if I might impose on your good offices, Doctor. Julianna has been complaining of chest pains these last two days. It is doubtless the unhealthy vapours from the Fens, but I would appreciate your advice on the matter. She can provide you with the details necessary to calculate her stars.'

Julianna smiled at him, coughing forgotten, and Bartholomew found himself unaccountably flustered. 'I cannot,' he said, thinking fast. 'I would need a set of astrological charts to calculate a horoscope, and mine were rendered useless when I fell in the river.'

'Do not worry about that,' said Julianna with a wide grin. 'I have a set here that belongs to the Countess.' She waved a scroll at him.

'But I do not usually conduct astrological consultations,' he objected. The more he practised medicine, the more he became convinced that the efficacy of his cures had nothing to do with the alignment of the celestial bodies. Because his personal beliefs did not exempt him from teaching his students how to do them, he performed the occasional horoscope just so he did not forget, but these were very few and far between, and he always resented the time he spent on them.

'Rubbish!' said Julianna, not to be deterred. 'You are a physician, and all physicians read their patients' stars. You saying you do not prepare horoscopes is like a merchant saying he does not like the feel of money!'

'Well, I prefer doing other things,' he said shortly. 'I seldom calculate horoscopes.'

'I would be grateful if you would make an exception,' said the Abbess, laying a hand on her niece's shoulder in motherly concern. 'Julianna is very young to be suffering from chest pains, and I do not want to send her to Ely to see the infirmarian while there are outlaws at large on the causeway.'

'Very well, then,' he said reluctantly, realising it would be churlish to decline a request from the Abbess, given that they had availed themselves of her hospitality. He turned to Julianna, trying to become professional to hide his irritation. 'Perhaps you can tell me when these pains started?'

'Oh no!' said Julianna with distaste. 'Not here! There is a small chamber on the floor above that is far more private for you to ask your intimate questions.' She looked pointedly at Michael.

'I will not ask any intimate questions,' said Bartholomew nervously. 'I only have to know the letters in your name – each letter of the alphabet has a specific astrological number and I need to add them together – and a few pertinent dates—'

'I want more than that!' said Julianna indignantly. 'I want a complete astrological prediction that will tell me whether I should be forced to remain among the dangerous miasmas of these marshes, or whether I should be allowed to move to somewhere more conducive to my health.'

So, thought Bartholomew, Julianna regarded him as her escape route from Denny to somewhere more lively. He could not blame her: the Fens were not his idea of paradise, either.

'You will see that your consultation will enable me to make the correct decision regarding my niece's future,' said the Abbess, a worried frown marring her face. 'I would truly appreciate any advice you could offer.'

'Upstairs, then,' said Julianna, standing and stretching out a hand to Bartholomew.

The physician swallowed hard. 'It would be better if there were another nun present,' he said quickly. A dozen would be preferable, he thought to himself. He saw a brief flash of anger in Julianna's eyes, and his discomfort intensified.

'I will chaperone Doctor Bartholomew and Julianna,' said Dame Pelagia, heaving her ancient body from her fireside chair.

'Let me think,' said the Abbess, as Michael slipped quickly into the chair Dame Pelagia had vacated, thus placing himself considerably closer to her. She stood and moved away, clasping her hands. Bartholomew could see her dilemma. Should she risk the reputation of her wanton niece with the physician, or should she risk her own at the hands of Brother Michael, whose interests were clearly not monastic? To send for another nun to chaperone them might be construed as offensive and the Abbess was far too well mannered to insult her guests.

'Doctor Bartholomew is a professional man,' pouted Julianna, 'and he is only going to ask me about my stars. Why would we need a chaperone?'

The Abbess eyed her niece suspiciously and came to a decision. She apparently trusted her own abilities to fend off manly attentions over those of Julianna, whose brazen gazes led Bartholomew to wonder whether the skill of repelling male attentions was ever a part of her education.

'Dame Pelagia will go with Julianna,' said the Abbess, 'while Brother Michael will defend my virtue.'

She smiled lightly, as if she had made a joke, but her

meaning was clear enough. Some of the glitter faded from Michael's eyes, but he nodded politely.

Filled with trepidation, both for the Abbess and for himself, Bartholomew followed Julianna up a narrow flight of stairs to an attic above the solar. The room was as elegantly furnished as the rest of the building, and Bartholomew was impressed to see glass in the windows that was so fine and clear he could see right through them and out to the fields and Fens beyond. Dame Pelagia finally heaved herself up the stairs and stood wheezing in the doorway. Bartholomew helped her to a chair.

'You seem more in need of a cure for chest pains than Julianna does,' he said pointedly, as the old lady collapsed into the chair with evident relief. Julianna grinned at him, totally unabashed, and perched herself on a table where she sat swinging her legs.

Bartholomew started to ask her about her birth date and various other significant events in her life, to keep matters purely medical, and to prevent her from embarking on some tangential discussion of her own choosing. Dame Pelagia began to nod and doze in her chair, watched attentively by both Bartholomew and Julianna for entirely different reasons. Dame Pelagia's head drooped and Bartholomew leapt noisily to his feet to pace the room. The old lady snapped awake, eyed him suspiciously and tried to pay attention to what was being said.

Several times he tried to bring the interview to an end, but Julianna knew as well as he did that ascertaining information to predict what would best favour a person's future health with any degree of accuracy took time. She also seemed aware that he did not want to offend the Abbess by providing her niece with a less than accurate consultation. Wearily, he sat at a table, unrolled the charts and began to make his calculations.

Dame Pelagia's head sank down onto her chest a second time and Bartholomew rapped the ink-well on the side of the table vigorously, pretending that its contents needed to be shaken. Pelagia looked up sleepily and resettled herself in the chair. But Bartholomew's ploys could not keep the old lady from her midday doze indefinitely and it was not long before she was soundly asleep, her gentle snores whispering about the room.

'Now,' said Bartholomew as he sharpened a pen noisily, hoping to waken her yet again. 'What phase was the moon in when you first experienced these pains?'

He pretended to drop the ink-well, sending it clattering to the floor, but Dame Pelagia did not even stir.

'Now she is asleep, you will not waken her with your contrived racket,' said Julianna, confident in her superior knowledge of the old lady's habits. 'We do not have long now you have successfully wasted so much time in keeping her awake. The bell for sext will ring at any moment and then our time alone together will be at an end.' She advanced on him meaningfully.

Bartholomew leapt to his feet and backed away, raising his hands to fend her off. 'Sister Julianna! You are a nun – remember your vows!'

'I am not a nun!' said Julianna in disdain, her voice low. 'And I have taken no vows. I am merely here in the care of my aunt until a suitable marriage can be arranged.'

Bartholomew glanced uneasily towards the door, assessing his chances of reaching it before Julianna blocked his way. He wondered whether being accused of seducing a nun was better or worse than being charged with ravishing the daughter of a nobleman. Julianna moved towards him and he edged away.

'Keep still,' Julianna whispered in sudden frustration. 'I am risking my life by speaking to you, while all you do is back away from me like some old priest!'

'Risking your life?' This was worse than he had thought. Her family must be powerful indeed!

'Yes. And I cannot say what I must too loudly, so come

closer, near the window and away from the door.' She waited impatiently and then raised her voice in exasperation. 'I do not bite for heaven's sake!' She grabbed his arm and yanked him towards the window. 'We must not be overheard.'

He was about to reply when the slightest of creaks from outside the door indicated that someone was there, listening.

'Saturn was at its zenith,' said Julianna loudly, her eyes wide with horror as she gazed at the door. Swallowing hard, she leaned close to him and spoke in a whisper. 'You must leave here today. You are in the gravest danger. Leave now – this afternoon – before it is too late!'

CHAPTER 6

BARTHOLOMEW REGARDED JULIANNA IN DISBELIEF, simultaneously they looked towards the door a second time as there was a slight, but distinctly audible, groan from the floorboards in the hallway.

'And what day of the month did you notice this change in your humours?' he asked, speaking as loudly as he could. Under the door, where there was a gap between wood and floor, a shadow moved, stopped and then passed on, while in her chair Dame Pelagia snored obliviously.

Julianna smiled quickly at him before becoming intense again. 'They suspect I know. I am no longer safe and neither are you.'

'Know what?' said Bartholomew in confusion. 'Safe from whom?'

'I have no idea,' said Julianna. 'That is the frustrating part. There are comings and goings in the depths of the night and something is amiss, but I do not know what.'

'Then how do you know you are in danger?' asked Bartholomew. Perhaps Julianna had been locked up in the convent for too long, and her desire for something to break the monotony of her daily life had gained the better of her common sense.

She fiddled with her veil and glanced at Dame Pelagia. 'There is not much time to explain. Last night, after compline, I went to the pantry for something to eat – I am always hungry here since the portions are so small – and I heard men in the kitchen. I heard one of them telling the others that you were not dead, but were recovering here along with that fat Benedictine and your servant. They were furious. Then I heard them say they would act tonight. As I went to leave, I knocked a plate off a shelf and they heard me. I escaped to the dormitory, but I think they guessed it was me who had been eavesdropping.'

'What were these men like?' asked Bartholomew. 'Mercenaries wearing boiled leather jerkins and helmets? Or a young man with a newly grown beard?'

Julianna shook her head. 'I did not see them. But at least one of them was gently spoken. He was not a common soldier.'

Bartholomew was nonplussed. By no stretch of the imagination could Alan or any of the soldiers be described as gently spoken. But while Bartholomew could believe that the mercenaries might have discovered their whereabouts and intended to attack them again, surely there was not a second group of people who wanted his death and Michael's? He wondered again if Julianna might be making up the story to inject some excitement into her life, or if she had misunderstood or misheard.

Julianna read the doubt in his face. Her eyes narrowed and her face became hard. 'You do not believe me! I risk myself to come to warn you, and you do not believe a word I say. Well you will find out I am right, but then it will be too late.'

She began to flounce away, but he caught her by the arm.

'Wait! You say you have risked your life to warn me, but people do not risk their lives for those they do not know. What were you intending to ask of me? Other than an astrological consultation to cure the cough we both know you do not have.'

Her eyes flashed with fury, but this was as quickly replaced by sudden humour. 'You are astute!' She looked towards

Dame Pelagia and then to the door. 'You have also guessed correctly. When you leave tonight, I want to go with you.'

He had been right: Julianna saw in Bartholomew and Michael an opportunity to escape from her tedious existence at Denny. Since she probably realised that there would be nothing in her horoscope to warrant the Abbess removing her from the Fens, she must have had an alternative plan to ensure she would be able to abscond.

'And if we take you to Cambridge, what will you do then?' he asked, to see how far she had considered her arrangements in advance. He was not disappointed.

'I will throw myself on the mercy of my uncle,' she said promptly. 'Thomas Deschalers, the grocer.'

It was a small world, he thought. 'Are Thomas Deschalers and the Abbess kinsmen, then?' he asked. 'You are the niece of both.'

'I know what I am,' said Julianna imperiously. 'But Thomas Deschalers is my father's brother and the Abbess is my mother's sister. They are not kinsmen really. When my parents died last year, he used my relationship with her to secure me here.'

'You did not want to come, I take it?' asked Bartholomew.

'I did not!' claimed Julianna vehemently. 'I preferred life in London, although Cambridge was proving it might have possibilities. Uncle Thomas did not really give me time to find out before he had arranged for me to come to this godforsaken bog.'

'You have not always been in a convent, then?'

Julianna grimaced. 'Unfortunately, yes, I have spent most of my life with nuns. I had a few weeks of freedom in London after the death of my parents, and then a few weeks in Cambridge when I lived with Uncle Thomas. But I would rather be anywhere but here. You must take me with you.'

'And what will you do if Uncle Thomas orders you straight back here?'

'He will not!' said Julianna defiantly. 'I will tell him of all the strange happenings and he will inform the Sheriff who will investigate.'

'What strange happenings?'

'I have already told you!' said Julianna impatiently. 'Comings and goings in the night, strange men in the kitchens between matins and lauds—'

'But there might be a dozen explanations for these things, Sis . . . Mistress Julianna,' said Bartholomew gently.

Perhaps some of the lay sisters had their menfolk into the kitchens to give them food, he thought, for even in the Fens, where fish and fowl were more abundant than elsewhere, food was still scarce and hideously expensive for the honest labourer. Or perhaps the explanation was less innocent, and some of the lay sisters, or even nuns, entertained men under cover of darkness. But regardless, Julianna's suspicions were scarcely something with which to bother the Sheriff.

'The wisest course of action for you to take would be to tell your aunt of your concerns and observations, and let her decide what to do about it,' he said eventually.

'You are worthless!' shouted Julianna with sudden vehemence, her eyes filling with tears. 'I should have known better than to trust you.'

Her furious words woke Dame Pelagia, who blinked in confusion at the scene in front of her. Julianna shoved Bartholomew away and fled from the room.

'And *you* should not be there!' he heard her yell, presumably to the person who had been trying to listen outside the door. He went to look, but there was no one to be seen.

'What ails Julianna?' asked Dame Pelagia, standing unsteadily. Her eyes widened accusingly. 'You did not seduce her while I was dozing?'

'Of course I did not!' said Bartholomew half indignant and half startled by the old nun's forthrightness. 'She is angry because she did not like the advice I gave her.'

He helped the old lady down the stairs and they entered the Abbess's solar again. She and Michael were positioned most decorously, she standing at the window, and he still sitting in the chair by the fire. He stood as Bartholomew entered with Dame Pelagia and offered her the chair.

'Have you worked out a course of treatment for my niece's ailment?' asked the Abbess. 'Or will I need to ask Thomas Deschalers to house her until I find her another convent in a more healthy part of the country? I was alarmed when she told me of her condition yesterday. It is not good for a person so young to have such complaints.'

'Indeed not,' said Bartholomew. He was saved from having to answer further by the sound of the bell ringing to call the nuns to sext. The Abbess moved from the window and offered her hand to Michael, who hastened to take it in his.

'Thank you for your company, Brother,' she said. 'You have been most charming and entertaining. You are welcome to join us for sext, if you like.'

Michael caught Bartholomew's look that he wanted to talk and said, with some reluctance, that he would say his offices at the prie-dieu in the guesthall. With a gracious smile, the Abbess took her leave, followed by Dame Pelagia, while the lay sister conducted Bartholomew and Michael out of the convent proper and back to their lodgings.

'Are you still in one piece?' asked Cynric anxiously, looking up from the fire in front of which he had been drowsing. 'I thought those women intended some serious mischief.'

'Some of them did,' said Michael slyly, looking at Bartholomew out of the corner of his eye.

'Not to the same extent as you,' retorted Bartholomew. 'Your lecherous attentions had that poor Abbess in a terrible quandary.'

'Matthew, Matthew!' said Michael in hurt tones. 'What do you think I am? I have sworn a vow of chastity.' The gleam in his green eyes was anything but chaste.

'Really?' said Bartholomew. 'And how well do you keep it?'

'That, my dear physician, is none of your business,' said Michael with a smug smile. 'But I can assure you I was nothing but decorous and gallant with that noble lady, the Abbess.'

Bartholomew looked at him sharply, but was unable to determine whether he was telling the truth. Michael's eyes shone with something other than their usual salaciousness, and Bartholomew hoped the monk did not imagine himself in love. If he did, the situation was bound to end in tragedy for Michael, if not for the Abbess.

Briefly, he told Michael what Julianna had said, but the monk dismissed it with a wave of his hand.

'Silly girl! The nuns ought to warn her about her behaviour. She was lucky it was you she enticed up into her secluded chambers, and not some lout who would have taken advantage of her.'

'What about what she says she overheard last night?'

Michael shook his head. 'You were right to have misgivings: she probably made it up to force you to take her to Cambridge. It is a clever tactic – what better way to make someone do what you want than to prey on his fears? You have just been viciously attacked and almost killed in the Fens, and so she warns you that it might happen again. Most men would be gone already!'

'Then we should go,' said Bartholomew promptly. 'There is a remote chance she is telling the truth and I want to return to Michaelhouse anyway.'

'Your leg needs more rest,' said Michael, after a moment's hesitation.

'It does not!' said Bartholomew, laughing at the feebleness of the excuse to stay.

'It is too late,' said Michael, studying the sky through the open shutters. 'If we set off now, it will be dark by the time we reach Cambridge and it would be dangerous to be on the road then.'

'Nonsense,' said Bartholomew. 'There are at least four

hours of daylight left and we can easily walk the eight miles to Cambridge before dusk.'

'Walk?' squawked Michael in horror. 'I cannot walk eight miles!'

'It will do you good, Brother,' said Bartholomew, eyeing Michael's substantial girth critically. 'You need some exercise.'

'I still feel weak from my experiences in the Fens,' said Michael, putting a flabby hand to his forehead. 'And I think I might have twisted my ankle.'

'Show me,' said Bartholomew unsympathetically. 'I am good with twisted ankles.'

Michael sighed. 'Just one more night, Matt!' he pleaded. 'One more! And then I will return to Cambridge with you. I will even walk if you so demand. But let us stay here one more night!'

'Why?' asked Bartholomew curiously. 'Do you have a tryst with the Abbess? I would advise against it if you do, Brother. No good can come of such an affair.'

'You sully that good lady's name,' said Michael coldly. 'Of course I have no tryst with her. She is a holy, decent woman.' He turned abruptly on his heel, and went to sit in one of the window seats at the opposite end of the hall, staring morosely out at the misty marshes.

Bartholomew exchanged a look of incomprehension with Cynric, who had watched the scene with considerable interest.

'Is he in love with this Abbess?' whispered Cynric, looking at Michael uncertainly.

'I hope not,' said Bartholomew. He sighed and paced restlessly. 'We are wasting time here, Cynric. If Gray fails his disputation a second time, he will have to repeat an entire year of studying. And that is something neither of us wants!'

'You work too hard, boy,' said Cynric. He gestured to the fire. 'Where is there a welcoming hearth like this in

Michaelhouse? Just draw up a stool and enjoy it while you can.'

Reluctantly, Bartholomew saw Cynric was right. Michael clearly had no intention of leaving Denny that day – although what could be keeping him except the possibility of an encounter with the Abbess, Bartholomew could not imagine – and he could not leave the fat monk behind. He perched on a stool and poked at the fire with a stick, watching sparks fly up the chimney. He realised there was a residual stiffness in his limbs from his night in the Fens and the rest would do him good – then they would be able to make better time on the road to Cambridge at first light the next morning.

The lay sister tapped tentatively on the door and entered, bearing a tray that was so heavily laden with food that Bartholomew, not anticipating such weight, almost dropped it when he hurried forward to help. Michael smacked his lips appreciatively at the large game pie, while Bartholomew ate the excellent bread, baked that day in the convent's own kitchens. Fresh bread was a rare commodity in Michaelhouse, where stale flour was usually used because it was cheaper. There was also some firm yellow cheese, a pat of creamy butter, a little dish of something covered by a linen cloth, and three oranges. Bartholomew picked up one of the fruits and turned it over in his hand.

'I have not seen one of these for years,' he said. It was wizened and hard after its long journey from Spain or Italy, and probably long past its best. But to see an orange at all in the Fens in winter was remarkable.

Cynric eyed it with suspicion. 'I heard those things poisoned Master Mortimer the baker.'

'That was lemons,' said Bartholomew. 'Oranges should not poison anyone. Try some.'

Cynric shook his head quickly and turned his attention back to his bread and cheese. Michael poked suspiciously at the green and lumpy substance in the small dish covered by the linen.

'What is that?' he asked with some disgust. 'It looks like something terrible has been done to a vegetable – and you know how I feel about vegetables.'

'Pickled eels and samphire,' said Bartholomew, recalling Stanmore bringing some as a gift for Edith many years before. His sister had eaten it only because she wanted to please her husband, and had paid for her courtesy by spending most of the night being sick. The next time Stanmore had presented some to her she had shown the good sense to feed it to the cat. 'It is considered a great delicacy and is very expensive. We should be honoured the abbey is sharing such a dish with us.'

'You eat it, then,' said Michael, pushing it towards Bartholomew after a brief and decisive sniff. 'It smells rank.'

Bartholomew shook his head. 'No, thank you, Brother. It tastes a good deal worse than it smells. That is why it is produced in such small quantities: like most delicacies, if it were common, no one would eat it. Oswald told me the King has a liking for pickled eels and samphire, and so, of course, it can be found in the houses of most people who consider themselves fashionable.'

Michael offered it to Cynric, who speared a piece of eel with his dagger and put it in his mouth. He spat it out again immediately, and pulled a face of such utter disgust that Michael and Bartholomew began to laugh.

'That is quite horrible,' said the Welshman, after he had taken a healthy swig of ale to wash away the flavour. 'It tastes like bitter medicine! Far from being honoured, I would say the abbey is trying to get rid of us! You can keep your local delicacies, boy. We Welsh know how to cook seaweed better than that.'

'Seaweed?' whispered Michael, aghast. 'They have given us seaweed?'

'A particular type,' said Bartholomew, feeling guilty that they were being uncharitable over the nuns' generous attempt to provide them with extravagant foods. 'It is not just any old weed picked up from the shores.'

'That makes no difference, Matt,' said Michael sagely, placing the dish as far away from him as possible. 'Seaweed is seaweed and we should not eat it. It is not natural. We are not crabs!'

Bartholomew smiled and went back to poking the fire while the others finished their dinner. Despite Michael's recovered humour, Bartholomew remained apprehensive about his determination that they stay in Denny for another night. He was certain that whatever it was that made him so insistent had nothing to do with the poisoned wine, or the attempt on their lives. Michael, thought Bartholomew, would not win his much-desired promotion from the Bishop if he indulged in a love affair with the Abbess of Denny!

Bartholomew awoke with a start to find a hand clamped firmly over his mouth. He was about to struggle when he saw Cynric's profile etched in the faint light from the embers of the fire. He relaxed and the hand was removed. When he had grown bored with sitting by the fire, he had fallen asleep on his bed and the room was now quite dark. He wondered what time it could be: he could hear no sounds coming from the convent and the guesthall was totally silent. He sat up on the bed and watched Cynric buckling his dagger to his belt.

'What is it?' he whispered.

Cynric edged nearer so that his voice would not carry. 'Michael has gone.'

'Gone where?' Bartholomew stood up and went towards Michael's bed, a pointless action since Cynric had just informed him that Michael was no longer there. He rubbed his eyes and tried to force himself to be more alert.

'Shh! I do not know. He went out a few moments ago. Should I follow him?' He drew his cloak around his shoulders in anticipation.

'We both will,' whispered Bartholomew, after a moment of indecision. He could sense Cynric's disapproval, but the Welshman kept his thoughts to himself. Bartholomew knew Cynric had a low opinion of his abilities to creep around undetected in the dark, but it was only Michael they were following and, if anything, Michael was even worse at stealth than was Bartholomew.

Absently slipping his medicines bag over his shoulder, he followed Cynric through the door.

'Why are you bringing that?' hissed Cynric, pulling at it in the dark. 'It will be in the way.'

Bartholomew shrugged: taking his bag was so instinctive, he had not even realised he had done it. His teacher, Ibn Ibrahim at the University in Paris, had taught him he should never be without it, not even in the bath. Bath! All very well in the civilised countries to the east, but Bartholomew had only ever seen one bath-house in England, and that was in the former villa of a Roman nobleman and had fallen into ruin many centuries before. It was all Bartholomew could do to persuade people to give their hands the most cursory of rinses before eating, despite the fact that he was sure it would prevent a veritable host of intestinal disorders if they did.

He forced his mind away from the perennial problems of medicine and back to Cynric's silent shadow moving ahead of him. Michael was nowhere to be seen, but Cynric led the way unhesitatingly around the side of the guesthall and into the gardens behind the church. An empty snail shell crunched loudly under Bartholomew's foot, making Cynric glance back at him with a weary look of warning to take more care.

The temperature had fallen dramatically with the coming of clearer weather, and the ground underfoot was crisp with rime. For the first time in many weeks, the stars could be seen glittering between the occasional drifting cloud and Bartholomew paused to gaze upwards before an impatient tug on his sleeve set him following Cynric through the fruit trees and rows of kitchen vegetables. Bartholomew shivered in the cold, and wished he had brought his cloak.

At first, he thought Cynric's instincts must have been wrong and that Michael had traipsed off elsewhere in the darkness. But then he saw a movement and there was Michael, all but invisible in his black habit. He appeared to be waiting for someone, because he paced back and forth with an agitation Bartholomew had seldom seen in the sardonic monk. Bartholomew began to have serious misgivings over spying on his friend, for it was apparent from his demeanour that Michael was not meeting just anybody: he was anxious and tense and Bartholomew had attended enough nocturnal meetings with Michael to know he was not easily unsettled from his habitual complacency.

'Come on,' said the physician softly, pulling at Cynric's sleeve. 'This is not right. We should not be spying on Michael and his lady-love.'

Wordlessly, Cynric led the way out of the garden and back towards the guesthall. When he stopped, it was so sudden that Bartholomew bumped into him from behind. Cynric raised his hand to warn him not to speak, but Bartholomew had already seen the dark shadow flitting along the side of the guesthall. The nun looked around carefully, before moving soundlessly through the fruit trees to where Michael waited. Cynric drew Bartholomew into the shadows until she had passed, and then led the way back to the guesthall door. He fiddled with the handle.

'Hurry up!' said Bartholomew, shivering. 'It is cold out here. It is all very well for you – you have your cloak, but I do not.'

'It is locked,' muttered Cynric. He stood back and studied the handle, perplexed.

'It cannot be,' whispered Bartholomew impatiently. 'Let me try.'

He fumbled around with the handle, and pushed and

pulled at the door, but Cynric was right: someone had locked it.

'How very odd,' he said, looking at Cynric's silhouette in the darkness. 'Do you think someone broke in to search our belongings?'

'If it were me, I would not lock the door while I was inside,' answered Cynric softly. 'It might interfere with a hasty escape.'

Puzzled, Bartholomew followed Cynric around to the side of the building to assess the chances of climbing through a window – they could hardly knock on the abbey door in the depths of night and say they had locked themselves out.

Cynric froze suddenly, motioning for Bartholomew not to move. There were two people kneeling at the foot of the wall below the window in the guesthall. Bartholomew peered into the darkness, trying to see what they were doing, but all he could see was their bent backs and something dark on the floor. Then there was a blaze of light and the two figures leapt to their feet. Both held a flaring torch in each hand. Bewildered, Bartholomew watched as one stood back and hurled the flaming missile upwards and towards the window. Leaving a trail of light behind it, the torch dipped and disappeared with a tinkle of breaking glass. The first torch was followed by a second and then a third. The fourth missed, and had to be retrieved and thrown again.

Cynric eased Bartholomew further back into the shadows as the two figures darted towards them, and watched them run out of the nunnery grounds through the gate next to the vegetable garden. Bartholomew was unable to take his eyes from the flames licking up inside the guesthall.

'Damn!' he whispered. 'My cloak is in there, and so are my new gloves. Just when I was beginning to like them!'

'I have your gloves here,' said Cynric, pushing them into Bartholomew's hand. 'I borrowed them yesterday when I went to look for Egil.'

Numbly, Bartholomew put them on. He jumped and

ducked as one of the windows blew out suddenly in a roar of flames, sending glass showering onto the ground below.

'We are meant to be in there,' Cynric whispered, stating the obvious. 'That door was locked so that we could not get out.'

'But we could still have jumped through the windows,' said Bartholomew.

Cynric shook his head, squinting up and assessing their size, vividly outlined by the flames behind. 'The mullions are too close together. I might have made it, but you would not and neither would Brother Michael.'

'Michael!' exclaimed Bartholomew loudly, suddenly afraid for the fat monk's safety. He turned and raced to the vegetable garden with Cynric at his heels.

Michael stood under the trees, talking softly to the nun who had passed them earlier. They stood closely together in an intimate fashion, and Bartholomew wondered how Michael would react at being caught red-handed at his dalliance. The Benedictine looked up as he heard their footsteps coming towards him, his expression unreadable. As Bartholomew came nearer, the nun turned around and he was brought up short.

'Dame Pelagia!' he exclaimed.

The elderly nun acknowledged Bartholomew's unexpected presence in the orchard with a curt inclination of her head, but Bartholomew was in utter confusion. Surely Dame Pelagia could not have been the object of Michael's amorous attentions? How could she be the reason Michael had insisted on remaining at the abbey? The monk regarded him coldly, clearly unamused at being interrupted.

'Someone has set light to the guesthall, thinking us to be inside,' explained Cynric, when he realised Bartholomew had been startled into silence.

Michael exchanged an enigmatic glance with the old lady.

'I wondered what that crash was,' she said. 'One of the windows blowing out?'

Bartholomew nodded, surprised that she should know about such things.

'I suggest we leave here right now and let these people think they have done their job this time,' said Cynric urgently, 'or else we shall never be free of their attentions.'

His plan made sense to Bartholomew, but Michael was uncertain. 'What are you suggesting? That we head to Cambridge now? In the dark?'

'Why not?' asked Cynric. 'I can scout ahead and make certain it is safe.'

'No,' said Michael. 'We will leave at first light.'

'And what do we do in the meantime?' asked Bartholomew, bemused by Michael's attitude. 'Go back to the abbey and wait for the killers to try again?'

'We need to collect our belongings,' said Michael, clearly temporising.

'The guesthall is on fire,' said Bartholomew. As he spoke, the abbey bell began to sound the alarm, and excited voices began to clamour in the silence. 'Everything will have been destroyed, including my only cloak and even the pickled eels and samphire.'

'Pickled eels and samphire?' asked Dame Pelagia sharply. 'I did not know the abbey possessed any of that. It is a favourite of mine.'

Michael patted her arm. 'I will buy you some when we reach Cambridge,' he said absently.

Bartholomew looked from one to the other. 'Forgive me, Brother,' he said hesitantly. 'But are you suggesting that Dame Pelagia will be travelling to Cambridge with us?'

Michael nodded. 'She will. We will leave as soon as it is light.'

'It is better we go now, boy,' said Cynric urgently, 'while all this confusion is on. When the fire is out, they will soon see there are no bodies and we will have lost the advantage. Then we might never get home.'

Michael hesitated in an agony of indecision.

'Leave me here, Michael,' said Dame Pelagia. 'Come back when you are better equipped.'

'No,' said Michael shortly. 'You will not be safe and leaving you is out of the question.'

'But I could slow you down,' she said gently. 'And it is imperative you return to Cambridge and send word to the Bishop in Ely that I have information for him or, better yet, inform Sheriff Tulyet what has been happening so that he can act before it is too late.'

'Information about what?' asked Bartholomew, his confusion growing by the moment.

'If I leave, you leave,' said Michael, ignoring him and speaking firmly to the nun, his tone brooking no argument.

The old lady sighed. 'Then we should go now, as your friend suggests.'

Michael put his hands over his face and scrubbed hard at his cheeks. 'Very well,' he said eventually. 'Fetch what you need and meet us here. But hurry. And take care!'

'Will you bring Julianna?' asked Bartholomew as she began to move away. She stopped and stared at him mystified. 'When you come back, bring Julianna with you,' he said again, thinking she had misheard. Wordlessly, she moved away, her progress through the trees stately, but sure-footed.

'What is this?' said Cynric, bewildered. 'Do we each get to choose a nun to take home with us?'

Michael turned to him. 'Can you follow her? Make sure she returns unmolested?'

Cynric's face registered confusion, but he slipped away soundlessly through the trees after the old lady.

'Explain yourself,' said Michael to Bartholomew peremptorily. 'What do you mean by imposing that young woman on us? She is a harlot!'

Bartholomew gazed at Michael in disbelief. 'Michael!' he chided gently. 'What is the matter with you? You know why she must come – she warned us that an attempt might be made on our lives tonight and she was right. And she said she believed she was in danger, so now we are under a moral obligation to try to protect her. But more to the point, why are you insisting that we bring Dame Pelagia? She is an old lady, and will not find such a journey easy, especially in the dark.'

'I know!' said Michael fiercely. 'That is why I wanted to leave in the morning.'

'But why bring her at all?'

Michael lunged at Bartholomew suddenly, catching him by a handful of his tabard. 'That is my affair and none of yours! Keep your questions to yourself!'

He thrust Bartholomew from him with such force that the physician lost his footing on the frozen soil and tumbled inelegantly to the ground. In an instant, Michael was kneeling next to him.

'Oh, Lord, Matt! I am sorry! I did not mean . . . sometimes I do not know my own strength,' he said apologetically, anxiety written all over his face.

'What is wrong with you?' demanded Bartholomew crossly, rubbing his leg. 'If there is something distressing you, tell me. Do not just push me around!'

The fat monk let out a great sigh and looked up at the stars. 'Dame Pelagia,' he said in a low voice, 'is my grandmother.'

'So? That is no reason for belligerence.' Bartholomew started to climb to his feet.

'You do not understand,' said Michael, grabbing his shoulder and hauling him up with ease. For all his obesity and lack of fitness, Michael was still a powerful man. 'You see, like me, Dame Pelagia is an agent for the Bishop of Ely.'

Bartholomew shook his head slowly, trying to work some sense into Michael's piecemeal revelations. 'Are you telling me that spying runs in your family, or just that your Bishop is prepared to use anyone to further his own ends – even an old lady?'

Michael sighed again. 'She is officially retired now. She was in all this business long before I was born, and was not always a nun.'

'Evidently not,' said Bartholomew, 'if she is your grandmother. But why the secrecy? It is not such a terrible thing to have grandparents. Even I had some once.'

'Because I know the Bishop would want me to leave her here to discover more about what is happening. But she is old and frail, and I am about to defy the Bishop and take her away,' said Michael. 'It is becoming too dangerous for her here.'

'I see,' said Bartholomew, understanding. That Michael was about to incur the Bishop's ire might have serious consequences for the advancement of the ambitious monk's career. The Bishop would not be pleased that Michael had taken matters into his own hands and removed a potentially valuable spy: he was possessive about people who provided him with information, as his insistence that Michael was to remain Proctor and not become Master of Valence Marie attested.

'But what makes you think she will not be safe here?' Bartholomew asked eventually. 'And why could you not have told me all this earlier?'

'No one knows Dame Pelagia is my grandmother except the Bishop,' said Michael. 'He decided it would be safer for everyone concerned if only he and I know that.'

'Dame Pelagia knows, I take it?' asked Bartholomew facetiously.

'Do not be flippant, Matt!' snapped Michael. 'This is no laughing matter!'

'I am sorry,' said Bartholomew, with a sigh of resignation. 'But I do not see why you deem all this secrecy so necessary.'

'Although my grandmother came to Denny to enjoy a well-earned retirement, old habits die hard. She told me yesterday that she has suspected for several months that something untoward has been going on in the area and, like Julianna, has observed strange comings and goings in the night. She has known since she arrived that Denny Abbey lies on a smuggling route. Goods are brought down the Fenland waterways from the coast, because the dry land around here is ideal for storing the contraband until it is sent on.'

'Smuggling?' asked Bartholomew, startled. 'Are you suggesting the Abbess is a smuggler?'

'Of course not!' snapped Michael. 'How could she be? The smugglers are the Fenfolk, some of whom have kin among the lay sisters at the abbey. It was these men whom that silly Julianna heard in the kitchens last night. My grandmother knows the identities of some of them, and she wants me to pass their names to either the Bishop or the Sheriff. I was also hoping to learn something from the Abbess earlier today, but I could tell she is innocent and knows nothing of all this.'

'Oh,' said Bartholomew, thinking guiltily of his conviction that Michael's intentions for the Abbess that afternoon had been rather different.

'Oh, indeed,' said Michael sardonically. 'You assumed I was trying to seduce the woman. You have a nasty imagination, Matthew! My intention was only to discover whether she might have heard or seen anything odd without raising her suspicions, or telling her why I wanted to know. I had to be subtle: I did not want her to endanger herself by beginning an investigation of her own, and so needed to be careful not to let slip that her abbey is the scene of untoward happenings.'

'The oranges!' said Bartholomew suddenly. 'And the lemons Deschalers sold Mortimer.'

'What are you talking about?' said Michael testily.

'Smuggled fruit,' said Bartholomew. 'The oranges we ate earlier tonight were probably smuggled through this route across the Fens.'

Michael considered. 'You are doubtless right. But, oranges aside, I feel that it is no longer safe for my grandmother to remain here. She has been asking questions in the kitchens all afternoon, so that she could provide me with information when we met tonight, and I am afraid her actions will have aroused the suspicions of the smugglers. I suppose your Julianna is equally vulnerable.'

'Not *my* Julianna,' said Bartholomew quickly. 'But you did not speak to your grandmother between the time we left the Abbess and the time you persuaded us to wait until tomorrow to leave. How did you know to meet her here tonight?'

'The Countess of Pembroke is a powerful lady,' said Michael, apparently changing the subject, 'and, like all ladies, she confides her secrets to her most trusted ladies in waiting. She is careful, but she often overlooks the presence of an old nun dozing on a bench, or doddering feebly around the cloisters. I have met my grandmother here, under this tree, many times since I undertook to act as the Bishop's agent. She often has vital information, which I then pass to him. My grandmother and I know each other well enough to arrange to meet without speaking.'

Bartholomew shuddered, appalled at the implications of Michael's words. The Bishop even had a spy in the Countess of Pembroke's bedchamber, and was using a frail old lady to obtain information that would enable him to manipulate his domain and maintain political power. But then, if Dame Pelagia acted in the way Michael described, she was anything but a frail old lady: she was a cunning manipulator – just like Michael himself – except that she seemed to have years of experience behind her. He was suddenly absolutely certain that she had not been asleep when Julianna spoke to him in the attic, and that the younger woman's intelligence of curious happenings might well have prompted her to go ferreting for further information to pass to Michael. He remembered the soft creak outside the attic door: someone else had heard what Julianna had to say, too.

A low hiss told him that Cynric was back. Dame Pelagia was with him, leaning on his arm, and Bartholomew wondered how Michael thought they were going to get her back to Cambridge. Behind them was Julianna, her face aglow with vindication.

'I told you so!' she whispered to Bartholomew, raising her eyebrows arrogantly. 'It is a good thing you heeded my advice, or you might now be dead.'

Bartholomew did not say that he and Michael had discounted her advice, and that it had been by chance they were away from the guesthall when the attack was made. 'Are you ready?' he asked. 'Do you have a cloak? It will be a long, cold walk.'

'Walk?' exclaimed Julianna in disbelief. 'I cannot walk! Where are your horses?'

'His is at the bottom of a bog,' said Michael archly, nodding at Bartholomew. 'And so will you be if you cause us trouble. This is no jaunt we are undertaking, madam, but a flight for our lives.'

Julianna's exuberance faded at Michael's hostility and the prospect of a dismal walk, and Bartholomew thought she looked as though she was having serious second thoughts about the whole adventure. Although the rain had stopped, a chill wind cut across the Fens, blowing clouds over the moon and obscuring its dim light. It would not be an easy journey, nor a pleasant one.

'Are you sure your uncle will take you in?' asked Bartholomew. 'Because if he refuses, we cannot take you to Michaelhouse. Women are not allowed in the Colleges.'

'Are you monks then?' asked Julianna in surprise.

'Virtually,' said Bartholomew, not without rancour. He understood that it would not be wise to allow women to roam freely around the Colleges and hostels, but the rule was sometimes carried too far. If it were not for his patients and the occasional case with Michael, Bartholomew would not have met any women at all.

'Listen,' said Cynric, gathering the small group around him. 'I will scout ahead and check all is clear. If something is amiss, I will make a sound like a nightjar – twice – and you should immediately take cover at the side of the road and stay there until I say it is safe to come out. You,' he said, turning to Bartholomew, 'should stay well behind and ensure we are not being followed, and Brother Michael can help the ladies in between.'

Without waiting for their agreement, he set off and almost instantly disappeared in the undergrowth. Julianna puffed out her cheeks in displeasure.

'Am I to take orders from that grubby little man?' she asked. 'He cannot even sew!'

'You do what he says or you can stay here,' said Bartholomew coldly, angered at her attitude towards the man who was a loyal friend and whose judgement Bartholomew respected. He was already beginning to doubt the wisdom of taking Julianna with them. She was the Abbess's niece, and would surely be secure under her care. But Julianna had seemed in genuine fear, and the more he came to know her, the more Bartholomew doubted her ability to look after herself. All he needed to do was to deposit her with Deschalers, and his responsibility would be at an end. If Deschalers thought Bartholomew had made a mistake, then he could return her to Denny with no harm done.

With Michael holding Dame Pelagia solicitously by the elbow and Julianna swaying along beside them, the small group set off. Bartholomew was about to drop behind, when Dame Pelagia caught his arm in a grip that was more powerful than he would have believed possible from someone who gave the appearance of being so frail.

'That pickled eel and samphire,' she whispered. 'The dish was on the kitchen table when I went to collect my cloak. I tasted it, and I am almost certain it contained some soporific drug. Had you three been more adventurous in your tastes – or more alert to the fashions of court – you would have eaten the dish that is such a favourite of the King. And then nothing would have woken you when the fire broke out in the guesthall.'

Bartholomew felt vulnerable trailing behind the others. Their progress was painfully slow along the road, and he could see that this was largely because Julianna had put on the light shoes nuns wore in the abbey, which were wholly inadequate for the rutted, sticky mud of the road. Even from his position far behind, he could hear her shrill complaints ringing out across the Fens. After they had travelled about a mile, Michael stopped and waited for Bartholomew to catch up with him.

'This is hopeless,' he grumbled, casting a venomous look at Julianna. 'We will never reach Cambridge if she is with us. She cannot walk and she will not be quiet.'

Julianna regarded him icily. 'He is going too quickly, and my feet hurt.'

'We must hurry, Julianna,' said Bartholomew gently. 'You said you were in fear of your life from these men, and you have good reason to be afraid. It is only a matter of time before they learn that we did not die in the fire – and they will guess where we are going, and will come after us. Do you want them to catch us?'

She shook her head miserably, and looked as though she was going to cry. Michael turned away in disgust and continued walking with his grandmother.

'And he pays far more attention to that old crone than me,' said Julianna bitterly.

So that was it, thought Bartholomew: spoiled Julianna resented not being the centre of attention.

'Stay with me then,' he said, reasoning that he might have better luck with her than Michael. 'But no talking.'

She smiled at him in the darkness, and he took her hand and led her to the side of the road. He waited for a while, peering back along the track to ensure that no one was following, before walking briskly a short distance and repeating the process. When the moon was out, there was enough light to see the road quite clearly, but when it went behind a cloud, the darkness was all but impenetrable. To make matters worse, strips of ghostly white mist trailed across the causeway, sheathing the undergrowth in a murky veil that made Bartholomew's task almost impossible.

It was not long before Julianna was bored, complaining that her wet feet became chilled during the periods of enforced stillness. She had opened her mouth to let off yet another litany of grumbles, when there was a sharp snap from the undergrowth, and she and Bartholomew froze into silence. At the same time, the moon slipped behind a cloud, and they were plunged into inky blackness.

Just when Bartholomew was beginning to think the noise had been made by an animal, and that it was safe to move on, he saw a shadow emerge from the bushes nearby and slip down the road after Michael.

'What do we do?' said Julianna, her voice high pitched with excitement. 'Will you kill him?'

Bartholomew regarded her askance. For a woman who had spent her life with nuns, she had a curiously vicious trait in her personality. 'Stay here,' he commanded. 'Do not move until I come back for you; you will be quite all right if you do what I say.'

'And what happens if you are slain?' she demanded indignantly. 'Do I just wait here in this foul place for ever?'

Bartholomew gave her another look of disbelief, and left, creeping along the side of the road after the figure with as much stealth as he could muster. Ahead of him, the man kept to the middle of the road, but then was lost to sight as a wisp of Fen mist curled across the path and enveloped him. Intent on watching him, Bartholomew did not pay as much attention to where he was treading as he might, and he stumbled into a pothole. Through the shifting fog, Bartholomew saw the man dart into the undergrowth in alarm.

Bartholomew picked himself up, found a spot where he would be well shielded by bushes, and prepared to wait. He shivered. It was cold without a cloak, and his hiding place had ankle-deep icy water that seeped through his boots.

One thing his years of friendship with Cynric had taught Bartholomew was that in situations like the one in which he now found himself, the safest option was to wait and see what happened next. Cynric had often told him that the art of travelling at night without being seen was merely a matter of patience and practice. Bartholomew had been given more opportunities to practise than he would have liked over the previous five years, while his work as a physician had forced him to learn patience. He knew that, eventually, the person ahead of him would grow tired of waiting, or would come to believe he had imagined the sound that had startled him, and would emerge from his hiding place.

With horror, Bartholomew saw another figure glide past him and make its way down the road. Julianna! The moon emerged from the clouds and she was clearly visible. To make matters worse, every so often, she would stop and call out his name. Bartholomew closed his eyes in despair. Stupid girl! He was deliberating whether to go after her and haul her to safety, or let her go and hope the man hiding further along the road would allow her to pass unmolested, when the matter was decided for him.

The stranger hurtled out of the undergrowth, and then he and Julianna were engaged in a violent skirmish. Bartholomew tore towards them, abandoning any attempt at stealth. But Julianna's screams were so loud and piercing, that Bartholomew imagined she would have alerted any outlaws for miles around that there was potential prey on the road anyway.

He reached the struggling pair, and hauled the man away from Julianna. The moon slipped behind a cloud again. The man tottered backwards, but then regained his balance and raced at Bartholomew. They collided, and Bartholomew realised in panic that the man was attempting to put him in one of the holds that wrestlers used. He tried to wriggle out of the man's grip, but powerful arms had locked around his chest.

'Hit him!' screamed Julianna, using a rotten branch to flail at the man. One of her wild blows caught Bartholomew on the neck, and he realised that he was in as much danger from her ill-aimed swipes as was the man who attacked her. He kicked backwards, aiming to drive his heels into the man's shins. With a grunt of pain, the man eased his hold for the instant that allowed Bartholomew to squirm free.

'Do something!' Julianna howled. Her voice distracted the man, and Bartholomew used the opportunity to dive at him. The man side-stepped neatly, and used Bartholomew's own momentum to throw him to the ground. Bartholomew scrambled away as fast as he could and managed to regain his footing. He had seen what happened to wrestlers once they had fallen on the floor, and he had no desire to have his arms bent into unnatural positions or his head twisted round on his neck.

The man grabbed at him before he had fully gained his balance and then they were both down, scrabbling about in the muddy road. While the wrestler tried to get a good grip on Bartholomew to render him helpless, Bartholomew fended him off with kicks and punches. Julianna, meanwhile, declined to come too close to the affray and began to throw stones. The first one fell harmlessly short; the second caught Bartholomew a painful blow on the arm.

'Julianna! Stop!' he yelled.

The man had managed to get a hand inside Bartholomew's collar, and was beginning to twist it. As his tunic was pulled tight around his neck, Bartholomew began to gasp for breath.

He balled his hand into a fist and punched as hard as he could, aiming for the sensitive region just under the ribs. But the man was solid muscle and, with the exception of a small grunt, Bartholomew's desperate measure had no impact on him at all. Just as Bartholomew was beginning to feel dizzy from lack of air, the man went limp and the grip on Bartholomew's collar was released.

'There!' said Julianna in satisfaction, dropping a heavy stone to the ground and brushing off her hands. 'That taught him a lesson!'

Bartholomew struggled out from under the unconscious man as Cynric and Michael, alerted by Julianna's screams, came hurrying towards them. Breathless and shaken, but still in one piece, Bartholomew bent to examine his opponent.

'Did he molest you?' Dame Pelagia asked Julianna, coming straight to the point.

Julianna shook her head. 'He asked me whom I was looking for,' she said. 'I attempted to run away, but he caught me and I screamed.'

'You most certainly did,' said Michael drily. 'I thought Judgement Day had come! What a racket! And now half the population of East Anglia knows we are here.'

'Oh no!' exclaimed Bartholomew in horror, breaking into their conversation.

Everyone turned to look at him, kneeling over the prostrate figure in the moonlit road.

'It is Egil!' he said in a voice filled with dismay. 'And we have killed him!'

chapter 7

'**B**UT HE WAS ATTACKING YOU!' PROTESTED JULIANNA, unrepentant. 'And what would I have done if he had killed you, all alone out here in this vile place?'

Cynric shot her an unpleasant glance. 'From what I saw, Egil did mean you harm, boy,' he said to Bartholomew. 'He was choking the life out of you.'

'He was!' agreed Julianna. 'I saved your life, but now you think I am a murderess.'

'Well, so you are,' said Michael unsympathetically. 'Where did you learn such things? Not at Denny, I am sure.'

'It came naturally,' said Julianna, not without pride. 'I just knew what needed to be done and I did it. My uncle, Thomas Deschalers, always said I should have been born a boy. Then I might have been a fine warrior.'

Bartholomew gazed at her in revulsion. The woman had just struck a man dead, so that even now her hands were red from the blood that had splattered onto them, and she was boasting about it. He sat back on his heels and felt a wave of sickness pass over him. Egil had been killed instantly, his skull smashed like an egg under the great rock she had used. Even in the pale light from the moon, Bartholomew could see the huge depression at the back of the man's head where the stone had dropped. What was he to tell Oswald? And what of Egil's family? How would they manage without him?

Cynric patted him consolingly on the shoulder. 'She saved your life,' he said softly. 'If she had not brained him, I might well have done.'

Bartholomew turned to look at him. 'But you would not, Cynric,' he said bitterly. 'You might have rendered him insensible, but you would never have struck him dead from behind in the dark.'

'What is done is done,' interrupted Dame Pelagia sharply, looking down at the body. 'This is neither the time nor the place for recriminations. Julianna believed this man was about to kill you, and so she took the action she considered appropriate. And now we should continue our journey before one of us comes to harm.'

Dame Pelagia's reaction to Egil's violent death was no more nun-like than Julianna's had been, and Bartholomew wondered afresh about the religious community in the Fens. Were they all smugglers, slipping out in the dead of night with their habits kilted around their knees to haul stolen goods along secret waterways? Was it the nuns of Denny who had hired Alan and the mercenaries to kill him and Michael? But that made no sense – Bartholomew had never been to Denny before and the nuns could have no reason for wanting him dead. Perhaps it was something to do with Michael and his grandmother. He looked at the old lady dubiously, wondering what intrigues and wicked deeds she had encountered while in the service of the Bishop. If she had been in the spying business for years, her skills must be outstanding in order to have allowed her to have reached her ripe old age unscathed.

Bartholomew stood and walked away from the others, looking up at the star-blasted sky and trying to pull himself together. His first inclination was to go to Julianna and shake her so hard that her teeth would fall out; his second was to run back to Michaelhouse as fast as he could, and put the whole business – the pointless deaths of young Armel and Master Grene; the brutal murder of Isaac; the vicious

attacks on him, Michael and Cynric; the Fen smugglers; and
Julianna's assault on Egil – out of his mind. He dismissed the
wish almost as soon as he had made it: he had no desire to see
Julianna tried for murder, since she had obviously acted in
the firm belief that Egil was trying to kill him. But the matter
would need to be handled very carefully, nevertheless, if the
Sheriff were to be convinced her action was justified. And,
Bartholomew admitted to himself, it was not so much the
manner of Egil's death that distressed him – horrifying
though it was – it was Julianna's total lack of remorse. He
had met some selfish people in his life, but none were quite
as cheerfully blatant about it as was Julianna.

Nothing would be gained from further delay, however, so
he took a deep breath, and walked back to where Cynric was
wrapping Egil in the dead man's cloak.

'We cannot carry him back with us now,' said Cynric,
tugging at the inert body and testing its weight. 'He is
too heavy for you to carry alone and I still need to scout
ahead.'

Bartholomew agreed. 'Our first priority is to get Dame
Pelagia and Julianna to safety. So, we will leave Egil at the
side of the road and come back for him in the morning.
Oswald . . .'

He had been going to say Oswald would lend him some of
his men, but, in view of what had happened to the last ones,
he was uncertain Stanmore would trust him with others.

'Perhaps the Sheriff . . .' he trailed off miserably, looking
at Michael.

'Master Stanmore will come for the body,' said Cynric
decisively. 'Help me carry him off the track before we lose
any more time.'

Between them, Michael, Bartholomew and Cynric managed to haul Egil's heavy body to the side of the road. A
dark trail dribbled from the bundle as they moved, and
Bartholomew glanced involuntarily at the huge stone that
Julianna had selected. She must surely have known that a

blow from such a large rock would kill. He glanced over to where she watched, hands on hips and a satisfied smile playing about her lips. He considered inviting her to paint her face with Egil's blood, as young hunters often did with their first kill, but was not entirely certain that she would not leap at the opportunity with enthusiasm.

As Bartholomew tucked the cloak tighter around the corpse, Cynric drove a stick into the ground as a marker. Although nothing was said, Bartholomew knew as well as Cynric that a corpse might attract wild animals, and if they dallied too long before returning, who could be certain that Egil would be where they had left him?

When they had finished, Cynric wordlessly slipped off into the darkness to check the road ahead again, while Michael took Dame Pelagia's arm and led her forward. Bartholomew was left with Julianna.

'You had better go with them,' he said, regarding her with distaste. 'It will be safer for you.'

'It will be safer for you if I am here,' she replied brightly. 'You would have been throttled by now, had I not saved you.'

'You killed my brother-in-law's servant,' said Bartholomew, feeling his anger rising again. 'There was no need to hit him so hard!'

'There was every need!' blazed Julianna. He shook his head and turned away from her, but she caught his arm. 'Listen! I am sorry he was someone you knew but, believe me, it was you or him as far as I was concerned.'

'All right,' said Bartholomew, relenting slightly. 'Now go with Dame Pelagia and Michael. I will check your screeching did not alert any outlaws.'

She opened her mouth to protest, but thought better of it, and flounced after Michael. The sadly inadequate shoes prevented her from walking in as dignified a fashion as she would have wished, but she managed to effect a respectable strut. Bartholomew watched her go, hearing her footsteps recede into the darkness. Overhead, the stars were beginning to fade and the sky was fractionally lighter than it had been. It would not be long until dawn. He stood looking down at Egil's body for some time before he followed the others.

Mercifully, the rest of their journey was uneventful, and they arrived at the Barnwell Gate just after prime. Julianna's flimsy shoes had finally disintegrated and Bartholomew and Michael had been forced to take turns to carry her for the last three miles. Dame Pelagia, however, had maintained a steady pace, and Bartholomew was impressed with her stamina, especially given her performance of frailty when he had helped her up the steep stairs to chaperone Julianna's astrological consultation. The old lady, Bartholomew thought begrudgingly, was a fine actress indeed. He supposed her habitual pretence of feebleness would go a long way in ensuring she was excused from some of the more rigorous duties of a convent nun – such as taking a turn in the vegetable garden or long vigils – and thus improve Dame Pelagia's quality of life immeasurably.

By the time they reached the town gate, all five of them were mud-spattered, cold and weary, and Michael was limping from where his wet sandals had chaffed his heels. Only Cynric and Dame Pelagia seemed to have any energy left. The soldiers on duty at the Barnwell Gate regarded the bedraggled party suspiciously, but allowed them in without comment when they recognised Michael.

'Cynric will inform the Sheriff of what has happened to us,' Michael announced to the guards imperiously, 'and should anyone come asking whether we have returned, Master Tulyet will not be pleased if you tell them we have, no matter how kindly seeming the enquirer.'

The guards nodded understanding and escaped gratefully to their small lodge out of the cold. It was not the first time Michael had made such a demand, and they knew his threat was not an idle one. Unlike most University officers, Michael often worked closely with the Sheriff to maintain peace in the town, and Tulyet would take seriously a request from him to reassign the soldiers to less pleasant duties.

As they walked towards Petty Cury, a narrow street lined with a random assortment of shops, Michael grabbed Bartholomew's arm and pulled him out of Dame Pelagia's hearing.

'When I made the decision to bring my grandmother with us, I had no clear notion but to get her away from Denny,' he whispered, glancing furtively over his shoulder. 'But what shall I do with her? I cannot take her to Michaelhouse: the other Fellows would have a fit if I took a woman there, regardless of her age and vocation.'

Bartholomew shrugged. 'You could lodge her with the nuns at St Radegund's Priory.'

Michael shook his head. 'The Priory lies too far outside the town to be safe and, anyway, that will be the first place the smugglers will look when they see she has gone.'

Bartholomew regarded him speculatively. 'You think they will come for her?'

'I am certain of it,' said Michael. 'They will want to know how much information she has gathered, so they will know which parts of their operation are secure and which need to be closed down. I mulled over what she told me all the way home. If those smugglers are well organised enough to carry out an elaborate plan to kill us, then a search of the town for an old nun will be child's play to them.'

'I suppose we could take her to Edith at Trumpington,' said Bartholomew, reluctant to involve his sister, but feeling obliged to offer.

Michael shook his head again. 'That will be the second place they will look. We need somewhere where they will never think of checking.'

Bartholomew thought for a moment. 'Is your grandmother easily shocked?' he asked.

Michael gave a snort of laughter. 'Grandmother? Shock-able? Never!'

'Then I know just the place,' said Bartholomew. 'But first, I want to get rid of Julianna before she kills someone else, and then I want to see Oswald.'

'You are being unfair to Julianna, Matt,' said Michael. 'Cynric was right. Egil looked as though he was going to kill you.' He pulled at Bartholomew's tunic and looked at his neck. 'There are still scratches on you from where he almost had you throttled. Let me tell Oswald what happened – if you relate the tale, he will have Julianna swinging for murder and you beside her as her accomplice!'

'Egil did not make these marks,' said Bartholomew, rubbing his throat. 'Julianna did that when she was flailing around with a stick – before she thought of using a more deadly weapon. I suppose I should be grateful it was Egil she brained and not me.'

'I see you are shocked that a young, well-bred woman could kill without compunction,' said Michael, eyeing Bartholomew with an amused expression. 'Well, you should not be. With all the teaching you do, you have forgotten what women are really like. You idolise them and think they are meek and gentle creatures. Do you think Edith would have hesitated to kill Egil if she thought he was harming you? Or that Philippa, of whom you were so enamoured during the Death? Or even Agatha our laundress? And look at my grandmother! How do you think she has lived so long in the sinister world of spying, if it were not for a certain ruthless streak and her inimitable cunning?'

Wondering how the monk came by his superior knowl-edge of women, Bartholomew conceded the point, and acknowledged that his attitude to Julianna was probably unreasonable. Part of his ambivalence to the incident, he accepted, was that he did not like her, and that was unfair. Both Cynric and Michael, whose opinions he trusted, had been convinced that Egil would have killed him had not

Julianna acted when she did. He gave Michael a weak smile, and tried to force his feelings of misgiving from his mind.

While Cynric went to St Mary's Church to report the attack to Vice-Chancellor Harling, and then to the castle to tell the Sheriff, the others made their way to Milne Street where Bartholomew rapped sharply on the bright new door of the house of Thomas Deschalers the grocer. A servant answered, and they were conducted to a chilly room overlooking the street while she went to fetch her master. Julianna was uncharacteristically subdued and Bartholomew had a sudden lurching doubt that she was related to Deschalers at all, and wondered if she had tricked him into bringing her from the abbey.

After a brief wait, during which Michael greedily devoured a dish of sugared almonds that someone had rashly left on the table, Deschalers entered. He had apparently been working in his yard, for he was wearing thick woollen hose of a russet red and a fur-lined cloak that looked comfortable and warm. Bartholomew thought of his own threadbare cloak, now a pile of ashes at Denny, and tried to imagine how he would survive the rest of the winter without it.

'Uncle!' exclaimed Julianna, racing across the room and hurling herself into her startled relative's arms. 'Uncle! I have had such a foul time! Look!' She pulled up her gown to reveal ankles that were scratched from grovelling around in the undergrowth, while her slippers dangled from her feet, hopelessly ruined.

Deschalers looked from the shoes to Bartholomew and Michael. 'What in God's name have you done to her?' he asked, his eyes blazing with a sudden anger. 'Why have you taken her from Denny Abbey? Dame Pelagia?'

'Your niece overheard some men talking there,' said Dame Pelagia soothingly. 'They seemed to be smugglers, and so we brought her here with us for her own safety.'

'Smugglers?' echoed Deschalers, bewildered. 'What are

you talking about? There are no men at Denny Abbey. It is a convent!'

'They are the menfolk of the lay sisters,' explained the elderly nun patiently. 'Brother Michael will inform the Sheriff. But, meanwhile, I think Julianna will be safer with you than at Denny.'

'But what about these smugglers?' queried Deschalers, looking from her to Michael. 'I have heard of no smugglers in that area. Why were they at the abbey?'

'Unfortunately, we know little about them,' said Michael, 'except that they are well organised and ruthless.' He paused, but then plunged on. 'On our way here, there was an unfortunate incident.' He glanced at Bartholomew, and quickly outlined the circumstances of Egil's death and the role Julianna had played in it. Deschalers paled and swept Julianna up in a protective hug.

'What have you done?' he asked in a whisper. At first, Bartholomew thought he was talking to Julianna, but Deschalers was looking at him. 'To what horrors have you subjected this innocent child? Is it not enough that you drag her off in the middle of the night in the company of rough men? And to compound your crime, you force her to fight for her life against an outlaw?'

This seemed a somewhat jaundiced interpretation of the circumstances. Bartholomew protested, goaded by Julianna's expression of gloating self-righteousness. 'Egil was not an outlaw. He was one of Oswald Stanmore's men. And no one forced her to fight – she joined in of her own accord.'

'I did no such thing!' said Julianna with dignified outrage. She turned to her uncle. 'Doctor Bartholomew abandoned me in the bushes by the side of the road while he went off in the dark. I grew so frightened on my own that I was forced to find my own way to Dame Pelagia. And then that man – Egil – attacked me. It was horrible!'

She buried her face in her uncle's shoulder, while Deschalers turned a furious face towards Bartholomew.

'What were you thinking of? You left my niece alone when there were outlaws nearby?'

Bartholomew's recollection of the incident was somewhat at variance with that of Julianna, and he was certain that it had been curiosity and impatience that had driven her from her hiding place, not fear as she had claimed. He regarded her with dislike. She lifted her face from the depths of her uncle's cloak, her bright, turquoise eyes blazing defiantly.

'And then, when Doctor Bartholomew finally came to my aid, this outlaw started to get the better of him. I struck Egil with a stone, and in so doing I saved all our lives!'

'Is this true?' Deschalers demanded, still holding his niece close to him.

'More or less,' said Michael, before Bartholomew could answer. 'She dispatched Egil with a single blow to the head using a rock, although I am unable to verify that we were in danger of our lives. He had no weapon with him.'

'He was throttling the physician,' said Julianna angrily, struggling from her uncle's grasp and striding across the room to wrench at Bartholomew's tunic. 'Look! See those marks and tell me Egil did not mean business.'

'It appears you owe my niece a great deal,' said Deschalers, moving forward to inspect the scratches on Bartholomew's neck. He smiled with sudden pride. 'If only she had been born a boy. What a wonderful heir she would have made!'

Bartholomew suspected that Julianna would make Deschalers a wonderful heir just as she was – she was resourceful, resilient, ruthless and wholly without remorse. She would be a splendid merchant, especially if she were able to learn how to use her brutish instincts with more discretion. He imagined what she might be like having acquired Deschalers' power and influence, and shuddered.

'I could still make you a wonderful heir, uncle,' she pouted. 'I am clever and determined, and no man has yet bested me in anything.'

That Bartholomew could well believe. 'You should make

her your chief henchman,' he said to Deschalers. 'You would never need fear anything again.'

Deschalers eyed him uncertainly, but Julianna took his words as a compliment and smiled. 'Perhaps you should hire me as your book-bearer,' she said to Bartholomew, with a predatory gleam in her eye. 'I would do a better job than that dirty little man you have now.'

'I doubt it,' said Bartholomew coldly.

'You know I would,' claimed Julianna haughtily. 'Who was it who saved your life, while your servant grubbed about doing the Lord knows what in the bushes up ahead? And I can sew. I certainly would not have mended brown leggings with a red patch!'

Bartholomew would have worn red patches on all his clothes if the alternative was Julianna's companionship. He gazed at her with undisguised dislike. 'We cannot stand around talking nonsense with you all day. I have patients to see.'

He ignored Michael's look of warning, and pushed his way past her to leave. Deschalers stepped into his path.

'You seem more shaken by this affair than the others, Bartholomew,' he said, waving a hand to where Michael and Julianna watched in anticipation of a confrontation. 'Even more than old Dame Pelagia. Therefore I will over-look your rudeness. But bear in mind that you owe my niece your life; perhaps she will require a favour in return one day.'

Outside, in the street, Bartholomew waited for Michael with his temper barely under control. Typical merchant, he thought with disgust, seizing every opportunity to turn it to some kind of advantage! His blood ran cold when he considered the kind of return favours Julianna was likely to demand. After a few moments, Michael joined him. Dame Pelagia had been persuaded to take some refreshment with Deschalers and Julianna, while Michael and Bartholomew went alone to perform the unpleasant task of informing Stanmore of the deaths of Egil and Jurnet.

'You might have been more gracious,' complained Michael as they walked to Stanmore's premises next door. 'You cannot just barge into the houses of the most influential people in the town and yell at them.'

'I did not yell!' snapped Bartholomew. 'And I do not care whether they are influential or not. That Julianna is positively gloating about how she killed Egil!'

'Then let her gloat,' said Michael pragmatically. 'She will learn in time that such an attitude is unbecoming, and it cannot harm Egil now.'

Bartholomew took a deep breath in an attempt to calm himself, and walked through the gates into Stanmore's yard. The clothier stood in the middle of it, shouting orders to a group of sweating apprentices who were struggling to fit more bales of black cloth onto the top of an already teetering pile. He saw Bartholomew coming towards him and gestured for the weary boys to take a break. Gratefully, they clattered off towards the kitchens in search of food. One hesitated, and watched them uncertainly before following the others. He looked vaguely familiar, but Bartholomew was often in Stanmore's yard and he had doubtless seen him there before. He thrust it from his mind, and tried to concentrate on finding the right words to break the news about Egil and Jurnet to his brother-in-law.

'Always hungry,' said Stanmore, shaking his head indulgently as he watched his apprentices go. 'Although they have been somewhat listless of late. Perhaps you might have a look at them when you have a moment, Matt. But you are back early – you told Edith that you might be gone for a week. I hope you were not so foolish as to travel the road at night. The Round Church was burgled two nights ago – inside the town itself and right under the noses of the Sheriff's patrols! These outlaws have grown bold indeed. I trust you took the proper precautions when you travelled—'

'Your suspicions about the Bishop's message were right,' said Bartholomew in a quiet voice, breaking into Stanmore's tirade. 'The whole thing was a ploy to get Michael and me out into the Fens and ambush us.'

Stanmore stared at him with his mouth open and Bartholomew continued. 'Jurnet was killed in the fight and Egil died on the way home.'

He waited. He would not have blamed Stanmore if he had raged and sworn. One of the traits Bartholomew most admired in his relative was the care he took of the people who worked for him, and Bartholomew would have been beside himself if someone had taken Cynric and returned to say that he was dead. Stanmore, however, neither raged nor swore. He took Bartholomew and Michael firmly by the elbows and led them towards the house. Although he did not live there, it was handsomely furnished, and the solar on the upper floor that he used as an office was a pleasant, although cluttered, room. He gestured that they were to sit by the fire and ordered a maid to bring mulled wine.

'And some bread,' called Michael opportunistically as the maid left. 'And perhaps a little cheese and a bit of bacon for a starving and exhausted monk.'

Stanmore sat opposite them and folded his arms. 'You look dreadful,' he said to Bartholomew. 'Tell me what happened.'

'I am sorry, Oswald,' said Bartholomew wearily. 'Father Paul warned me that the Bishop's summons was odd; then you and Edith voiced doubts; then Harling expressed fears. But we paid no heed to any of you, and now Egil and Jurnet are dead.'

Oswald reached out to touch him lightly on the knee. 'I am sure you are not to blame,' he said gently. 'Now, put aside your remorse and tell me what occurred.'

Michael began to speak before Bartholomew could collect himself, and gave a reasonably accurate account of the events of the previous two days, omitting reference to his grandmother and to Julianna's evident satisfaction at having killed Egil. When he had finished, Stanmore sat back and sipped his mulled wine.

'Smugglers, you say,' he said, setting down the cup and frowning thoughtfully. 'It is common knowledge that there are smugglers in the Fens – there have been for years – but I had no idea that they were at the abbey itself.'

'You know of these smugglers?' asked Michael in surprise. 'What exactly have you heard?'

'Not much,' said Stanmore with a regretful shrug. 'Goods are brought from France and the Low Countries to the Wash, and then dispersed around the country via the Fens. It is, by all accounts, an easy matter to use the channels there to keep out of the sight of the men who collect the King's taxes on imported goods. It is nothing new, however, as I said, although I imagine there has been more smuggling this year than last because the mild weather has kept the waterways from freezing. And, of course, taxes are high to finance the King's wars in France, so contrabanding is a lucrative business.'

'I thought hostilities with France had ended because of the plague,' said Bartholomew, looking up from the cup he held in both hands in an attempt to warm them.

Michael and Stanmore looked at him pityingly. 'The King still has debts to pay and his soldiers' wages to find,' said Stanmore.

'And he still needs to keep his spy network in place,' continued Michael. 'Spies are expensive. Then there are officials to bribe, enemies to be deposed and friends to be bought. And although fighting might have temporarily ceased in France, Brittany is still a hotbed of violence and looting.'

'Sheriff Tulyet told me that bands of Englishmen roam Brittany at the King's command, ambushing traders, attacking villages and plundering religious houses,' said Stanmore, shaking his head in disapproval. 'Brittany is an unsafe place to be.'

'Sounds like the Fens,' remarked Bartholomew, looking down at the dark wine in his cup.

'It is curious,' mused Michael, 'but Master Deschalers seemed surprised when we told him about the smugglers. Have you not discussed this with the other merchants?'

'Of course,' said Stanmore, as though it was obvious. 'He knows as much as I do – or possibly more, since most of his goods come from the Wash via the river. Most of mine come from the south, and I use the roads not the waterways.'

'Then why did he deny that he was aware there is smuggling in the Fens?' asked Bartholomew. 'Surely he would guess that we would discuss the matter with you, and that you would reveal he knew all about it.'

Stanmore shrugged. 'Perhaps he thought you would accuse him of being involved if he acknowledged what he knew.'

'Now that I rethink his actual words, Deschalers did not deny that he was aware of smuggling in the Fens, Matt,' said Michael, frowning. 'What he said was that he did not know there was smuggling *in that area.* That is an entirely different statement.'

'Do you think it is likely that he is involved in it?' asked Bartholomew of Stanmore.

Stanmore scratched his head. 'I really could not say. And anyway, he is a fellow tradesman. It would be very wrong of me to besmirch his reputation with unfounded suspicions.'

'Your reticence does you credit, Sir Oswald,' said Michael comfortably. 'Now, tell us what you suspect, if you please.'

Stanmore leaned back in his chair, and blew out his cheeks. 'Well, Deschalers has been selling lemons recently. It is possible they came via these smuggling routes. But I have no evidence to support such a claim, and I would rather you did not tell him it was I who put the idea into your heads.'

Bartholomew sensed immediately that he and Michael had stumbled into a trade war. No matter how Stanmore stressed that his relations with his powerful neighbours – Mortimer,

Cheney and Deschalers – were friendly, Bartholomew was not fooled. He had spent his childhood in Stanmore's house, and knew only too well how bitter the competition between merchants could be. Even though Deschalers was a grocer, Mortimer a baker, Cheney a spice-dealer and Stanmore a clothier, they were still rivals in the hard world of commerce. They fought over use of the river wharves, the size of their stalls in the Market Square and even their relative positions in the ceremonial processions through the town. Their dealings with each other appeared cordial enough, but in fact they watched each other like predators, waiting for signs of weakness. Deschalers and Cheney seemed to have taken young Edward Mortimer under their wings, but Bartholomew was certain it was not for altruistic reasons – they were probably already looking ahead to the day when Edward inherited his father's business, and were securing their influence over him for the future.

'Is there anything else you can tell us?' asked Michael, pouring the last of the wine into his cup. 'I know the day is wearing on, and we have already taken up too much of your time, but I would appreciate any more information about this smuggling you might have.'

Stanmore frowned. 'I really have little more to share with you, Brother. I am certain this has been a good year for smuggling. In the summer, the waterways teem with legally loaded vessels and the long hours of daylight make secret voyages difficult. In the winter, trading usually stops when the Fen waterways become frozen. But this year, the heavy rains have not only kept the ice away, but have provided deep water and more channels for the smugglers' crafts. They have doubtless become more brazen because business is good and profits have been high – hence Deschalers's lemons wherever you look.'

'But why should these smugglers want to kill Michael and me?' asked Bartholomew, shaking his head as Michael offered him the last piece of bread. 'We had no idea that any of this went on until we arrived at Denny Abbey.'

'You would know the answer to that better than I,' said Stanmore. 'It must be something to do with that poisoned wine you were investigating before you left. I suppose it is possible that the brew which caused all those deaths was smuggled through the Fens.'

'It must have been,' said Michael, nodding. 'Some rascal named Sacks was selling it in the Brazen George and, according to Matt's students, Sacks seldom comes by anything honestly.'

'Well, there you are then,' said Stanmore. 'In the wine lies the solution to all this. Discover more about that, and you will know who is prepared to kill you, rather than risk letting you make your inquiries.'

'I do not care about smuggling and tax evasion,' said Bartholomew gloomily. 'I only want to make certain no more of this deadly claret is sold to our scholars.'

Stanmore picked up his cup, but then set it back on the table without drinking. 'Do you think someone is trying to foul University–town relations? It would be an easy matter to sell tainted goods to scholars and make them think someone in the town was trying to kill them. I hope that is not the case – it would be devastating for commerce!'

'I understand that trade is very good for most merchants at the moment, which is unusual for winter,' said Michael conversationally.

Stanmore agreed. 'The cloth trade is an exception – it is always better in the winter than in the summer because people need warm clothes in the colder months. Unfortunately for me, the open waterways mean that there are fewer travellers on the roads, and so my goods are more vulnerable. Two of my carts have been attacked on their way from London within the last month. The Sheriff is out daily looking for these outlaws, and I have had to place my merchandise under an armed escort.'

Bartholomew glanced at him guiltily, thinking that he would be two guards short following the loss of Egil and Jurnet.

Stanmore read his thoughts and patted his hand. 'I do not blame you for their deaths, Matt. Egil came looking for work last autumn. He was an adequate guard, but hated life in the town. When I needed him here, he pleased himself whether he would come, and might spend the day fishing in the Fens if the mood took him. I was on the verge of dismissing him. And Jurnet has been with me only since Christmas. I needed a strong arm, and he served his purpose, but he was a lout. He bullied my apprentices, and I suspect his wife had good reason for not leaving her house in Ely to live with him here. I am sorry they are dead, and will help their families if I can, but I am not surprised either came to a violent end.'

That Stanmore did not like the men who had died was of small comfort to Bartholomew. He stood to leave. 'I am sorry anyway. And next time I will pay more attention to my friends' misgivings.'

'In that case, Matt, heed this. The attack on you sounded well organised and elaborate. It is not cheap to hire men to commit murder. Either drop this poisoned wine business, or solve it quickly, because men who have organised one such ambush will easily be able to arrange another.'

Bartholomew did not need to be reminded. He gave his brother-in-law a weak smile and looked around for his cloak, before he realised he no longer had one. He picked up his gloves from where they had been drying near the fire and pulled them on.

'Those are fine gloves,' said Stanmore, regarding them with the eye of a professional. 'Who gave them to you? I am sure you did not pay for them while there are still books in the world to be bought.'

'Constantine Mortimer,' replied Bartholomew, leaning down to retrieve his medicines bag from the floor. 'Actually, he wanted to sell them to me, but his wife said they would compensate me for missing the installation.'

'Then Mortimer must have felt wretched indeed,' said Stanmore. 'He rules that poor woman with a fist of iron and does not usually take heed of her suggestions. But how did he come to have such things to sell anyway? He is a baker not a glover.'

'I have no idea,' replied Bartholomew, uninterested. 'I have not given it much thought.'

'If I were you,' said Stanmore, watching him stretch stiff limbs, 'I would leave Cambridge until all this has died down. Come to Trumpington. Edith would love you to stay with her, and you know we will both fret over you until all this is resolved and you are safe again.'

'They would find him,' said Michael bluntly. 'The more I learn about these men, the more I fear them. The only way we will be safe from another attack is to catch them and hand them to the Sheriff.'

They left Stanmore to arrange for his steward to fetch Egil's body, and collected Dame Pelagia from Deschalers's house. She had borrowed a dark blue cloak from Julianna and removed part of her veil, so that she looked like any anonymous old crone and not a nun. Bartholomew was impressed that she had thought to disguise herself on the way to her hiding place, but then remembered that she was Michael's grandmother and an agent of the Bishop. He glanced down at her and she gave him a beneficent smile, which made her look sweet and gentle. But when the smile faded and he looked at her again, he saw her hard green eyes taking in every detail as they walked and, although her progress was slow, there was nothing shaky or frail about her movements. Michael was walking awkwardly, stiff after his long walk, but Dame Pelagia showed no such weakness.

Bartholomew led the way up the High Street towards the

area known as The Jewry, which had been the domain of Jewish merchants until their expulsion from England in 1290. It was here that Matilde had her small, neat house. Michael realised where they were heading in an instant, and rubbed his hands together in glee.

'Excellent, Matt! Who would ever think that we would secrete an elderly nun in the house of the town's most exclusive prostitute?'

'No one, I hope,' said Bartholomew, casting an anxious glance at the old lady. He was already beginning to have second thoughts. 'Perhaps this is not such a good idea.'

'Nonsense. It is a superb idea. She will have the time of her life.'

'Who? Matilde or your grandmother?' asked Bartholomew, knocking at the door hesitantly.

Before Michael could answer, the door was opened and Matilde stood smiling at them. To Bartholomew, she was one of the most attractive women in Cambridge, with long silky hair that almost reached her knees, and bright blue eyes. Known as 'Lady' Matilde for her fine manners and literacy, she and Bartholomew had struck up an unlikely friendship that was proving increasingly valuable to both of them.

'Have you come to barter for my services?' she asked pertly, continuing the ongoing battle in which she and Michael attempted to embarrass each other. To her great astonishment, she succeeded, and he blushed and studied his feet in abashed silence. Matilde looked at Bartholomew with a startled grin.

'This is Dame Pelagia from Denny Abbey,' said Bartholomew, hiding his amusement, and gesturing to the elderly nun. 'She is Brother Michael's grandmother and needs somewhere to stay for a few days.'

For the first time since he had known her, Matilde was at a loss for words.

'We wondered whether we might impose on your generosity for a brief while,' Bartholomew continued, still doubtful about thrusting the two women together. Despite her dubious past, Dame Pelagia was still a nun, and Matilde, for all her courtliness and grace, was still a prostitute.

Matilde recovered her poise and her customary charm returned. 'Of course,' she said, holding out a welcoming hand towards Dame Pelagia. 'Please come in. May I offer you some ale?' She looked appraisingly at the old nun. 'Or perhaps you would prefer strong French wine?'

Dame Pelagia's beatific features broke into a acquisitive grin, looking so much like her grandson that the effect was disconcerting. She elbowed Michael out of the way and followed Matilde into the house. While Michael solicitously helped her to a chair, Bartholomew perched on a stool and edged closer to the fire. The biting Fen wind had chilled him just from walking the short distance from Stanmore's house to Matilde's, and he wondered again how he would manage the rest of the winter without his cloak.

While Michael gave a brief, and not wholly truthful, explanation as to why an elderly nun was seeking refuge in the house of a prostitute, Bartholomew reconsidered the matter of the poisoned wine and the smugglers. He could see that the two might well be related, but since Michael had barely started to investigate the deaths of Armel, Grene and Isaac, he did not understand why someone should try to kill them because of it. He wondered whether they should interpret the incident in the Fens as a warning, and abandon the investigation altogether. But then, as Michael had pointed out to Stanmore, they would constantly be looking over their shoulders, waiting for the next attack. Bartholomew would not even be able to answer summonses from his patients without his suspicions being aroused.

'Julianna, did you say?' Matilde was asking. 'The niece of Deschalers the grocer?'

Bartholomew dragged himself away from his thoughts, and concentrated on the conversation between Matilde and Michael.

'The very same,' said the monk. 'How do you know her?'

'Through the usual means,' said Matilde, referring to the way in which she and the other prostitutes provided each other with information, so that they were almost as well informed of events in the town as was Stanmore from his spies. 'I have heard she is a woman who knows what she wants and how to get it.'

'That is certainly true,' muttered Bartholomew. 'She knew how to wrangle herself an escape from Denny Abbey, although I suspect she did not enjoy the journey.'

Matilde seemed amused. 'You do not like her, do you?'

'Am I so transparent?' he asked, unsettled that she should read his feelings with such ease.

'Sometimes,' said Matilde, regarding him with eyes that twinkled with mischief.

'Like most men,' put in Dame Pelagia with a wink, and the two women laughed uproariously together. Bartholomew and Michael exchanged a look of incomprehension. When he had first thought of leaving Dame Pelagia with Matilde, Bartholomew's concerns had been whether the elderly nun would find Matilde's occupation offensive. But now he felt more anxious that Dame Pelagia might have a corrupting influence on Matilde. He regarded the nun again, impressed at the way she was gulping the potent claret without grimacing – as he had done – and reappraising her sharp green eyes and intelligent face.

'How long have you been a nun, Dame Pelagia?' he asked.

Matilde and Michael seemed startled at his question from out of the blue, but Dame Pelagia did not seem surprised at all. She looked him up and down shamelessly.

'Since before you were born,' she said, deliberately vague. 'I led a somewhat different life before that.'

'Really?' asked Matilde with interest. 'Do tell.'

'Not now,' said Michael quickly. 'Matilde, what do you know about Julianna?'

Matilde looked disappointed, but the old nun gave her a glance that indicated Matilde was in store for quite a story once Bartholomew and Michael had left. Matilde gave her a quick smile, and began to answer Michael's question. 'She is betrothed to Edward Mortimer.'

'To Edward Mortimer – son of the baker who was greedy with his lemons?' asked Michael, scratching at a spot on his face. 'No wonder Deschalers is taking such an interest in him! Poor Julianna! Edward Mortimer is a pathetic specimen of manhood – there is no backbone to him.'

'Apparently she feels the same way,' replied Matilde. 'Rumour has it that she prefers the attentions of another who lives in Cambridge.'

'I suppose that is why she was so keen to escape from the abbey,' said Michael. 'To return to the arms of her paramour. Do you know the name of this fortunate fellow?'

'Not for sure,' said Matilde. She would not meet Michael's eyes.

'It would be helpful to know,' pressed Michael. 'It might help us with our investigation.'

'I am not sufficiently certain to tell you,' protested Matilde, uncharacteristically indecisive.

'Please Matilde,' said Bartholomew wearily. 'We will be discreet.'

She leaned forward and touched him on the knee. 'I know you will,' she said. 'I am only reluctant to tell you because it may lead you down a false trail, and make you waste time, when it seems to be important that you solve this business quickly. I could not bear it if anything were to happen to you.'

Bartholomew looked up sharply, but Matilde was staring down at her hands, long and graceful, which were folded demurely in her lap.

'The rumour is that it was Ralph de Langelee, Michael-house's new Fellow of philosophy, who took her fancy before she was sent away to Denny,' she said reluctantly.

'Langelee?' exclaimed Michael in disbelief. 'That great, stupid brute?'

'He is a handsome man,' said Matilde, fixing him with her steady gaze. 'And he has not yet taken any vows of chastity that might put him out of a woman's reach.'

She and Michael exchanged a look that Bartholomew found impossible to interpret. Surely the monk would not have availed himself of Matilde's services, he thought suddenly. For some reason, the notion disturbed him.

'But Langelee is aggressive and arrogant,' he said, forcing the unpleasant image of Matilde and Michael dishabille from his mind.

'So is Julianna,' Matilde pointed out. 'I imagine they would be rather well suited.'

'But you said she was betrothed to Edward Mortimer,' said Michael, 'so there can be no future in her yearnings for our loutish philosopher.'

'Yearnings are not so easily cast aside,' said Matilde. 'Especially when one is young.'

'Why does she not like Edward?' asked Bartholomew. 'He seems comely enough to me.'

'But you are not a young woman of twenty-two, Matthew,' said Matilde. 'Edward is three years younger than Julianna, and probably seems like a baby to her. Given the choice, I would take Ralph de Langelee over Edward: Edward has not seen enough of the world to make him interesting, and he had been too long under the thumb of his father. Julianna doubtless wants to cast her net wider.'

Did Matilde know Edward and Langelee so well? Barth-olomew wondered, regarding her with renewed curiosity. Matilde's customers were a subject that, by mutual consent, they did not discuss. He doubted she would have told him even if he asked. Not for the first time in their friendship, he found himself wishing she had chosen another profession, and that she was someone he might ask to walk with him in the meadows by the river, or take to the mystery plays in St Mary's Church.

The last time he had invited her to spend some time with him, she had felt obliged to disguise herself as an old woman to protect both their reputations. Despite the fact that they had laughed about it since, Bartholomew regretted that he had been unable to enjoy her company without her resorting to subterfuge and heavy cosmetics. He wondered what his sister would say if he took Matilde to Trumpington, so that they might see the early-born lambs together, or she might sit with him in the kitchen stealing hot cakes from the griddle.

Reluctantly, he forced his thoughts away from Matilde, and began to consider Julianna. She was evidently not all she seemed. Could *she* be involved in the smuggling, perhaps escaping from Denny to warn her uncle that Dame Pelagia had incriminating evidence against him? Deschalers claimed he had discovered a way of storing lemons in his cellars that kept them fresh. But what if he were lying, and his lemons came from the illicit trading routes through the Fens, as Stanmore believed?

'Deschalers might have made a worse match for Julianna than Edward,' he said, standing and placing his unfinished wine on the table. 'Old Master Cheney has been looking for a young wife ever since his own died during the plague. Julianna is lucky her uncle does not press Cheney on her.'

'But Cheney knows about her past,' said Matilde, rising to see him to the door. 'Julianna was sent to Denny because Langelee was just one in a line of alliances completed within a matter of weeks that impresses even me.'

Bartholomew supposed he should not be surprised to hear that Julianna had made the most of her time in Cambridge, and realised that Michael had been right – living in Michaelhouse was blinding him to the ways of the world. He smiled at Matilde and thanked her for her hospitality.

Michael glanced at his grandmother, who appeared to be asleep, and made no move to leave.

'Your grandmother has a habit of pretending to doze when she is fully awake,' said Bartholomew tartly, reluctant to leave the fat monk alone with Matilde. 'I would not tarry here if I were you, Brother.'

Michael sighed, and levered his massive bulk from Matilde's best chair to follow Bartholomew out into the street. As Matilde stood on the doorstep to bid them farewell, Bartholomew saw Dame Pelagia snap awake and reach for the wine he had left in his cup.

'Thank you for looking after my grandmother,' said Michael. 'You will find she will be no trouble, and will know when to make herself scarce.'

Matilde looked through the half-open door at the old lady, who had drained the remains of Bartholomew's wine, and was now looking to see if the other cups were empty. 'I will enjoy the company,' she said, smiling. 'I have a feeling she has a great many fascinating stories to help pass the long winter evenings.'

Bartholomew, watching the old lady settle herself comfortably by the fire with a cup in either hand, was sure she had.

The rest of the day was spent at Michaelhouse, teaching in the chilly hall. Great grey clouds that threatened more rain had rolled in, and the room was dark and gloomy. In one corner, a student of Alcote's strained his eyes to read Cicero's *Rhetoric* in a flat monotone to a group of first years, while Alcote himself was relaxing by the fire in his own sumptuous quarters, having declined to grace the dismal hall with his presence. In another corner, Father William ranted about the Devil being in unexpected places to his little band of similarly fanatical Franciscans in a voice sufficiently loud to be heard in the High Street. At regular intervals, the other Fellows asked him to moderate the volume so that

they could concentrate on their own teaching, his rabid
diatribes distracting even the tolerant Master Kenyngham.

In front of the empty hearth, Ralph de Langelee strutted back and forth, waving his meaty arms around as he
expounded Aristotle to three bemused students who would
fail their degrees if they repeated his peculiar logic in
their disputations. John Runham was giving a lecture on
the *Corpus juris civilis* in the conclave, a smaller and far
more pleasant room at the far end of the hall, but since
he had at least fifteen students hanging on his every word,
there was no space for any of the other Fellows to share it
with him. Bartholomew was not the only one who resented
being excluded from the conclave: it was the only room in
Michaelhouse with glass in the windows, and therefore was
by far the warmest place in the College and easily the most
popular spot after the kitchen.

Like Alcote's students, Michael's Benedictines were obliged
to manage without him – he was with Vice-Chancellor
Harling at St Mary's Church discussing the ambush and
composing a message to inform the Bishop of what had
happened – and they sat quietly in the middle of the
room analysing one of St Augustine's *Sermons* in low voices,
although occasional laughter and a good deal of grinning
made Bartholomew suspect their conversation had wandered somewhat from the original topic. Bartholomew's
own students sat in two lines on wall benches under the
unglazed windows, shivering in the draught and wrapped
in an odd assortment of cloaks and blankets.

Michaelhouse Fellows had a choice as far as teaching in
the hall was concerned: they could close the shutters and
sit in the dark, or they could open the shutters and have
daylight – along with the full force of the elements that
blasted in through the glassless tracery. Since reading was
difficult in the dark – and Michaelhouse finances did not
stretch to providing candles during the night, let alone in
the daylight hours – wintertime lectures were usually given

to rows of pinched, frozen faces poking out from improbable collections of bed covers, extra clothes and even rugs.

The disputations for students of medicine had been scheduled for the next afternoon and, feeling a huge sense of urgency that his class should succeed, given the chronic shortage of qualified physicians since the plague, Bartholomew grilled the would-be healers relentlessly, firing questions in rapid succession that had them reeling.

When the bell rang to announce the end of the morning's teaching, so that the hall could be cleared and made ready for the midday meal, the students heaved sighs of relief, and escaped from their demanding master as quickly as they could. Bartholomew, however, was worried. While not even in his wildest dreams did he imagine Deynman would be successful, he had expected Bulbeck, Gray and the others to do well, and was perturbed that their answers to his questions were hesitant and incomplete.

While the Bible Scholar stumbled his way through some incomprehensible genealogy from the Old Testament as they ate, Bartholomew toyed listlessly with his boiled barley and soggy cabbage, his appetite waning further still when he discovered a well-cooked slug among the greens. The more he thought about it, the more he resented losing two valuable days to the ambush in the Fens when he should have been concentrating on his work.

After Kenyngham had ended the meal by reading grace, Bartholomew rounded up his students, and marched them off to the conclave for some additional lessons, abandoning his own plans to work on his treatise on fevers that afternoon. He taught until the light faded and the young men were no more than dark shapes with voices that were hoarse with tiredness, and then he continued until he became aware that at least two of them were asleep, exhaustion and the dark taking their toll. Reluctantly, he released them and went to his room, feeling far more anxious about their impending examinations than they were. He sat at his table and lit a vile-smelling tallow candle, intending to write a paragraph or two about contagion before he retired to bed.

He heard one of Michael's room-mates snoring in the chamber above him, and the slap of sandals on the wooden floor as someone moved around. Agatha's favourite cockerel crowed once in the darkness, and somewhere in the town a group of people was singing at the tops of their voices. Firelight flickered temptingly from the kitchen, and Agatha's raucous laughter wafted across the yard as she sat chatting with the other servants. And then it was silent. He wrote three sentences and promptly dozed off, waking abruptly when he almost set his hair alight as his head nodded towards the candle. With a sigh, he doused the flame, and groped his way over to the bed, wrapping himself in his blanket and shivering until he fell asleep.

He awoke the following morning feeling refreshed and far more hopeful about his students' chances of passing their disputations than he had been the day before. He went with Father Paul to prepare the church for the morning service, ate a hearty breakfast of warmish oatmeal and grey, grainy bread, and set about his teaching with renewed enthusiasm. By the time the bell rang to announce the end of the day's lessons, he was pleased with the progress his students had made, and felt that all but Deynman should do his hard work justice – Deynman's was a case beyond all earthly help.

He visited three patients with a recurrence of the winter fever that he was certain was caused by drinking from the well in Water Lane. Because it was easier and quicker to use the Water Lane well than the one in the Market Square, people were still becoming ill and, short of sealing it up, Bartholomew did not know how to stop them: claiming that invisible substances were seeping into it from the river was not a sufficiently convincing reason to make them change the habits of a lifetime.

When he had finished with the winter-fever patients, Bartholomew then went to St John's Hospital to tend a man with a palsy. On the way back, he met Michael, who had been investigating a burglary in nearby St Clement's Hostel – the outlaws had struck again.

Since they were close, Bartholomew persuaded Michael to walk up Castle Hill to see Sheriff Tulyet and describe to him, first hand, their experiences with the outlaws on the Cambridge to Ely causeway. Michael regarded the hill with apprehensive eyes, but agreed that it would be courteous to visit the beleaguered Sheriff, to see if their personal account of the ambush in the Fens might help him to catch the men who were terrorising the public highways and attacking property in the town.

They walked towards the Great Bridge, and paid the toll to be allowed to cross it. They trod carefully, wary of the rotten timbers that had crumbled away to reveal the swollen, stinking river below, and of the low sides, where the stone had been plundered to repair buildings in the town. Carts creaked across it, horses picking their way cautiously and stumbling as their hooves turned on the uneven surface. Their owners yelled, cajoled and urged, making almost as much noise as they did when they sold their wares at the market. Beyond the bridge, the road rose in a muddy trail to the churches of St Giles and St Peter, standing almost opposite each other, and then to the mighty castle beyond.

Michael complained bitterly about the exercise, although the hill was neither steep nor tall, and by the time they reached the top, the fat monk's face was covered in a sheen of sweat and his scanty supply of patience had evaporated. When a pardoner sidled up to them and invited them to look at his goods, Michael's face assumed such an expression of anger that the man scuttled away as fast as his legs would carry him.

'That was unnecessary, Brother,' said Bartholomew reprovingly, watching the pardoner run. 'He needs to make a living and life is not easy for itinerants in the winter.'

'He should know monks do not buy pardons,' retorted

Michael, unrepentant. 'And anyway, I have sworn a vow of poverty and have no money to spend on such foolishness.'

'That is not what you told Walter,' said Bartholomew mildly. 'What of these silver candlesticks from the Holy Land and your illustrated manuscripts?'

'I possess no such things!' snapped Michael irritably. 'Really, Matt! Do you believe everything I say? What I do have, however, is important documents and writs. I cannot have that good-for-nothing porter not bothering to protect my room because he thinks I own nothing of value. Now he believes I own a veritable treasure trove, he will be more careful.'

That was probably true, thought Bartholomew. Walter would not wish to risk being held responsible for the loss of Michael's fictitious treasures – although he would care nothing for scrolls – and would doubtless make more of an effort to ensure the monk's chamber was secure from now on.

The castle, dominating the town from its hill, was a collection of squat, grey buildings surrounded by a sturdy curtain wall. The curtain enclosed a wide expanse of muddy ground that was nearly always active with some kind of military training, and was overlooked by the great round keep at the far end. Tulyet's office was on the first floor of this austere Norman tower, the jagged crenellations of which pierced the white winter sky like blackened teeth.

Unusually, the bailey was almost deserted. There was a sergeant at the gate, and one or two archers lounged around the wall-walk, but the bulk of the garrison was out, attempting to hunt down the outlaws. It was an almost impossible task: the daylight hours were few, and the Fenlands to the north and the great forests to the south provided excellent cover for thieves and robbers. The sergeant, who had admitted Michael to the castle on many occasions, let them in and left them to find their own way to the Sheriff's office. Hearing their voices as they climbed the newel stair, Richard Tulyet came to greet them.

'Cynric told me about your experience with these outlaws,' he said without preamble, waving them to seats on a bench that ran the length of two of the walls. 'He was able to give me an excellent description of them, which will be useful, but I am concerned that they so shamelessly strutted into the town and had a drink at the Brazen George before leaving on their murderous mission.'

Bartholomew sat on the bench nearest the fire. Michael might be hot and sweaty from his exertions, but the physician was frozen to the bone. 'They were confident,' he agreed. 'And well-organised.'

'So Cynric said,' said Tulyet, sitting at his desk and leaning back in the chair. 'I have a strong suspicion that the outlaws I have been hunting this winter and the men who attacked you are one and the same. It is unlikely that there are two well-run criminal bands operating in the same area. At least, I hope not!'

'Did you know about the smuggling that takes place in the Fens?' asked Bartholomew.

'Yes, of course,' replied Tulyet. 'And I know it has become far more prevalent this year because the mild winter has kept the waterways open.'

'So, you think these smugglers are also responsible for the burglaries in the town and the robberies on the roads of which Sir Oswald Stanmore has been complaining?' asked Michael.

Tulyet picked up a quill and began to chew the end. 'I do. But speaking of Stanmore, what about the deaths of his men – Egil and Jurnet? Have you told him about that yet? It is not a task I envy you; Stanmore is protective over the people who work for him.'

Bartholomew nodded. 'We told him yesterday. Alan of Norwich killed Jurnet and Julianna did away with Egil.'

Tulyet looked up sharply and Michael gave a sigh. 'Ignore

him, Dick,' said the monk in a voice that bespoke long suffering. 'I saw the grip Egil had around Matt's throat, and so did Cynric. I would have brained the man myself had he been within my reach. Julianna saved Matt's life.'

'Did you not recognise Egil as you fought?' asked Tulyet of Bartholomew.

Bartholomew shook his head. 'The moon was in and out, and it was difficult to see clearly. I imagine the poor man had been wandering in the Fens for the previous two days and, quite reasonably, assumed that anyone on the highway in the dead of night, walking as furtively as we were, was up to no good. He attacked without trying to discover who we were.'

'I spoke with Egil when he first arrived in Cambridge,' said Tulyet, frowning. 'I interview any stranger who stays here longer than a week – we cannot be too careful with strangers these days – and he told me that he knew the Fens around Ely like the back of his hand.'

'So?' asked Bartholomew, uncertain of the point the Sheriff was trying to make.

'So if he knew the Fens so well, he would not have wandered for two days before finding the road again,' said Tulyet impatiently.

'True,' said Michael, thinking hard. 'Oswald Stanmore said that Egil preferred the Fens to the town, and often went fishing there. And he certainly knew where the Ely causeway went when it disappeared underwater on our outward journey. No, Matt. Egil would not have been lost.'

'Perhaps he was injured,' said Bartholomew, 'and left for dead by the smugglers.'

'Possibly,' said Tulyet. 'But we will know that for certain when you examine the body properly. I take it Stanmore has gone to fetch it back?'

Bartholomew nodded, wondering whether it was worth protesting at Tulyet's cavalier assumption that he would act as coroner for him.

'I arrested Thomas Bingham – the University's newest Master – for the murder of James Grene this morning,' said Tulyet, almost casually. 'We have him locked in a room upstairs.'

Michael leapt to his feet. 'What? Bingham? On what evidence?'

'On the evidence we all saw,' said Tulyet. 'Grene was poisoned at Bingham's installation. Apparently, his Fellows began their own investigation when Vice-Chancellor Harling told them you had been called away, and Father Eligius came to me and made a case for his arrest earlier today. Essentially, he pointed out that someone killed Grene, and the only person to benefit from his death was Bingham. And perhaps even more damning was the fact Grene confided he was in fear of his life from Bingham shortly before his death to Eligius and to two other Valence Marie Fellows.'

'Grene confided his fear to *three* Fellows?' asked Michael. 'That is damning. But why did *you* arrest Bingham? This is a matter for the Proctors, not the Sheriff. It is a crime against the University, committed on University property.'

'You were busy investigating the outlaws' attack on St Clement's Hostel, and could not be found. And Harling thought Bingham would be safer with me than in the Proctors' gaol. Despite the fact that no one much cared for Grene while he was alive, sympathy for him dead has exceeded the bounds of all reason, because so many people witnessed his murder. Harling was afraid Grene's supporters might march against the less-secure Proctors' prison, and try to lynch Bingham.'

Michael puffed out his cheeks. 'Harling is probably right. And it is all down to this damned relic of Valence Marie's!'

'The relic found last year?' asked Tulyet, startled. 'What is that to do with Grene's murder?'

'Because since we returned from Denny, I have lost track of the times that I have been asked when the Chancellor plans to reinstate that wretched hand to Valence Marie.

People believe Grene died for the thing – and that Bingham is leading a sinister plot to discredit it.'

'How can people be so gullible?' asked Bartholomew tiredly. 'I thought we had exposed that horrible thing as a fake – and, perhaps even more importantly, proved that the saint it was said to have come from was no more a martyr than I am.'

'There speaks a man of science,' said Tulyet, grimly amused. 'People do not need facts to whip them up into a fanatical frenzy about something, Matt. If you made a convincing case that cows could fly, you would find people willing to believe it – and even to die for it – despite what their experience and common sense dictates to them.'

'I am concerned that Grene expressed fears for his safety to *three* Valence Marie Fellows,' said Michael, gnawing on his lower lip. 'This is beginning to look very bad for Bingham.'

'Can we be sure all three are telling the truth?' asked Bartholomew. 'What if they are the same three who voted for Grene in the election, and this is no more than College politics running wild?'

'Are you suggesting that Father Eligius is lying?' asked Tulyet, surprised. 'He is one of the University's foremost scholars.'

'No one saw Bingham give Grene the poisoned wine,' said Bartholomew, standing and beginning to pace. 'And murdering him would be a foolish thing to do in front of half the town. I cannot believe Bingham did it.'

'Then who did?' asked Tulyet, watching him move back and forth across the small room. 'Who else might gain?'

'Father Eligius himself,' suggested Michael quietly.

'Why?' asked Bartholomew in frustration. 'He was offered the Mastership and he did not want it. He has no motive for wanting Grene dead.'

'He has no motive that we know about,' corrected Michael. 'But there is always the relic that he feels so strongly about. Perhaps Grene's death is somehow connected to that.'

'I suppose he was very quick to accuse Bingham of Grene's murder,' admitted Bartholomew reluctantly. 'That might be significant.'

'But so were you,' Michael pointed out. 'If you recall.'

'Only to you,' protested Bartholomew. 'But what of these other two Fellows who say Grene professed he was in fear of his life? Why did they wait for Eligius to instigate an investigation before telling their stories? It all strikes me as very odd.'

'Do you think Bingham is guilty?' Michael asked Tulyet.

Tulyet shrugged. 'As you say, the installation was a foolish place to dispatch a rival. But people are often foolish and live to regret their actions. I see plenty of evidence to suggest his guilt, and none to support his innocence. He claims he is blameless, of course. Do you want to speak to him?'

Michael nodded, and Tulyet led them up to the second floor, where a sleepy guard unlocked the door of a small chamber set in the thickness of the wall. The room was gloomy – only a narrow slit allowed the daylight to filter in – but was reasonably comfortable. The remains of a sizeable meal lay on the table, and Bingham had been provided with better, warmer blankets than the ones Bartholomew had at Michaelhouse.

Bingham recognised Michael and came towards him, his face haggard. 'I did not kill Grene,' he began immediately, his voice a throaty whisper. 'I did not like the man, but I did not kill him.'

'Then how did the poison find its way into his cup?' asked Michael harshly. 'It is strange that only he was stricken at the installation, would you not say?'

'I do not know!' said Bingham, in the weary tones of a man who had said as much many times before. 'I was as shocked by his death as was everyone else. I did not kill Grene and I have no idea how poison came to be in his wine. When he died, I assumed it had been simple gluttony that had brought about a seizure. The serving lad behind him had been filling his cup all night.'

Bartholomew had never been good at ascertaining whether people were telling the truth, but Bingham was convincing. It would have been difficult for him to pass a poisoned bottle to Grene without having it intercepted or seen by another person – unless he had an accomplice, of course. But then, surely the accomplice would be working to quell the allegations that Bingham was the murderer – for his own sake as much as Bingham's – and yet no one was speaking in Bingham's defence. The tall, willowy figure of Eligius sprung into Bartholomew's mind again. But what was his motive? Eligius did not want to be Master, so why should he want Bingham convicted of Grene's murder? Was it to promote the relic in some bizarre way – slaying one of its proponents to make people believe it was worth dying for?

A commotion in the bailey drew Tulyet over to the narrow window. He threw open the shutter and leaned out.

'Let him in,' he yelled to the sergeant on the gates. Moments later, feet pounded on the newel stair, and Cynric burst breathlessly into the room.

'Thought I would find you here,' he gasped, ignoring the Sheriff and addressing Bartholomew. 'Master Colton of Gonville asks that you come immediately. Father Philius is dead!'

CHAPTER 8

ALTHOUGH THE DEATH OF A SCHOLAR WAS NOT the concern of the Sheriff, Tulyet went with Bartholomew and Michael as they hurried down Castle Hill towards Gonville Hall.

'You seem to have most of your soldiers out in the Fens, Dick,' said Michael. 'Given that the outlaws have started to attack places in the town itself – the Round Church and poor little St Clement's Hostel to name but two – perhaps you would be better advised to keep a few back to patrol the streets.'

'Damn these villains!' spat Tulyet in sudden anger. 'What am I supposed to do? It is like looking for a needle in a haystack! Do I concentrate my searches on the Fens, or do I withdraw men, as you suggest, and look for them here? Your descriptions will help, but names would have been better.'

'I think we can provide you with some of those,' said Michael comfortably. 'I have an informant who knows the identities of several of these smugglers. The attack I was investigating on St Clement's Hostel distracted me – I should have told you before now.'

Tulyet stopped walking abruptly, and seized the fat monk's sleeve. 'How have you come by such information?' He shook his head quickly. 'Never mind. Just give me the names.'

'A nun has all the information you need,' said Michael. 'We brought her with us from Denny.'

'Well, where is she? Can I speak with her now?'

'I thought she would have passed this information to you on the way back from Denny,' said Bartholomew, reluctant for a well-known public figure like the Sheriff to visit Matilde's house and alert the outlaws to Dame Pelagia's whereabouts. 'She had plenty of time.'

'Of course she did not,' said Michael, treating Bartholomew to the kind of look that he normally reserved for students who made exceptionally stupid observations. 'First, it would not have been wise to discuss such matters on an open trackway – who knows who might have been listening from among the bushes at the roadside? Second, the fewer the people privy to this kind of information, the better – what one does not know, one cannot be forced to tell – and, anyway, Julianna was with us a good deal of the way, and I did not want her knowing more than she already does. And, third, Dame Pelagia is an old lady and needed all her energy for walking. She did not have excess breath to be chattering with me.'

Bartholomew's recollections of their journey suggested that it was probably Michael who had needed all his breath for walking, while Dame Pelagia had remained very sprightly, even at the end of the walk.

Tulyet made an impatient sound at their digression. 'Never mind all that. I want to speak with her immediately!'

Michael shook his head. 'I do not want anyone to know her whereabouts because I believe her to be in grave danger from these outlaws. I will ask her for the information and pass it to you as soon as we have finished with Father Philius.'

'No,' said Tulyet, hauling on Michael's sleeve as he made to walk on. He gestured up at the sky. 'If you tell me now, I can set about hunting these rogues immediately, while there is enough daylight. If you tell me later, I will have to wait until tomorrow, and by then who knows what might have happened? Go now. I will accompany Matt to see about Father Philius.'

Michael made as if to demur, but Tulyet stood firm. The Sheriff was right: the sooner the outlaws were rounded up, the sooner he, Bartholomew and Dame Pelagia would be safe. Michael nodded acquiescence, and headed off towards The Jewry. After a moment of hesitation, Cynric slipped away after him, and Bartholomew was reminded, yet again, what a dangerous position they were in.

A student was waiting outside Gonville Hall to conduct them to Father Philius's room. In it, Master Colton paced back and forth, pulling at his beard in agitation, while Bartholomew stopped dead in his tracks and stared. Philius's room looked as though a fierce wind had blown through it. Parchments were scattered everywhere, and the table and several stools had been overturned. The collection of fine crucifixes had gone, too – the hooks where they had hung were empty. As Bartholomew recovered himself, and walked towards the body that lay on the bed, glass and pottery crunched under his feet from the bottles and cups that had been shattered.

He knelt on the floor, and eased the dead scholar over onto his back. Philius's eyes were wide open, there were traces of blood around his white lips, and his face revealed an expression of profound shock. Tulyet leaned over Bartholomew's shoulder to look, and crossed himself hurriedly.

'It seems to me that the evil humours, for which you treated Philius recently, must have burst from him,' said Colton from the doorway as he watched. He gestured around the room. 'He must have done all this in his death throes. We decided we should leave everything as we found it, so that you could be certain it was these evil humours that killed him. I cannot have lies circulating that Philius died in suspicious circumstances, not so soon after the rumours that he was poisoned by his own book-bearer. What will people think of us?'

Bartholomew stood up, and turned to face Colton.

'But I think Father Philius has been murdered,' he said quietly. He looked around the room. 'And it seems he put up quite a fight.'

'Murdered?' echoed Colton nervously. 'But that cannot be so! The porter heard and saw nothing, and these days – with the outlaws at large – we keep our gates locked during the day as well as the night.'

'But he must have heard something,' said Bartholomew. 'Surely the sound of that table falling would have been audible from the porter's lodge?'

'Send for him,' ordered Tulyet. 'We shall see.'

With a long-suffering sigh, Colton hailed a passing student, and instructed him to fetch the porter.

'We might know what happened for certain once I have looked more closely at Philius's body,' said Bartholomew. He crouched next to the dead Franciscan, and inspected his face. Colton reached past him and hauled the bed-cover up, so that it covered the body. Bartholomew twisted round to gaze at the Master of Gonville Hall in astonishment.

Colton shook his head firmly. 'I am sorry, Bartholomew, but I cannot permit this. I will not have it put about that a murder has taken place in my College in the wake of this nasty affair of the poisoned wine. If I had thought you would try to prove Philius had been murdered, I would never have allowed you to come here. I expected you simply to confirm that Philius died as a result of his earlier affliction.'

'Did you ask me to come because you want to know what really happened, or because you want me to say what you hope to be true?' asked Bartholomew quietly. 'Because I will not lie for you.'

Colton looked angry. 'Philius could not have been murdered! I ate breakfast with him this morning! He had been very careful about his personal safety after Isaac's death: he locked his room at all times, even when he was in it. You are mistaken if you suspect foul play. I tell you, poor Philius had an attack of the same evil humours that struck him before.'

Bartholomew disagreed. 'He seemed to have recovered from that.'

'Seemed, yes,' insisted Colton. 'But you know diseases appear to be healed and then return with greater vigour. You must have seen how that happened with the Death?'

That was true. Bartholomew had seen many plague victims who seemed to be mending, but promptly died just as their family and friends were giving thanks for their deliverance. But he was certain that was not what had happened to Philius. He looked reappraisingly at Gonville Hall's Master. Did he have something more to hide than a desire to suppress rumours that might damage his College's reputation? Colton had been present in his College when Isaac was murdered and now, it seemed, he had seen Philius at breakfast – a matter of hours before the man had been dispatched. And Colton had been at the feast where Grene had died.

'If the humours had burst forth from his body as you suggest,' said Bartholomew, 'then we would see signs of it. He would have vomited, or had some other kind of flux, and there would be a recurrence of the small blisters I saw earlier.'

'What are you saying, Matt? That someone forced his way in and killed him?' asked Tulyet.

Bartholomew nodded slowly.

'That is ridiculous!' snapped Colton dismissively. 'I have told you already that Philius has been careful since Isaac's death. He kept his door locked at all times, and allowed few people in. And you are asking me to believe that someone entered the College, and killed him in broad daylight? As I told you, I saw him fit and well at breakfast when I joined him here, in this very room, this morning.'

'If he had been fit and well at breakfast, why should he suddenly die a couple of hours later?' asked Bartholomew. 'If his humours were unbalanced, he would have complained about it then.'

'Perhaps it came upon him all of a sudden,' said Colton, exasperated. 'And how could a murderer gain access to his room? The door was locked.'

'Was it locked when you found his body?' asked Bartholomew. 'With him dead inside?'

Colton considered. 'Well, no. It was unlocked when I found him like this, but he might have opened it as these evil humours burst forth in an attempt to call for help.'

'Then why did he not die outside in the yard?' persisted Bartholomew. 'Unless you moved the body?'

'I have touched nothing!' said Colton angrily, enunciating each word. 'And the reason I have touched nothing is so that we might quell any vicious rumours that Philius's death was anything but natural. I did not want you claiming that I have tampered with evidence. And, anyway, see reason, man! You are reading far too much into all this. Philius died, purely and simply, of a surplus of the evil humours that sickened him a few days ago.'

'Why do you keep saying Philius's last illness was caused by evil humours?' demanded Bartholomew. 'We both know very well that he was poisoned with the same substance that killed Grene and Armel.'

'*I* know nothing of the sort!' retorted Colton. 'I suggested to Philius, only this morning, that his ailment a few nights ago was a case of an overly acidic purge. He was *not* poisoned.'

Bartholomew stared at Colton in disbelief. 'Really? And I suppose this new diagnosis has nothing to do with the fact that you do not want your College associated with the murder of University scholars? Did you and Philius sit down together and discuss how you might best protect Gonville Hall from unseemly rumours?'

Or, he thought, perhaps it was more sinister than that, and Colton had ensured Philius would not live to spread tales of tainted purges and slain book-bearers.

Colton flushed furiously. 'I resent that implication,

Bartholomew. You are accusing me, and one of your own medical colleagues, of plotting to tell the most atrocious lies!'

Bartholomew sighed, weary of argument. 'But even you must see there are problems with your conviction that Philius's illness and subsequent death were natural, Master Colton – such as why did Philius display the same symptoms of poisoning as did Armel and Grene, if his ailment was caused by an excess of bad humours? And why was Philius so careful to lock his door, if he had nothing to fear?'

Colton said nothing, but glowered at Bartholomew, clenching and unclenching his fists.

'You said Philius secured his door,' Bartholomew continued relentlessly, 'but why was his room unlocked when you discovered his body? The answer to that is because his killer did not latch it when he left.'

'That is dangerous, unfounded speculation!' hissed Colton. 'How can all this be true? Philius would hardly unlock the door and allow a killer in his room!'

'He probably did not know this person was a killer when he admitted him,' said Bartholomew, with more patience than he felt Colton deserved, 'but it is clear from the state of the room that they struggled.'

Colton shook his head angrily, and gestured at Philius. 'There is no blood to suggest a wound, and his head is not caved in. There are no marks on his corpse at all. You should have evidence before you make such horrible assertions.'

'Give me a few moments to inspect the body, and I might be able to provide you with some,' said Bartholomew, fighting not to lose his temper. He felt vulnerable in the room where Philius had probably been murdered, even with Tulyet standing behind him, and Colton's unsettling attitude was not making him feel any better. He considered giving in to Colton's demands, just to ensure measures were not taken to ensure *his* silence over Gonville's precious reputation. He had not wanted to become involved in the investigation of the suspicious deaths in the first place, and bitterly resented the fact that it seemed to have placed him in such a dangerous position.

Colton scowled at him, but then, to Bartholomew's surprise, he yielded. 'Very well, then. I suppose that unless you satisfy yourself that poor Philius died of a flux of bad humours, rumours will follow that Gonville is seeking to hide the truth. But, be assured, Bartholomew, I will ask Doctor Lynton from Peterhouse to verify anything you find. I will not have my College dragged through the mire because you are unwilling to admit that you misdiagnosed Philius's illness the first time.'

He walked to the other end of the room so he would not have to watch, and began to pare his nails with a small knife in the light from the window.

Bartholomew bit back several scathing remarks that flooded into his mind, and bent to inspect Philius once again. It appeared that the Franciscan had prepared himself for bed when he was struck down – wary of over-exerting himself following his close brush with death a few days before – because he wore a long brown nightgown with a silk robe over the top. His feet were bare, so perhaps he had already been asleep. Bartholomew felt carefully around the friar's head, but Colton was right in saying there was no wound. Then he looked at the dead man's neck, but there was no bruising and no marks to suggest throttling. Finally, he drew the gown up, and looked for puncture wounds. With Tulyet's help, he turned the body over, but there was nothing to be seen.

Perhaps he had been wrong after all, he mused, and the internal damage sustained from the poison Philius had swallowed earlier *had* killed him. Bartholomew had worried about the long-term effects of the poison when he first attended the friar. But the expression on Philius's face did not seem right somehow. Bartholomew knew this was insufficient evidence on its own, but it set bells of warning jangling in his mind. He turned the corpse onto its back, and stared down at it, perplexed. And then a tiny glitter caught his eye.

On the left side of Philius's chest, a sliver of metal was embedded, all but invisible among the hair. Bartholomew leaned closer and saw that only the merest fraction protruded. Someone had clearly forced it in as far as it would go to hide it from view. Bartholomew took it between thumb and forefinger, and drew it out with some difficulty. Tulyet edged closer to watch, while Colton abandoned his manicure and stood next to him, his mouth agape with horror. The metal object was a nail, as long as Bartholomew's hand was wide, and whoever had used it had known exactly where to strike to bring about almost instant death.

'It penetrated his heart,' explained Bartholomew, holding it up for Colton to inspect. Colton's eyes were wide in a face that was suddenly bloodless. 'He would have died quickly and, as you can see, the wound did not bleed much. My interpretation of what happened is that Philius was asleep, but was roused by a knock at his door. The killer forced his way in and Philius began to fight – hence the scattered parchments and the upturned furniture. The killer then must have thrust the nail into Philius's chest. If you look here, you can see a little hole in his gown, and there is a small bloodstain that barely shows because of the dark colour.'

'There must have been two of them, Matt,' said Tulyet, putting both hands firmly behind his back as Bartholomew offered him the nail to examine. 'Philius would hardly stand still while someone stabbed him. One must have held him while the other drove the nail into him.'

'Not necessarily,' said Bartholomew. He stood behind Tulyet, and wrapped an arm around his throat to demonstrate. 'Philius was not a large man. His assailant might have managed to grab him from behind, and hold him still, like this, and the rest would be easy.' He made a quick, downwards motion with the nail in his hand to illustrate his point, making Colton flinch.

'This nail,' said Colton, unable to drag his eyes from the grisly object. 'Why did the killer not take it back?'

'Probably because it prevented the wound from bleeding,' said Bartholomew. 'And because it was virtually invisible anyway. The gown Philius is wearing will do well enough as a shroud, and I imagine the killer did not anticipate anyone taking it off to conduct a more rigorous investigation. You were meant to believe he died naturally. As indeed you have been suggesting.'

Colton slumped down on a stool, and clasped unsteady hands together. 'This is dreadful! We said a mass yesterday to give thanks for his recovery. Afterwards, he and I went for a walk to the Franciscan Friary.' He gazed at Philius's body, swallowed hard, and looked up at Bartholomew. 'Are you certain this nail killed him? Could it not have been there some time before today?'

Bartholomew raised his eyebrows in surprise. 'Hardly! It was driven into his heart. Call Lynton to confirm it, if you like. Or Robin of Grantchester. Both will tell you the same. The wound was a fatal one.'

Just then, the student returned with the porter who had been on duty that day. Bartholomew took one look at his heavy eyes and rumpled clothes, and guessed exactly why he had not heard anything from Philius's room.

'Do you sleep all the time you are supposed to be guarding your College?' he asked coolly.

'No, not all the time,' said the porter, and bit his lip when he realised what he had said.

Colton gave him a withering look. 'John!' he said tiredly. 'How could you? You know what happened here three days ago. I trusted you to be vigilant.'

'I was vigilant!' protested John. 'But there was nothing going on, and the whole place was as still as the grave. All the students were studying with the masters in the hall, and the cooks were busy in the kitchen. The College was so quiet, it was almost like the middle of the night. So, I thought there would be no harm if I just closed my eyes for a moment.'

'And you heard nothing?' asked Colton, looking at the porter in weary resignation.

'Nothing!' said John. 'Nothing at all. The first I knew of this . . .' his eyes strayed to Philius's body on the bed, 'was when you raised the alarm. I swear, I heard nothing!'

'And then, when you went to unlock the main gate to send for Matt and the Proctors you found it already open,' said Tulyet, walking to the window and leaning his elbows on the sill.

'Yes. No!' John gaped at the Sheriff, aghast at having been so easily tricked.

'And how much were you paid to leave the door unlocked, John?' Tulyet continued softly.

Colton stared at the Sheriff in mute horror. Disgusted by the porter's treachery, Bartholomew turned his attention back to Philius, straightening the stiffening limbs, and smoothing down the rumpled gown. Philius was not a man whom Bartholomew had especially liked, but he was a colleague and he would miss him – even if only for the dubious pleasure of disagreeing with his theories.

'I did not . . . they made me!' John said in a wail. 'They said they would kill me if I did not do what they said. I was to leave the door open and ask no questions. I decided it would be safer for me if I was asleep when it happened.'

'Who, John?' asked Tulyet calmly, still looking out of the window. 'Who told you to do this?'

'Them!' insisted John. 'The outlaws!'

'And how do you know they were outlaws?' asked Tulyet, his voice deceptively quiet. Bartholomew, who knew him well, was aware that his measured tones concealed a deep anger – partly at John's selfishness, but mostly that the outlaws who were outwitting him at every turn had succeeded yet again.

John clasped his hands together and gnawed at his knuckles. 'I just know,' he said, his voice shaky. 'They were the outlaws who killed Isaac and are robbing houses and church in the town.'

'But how do you know?' persisted Tulyet.

He spun round as John bolted from the room, slamming the door closed behind him. They heard a thump as the bench in the hallway – on which Philius's patients sat while they waited to be seen – was jammed against the door to prevent their escape. By the time Tulyet had forced it away, John was out of the yard and through the front gate. Tulyet tore after him, Bartholomew and Colton at his heels.

'Damn!'

Tulyet kicked the gate in frustration and pressed his palms into the sides of his head as he walked in a tight circle, every movement betraying the fury and helplessness he felt.

The lane was deserted: nothing moved and all was silent. In the middle of it lay John. The porter was slumped on his side, a crossbow quarrel embedded in his back and a thin trickle of blood oozing from his nose.

As the sun disappeared from the sky, Michael eased himself into Agatha's great chair by Michaelhouse's kitchen fire, and allowed her to fuss over him. He accepted yet another oatcake smeared with honey, and washed it down with the cup of ale that she had placed at his elbow. Next to the cup was a small dish of roasted nuts and a wizened pomegranate.

'Where did these come from?' he asked, shovelling a handful of the nuts into his mouth.

'I bought them from the market,' replied Agatha evasively. She picked up the pomegranate and studied it curiously. 'Just look at this peculiar thing! Have you ever seen its like?'

'What is it?' asked Michael, taking it from her and inspecting its rough pinkish-yellow skin with deep suspicion. 'You do not expect me to eat it do you?'

'It is a pomegranate,' said Bartholomew. 'I have never seen one in England before.'

'What do you propose we do with it?' asked Michael, tossing it to him and taking another handful of nuts.

'You can eat the fruit, or make it into a drink. The seeds can be used as a preservative,' Bartholomew answered. He threw it back to Michael. 'But we have more important things to be discussing than pomegranates. Like what happened to you.'

'That was outrageous!' muttered Agatha indignantly. 'What is the town coming to?'

Bartholomew sat on a stool near the fire and began to poke at the flames with a stick. 'Tell me again,' he said. 'What happened?'

Michael gave a great sigh. 'Not again, Matt! I am too tired.'

'He has told you once already,' said Agatha, prodding Bartholomew in the back with a spoon handle. 'The poor lad needs to rest.'

'We will never get to the bottom of this if we rest!' shouted Bartholomew, standing so abruptly that the stool went skittering across the kitchen floor.

Michael and Agatha gazed at him, startled. Bartholomew rubbed a hand through his hair, retrieved the stool and sat again.

'Sorry, Agatha,' he mumbled. 'But we must reason this out before anyone else comes to harm.'

Agatha continued to stare. She had known the mild-mannered physician since he had come to take up his post as Master of Medicine at Michaelhouse nine years before and, during all that time, he had never once raised his voice to her. She had heard him shouting at his students from time to time, but he did so far less than the other Fellows, and it was usually frustration with their speed of learning rather than genuine anger. But it had been anger that had prompted him to yell at her now.

He twisted round when she did not reply, and saw the hurt expression on her rounded features. He was surprised. Agatha won, and maintained, her position of power over the other College servants on her claim that she was more of a man than any of them or any of the scholars. It was an assertion none was brave enough to dispute, and she ruled the domestic side of the College with a ruthless efficiency no one dared question. Even the forceful fanatic Father William had never won an argument with Agatha, yet Bartholomew had silenced her with a few words.

He rubbed at his hair again and stood with a sigh. 'Sorry, Agatha,' he said again. 'I should not have shouted at you.' He took her arm and brought her over to the fire. While she descended ponderously onto the stool, he sat on the edge of the hearth, oblivious to the occasional sparks that spat from the damp wood and burned small holes in his tabard.

'You are worried about Matilde!' said Agatha with sudden insight.

'No!' he protested, embarrassed that she had so adeptly read his thoughts. 'It is this entire business. Philius brutally murdered, and now this attack on Michael . . .'

Michael leaned forward and tapped Bartholomew gently on the head with a fat, white forefinger. 'But it failed,' he said soothingly. 'And I am fine.'

'He needs another oatcake,' said Agatha, struggling up from the stool to fetch him one.

'He does not,' said Bartholomew, looking at Michael's ample girth and hauling her back down. 'He needs to lose some weight. If you feed him much more, one day you will find him unable to get out of that chair of yours.'

Agatha screeched with laughter, a familiar sound that echoed around Michaelhouse's yard several times each day. Michael smiled, too, and settled himself back comfortably.

'Once again, then,' he said, folding his hands across his stomach. 'I was approaching All Saints' Church on my way to see Matilde, when an ill-dressed villain came racing towards me from the direction of the Great Bridge. I took no notice, thinking it to be some apprentice late for his chores, but, as he drew nearer, I saw his eyes were fixed on me with more than a passing interest. He had a knife in his hand, and as he collided with me, he attempted to stab me with it. As you know, I am not a small man, and not easily tumbled to the ground. And more drunken students have taken swings at me with weapons than I care to remember. This little chap did not stand a chance. I wrested the knife from him, but then he was away, and was too quick for me to follow.'

Agatha pursed her lips and she shook her head disapprovingly. 'That was why the Death came!'

Bartholomew stared at her, somewhat taken aback. 'Because Michael is too fat to chase the man who tried to kill him?'

Agatha shot him a long-suffering look. 'Of course not! Because of sinful acts – murders and ambushes and people riding horses too fast along the High Street. That was why the pestilence came in the first place, and that is why it is only a matter of time before it returns. You mark my words! Those of you who are not God's chosen should beware.'

'And why do you think you are God's chosen and not us?' asked Bartholomew warily. He had heard a good many explanations for why the plague had swept across the country, but reckless riding had not usually been among them.

Agatha drew herself up to her full height. 'Because I walked daily among the victims of the pestilence and I was not struck down,' she said grandly. 'I did not die!'

'But we did not die either,' Michael pointed out. 'And neither did the maniac who tried to stab me.'

There was silence as Agatha digested this, and Michael took the opportunity to continue with his tale.

'I went to All Saints' Hostel to recover with a drop of mulled wine, while Cynric tried to pursue this lout. But Cynric had been too far behind to start with – he had met that woman of his from Stanmore's house, and had dallied talking with her – and he lost my would-be killer in

the Market Square. We slipped out of the back door of All
Saints' to continue to Matilde's house. Cynric is certain we
were not followed and so am I. When we left Matilde's, we
went back through All Saints' Hostel and emerged through
the front door, so that anyone watching will have assumed
we were there the entire time.'

'These smugglers are clever and resourceful,' said
Bartholomew, biting his lower lip. 'It was a stupid idea
to leave Dame Pelagia with Matilde. Now neither of them
is safe.'

'Come on, Matt,' said Michael. 'They will be perfectly all
right. Now Tulyet has the list of names from Dame Pelagia,
we will not need to visit them again until this is over.'

'That is what he is cross about!' said Agatha with another
ear-shattering howl of laughter. 'Where will he spend his
nights now that Matilde's house is out of bounds?'

'Agatha!' exclaimed Bartholomew, shocked. 'What are
you saying?'

'All these night visits to people with winter fever,' leered
Agatha. 'Likely story!'

'But it is true!' protested Bartholomew, horrified to feel
himself blushing. 'Matilde and I have never . . .'

He faltered and Agatha guffawed again. Michael came to
his rescue.

'Now, what about Philius? Agatha, more oatcakes, please.
And do you have a little bacon fat to spread on them?'

While Agatha went to fetch the bacon fat from the pantry,
Bartholomew told Michael about his findings regarding
Philius's death, and how John the porter had been killed.

'We are left with a good many unanswered questions
regarding Philius,' he concluded. 'We still cannot be sure
where the wine that killed him came from – Oswald vehemently denies one of his apprentices is missing, and now
both Philius and Isaac are dead there is no one we can ask
to verify who is telling the truth.'

'This crossbow business bothers me,' said Michael. 'It

seems very convenient that an archer just happened to be in place at the precise moment when John ran from the College.'

'What do you mean?' asked Bartholomew warily.

Michael rubbed at the whiskers on his chin. 'I think this archer was waiting for you, not John. He was going to kill you, just as the knifeman attempted to dispatch me. When John came racing out, obviously in some distress – and it would not take a genius to guess why, with the Sheriff in the College and Philius's body just found – this archer decided to prevent John from telling any more than he might have revealed already. It takes a while to rewind a crossbow, and no murderer wants to tarry too long at the scene of his crime. Rather than take the risk of waiting for you after he had slain John, he decided to slip away while he could.'

Bartholomew had a sudden unpleasant thought. 'If you are correct, could he have been forewarned that we might be visiting Gonville Hall? By someone who had called us and knew that we would not refuse to attend? Someone such as Colton? He was unduly nervous about the whole thing. And he had cooked up some ungodly lies – supposedly with Philius's blesssing, he was claiming that Philius had never been poisoned, but was suffering from an excess of evil humours.'

Michael scratched his head. 'Colton cannot be ruled out as a suspect. I have known him for years, and he is clever and ambitious. But so are most Masters. I would not have marked Colton down as the kind of man who would be an accessory to murder, but who knows?'

Bartholomew groaned. 'What is happening? Why are these men so intent on killing us? What have we done to incur such a reaction?'

'It must be this poisoned wine,' said Michael, picking at a food stain on his habit. 'It is the only common factor.'

'Or perhaps we have yet to learn what this common factor is,' said Bartholomew, rubbing his eyes tiredly. 'Perhaps we are overlooking something.' He paused. 'And I do not know what to believe about Grene. It seems something of a coincidence that he should be murdered the day after confessing to Eligius that he was in fear of his life from Bingham. Yet I am not completely convinced of Bingham's guilt.'

'But it does not look good for Bingham. Eligius is a highly respected scholar and I know of no reason why he and his two colleagues should lie.'

'I just cannot see how Bingham could have passed this wine to Grene at the feast,' said Bartholomew, frowning. 'They did not sit next to each other. How could Bingham be certain that the bottle would reach its intended victim? You said yourself that everyone was watching to see how Grene was taking his defeat – it would have been impossible. And if Grene really did believe himself to be in danger, why should he drink from a bottle given to him by the man he feared?'

'I agree,' said Michael. 'Had I been in that position, I would have eaten nothing at the feast, yet Grene positively gorged himself. Perhaps Eligius and the other two are lying after all. Grene's death has provided them with a splendid opportunity to rid themselves of Bingham – the Master for whom they did not vote.'

'I am so tired I can barely think,' said Bartholomew, his mind whirling as he tried to sort the facts into some semblance of order. 'Everything seems connected, yet is jumbled – the attack on us in the Fens; the poisoned wine; Bingham, Grene, Eligius and that stupid relic; Philius and Colton and their concoction of lies about Philius's illness; the smugglers and Julianna . . .'

'It has been a long day and we should both rest,' said Michael. He stood up, and glanced out of the window. 'There are your students back from their disputations. You cannot expect Deynman to have passed, but the others should have good news for you.'

He grinned at Agatha as she returned with a huge plate of

oatcakes heavily smeared with the salty white fat that Michael loved. Bartholomew felt sick just looking at them, but Agatha presented him with a piece of seedcake instead. He leaned over and, before she could guess what he was going to do, kissed her cheek and fled the kitchen. Michael roared with laughter as Agatha's astonishment changed to delight. She beckoned Michael back to the fireplace, and the two of them proceeded to devour the entire greasy repast.

Wiping cake crumbs from his face with the back of his hand, Bartholomew tapped at the door of the room Gray shared with Bulbeck, and entered. He sensed in an instant all was not well. He raised his eyebrows questioningly, and sat on the window sill, silhouetted against the remaining light of the darkening evening.

'They asked me about trepanation.' said Gray in an accusatory tone. 'You never taught us about that! How am I supposed to know things you have never told us?'

'We discussed trepanation last summer, Sam,' said Bartholomew wearily, 'when Brother Boniface was with us. I take it you did not pass?'

'It was not fair!' shouted Gray petulantly, kicking off his boots so that they fell with a crash against the wall. 'Then they asked me to debate the question: Did God create the world out of nothing or out of the primordial darkness?'

'And?'

'And how should I know?' snapped Gray. 'I was not there!' His two friends looked aghast at his blasphemy, and he relented. 'I did my best, but the examiners did not like my answers.'

'I hope you were not flippant with them,' said Bartholomew, concerned. His own reputation for unorthodoxy was as much as he could handle, and he did not want to be blamed for teaching Gray bad habits, too.

'He was not flippant,' said Bulbeck, from where he lay on the bed with his arm across his eyes. 'He was just unfortunate in the questions they asked. If he had got Rob's questions, he would have been fine.'

'I did not pass,' said Deynman gloomily. 'I cannot think why – I answered all they asked me.'

Bartholomew did not want to know what Deynman's answers to the questions were, but the student was relentless.

'They asked me what I would do for a patient bleeding from a serious wound on his head, so I told them I would check his legs were not broken—'

'His legs?' asked Bartholomew, startled. 'Whatever for?'

'In case he had sustained the injury falling from a horse,' replied Deynman with confidence. 'Then I said I would see if there was another wound underneath the one in his head—'

'Underneath it?' interrupted Bartholomew, not understanding. 'What do you mean?'

'You told us we should be careful that one symptom does not mask another. So I would poke about under the wound to make sure there was not another, more serious, injury underneath.'

'That was not really what I meant,' said Bartholomew, rubbing his hand through his hair, too tired to feel exasperated. 'I meant symptoms for diseases and ailments, not wounds. And while you are looking at his legs and prodding about with his head, this poor patient of yours might have bled to death.'

Deynman looked crestfallen, but continued with his answer anyway. 'Then I said I would bind the injury with a poultice of clean water and henbane—'

'And a pinch of arsenic to kill the infection, you said,' interrupted Gray scornfully. Bartholomew regarded Deynman with awe, wondering if there was anything of his lectures the student remembered even remotely accurately.

'Then they asked me to debate the question: When a man takes a pig to market on a rope, is the pig taken by the man or by the rope? I told them it mattered neither one way nor the other to the pig.'

'So the debate was a short one, then?' asked Bartholomew drily. 'And you did not reveal to the examiners the true extent of your incisive and orderly grip of logic?'

'He did. That was the problem,' muttered Gray.

'But you passed, Tom,' said Bartholomew, looking at his best student. He had certainly not expected Deynman to be successful, but he was disappointed in Gray's performance. They had discussed trepanation at some length, and Gray should have been able to answer questions about it. Gray was also a consummate liar and was good at twisting people's words and meanings. He should have excelled in his disputation.

'I failed,' said Bulbeck.

Bartholomew closed his eyes and tipped his head back to rest on the wall behind him. His three students were silent, aware that they had let him down, but not certain what they could do to make amends. Bartholomew wondered where he had gone wrong: perhaps he should have done more to curtail the illicit drinking in taverns that had been taking place, or perhaps he should have spent less time on his treatise about fevers and given them additional lessons. Their lack of success would not have been so bad, but the country was in desperate need of trained physicians to replace those who had died during the plague.

'All the others passed,' Deynman ventured. 'It was only us who . . . did not do so well.'

'But you, Tom!' groaned Bartholomew, regarding Bulbeck in despair. 'I expected better things of you.'

'I feel ill,' said Bulbeck in a weak voice. Bartholomew went to his side, and rested a hand on his forehead. He was feverish and looked pale.

'How long have you been unwell?' he asked, wondering whether he had put too much pressure on the student, and made him sick from worry.

'Since midday,' said Bulbeck. He pulled his knees up to his chest, and put both hands on his stomach, closing his eyes tightly in pain.

'Have you drunk any wine? Or eaten anything from outside Michaelhouse?' asked Bartholomew uneasily, reaching for a cloth with which to wipe Bulbeck's face.

Bulbeck shook his head. 'You told us not to,' he said.

'You had that cup of water,' said Gray. 'From the well.'

'Water does not count,' said Deynman disdainfully. 'Doctor Bartholomew meant that we should not touch foods and wines from outside the College. Water is nothing!'

'Which well?' asked Bartholomew, already guessing the answer.

'The one near the river,' said Deynman. 'Winter fever!' He exclaimed suddenly, pleased with himself. 'Tom has winter fever!'

Bartholomew could think of no other explanation. Since he had advised people against using the well in Water Lane – on the grounds that the river had somehow invaded it – the number of cases of fever had dropped and only the stubborn or lazy, who ignored his advice, were stricken. Bartholomew supposed that the contagion must increase in still-standing water, because those who drank straight from the river did not seem to catch the sickness. Several, however, were afflicted with other ailments, for which Bartholomew was reasonably certain that the foul, refuse-filled Cam was responsible.

'I was thirsty,' said Bulbeck in a small voice. 'And I forgot what you said about the well. I know you said we were not to eat or drink anything outside Michaelhouse, but I thought a sip of water would not harm me.'

Bartholomew patted his shoulder and went to make up a potion to ease Bulbeck's stomach cramps. When he returned, Gray and Deynman had put the ailing student to bed and closed the window shutters to keep some of the cold from the room. He saw that Bulbeck finished the medicine, and left the others to watch over him while he slept. Although this particular fever was unpleasant, it was not usually fatal, and Bartholomew was sure Bulbeck would make a full recovery, given rest and a carefully selected diet for a few days.

He closed the door and began to walk across the yard to his own room. He rubbed his eyes as he walked, feeling them dry and sore under his fingers. Then he collided so heavily with someone that he staggered, and almost lost his footing in the slippery mud of the yard.

'Watch where you are going!' yelled Langelee, his voice drawing the attention of several scholars who were talking together near the door to the hall.

'Sorry,' said Bartholomew. He tried to step round the philosopher, but Langelee stopped him.

'Sorry?' he sneered. 'Is that all?'

'What more do you want?' asked Bartholomew, puzzled.

Langelee leaned nearer, and Bartholomew detected a strong odour of wine.

'It is a disgrace the way you and Brother Michael have leave to come and go all hours of the night,' he hissed. 'And I know where you go.'

'I go to see my patients,' said Bartholomew coldly. 'You can come with me next time if you wish.' He pushed past Langelee, intending to end the conversation there and then.

'Maybe I will,' said Langelee, turning to follow Bartholomew to his room.

'Fine,' said Bartholomew. 'I will send Cynric for you when I am called.' He wondered what he had agreed to, but reasoned it might not be a bad thing to have the company of the brawny philosopher – his presence would certainly make opportunistic outlaws think twice before attempting to rob him. But he saw it would be foolish to go out at night – even with Langelee – when there were people who wanted him dead. He had been lured out of the safety of Michaelhouse and attacked while trying to solve other mysteries in the past, and would not allow himself to fall for such an obvious ploy again.

He pushed open the door to his room and threw himself on his bed. He closed his eyes, but opened them again when he sensed the presence of another person.

'What do you want, Langelee?' he asked irritably, when he saw the philosopher close the door behind him and gaze around the room speculatively. 'I am tired and would like to sleep.'

Langelee perched on the edge of the table and crossed his ankles. 'Sleep? When three of your students have disgraced the College by failing their disputations?'

Bartholomew sat up. 'Were you one of their examiners?'

Langelee nodded, his face smug. 'I was assessing their grasp of philosophical issues, and I have never seen such a miserable performance. Even Tom Bulbeck was dreadful, and he is said to be your best student.'

'He has a fever,' said Bartholomew. 'I have just made him a physic.'

'I hope you told him to wash his hands before he took it,' said Langelee with a sneer. 'If you taught traditional medicine instead of all this cleanliness nonsense they would have passed. All three are quick enough.'

'Can we discuss this another time?' asked Bartholomew, refusing to be drawn. If Langelee considered Deynman quick, he must be drunk indeed.

Langelee stared down at him. 'And why are you so weary? Worn out after a night with your harlot Matilde? I suppose she offers you her services for free. The rest of us pay, of course.'

Bartholomew glared at him, fighting a wild impulse to shove the man backwards through the window. Was there anyone in the College who was not intimately acquainted with his harmless affection for the town's most exclusive prostitute? He wondered whether his students knew, and the dour Franciscans. But they could not, he reasoned, because Father William would certainly have challenged him about it if they had. He frowned. It was not as if he had anything about which to feel guilty: he and Matilde had never been anything but friends. She had, however, told him that she considered Langelee an attractive man, although looking at the philosopher now, when his pugilistic features were stained red with drink, Bartholomew seriously doubted her good taste.

'Go away,' he said, leaning back on the bed again and closing his eyes.

Langelee picked up a scroll from the table and squinted to read it. Bartholomew sighed. So far, he had responded to Langelee's goading with admirable calm, but his patience was beginning to fray and it would not be long before they ended up arguing. It did not take a genius to deduce that Langelee wanted a fight: his fingers twitched and flexed as if in anticipation of action. But Bartholomew knew who would win such an encounter, and he was not foolish enough to allow himself to be battered to a pulp merely to satisfy Langelee's abnormal craving for violence.

'Aristotle,' announced Langelee, laying the scroll down and picking up another. 'And Galen, of course. What about Albucasis, the Arab surgeon? Do you use his works to teach your students?'

'Of course,' said Bartholomew cautiously, wondering where all this was leading. 'And Masawaih al-Mardini and Al-Ruhawi. There is much to be learned from Arab medical practice.'

'Ah, yes,' said Langelee. 'I was told that you had studied with an Arab in Paris. A curious choice of master, was it not?'

'I heard you studied with Father Eligius at Valence Marie,' said Bartholomew, deftly changing the subject before Langelee could attack him about his training. 'He must have made a fascinating teacher.'

'Oh, he was,' agreed Langelee. 'It is good to be in the same town with him again. I can debate with him and keep my skills honed.'

Bartholomew was surprised that the eminent Dominican logician had either the time or the inclination to help Langelee keep his mediocre skills honed, but said nothing.

'Now I should see your students,' said Langelee, dropping the scroll back on the table and standing up. 'I should let them know where they went wrong in their disputations.'

'Tomorrow,' said Bartholomew hastily. 'It would be very kind of you to take the trouble. I am sure they will appreciate your help.'

He was sure they would not, and was certain that Gray would make some insolent remark that might lead Langelee to respond with physical force. But by the following day, Langelee would probably have forgotten his offer, Gray would be less angry about failing his examination, and an unpleasant scene would have been averted.

'Now would be better,' said Langelee. He tapped his temple. 'While it is still fresh.'

'I have given Bulbeck a sleeping draught,' said Bartholomew patiently. 'He has a fever. Please leave him alone this evening. Speak to them tomorrow.'

Langelee shook his head. 'You are too soft with them. I will speak with them now. I know how to make them listen.'

Bartholomew stood. 'No,' he said firmly. 'See to your own students. I am sure they will be missing the benefits of your learning if you have been conducting disputations all afternoon.'

Langelee narrowed his eyes and Bartholomew opened the door for him. Then, in a blur of movement, Langelee had lunged across the room and had placed two meaty hands around Bartholomew's throat.

Bartholomew, however, had sensed that Langelee would not leave his room without some display of aggression, and was ready for him. Calmly, he lifted the small surgical knife he had kept hidden in his sleeve, and pointed it at Langelee's neck. Horrified at the touch of cold steel, Langelee immediately lowered his hands.

'Matthew!' Kenyngham's appalled voice startled Bartholomew and Langelee alike. The physician let the knife drop from Langelee's throat, and they both turned to face the Master of the College who stood in the doorway. Bartholomew had never seen him quite so angry. His face was white, and his eyes had lost their customary dreaminess and were a hard, cold blue. Behind him was Michael, taking in the scene with horrified amazement.

'What do you two think you are doing?' demanded Kenyngham, his voice tight with fury.

Langelee shrugged. 'I came to tell Bartholomew about his students' disputations – and I am not obliged to do so, I was doing him a favour – when he became belligerent and attacked me with his knife.' He raised his hands. 'You can see I am unarmed.'

'You are drunk,' said Kenyngham in disgust. 'Go to your own room, and do not come out again until you are sober.'

He stood aside for Langelee to leave. Langelee looked as if he would argue, but Kenyngham fixed him with a look of such hostility that the philosopher left without another word. Kenyngham watched him walk across the yard, and then turned to Bartholomew.

'Well?' he asked, his tone chilling. 'What have you to say for yourself?'

Bartholomew could think of no excuse that would mitigate the fact that he had been caught holding a weapon at the throat of one of his colleagues. It sounded churlish to claim that Langelee had followed him to his room with the clear intention of provoking him to fight: the philosopher had known exactly which subjects might be expected to evince a response from him – his unorthodox medical training, Matilde and then threatening to disturb the ailing

Bulbeck. He shrugged apologetically, while Kenyngham glared at him.

'I will not have my Fellows setting a poor example to the students,' he said icily. 'If I catch you menacing Langelee – or anyone else – with knives again, I will be forced to terminate your Fellowship. You think I will not do what I threaten, because we will be unable to replace you, but I would rather Michaelhouse had no Master of Medicine than one who uses the tools of his trade to intimidate the other scholars!'

He turned on his heel and strode out. Bartholomew sank on to the bed, feeling drained, and Michael closed the door.

'What were you doing?' asked the monk, regarding Bartholomew in disbelief. 'Threatening a colleague with a dagger? Matt! What is wrong with you? You are usually so opposed to that sort of thing.'

'He came looking for a fight,' said Bartholomew, pulling off his boots and lying on the bed with a sigh. 'I reacted with admirable restraint – right up until moments before you and the Master barged in. It was unfortunate that you did not come a few moments earlier, or a few moments later.'

'It looked terrible,' said Michael, eyeing Bartholomew dubiously. 'Langelee standing there looking frightened to death, while you waved that sharp little knife at his throat. I was with Kenyngham when I saw him follow you into your room. We came because I was afraid he meant you harm, but it seems he was the one who needed our protection! I am not surprised Kenyngham threatened you with dismissal. What else could he do? You offered no defence of yourself.'

'What could I say?' said Bartholomew helplessly. 'Damn! Do you really think Kenyngham believes I was the aggressor?'

'Matt, *I* thought you were the aggressor,' said Michael, sitting on the end of the bed. 'I thought you disapproved of brawling.'

'I do. Usually,' replied Bartholomew. He reflected.

'Kenyngham was serious: he would terminate my Fellowship over a set-to with Langelee.'

Michael nodded. 'I believe he would. He has always liked you, and has often spoken out in your defence. Either the sight of you armed and dangerous forced him to see you in a new light, or Langelee must have some powerful supporters to whom Kenyngham is forced to yield.'

'What do you mean?' asked Bartholomew, folding his arms behind his head. 'What kind of supporters?'

'Perhaps Langelee is a relative of one of Michaelhouse's benefactors,' said Michael. 'Or perhaps he has made the College the sole beneficiary of his will. Whatever, it is clear that he has some kind of advantage over you, if it comes to Kenyngham choosing between you or him. I would advise you to stay away from that lout in future. What did he say to drive you to such extremes?'

Bartholomew told him and Michael looked thoughtful.

'Matilde said Ralph de Langelee was the man of Julianna's choice. Perhaps Julianna has told him about our midnight flight through the Fens, and he was needling you because he is jealous.'

'Jealous of what?' protested Bartholomew. 'I loathe the woman. That pair deserve each other!'

'Perhaps that is not what she led him to believe,' said Michael. 'Matilde said Julianna knows how to get her own way. It is possible she is using you to make him more enamoured of her.'

'And what would you know of such things?' asked Bartholomew, closing his eyes. 'You are not a love-sick woman of twenty-two – as Matilde pointed out to us recently.'

Michael stood to close the window shutters. A wind had picked up, and was sending chilly blasts across the room, sending parchments and scrolls tumbling from the table onto the floor. When he turned around again, Bartholomew was asleep.

*   *   *

The scrawny cockerel, which Agatha fed on kitchen scraps, crowed yet again outside Bartholomew's window and woke him up. Exasperated, he hurled a boot at the shutter, hoping the sudden thump would be sufficient to drive the bird away without his needing to climb out of bed to see to it. It was pitch dark in his chamber, and he was certain it could not yet be time to rise for mass. He was just allowing himself to slide back into the uncertain area between sleep and wakefulness, when Michael tiptoed into his room.

'It is morning, Matt!' he whispered. 'Although you might not believe it. It is dark and cold, and no time for sane men to be up and about.'

'Then go back to bed and leave me alone,' mumbled Bartholomew, pulling the blanket over his head in an attempt to escape the cold draught that flooded the chamber as Michael opened the window shutters. There was a flapping sound as the cockerel was startled into removing itself to crow outside someone else's quarters.

'I will have that thing in a stew with onions one of these days,' muttered Michael viciously. 'It is the third time this month it has kept me awake half the night. But come on, Matt, or we will be late. Do not look so irritable! You said you would take mass duties today, because Father William did your turn while you were enjoying yourself at Denny.'

Still half asleep, Bartholomew hauled himself out of bed, and hopped from foot to foot on the icy flagstones while he washed and shaved. He grabbed a clean shirt with frozen fingers, and struggled into it, tugging hard enough to rip the stitches in one sleeve when it clung to his wet skin. It was several moments before he located his leggings in the dark and, by the time he was ready, Michael had already left for the church. Racing along the lane as fast as he could in a vain attempt to warm himself up, he almost collided with the solemn procession of scholars from Physwick Hostel, also making their way to St Michael's Church for the early morning service.

Michael had been unable to light the temperamental lamp, and was fumbling around the chancel in the dark, grumbling to himself, and swearing foully when he stubbed his toe against the sharp corner of Master Wilson's marble tomb.

'That man continues to be a bane in my life, even though he is five years dead!' the monk snapped, pushing Bartholomew out of his way as he groped towards the altar.

There was a loud crash that reverberated around the silent building, and made several of the Physwick scholars jump and cross themselves hurriedly. Michael's stream of obscenities grew more expressive as he realised he had knocked over the vase of flowers Runham insisted on leaving on his cousin's grave. Bartholomew lit the lamp quickly, and went to the monk's rescue before he did any more damage. While he gathered up the wilting blooms and shoved them back into the now dented jug, Michael slapped the sacred vessels on the altar in an undisguised display of temper, limping far more than was necessary, and not always favouring the same foot.

Michael had completed his preparations and Bartholomew had just kicked the flowers that remained on the floor out of sight under a bench, when the Michaelhouse procession entered the church, sleepy and shivering in their scholar's tabards – with the exception of Alcote, who was clad in a gorgeous, fur-lined cloak that an earl would have been proud to wear.

Father William's leather-soled sandals skidded in the water that had been spilled from the vase, and he gazed up at the roof in concern, seeking signs of another leak. Runham frowned when he saw the state of his blooms, as many stalks pointing upwards as flower heads, and Bartholomew heard him muttering disparaging remarks about the parish children who sometimes played in the church when it was empty.

Because it was the festival of the Conversion of St Paul, and therefore a feast day, a few parishioners had dragged themselves from their beds to attend the mass. Most of them were members of Michael's choir, present because the College provided oatmeal and sour ale to anyone who sang on special occasions. Also present were Thomas Deschalers and his niece Julianna. Julianna stood at the front of the small congregation, watching everything with open interest. She caught Bartholomew's eye and gave him a wink, and then did the same to Langelee. Afraid that the philosopher would see her smiling at him so brazenly and start some kind of fight over it, Bartholomew studiously avoided looking at her for the remainder of the service.

When it was over, he waited until he was sure her attentions were fixed on Langelee, and then slipped past her quickly to walk back to Michaelhouse, without waiting for his colleagues. As he shoved open the wicket door, Walter started guiltily, and Agatha's cockerel flapped out from under his arm. It rushed across the yard in a huff of bristling feathers and disappeared over the orchard wall. Bartholomew said nothing, although he suspected that he and Michael were not the only ones that the irritating bird was keeping from their sleep.

Master Kenyngham's procession – with the marked absence of Langelee – was not long in following, and Walter went to ring the bell for breakfast. Bartholomew was in his room, putting dirty clothes in a pile for Cynric to take to the laundry, and folding the others, when the book-bearer tapped on the door.

'A messenger has just arrived to say that Master Stanmore's steward returned with Egil's body late last night,' said the Welshman. 'Master Stanmore and your sister have spent the night in town, and he wants you and Brother Michael to go to his premises immediately.'

'Now?' asked Bartholomew, thinking about the warm oatmeal flavoured with honey and cinnamon that would be waiting for him in the hall. 'Can it not wait a while?'

'It sounded urgent,' said Cynric. 'Master Stanmore would not issue such a demand lightly.'

Bartholomew sighed and told Cynric to fetch Michael, who was already at his place at the breakfast table. He waited in the yard and shivered. It was beginning to rain: the dry spell of the past two days seemed to be over, and the weather was reverting to its customary dampness. He leaned against the wall and kicked absently at the weeds that grew around the door. He saw Father Paul walking hesitantly from his room to the hall, and he went to offer him his arm when the blind friar skidded in the mud.

Paul smiled. 'How cold you are!' he exclaimed, taking Bartholomew's hand in both of his.

'A problem with winter,' said Bartholomew. 'Especially with no fires anywhere and Alcote the only one of us with enough money to buy wood to burn.'

'Then you should inveigle yourself an invitation to his room,' said Paul wisely. 'Not only does he have roaring fires, but he has a lamp and comfortable chairs with woollen rugs.'

'He is still indignant about three logs he thinks I stole,' said Bartholomew ruefully. It was a shame, though: it would be worth enduring Alcote's company for the pleasure of sitting in a comfortable chair by a fire with a lamp to read by.

'Brother Michael took those logs,' said Paul. 'I quite clearly heard his distinctive puffing as he wrested with the stable door the night they disappeared. I put Alcote right about that, although you should not allow yourself to take the blame for things Michael does.'

Bartholomew smiled, amused that Paul should consider him in need of advice about how to deal with Michael.

Still clutching Bartholomew's hand, Paul lifted his face to

the sky. 'It is beginning to rain; you are about to go out and you are not wearing your cloak.'

'And how do you know all that?' asked Bartholomew, laughing. He knew the friar relished playing such games, showing off his superior skills of detection.

'The rain is simple,' said Paul, showing an upturned palm. 'I know you are going out because I heard Michael grumbling about missing breakfast; you are apparently waiting for him, which means you are going, too. And I know you are not wearing your cloak, because I would hear it moving around your legs. And I cannot.'

'I lost it,' said Bartholomew. 'Shall I tell you how, or will you tell me?'

It was Paul's turn to laugh. 'Tell me when Brother Michael is not glowering at you to hurry,' he said. Bartholomew gazed at him in surprise. 'I just heard his thundering footsteps coming down the stairs from his room,' Paul explained.

Bartholomew looked to where Michael waited impatiently by the gate.

'I have several cloaks,' said Paul. 'I insist you borrow one.'

'Thank you,' said Bartholomew, 'but I could not. First, I do not seem able to take good care of clothes and will be sure to spoil it. Second, I cannot wear a cloak that is part of a Franciscan habit – Father William would construe it as heretical, and would have me burned in the Market Square.'

'It is just a plain grey one,' said Paul. 'It is not part of my habit. And, as I said, I have several. If you find you like it, I can sell you one.'

The rain began to come down harder, and Bartholomew relented and accepted Paul's kind offer. He waited while the friar fetched it, and then ran across to meet Michael.

'Oh, very nice,' said Michael, eyeing the long garment with amusement. 'Now you look like one of the Four Horsemen of the Apocalypse. Pestilence!' He laughed uproariously, while Cynric crossed himself hurriedly, and muttered about the dangers of jesting about the plague.

Stanmore had left an apprentice to direct them to the room to which Egil's body had been taken. It was an empty storeroom, and the corpse had been placed on a table and covered with a large piece of black cloth. Bartholomew saw dark red stains on the floor, and winced. Edith was ushering the fascinated apprentices away from the window, but when she saw Bartholomew she abandoned them to their own devices, and ran into his arms.

'Oh Matt!' she sobbed. 'What vile business have you been dragged into this time?'

'It will all be solved soon,' said Bartholomew gently.

She wiped her eyes and stood back to look at him. 'How did you come by those scratches on your neck? This is not your cloak! And who put that awful red patch on your hose?'

Bartholomew put his hands on her shoulders. 'There is nothing to worry about. And I borrowed this cloak from Father Paul. I lost mine.'

'It is fine cloth,' said Stanmore, coming up behind him to feel it. 'Best quality wool. He is a fool to lend it to you – you will have it spoiled in no time. I would recommend you use a hard-wearing Worsted of some kind, perhaps—'

'Oswald,' prompted Edith, quelling the lecture that was about to begin. 'We did not drag Matt from his breakfast to talk about cloth.'

Stanmore's face became sombre. 'I know,' he said softly. 'Putting off the moment, I suppose.' He cleared his throat. 'It took some time to find Egil's corpse – your directions were understandably vague, and my steward had to make three journeys to the Fens before he could locate it. It had been moved, and Cynric's stick-marker was some distance away from it. It is Egil's body, without question, because I recall he had a prominent scar on his left calf. But . . .' His voice trailed off, and his eyes went to the body lying on the table. Since Stanmore made no move towards it, and was clearly reluctant to offer a further explanation, Bartholomew walked over and lifted the cloth. And drew in a sharp breath of horror. Egil's heavy body, clad in its thick, homespun clothes, lay under the sheet. But someone had hacked off his head and both of his hands.

'I take it this is not how you left him?' asked Stanmore, watching Bartholomew's expression of shock. 'You said he had been hit on the head. You did not say the blow had taken his skull from his shoulders.'

Michael took a cautious peep and backed away hastily. Bartholomew inspected the rest of the body, and then covered it again with the cloth. There were no other injuries. He thought about what Tulyet had said – that Egil was a Fenman who knew his way around the area. If Egil had not been lying injured for two days – and there was nothing on what remained of his corpse to suggest that he had – then where had he been? And what had he been doing? Bartholomew wondered if Egil had somehow stumbled on an outlaw lair, and had been fleeing from them when he had his fatal encounter with the aggressive Julianna.

'Who could have done this?' asked Stanmore, looking at the corpse with a shudder. 'Do you think the mutilation might be related to some satanic ritual?'

'Well, I think we know who did it,' said Michael, his face pale. 'Some of these Fenland smugglers – such as that Alan of Norwich and his men. What we do not know is why, although I cannot believe the answer lies in witchcraft.'

They were silent, and the only sounds were the apprentices shuffling and whispering outside, daring each other to sneak a look through the window. One, bolder than his fellows, hauled himself up onto the sill, his feet scrabbling against the wall. Stanmore pursed his lips and closed the shutters firmly.

'Youthful curiosity,' he said, shutting the door as well. 'And Rob is always the first.'

'He looks familiar,' said Bartholomew, the young man's long, thin nose and hooded eyes ringing the same bell of recognition he had experienced the last time he had seen him in Stanmore's yard. He shook his head. 'I have probably seen him working here.'

'Probably not,' said Stanmore. 'He is more often at my shop in Ely, although business has not been good there and I have had him here for the past few weeks. He is Robert Thorpe's boy.'

Bartholomew and Michael looked blankly at him. 'Robert Thorpe,' repeated Stanmore. 'The disgraced Master of Valence Marie. The elder Thorpe took to teaching when his wife died, and he left his son in the care of relatives. They apprenticed him to me when he declared he did not want to follow in his sire's footsteps and become a scholar.'

'Who can blame him, given what happened to his father,' said Michael. He scratched his chin thoughtfully. 'Yes. There is a resemblance now that you mention it – around the eyes and nose.'

'No!' said Bartholomew suddenly, his raised voice making the others jump. 'That is not it. I remember where I saw him before.'

He walked briskly to the door and flung it open. The group of apprentices was startled into silence as Bartholomew strode purposefully towards Rob Thorpe. Thorpe stood his ground, looking insolently at Bartholomew, but his nerve failed him at the last moment, and he made a sudden dart towards the gate. Bartholomew was anticipating such a move, however, and reacted quickly. He dived after the young man and had a good handful of his tunic before he had reached the lane.

Stanmore ran towards them, followed by the others.

'What is happening?' he demanded. 'Matt! Leave him alone! You are frightening him.'

'I know exactly where I have seen you before,' said Bartholomew, not relinquishing his hold on Thorpe's clothes. 'You were standing behind Grene at Bingham's installation. You helped me carry his body to the chapel.'

'Not me!' protested Thorpe, struggling free of Bartholomew's grip. He brushed himself down indignantly, small eyes flicking from Bartholomew to Stanmore. 'I was here all night.'

The other apprentices, who had clustered round to watch the excitement, nodded, although Bartholomew noted not all did so with conviction.

'You were not,' he said firmly. 'You were at the installation, wearing a light blue tabard and serving wine at the high table.'

Thorpe brandished a handful of his dark green tunic at Bartholomew with a sneer. 'Does this look light blue to you? And before you ask, I have another and that is green, too. You can go and look if you want.'

'Matt!' said Stanmore, trying to pull Bartholomew away. 'The lad is telling the truth. You know that all my apprentices' tunics are this colour. It helps me to keep an eye on them in a crowd.'

Bartholomew grabbed Thorpe by the scruff of the neck. 'We are going to see Harling.'

'Whatever for?' said Stanmore, indignant for his apprentice. 'You have heard what Rob has to say. He has done nothing wrong.'

'If he has done nothing wrong, why did he try to run away from me?' demanded Bartholomew.

'I would have run if I had seen you bearing down on me like something from hell!' retorted Stanmore, becoming irate. He tried to prise Bartholomew's fingers from his apprentice's collar. Bartholomew pushed him away, and took a few steps towards the gate, the wriggling Thorpe firmly in his grasp.

Edith blocked his way. 'Matthew, let him go!' she ordered,

incensed. Startled by the fury in her voice, Bartholomew obeyed. 'Rob has told you he was here on Saturday night and the other apprentices have supported his claim. They have no reason to lie. Do you think I would not have noticed one of our lads serving at the installation? Or Oswald?'

She had a point. Bartholomew backed away, and Stanmore ushered the apprentices out of the yard and back to work.

The merchant turned to Bartholomew, his temper only just under control. 'I suppose you are still thinking about that accusation of Father Philius's – that he came here to see one of my apprentices die? Well, I hear Philius is dead himself – murdered in fact – and so it is quite clear that he is involved in all this foul business, and was lying to you. Look to him and to his acquaintances for your poisoner, but leave my lads alone! Rob is a good boy. If you cannot bring yourself to believe your own family, then you can ask the priests at St Botolph's Church; he does odd jobs for them in his spare time and they think very highly of him.'

Bartholomew had rarely seen Stanmore so enraged and certainly never with him. He looked at Edith, standing with her hands on her hips and regarding him furiously. Edith had always taken a close interest in the apprentices, and she watched over them like a mother hen. Her instinct to protect one of them now was apparently stronger than her trust in her brother's accusations. Bartholomew glanced over her head to where Thorpe walked with his friends towards the kitchens. The apprentice twisted round and favoured Bartholomew with a triumphant sneer that was anything but innocent.

'He is the deposed Master Thorpe's son, and he was at the installation,' said Bartholomew, goaded into making rash accusations by Thorpe's gloating. 'He is the killer of poor James Grene!'

Edith and Stanmore gaped at him.

'That seems to represent something of a leap in logic,' remarked Michael, his eyebrows almost disappearing under his hair in his astonishment. He leaned over and whispered in Bartholomew's ear. 'Have a care, Matt. You are distressing your sister.'

'Rob is seventeen years old!' said Edith hotly. 'How can you accuse a young lad of so vile a crime? First, he was here all night and nowhere near Valence Marie. Second, he has alibis to prove it. Third, how would he come by poisoned wine with which to kill anyway? Fourth, Oswald and I would have seen him had he been at the installation – which he was not. And, fifth, since you seem to believe that wicked Father Philius rather than Oswald, you imply that our household is involved in something sinister.'

'No!' exclaimed Bartholomew, shocked. 'I only—'

Edith cut across his words. 'I think it would be best if you left us now, Matthew. Go and catch your poisoner. But you will not be welcome in our house again if you come only to make horrible accusations. And if I see you anywhere near Rob Thorpe, I will tell Tulyet to arrest you for assaulting a child!'

She turned on her heel and stalked across the yard to the kitchen. After a moment, Stanmore followed. The door slammed, and Bartholomew and Michael were left standing alone in the yard.

'You handled that well,' remarked Michael, beginning to walk away.

Bartholomew was rooted to the spot. 'She believes I am trying to implicate Oswald in all this,' he whispered, appalled.

Michael took his sleeve and steered him out of the yard. 'She spoke in anger,' he said soothingly. 'She will come to her senses in a day or two. And anyway, you *did* imply you did not believe her or Oswald when they told you Rob Thorpe was not at the installation.'

'I have never seen her so fierce,' said Bartholomew, still shocked.

'I have,' said Michael, with a wry smile. 'And so have you

if you allow yourself to admit it – only last week, in fact, when she caught that water-seller using the well near the river after you had told people not to drink from it. She had the man terrified out of his meagre wits. What you have *not* seen, Matt, is her ire directed towards you. Now you know how the rest of us feel when your beloved sister goes on the rampage.'

'You make her sound like a tyrant,' said Bartholomew resentfully. 'She is not.'

'She has a quick temper,' said Michael. 'And you rashly attacked one of her charges. But her wrath is always short-lived, and all will be well again tomorrow. Now, we both have duties to perform that we have been neglecting while we have been here – you should ascertain what caused Gray to put on such a disgraceful performance at his disputation, and give Bulbeck his medicine. Then, at noon you should come to dine with me in the Brazen George. It is time we treated ourselves to a little decent refreshment, and we need to talk undisturbed. Cynric?'

The small Welshman appeared behind him.

'Watch Master Stanmore's gates and tell us when Rob Thorpe emerges. If we are not teaching in College, we will be in the chapel. You know which one I mean.' He winked meaningfully.

Cynric gave him a knowing grin and trotted away, leaving Bartholomew bewildered. He tried to make Michael tell him what was happening, but the fat monk would say nothing.

Several hours later, they were comfortably settled in a pleasant chamber at the rear of the Brazen George, with a plateful of lamb and boiled onions. The room was one of Michael's favourite haunts when inclement weather rendered the garden impractical. The taverner kept it free for the exclusive use of ranking scholars who should not have been there, and there was a small door that led directly out into an alley that ran perpendicular to the High Street, thus allowing discreet exits to be made should an occasion arise when it became necessary. It was a comfortable place – small and cosy, with a fire burning cheerfully in a brazier and colourful tapestries hanging on the walls. The beaten-earth floor was liberally scattered with reeds collected daily from the river bank, while bowls of herbs on the window sill made the chamber smell clean and fragrant.

'I call this the chapel,' said Michael, gesturing around him with a grin. 'It is an excellent place for uninterrupted contemplation, where the troubled spirit can be restored with a good meal and a goblet or two of fine wine.'

Bartholomew was about to speak, when the landlord entered, bringing a dish of dried figs, which he presented with a flourish.

'Try these, Brother,' he said ingratiatingly to Michael. 'They are quite delicious.'

'What are they?' asked Michael suspiciously, poking at the wizened brown objects with the handle of his spoon, as if he imagined they might leap up and devour him.

'I have no idea,' admitted the taverner. 'My wife bought them yesterday, but she says they are quite the fashion at the King's table.'

'The King can keep them!' muttered Michael ungraciously. 'I would rather have some tart, if you have it. And not one made of these things! Apple. Or sugared pears. Something normal.'

The landlord left, crestfallen, while Michael regarded the figs with a shudder.

'They look as though someone has eaten them already,' he said, pushing them away.

Bartholomew frowned. 'Lemons at the feast at Valence Marie; pomegranates at Michaelhouse; sugared almonds at Deschalers's house; oranges at Denny Abbey. The whole town seems flooded with unusual foods. Deschalers must be making a fortune. Winter is usually a time when only apples left over from the summer are available. Now every house in Cambridge is attempting to dine like the King. Even Agatha was persuaded to buy a pomegranate and she did not even know what to do with it!'

'You will be having problems with people's digestions if they go round eating this kind of thing,' said Michael, pushing the figs further away from him.

Bartholomew stared at him, a notion beginning to unfold in his mind.

But Michael was speaking. 'You were right about that snivelling apprentice Rob Thorpe, Matt,' he said. 'He *was* at the installation. I saw him too.'

CHAPTER 9

'**B**UT WHY DID YOU NOT SAY YOU SAW ROB THORPE at the installation ceremony?' cried Bartholomew angrily, leaping to his feet and sending the figs scattering over the table in the little room at the back of the Brazen George. 'You might have saved me that ugly scene with Edith!'

'Your family is in fine form today,' said Michael with irritating calm. 'This morning Oswald and Edith holler at you and now you yell at me. Sit down and drink some ale. I will explain if you let me.'

'I do not want any ale!' snapped Bartholomew. 'Just tell me what game you are playing now.'

'No game,' said Michael, suddenly serious. 'Lives are at stake here, Matt: Bingham's for one. As soon as you had collared that young rat Thorpe, I knew you were right: it *was* him at the installation behind Grene, and he did indeed help you carry Grene's body to the chapel. Yet he was different – his hair was black, not light brown, and his eyebrows were darker and heavier. He had disguised himself. And Edith was wrong when she said she would have noticed him at the installation – she was not expecting him to be there and so she had no reason to look. The hall at Valence Marie is huge and with all those people crushed into it, it is not surprising that she failed to notice a single servant at a table a long way from her own.'

'Could you not have pointed this out to her?' asked

Bartholomew bitterly. 'It might have gone some way to making her believe I am not an ogre blaming a murder on an innocent child.'

Michael took a hearty mouthful of meat and swallowed it with the most superficial of chews. Bartholomew watched in distaste as the monk wiped the grease from his mouth on his sleeve and turned his attentions to the onions bobbing around in the thick gravy.

'I tried to stop you from continuing with your accusations, Matt,' he said, in the same maddeningly tranquil voice. 'I knew Edith and Oswald would never believe ill of one of their apprentices: they treat them like their own children. But you insisted in blundering on.'

Bartholomew wanted to grab him by the front of his habit and yell at him to stop being so infuriatingly smug. He chewed at his lip and wondered about the number of times he had recently felt moved to violence – towards Julianna for her attitude to Egil; towards Langelee for goading him about Matilde; towards Rob Thorpe for his gloating smile; and now even towards Michael.

'It was better that I said nothing,' Michael continued placidly. 'Rob Thorpe would simply have continued to deny the accusations, and had I told Edith that I, too, had seen him at the installation, she would have assumed I was lying to support you. Nothing I could have said would have made any difference.'

'So what do we do now?' demanded Bartholomew. He sat down with an exhausted sigh. 'What a mess!'

'We wait,' said Michael, taking another mouthful of boiled onions and smiling at his friend.

'Wait for what?' asked Bartholomew, putting his elbows on the table and resting his chin in his hands. 'For Thorpe to deliver us a bottle of poisoned wine? I might be tempted to drink it: I have had my fill of all this subterfuge.'

'Now, now,' said Michael, gently chiding. 'What would Matilde do without you?' He favoured Bartholomew with one of his leering winks and coaxed the ghost of a smile from his morose friend. 'But, meanwhile, we will wait for Rob Thorpe to go running off to the person who led him into all this murder and mayhem in the first place – his accomplice!'

Bartholomew lifted his head. 'And what makes you so sure there is such a person?'

'As your sister pointed out, Thorpe is seventeen years old. He would hardly be able to get himself into Valence Marie for the night without help.'

'So you *do* think he killed Grene?'

'Without a doubt,' said Michael, waving a greasy hand in the air. 'Although I cannot believe he did so alone. Gray and his cronies claim they saw an apprentice buying wine from Sacks on a Saturday night about a month ago. Philius was summoned to Stanmore's house later that night because someone there was stricken by an ailment – which you and he later discovered had the same symptoms of the poisonings of Grene and Armel. I suspect that the apprentice was Thorpe and that he probably bought the wine in total innocence. Then, another lad drank the wine Thorpe bought and died most horribly. It was his death that gave Thorpe the idea of killing Grene.'

'But wait a moment!' said Bartholomew. 'This is all very well. But what of the motive? Why should Thorpe want Grene dead? Why not Bingham who, after all, was the man elected into the position left vacant by his father's dismissal?'

Michael rubbed hard at the whiskers that stubbled his jowls, making a rasping sound. 'By killing Grene, Thorpe has struck a blow at both rivals for his father's position, not just one,' he said. 'Grene is dead and it is Bingham who is accused of his murder.'

Bartholomew considered. 'But if Isaac took the poisoned wine from Thorpe – and we know he did because Philius saw him – how did Thorpe acquire another bottle with which to kill Grene?'

'We can surmise he bought two bottles from Sacks,' said Michael. 'Gray said Sacks had six bottles initially. A few weeks later, Sacks was still trying to sell four of them. Four, Matt, not five.'

'I see,' said Bartholomew. 'So Thorpe bought two bottles – Isaac stole one and the other came briefly into our possession after it had killed Grene at the feast. Armel bought three – stolen from us at Michaelhouse. Which leaves one. Whoever has that will be in for an unpleasant shock.'

'We must to talk to Sacks,' said Michael. 'If we can discover to whom he sold the sixth bottle, we may yet save a life. I have had two beadles looking for him since this business began, but he seems to have fled the town. And who can blame him, given what he has done?'

'This accomplice of Thorpe's,' said Bartholomew, unable to banish the vision of the apprentice's gloating face from his mind, 'do you think it may be Father Eligius at Valence Marie?'

Michael puffed out his cheeks, and nodded. 'I must confess, it has crossed my mind. We have already discussed the possibility that Eligius had a hand in Grene's death.'

'We know Eligius is a firm believer that Bingham is responsible for Grene's murder,' said Bartholomew thoughtfully. 'He even arranged to have Bingham arrested – and he wanted it done with such haste that he could not even wait until you had finished looking into that burglary at St Clement's Hostel, and asked the Sheriff to do it instead.'

'True,' said Michael. 'And what better way to hide his own guilt than to blame someone else? And, if you remember, Eligius was also the first Fellow to claim that Grene had confided that he was in fear of his life from Bingham.'

'But what of the other two Fellows who claimed Grene had made a similar confession to them?' asked Bartholomew uncertainly. 'Do you think they are lying, too?'

'"Claimed" is the pertinent word,' said Michael. 'Once

Eligius stated that Grene had confessed himself in fear of his life, the other two might have thought back to conversations they had with Grene and read a significance into his words that was never there. Eligius is a brilliant logician, skilled at wrapping the arguments of others around their ears with his word-play. I imagine it would be easy for him to plant doubts in the minds of the others about supposed hidden meanings in Grene's statements.'

'All very well,' said Bartholomew. 'But I still cannot see why a renowned scholar like Eligius should risk all to help some apprentice commit murder.'

'If we knew that, we would have the evidence we need to tackle him,' said Michael. 'But it would have been simple for him, as a Fellow of Valence Marie, to help Rob Thorpe to slip into the College and to secure him a place near Grene at the high table. Then Thorpe could have given Grene the poisoned wine unobtrusively.'

They were silent for a while, thinking about what they had reasoned. Bartholomew wondered whether a seventeen-year-old apprentice would be able to conceive and execute such a plan alone and decided it was unlikely. In which case, why should Eligius help Thorpe in his warped desire for vengeance? It seemed a dangerous game to play, especially if Thorpe's nerve broke and he revealed the identity of his accomplice to the Proctors.

When Bartholomew and Michael had been examining Grene's body in St Botolph's Church, Eligius had made it clear that he believed Bingham to be responsible. Was that to ensure Michael's investigation concentrated on Bingham, and did not attempt to seek other possible culprits? But the niggling doubt at the back of Bartholomew's mind was Eligius's apparent lack of motive. Bartholomew could conceive of no earthly reason why Eligius should want to rid Valence Marie of Grene and Bingham in so dramatic a manner, just because he was unimpressed with their intellectual abilities. He had not wanted the Mastership for himself or he would have taken it when it had been offered to him.

Bartholomew turned his thoughts to the wine. 'There are aspects to this poison I do not understand,' he said aloud. 'I saw that cat drink from the broken bottle and it did not die; but the rat did, instantly. And Philius became ill from the poison, but he did not die, despite the fact that it was strong enough to cause that burn on Isaac's hand.'

'Armel seems to have died as quickly as Grene,' said Michael. 'And the porter at Valence Marie, who was overly curious about the three bottles we left in his care, also burned his hand on them. Perhaps Philius and the cat had a greater resistance to the poison than had Grene and Armel. You are always telling me that people react differently to the same disease and the same treatments.'

'But not usually to poisons,' said Bartholomew. 'At least, not to that extent. A poison strong enough to kill a person from a single sip is hardly likely to have no effect at all on a cat. But we still do not know why Sacks sold this poisoned wine in the first place. Gray says Sacks often sells stolen goods to students, so he would hardly want to deprive himself of their custom by killing them. He must have stolen them from someone else.'

'That is it!' said Michael, clicking his fingers with sudden insight. 'Of course! You have it! He stole them. They were never meant to be sold around the town taverns, and that is why someone went to such pains to retrieve them – as you pointed out days ago. Someone wanted the evidence back. This is beginning to make sense.'

'Not to me,' said Bartholomew. 'So, what you are suggesting is that Sacks stole these six bottles of wine and began selling them in the Brazen George. Thorpe and his cronies, perhaps out of fear of Oswald's anger at their disobedience, covered up the death of the apprentice Oswald denies losing. Thorpe kept the second bottle to use at a later date—'

'And that meant that the people trying to retrieve their

wine would have no clue where to look,' interrupted Michael, nodding. 'There were no tales of sudden and violent death for four weeks to reveal the bottles' whereabouts – although Sacks sold the first of the wine four weeks ago, the first public death did not occur until last Saturday.'

He took a bone from his plate and gnawed it thoughtfully, while Bartholomew watched him, wondering whether all their reasoning was correct. Michael waved the bone in the air and continued.

'At the installation I did not announce the fact that I had taken the bottle from which Grene had been drinking to look for poison, but I did not take it with stealth. Anyone might have seen me remove it. I imagine that, first, these people went to Michaelhouse, where they found not one but four of their bottles. Then they went to Gonville Hall where they retrieved the fifth one and killed Isaac at the same time.'

'But why go to Gonville at all?' asked Bartholomew. 'No one knew that Philius had been poisoned until I diagnosed it. And why was Isaac's death so brutal?'

Michael shrugged and then stretched his meaty arms. 'I confess I do not know. But we have made good headway with this mystery. At least we have the answer to some of our questions.'

'But not the identities of the people trying to kill us,' said Bartholomew glumly. 'And not why someone chopped Egil's head and hands from his body. Nor why Eligius should help a misguided adolescent commit murder. And I am still uncomfortable with the roles Colton and Julianna are playing in all this.'

'And we know a little of the smugglers that my grandmother uncovered,' said Michael, ignoring Bartholomew's pessimism. He gestured at the figs. 'The town is flooded with foods not normally seen at this time of year. Deschalers is a grocer – these figs, lemons, nuts and Agatha's pomegranate must have come from him. I am not sure I believe

Deschalers's claim that he stores them in his cellars. Gathers them from the Fens, more like.'

'Deschalers said he did not know the smugglers were operating in the area around Denny,' said Bartholomew slowly, 'suggesting that he knows about smuggling elsewhere. Was his name one of the ones Dame Pelagia gave to Tulyet?'

Michael waved his hand expansively. 'No, but once Tulyet has a couple of these smugglers in his cells, they will soon reveal who the ringleaders are. He should be rounding them up even as we speak.' He swirled the wine around in his cup as Bartholomew paced restlessly.

'I do not see why the mutilation of Egil was necessary,' said Bartholomew. 'The man was dead. There was nothing to be gained from it. Unless . . .'

'Unless what?' asked Michael, looking up from his wine.

'Something Deynman said,' said Bartholomew, frowning.

'I can tell I am about to be treated to some great pearl of wisdom,' said Michael drily. 'What could Deynman say that would possibly stick in your mind?'

'When he was asked how he would treat a head wound in his disputation, he said he would poke about in it to make certain there was nothing more serious hidden underneath.'

'Oh, Matt!' said Michael with a face of disgust. 'The boy is deranged. I take it you did not teach him that? God forbid he should ever come near me if I am injured!'

'But what he says might make sense in the case of Egil,' said Bartholomew, sitting down abruptly. 'I wonder if that was why his head was taken – to hide another wound.'

'But we saw the wound,' said Michael. 'A great soggy mess at the back of his skull where sweet Julianna brained him.'

'No, not that wound,' said Bartholomew. 'But there might have been others. Like blisters in his mouth and burns on his hands.'

Michael stared at him. 'What are you saying? That Egil was poisoned?'

Bartholomew stood and began to pace again. 'No. He could not have been – he was certainly not lacking in strength when he fought me. Forget what I said. It was foolish and implausible, even for this unsavoury affair.'

'But removing a head from a corpse is an implausible action,' said Michael, leaning forward with his elbows on the table. 'Let us think through this notion of yours, before dismissing it out of hand. Tulyet and Stanmore said that Egil was a Fenman – and we know smuggling has been a source of income for Fenland families for generations. It is entirely possible that Egil was involved in smuggling. You saw his body, and you said there were no injuries – other than the fact that he was missing his head and hands – so it seems he was not harmed as Alan and his men attacked us. In which case, we can assume that he was known to them. It is even possible he was sent to hunt us down after we escaped the fire at Denny.'

'And so his head and hands were taken because his associates were afraid that they might reveal something to us,' said Bartholomew. 'They did not take his clothes, so it was clearly not his identity that they were trying to hide. I keep coming back to the poisoned wine and tell-tale burns. It is the only reason I can think of for which these people might go to such extremes.'

The door opened silently and Cynric stepped lightly into the room. Abandoning the remains of his repast, Michael stood to greet him, his eyebrows raised expectantly.

'I was afraid I would lose Rob Thorpe if I stopped to fetch you first,' said Cynric without preamble, 'so I followed him to see where he went.'

'And where did he go?' asked Michael, folding his arms, and throwing a superior glance at Bartholomew. 'Now we will see, my friend. I wager you anything you like that Rob Thorpe will have fled straight to his accomplice to discuss how best to deal with the unwanted attentions of the Senior Proctor and his colleagues.'

'No, he did not,' said Cynric. 'He went to St Botolph's Church. He knelt at the altar for a while – alone – and then he went back to Master Stanmore's house without having spoken to anyone.'

'Nothing!' spat Michael in disgust at breakfast the following day, ignoring the admonishing looks of Alcote and Father William for speaking. 'Cynric watched Oswald Stanmore's premises all night and Rob Thorpe did not so much as put a foot outside. Are you certain there is no other way out?'

Bartholomew nodded. 'The only door is at the front. Perhaps we are wrong and Thorpe has no ally at Valence Marie after all. Perhaps Edith and Oswald are right and we are mistaken.'

'We are not mistaken!' snapped Michael in frustration, drawing further disapproving glares from his colleagues and the interested attentions of the students at the next table. He grabbed a lump of bread made from grey, grainy flour and gnawed at it so that crumbs snowed down the front of his habit. 'Gray and the others saw Thorpe buying the poisoned wine from Sacks; Father Philius attended a dead apprentice at Stanmore's business premises; you and I know it was Thorpe who helped us carry Grene's body from Valence Marie's hall. Even if we have misinterpreted some of the facts, the evidence that remains is overwhelming: Thorpe is involved in Grene's death without question. And he could not have gained access to Valence Marie without help.'

'I wonder why he went to St Botolph's,' said Bartholomew, deliberately not looking at Alcote, who was trying to catch his eye to warn him against talking without breaking silence himself. Had he not been discussing something as sombre as murder, Bartholomew would have found his antics amusing. On Alcote's other side, the surly Langelee sipped his watered ale carefully, his red-rimmed eyes and unsteady hands suggesting he was not in much of a condition to care whether his colleagues talked during the meal or not, as long as they kept their voices low.

Next to Kenyngham, whose anger of the previous day had faded so that he was back to his usual absent-minded geniality, Runham regarded the restless students with his heavily lidded eyes. Gray stared back, although even his insolence and confidence was no match for Runham, and he was the first to look away. Runham shifted his gaze to Deynman who, knowing he was in disgrace for failing his disputation, at least had the grace to turn red and shuffle his feet uncomfortably on the floor.

'Oh, why Thorpe went to church is no mystery,' replied Michael with a flap of a flabby hand. 'I spoke to the priests there last night – just as your brother-in-law advised us to do. Thorpe earns extra pennies by sweeping their church, and apparently, over the last few weeks, has taken to haunting the place even when there is no sweeping to be done. He told the priests that he likes to be there to escape from the childish behaviour of Stanmore's younger apprentices.'

'So, what shall we do next?' asked Bartholomew, sipping Michaelhouse's cloudy breakfast ale with a grimace. 'Cynric needs to rest, and I am not going to watch Oswald's house all day. Supposing Edith spotted me?'

Michael leaned plump elbows on the table and sighed. 'Perhaps Tulyet's excursions of the past two days will yield some results. At least we no longer need to worry about the smugglers – that is in his hands now.'

'We certainly do need to worry, Brother,' said Bartholomew fervently. 'They tried to kill us, and I will continue to worry until I am certain they are all secured in Tulyet's prison cells.'

They stood for grace, and then trailed across the muddy yard towards their rooms. It was almost six o'clock and time for teaching to begin, but Bartholomew felt strangely apathetic towards it. Bulbeck's failure – whatever the excuse – had been an unpleasant shock, and he wondered whether

Langelee was right, and that he should concentrate more on teaching traditional medicine than on telling his students his own theories – regardless of his personal beliefs.

Just as this thought crossed Bartholomew's mind, Langelee swaggered towards them, and intercepted their perilous journey across the morass that claimed to be Michaelhouse's courtyard. He went through an elaborate pantomime of showing Bartholomew his hands, to prove that he was unarmed and that the physician had no need to draw his own weapon. Bartholomew raised his eyes heavenwards, and tried to walk past him without speaking. Langelee grabbed his shoulder, and Bartholomew flinched backwards at the strong smell of wine that wafted into his face. No wonder he had been fragile at breakfast – he was still drunk from the night before.

'I wondered if I might borrow the copy of Aristotle's *De Caelo* that you have been hogging all term,' he said, with an unpleasant smile. 'I am to be the presiding master at a public debate, the title of which is "Let us enquire whether the world is created or eternal", and I need to refresh my memory about what Aristotle says on the matter.'

'It is my own copy, not Michaelhouse's,' said Bartholomew. 'But you may borrow it if you like. I find it a difficult text, and would like to come to listen to your debate.'

Michael seized the physician's sleeve and tried to pull him away, guessing that Bartholomew's motive for attending Langelee's debate would not be to learn. *De Caelo* was one of Bartholomew's favourite books, and the fact that it was one of only two texts he owned meant that he knew it inside out. Michael knew Bartholomew and Langelee well enough to predict which one would emerge victorious from a battle of intellects and which one would be left looking foolish.

He saw Kenyngham watching them from the window of his chamber, and sensed, once again, that Bartholomew should steer clear of encounters with Langelee if he wanted to continue to teach at Michaelhouse. He tightened his grip on Bartholomew's sleeve.

Langelee looked surprised – both at Bartholomew's request and Michael's reaction. He narrowed his eyes. 'You should come to hear me,' he said. 'You might learn something, although it is a difficult question and you probably will not understand all the arguments I make.'

'Really?' asked Bartholomew guilelessly. 'And which of the two positions do you believe is the more viable: that the world was created or that it is eternal?'

'That it is infinite,' said Langelee without hesitation. 'Any fool can see that. Otherwise everything in nature would have a much newer feel to it – like rivers and rocks and the oceans.'

'But that would mean that the world had no beginning,' said Bartholomew, trying to disengage his arm from Michael's insistent tug. 'And, the logical conclusion to be drawn from that is that an infinite number of celestial revolutions must have occurred to bring us to the present. But, because an infinite number of revolutions can never be completed, it stands that the revolution we are in now cannot have been reached. And that, of course, is absurd.'

'Eh?' said Langelee, blinking.

'And further,' said Bartholomew, prising Michael's fingers from his sleeve, 'as St Bonaventure argues, if an infinite number of revolutions have occurred until the present, the ones that will occur tomorrow will have to be added to that infinite number, which, I think you will agree, is impossible.'

'I . . . well,' said Langelee uncertainly.

'That is enough, Matt,' said Michael sharply, glancing up to where Kenyngham watched them from the window of his room. 'Master Langelee is perfectly capable of refuting St Bonaventure's arguments should he so desire. We all know that neither the creation of the world nor its eternity are scientifically demonstrable – as indeed Thomas Aquinas

points out – and that, as such, they are equally probable.'
He grabbed Bartholomew's tabard again.

'Hmm,' said Langelee non-committally.

'If we cannot discuss philosophy, then perhaps we can talk about common acquaintances,' said Bartholomew pleasantly, still attempting to extricate himself from Michael's grip. 'I hear you are acquainted with Julianna, the Abbess of Denny's niece.'

Langelee's eyes narrowed again. 'So? At least she is not a harlot like your Matilde. She is also the niece of Thomas Deschalers the merchant, and so is very well connected.'

'She is betrothed to Edward Mortimer,' said Bartholomew. 'Did you know that?'

The suspicion vanished from Langelee's face to be replaced by patent disbelief. 'What? Julianna is not betrothed to anyone!'

'You are right. She is not,' said Michael, hauling on Bartholomew's gown so hard that there was a sharp snap of ripped stitches. 'Matt has been listening to too much town gossip.'

Langelee moved like lightning to prevent the monk from pulling Bartholomew away from him, and Bartholomew, standing awkwardly because of the way Michael was tugging on his tabard, tripped over the philosopher's foot. He skidded in the mud, and only saved himself from a tumble by snatching at Michael's habit. Langelee raised his eyebrows as the physician struggled to regain his footing.

'You should go more easily on the ale, Bartholomew,' he said. 'Drinking in the mornings, I am sure, is bad for the balance of the humours.'

'You should know,' muttered Bartholomew.

Langelee's heavy eyebrows drew together, and he opened his mouth to reply. Michael intervened hastily, realising that an argument would ensue between his friend and the aggressive philosopher unless he prevented it – and Kenyngham was still at his window. He decided the best way to silence Langelee was to go on the offensive himself.

'You seem to be a little unsteady yourself, Master Langelee,' he said. 'As Senior Proctor, I must warn you that such behaviour is insupportable. My advice to you is that you remain in your chamber until you are certain you are no longer under the influence of last night's wine.'

Before Langelee could reply, Michael had gained a powerful hold on Bartholomew's arm, and was away with him across the courtyard, leaving the philosopher spluttering with impotent rage.

'The more I speak with that fellow, the less I like him,' said the obese monk pompously. 'I do not know why he insists on holding conversations when his sole intention is to needle people. Borrow Aristotle indeed! He would not know one end of *De Caelo* from the other!'

'He also does not know of Julianna's betrothal,' said Bartholomew thoughtfully. He rubbed his arm where Michael's fingers had pinched. 'He seemed quite disappointed to learn she was unavailable. Maybe I should let him know he has had a lucky escape. Or is the luck Julianna's?'

'You will do no such thing,' said Michael firmly. 'That man clearly has some kind of grudge against you, and you would be well advised to stay clear of him until I can have quiet words in high places and see about getting him transferred to another College – Valence Marie, perhaps, or King's Hall.' He glanced up at Kenyngham, still watching from his window. 'Assuming, of course, that words in high places were not had to bring him here in the first place.'

Bartholomew was spared from answering by someone shouting for Michael. They turned and saw Vice-Chancellor Harling picking his way cautiously across the yard.

'Can you do nothing about this foul mire?' he grumbled, looking at his splattered boots in dismay. 'Physwick Hostel does not boast such a mud bath.'

'Physwick Hostel does not have a yard,' retorted Michael. He smiled before Harling could take offence. 'I was about to come to see you.'

'Well, then, I have saved you the trouble,' said Harling. 'At the expense of my boots! But I wanted to tell you personally, Matthew, how appalled I was when Brother Michael told me about the attack on you when you went to see to the Bishop. I wish I had tried harder to dissuade you from going. I shall say a mass today to give thanks for your deliverance.'

Bartholomew smiled. 'Thank you. If we had listened to your misgivings about the journey none of it would have happened.'

'True,' said Harling. 'Although I did not come here to gloat. I came to ask whether you had discovered anything new.' The Vice-Chancellor shook his head as Deynman, hurrying to attend one of Alcote's basic grammar lectures in the hall, fell flat on his back in the mud and slid some distance before coming to a halt.

'Not really,' said Michael. 'Today I plan to visit St Bernard's Hostel to see if I can learn anything further about Armel's death, and then I will go to the castle to see how Tulyet has fared.'

'What is the Sheriff doing?'

'I was given the names of a ring of smugglers in the area by an informant,' said Michael vaguely. 'We believe it was the smugglers who made the attempt on our lives.'

'Your informant is the nun you brought from Denny?' asked Harling. Michael stared at him in surprise and Harling smiled. 'You chose an unfortunate accomplice in Mistress Julianna, Brother. She has been bragging all over the town how she and an elderly cleric escaped certain death from ruthless outlaws.'

Michael was horrified. 'I thought we could rely on her discretion when a life was at stake!'

'Whatever gave you that idea, Brother?' muttered Bartholomew.

Harling patted the monk's arm in a soothing gesture. 'Do not fear. Julianna thinks you have secreted this old nun here, in Michaelhouse.' He watched the grey-robed Franciscans assembling to process to the church for another mass. 'Although how she imagines you could hide a woman here with Father William and Master Alcote at large, I cannot imagine. Those are men who would not budge an inch in their conviction that women have no place in a College – even an elderly nun in fear of her life.'

'Yes, Michaelhouse is not noted for its tolerance and compassion,' said Bartholomew, looking to where Langelee was berating Agatha for taking too long to mend one of his shirts. The formidable laundress put her hands on her hips and glowered, looking so dangerous that the philosopher prudently backed down and slunk away while he was still able. 'Apart from Master Kenyngham, who I am not sure lives in the same world as us most of the time, our Fellows are a band of bigoted fanatics who would rather see someone die than one of our rules broken.'

'Dame Pelagia will not die,' said Michael, quietly firm. 'Even if it means I have to take that loose-mouthed Julianna back to Denny to shut her up.'

'Do not worry about Julianna,' said Harling. 'It is clear she knows nothing that can harm anyone, least of all your old nun. But why did you bring them to Cambridge in the first place?'

Michael scratched his chin. 'I was forced to remove Dame Pelagia from Denny for her own safety. She knew too much for her own good about these smugglers.'

'That was prudent of you,' said Harling approvingly. 'It would be unfortunate for the University if enquiries by one of its Proctors brought about the death of a nun. Do you have her in a safe place? If not, Physwick owns a small house in Trumpington that is seldom used. I can arrange for you to have it for a few days without the knowledge of my colleagues, should you need it.'

'Thank you,' said Michael with a grateful grin. 'That may become necessary and I appreciate your kindness.'

'However,' continued Harling, 'I am concerned about your close association with the Sheriff. If a dispute between canon and secular law arises – with the Chancellor on one side and the Sheriff on the other – your relationship with Tulyet might put you in a difficult position.'

Michael considered. 'You are right,' he said after a moment. 'Thank you for your concern. Let us hope such a rift will not occur until this smuggling business is solved.'

Harling nodded. 'I must not detain you.' He paused uncertainly but then plunged on. 'I appreciate what you have sacrificed in order to continue your duties as Senior Proctor, Brother. I would like you to know that I am not the only one to admire your loyalty and good service to the University, the town and the Bishop.'

Michael smiled, showing his small, yellow teeth. 'Be assured, Master Harling, that Matt and I will do all in our power to bring this business to an acceptable end – acceptable for the University, and for us.'

Such declarations of loyalty and gratitude were too much for Bartholomew. Michael, he knew very well, would not hesitate to double-cross Harling if he felt he might gain something from it, while Harling probably had very good reasons for soliciting Michael's allegiance and support. Perhaps Harling was planning to discredit the Chancellor – who was, by anyone's standards, taking an inordinately long time enjoying the luxuries of the Bishop's Palace at Ely – and was going to force another election. Bartholomew was also bothered by Michael's promise to bring about an 'acceptable end' to the poisoned wine affair: it bespoke of corruption and secrecy.

Smiling politely, he made his farewells to Harling and Michael, and went to see Bulbeck, who was slowly mending. He found the student sitting up in bed and pestering Gray to fetch him something to eat. Bartholomew sent Gray for some watered oatmeal and, satisfied that his patient was on the way to recovery, relinquished him to the rough, but sincere attentions of his friends. Even before he left the room, Bartholomew's mind began to mull over the symptoms of Bulbeck's sickness. If Bulbeck had taken only a sip of water from the well, and had become ill so quickly, then the well must be tainted more heavily than he had imagined. He decided to postpone his teaching and to go to inspect it himself, thinking that he might be able to persuade the Mayor to have it boarded over until the river level began to fall again.

The well stood in Water Lane, a seedy alley of deeply rutted mud that ran between Milne Street and the wharves. Unstable looking houses clustered closely along both sides, and Bartholomew was certain that if one fell they would all collapse, like a group of drunks clinging to each other for support. The ground underfoot was soft with human and animal dung that had been deposited there over many years, and the sharp stench of urine, rotting vegetables and offal made his eyes water.

The lane opened out into a small square around the well. A group of children played there, thin legs and arms poking from brown rags, as they scampered after a mangy dog with a filthy red ribbon tied around its neck. When Bartholomew crossed the square, they abandoned their game and besieged him, tugging at his tabard with grimy fingers and chanting their demands for pennies in high-pitched monotones. He flung them a handful of coins and approached the well.

Above ground, it was a simple wooden structure with a stone wall that stood to waist height, and a thatched roof, so that people winching up the water could stand out of the rain; below ground it was a narrow stone tube that dropped into deep darkness. Bartholomew leaned his elbows on the wall and peered down into the blackness. He could see the silvery glint of water at its foot, but jolted his head back sharply as an unpleasant odour drifted up.

'That is disgusting!' he muttered.

'Talking to yourself?' came Tulyet's voice at his elbow. The Sheriff perched on the wall's rim and grinned at Bartholomew. The children closed in again, and Tulyet tossed a few half-pennies towards them, more to be rid of their clamouring than as an act of charity. 'I had hopes you were a smuggler hiding his ill-gotten gains when I saw you here,' he said to the physician.

'This water must be foul indeed to emit such a stench,' said Bartholomew, his mind on the well and not on the Sheriff's banter. 'No wonder people become sick when they drink it.'

The bucket for drawing water was usually secured on a hook to one side, but the last person to use it had left it down inside the well. Bartholomew began to pull it up, so that he could inspect the water more closely. It was stuck, and Tulyet helped him to heave it free, before sitting down again and relating a tale of how he had found an outlaw camp so recently abandoned that the fire still smouldered. Bartholomew's mind was half on his task and half on Tulyet's story.

'God's teeth!' exclaimed Bartholomew, so violently that Tulyet jumped and almost toppled into the well himself. The Sheriff recovered his balance and twisted round to see the cause of Bartholomew's shock, gasping in horror when he saw what had snagged on the metal handle of the bucket.

'Is that what I think it is?' he asked in a whisper, tearing his gaze from the grisly object to look at Bartholomew.

Bartholomew met his eyes. 'It is a human ear,' he said.

'I think that is all,' yelled Bartholomew from the depths of the well. His voice echoed eerily around the stone walls, muffled by the scarf he wore wound tightly round his mouth and nose. He glanced up, seeing the sky as a circle of bright white high above, broken by dark shapes as Tulyet and Michael peered down. He coughed, beginning to feel nauseated by the sulphurous stench of foul water and the still air that sat at the bottom of the shaft.

He poked around for the last time with the pole he held, and then felt the bucket in which he stood precariously begin to rise. His balance went and he all but fell into the fetid water. The bucket stopped moving.

'Are you all right?' came Tulyet's voice.

Bartholomew tried to shout back, but he was becoming overwhelmed from inhaling the rank odour of bad water, and he was not certain that the sound he made had carried to Tulyet above. The bucket began to move again, more quickly this time, swinging to and fro, and bumping him against the sides of the well. He felt his cold hands begin to slip on the rope and forced himself to hold on tighter. He glanced upwards. The circle of white was still a long way off.

He closed his eyes tightly, and tried to concentrate on remaining upright in the swaying bucket. He should have tied himself in, he thought, wincing as the wooden container slammed against the stone shaft, sending booming echoes all around. The pole slipped from under his arm and clattered down to the black depths beneath him, entering the water with a dull splash. He opened his eyes and saw with relief that he was almost at the top. As his head drew level with the rim of the well wall, he gulped in mouthfuls of fresh air.

'Take my arm,' said Michael, leaning in.

Bartholomew released the rope with one hand and reached towards Michael, but his other hand was simply too cold and numb to support his weight on its own. With horror, Bartholomew felt it slide off the rope and the bucket tip sideways to pitch him back down the well. But his fall was jolted to a stop almost before it had begun, and he felt Michael grip his wrist, all but dislocating his shoulder as he hung suspended by one hand. Others reached down to grab him and he was hauled out of the well, to kneel gasping and choking for breath on the ground nearby.

'That was close,' said Michael shakily, wiping his fore-head with a mucky rag. 'You almost had me down there with you.'

Bartholomew tugged the scarf from his face and gratefully accepted a cup of wine someone pushed into his hand.

'Matilde!' he exclaimed in pleasure. 'Why are you here?'

'Half the town is here,' she said, gesturing to where a crowd had gathered. 'It would look suspicious if I remained at home. It is not every day that a corpse is discovered in one of our wells.'

Bartholomew coughed again and Matilde thumped him on his back.

'You are getting too old for this kind of thing,' she teased. 'You should let your students do it. Rob Deynman offered to go.'

Bartholomew looked to where his student was warding off those people who would have come to ask Bartholomew questions before he had recovered his breath – including Harling, which was risky, and Edith, which was downright rash – and smiled.

'How is Dame Pelagia?' he asked softly, even though no one else was near.

Matilde smiled. 'In better health than you at the moment, and splendid company. She had told me stories beyond my wildest imaginings.'

Bartholomew shot her a curious glance and wondered what kind of life Dame Pelagia had led to enable her to tell tales to astonish the worldly-wise Matilde. The uncharitable thought flashed through his mind that they might have been in the same business before Pelagia undertook her monastic vocation. Or was he being unfair?

Matilde helped Bartholomew to his feet and Edith came rushing towards him.

'What were you thinking of, volunteering to go down there?' she demanded angrily, hands on hips. 'It was a dangerous thing to do!'

'Someone had to do it,' he said, fending her off. 'And I am less sensitive about this kind of thing than most.'

Edith sighed and exchanged a look of resignation with Matilde. 'You do not deserve good women to worry over you,' she said. She hesitated and looked away towards the river. 'My words were over-hasty yesterday. I know you meant no offence to Oswald and I am sorry we quarrelled with each other.'

Bartholomew rubbed his eyes and smiled wanly. 'I should have thought before I made such an accusation. But Thorpe—'

Edith raised her finger to stop him from speaking. 'We will only argue again if we pursue that subject. It is enough that we are friends again.' She embraced him in a sudden fierce hug. 'There. Now Master Harling wants you, and the Sheriff is waiting.'

Bartholomew left her, and went to where Michael and Tulyet stood over the body that he had recovered from the well. Harling bustled up, smoothing down his immaculate tabard where Deynman had dared to lay his hands on it.

'That boy is a menace,' he said to Bartholomew, glowering at Deynman over his shoulder. 'I am tempted to pass him through his disputations simply to remove him from the town.'

'I might hold you to that,' said Michael opportunistically. 'I have been wondering how Michaelhouse might raise sufficient funds to buy him a degree.'

Tulyet bent down to lift the cover from the face of the dead man, so that Bartholomew could see it. He was not familiar, but had been in the water for at least a month and his features were all but unrecognisable. Harling glanced down and shuddered, looking away quickly.

'His own mother would not know him,' said Tulyet, regarding the Vice-Chancellor sympathetically. 'But his red tunic suggested to me that he might be one of Thomas Deschalers's lads. I just asked Deschalers if any are missing, and he informed me that one of his apprentices left

Cambridge about a month ago, rather abruptly, leaving a note that said he was going to become a monk. Apparently the lad was given to unpredictable behaviour, and Deschalers did not give it another thought. I suspect this is him, and that he found God in a way he did not anticipate. His death cannot be natural.'

'He must be the apprentice Father Philius was called to attend at Oswald's house,' said Bartholomew, kneeling next to the body. 'There are still blisters just visible on his lips and if I look in his mouth—'

'Not here, Matthew,' said Harling, touching him on the shoulder and glancing nervously at the crowd that watched them.

'Why not?' muttered Michael. 'You realise, Master Harling, that you are depriving Matt of a God-sent opportunity to revolt at least thirty people all at once – Edith and Matilde among them.'

Bartholomew glanced up at the crowd, many looking with horrified eyes at the bloated features of the apprentice. He pulled the cover over the dead man's face to hide it from sight and stood up, brushing mud from his knees.

'I would say, from the blisters and the time he has been in the water, that he is almost certainly the apprentice Philius saw dead,' said Bartholomew. 'What was his name?'

'Will Harper,' said Tulyet.

'So that solves one mystery,' said Michael to Bartholomew. 'Philius was summoned in a belated attempt to help an apprentice who died after drinking poisoned wine. After Philius left, the body must have been bundled down the well to hide it.'

'And the cases of fever started about three weeks ago,' said Bartholomew. 'Which would be about sufficient time for the body to begin festering in the water. No wonder people became ill! I was wrong about the river after all.'

'But correct in your theory that the fever was caused by poisoned water from this well,' said Michael. 'That a corpse was responsible is not an explanation that springs readily to mind. You cannot be blamed for not guessing that.'

Bartholomew shook his head, disgusted with himself. 'I should have checked the well earlier. I even told you about the similar case I had seen in Greece, where the cause was a dead goat in a stream. I should have known.'

Tulyet's men loaded the body onto a cart and took it away, leaving an ominous trail of water behind it. Realising there was nothing more to be seen, the crowd began to break up, talking about the incident in hushed voices as they went. Bartholomew looked around for Matilde, but she had already gone, and Edith was busily ushering her husband's apprentices homewards.

'So,' said Michael, to distract Bartholomew from looking too obviously for Matilde as they began to walk back to Michaelhouse. 'We can now be certain that Philius spoke the truth. He claimed to have seen a dead apprentice and here is the body. Philius assumed the lad was Stanmore's because he had been called to Stanmore's premises, and thus misled us. And the blisters around this apprentice's mouth suggest that he met his death in the same way as did Armel.'

'Oswald does not approve of his apprentices drinking,' said Bartholomew, 'although they have developed a number of ingenious plans to deceive him. I suspect that this was one such plan that went terribly wrong.'

'Let us recap what we know. One of Oswald's lads – Thorpe, no doubt – bought the wine in the Brazen George, as seen by Gray and his cronies, but it was Will Harper who drank it. When he became ill, they called Philius – not you, because they knew you would have told Stanmore – but when Philius declared him dead, they decided to hide the body and send Deschalers a note purporting to be from Harper saying he was bound for the cloister.'

Bartholomew nodded. 'The whole plan is the kind of ill-conceived venture frightened teenagers might dream up, not anticipating that the corpse would poison the well or that Father Philius might mention the incident to someone else. Poor Isaac probably felt perfectly justified in confiscating the wine from them when he went with Philius to Oswald's house that night.'

'But he died for it,' said Michael soberly. 'And so did Philius. Did these apprentices, emboldened by their success in ridding themselves of Will Harper's corpse, kill Isaac for stealing their wine?'

'No,' said Bartholomew, frowning in concentration. 'The people who killed Isaac also stole the bottles from Michaelhouse and terrified Walter out of his wits. And, anyway, you saw the killers as they knocked you over – you did not mention that they were the size of Oswald's apprentices.'

'They were not,' said Michael as they stepped through the wicket-gate into Michaelhouse. 'Two at least were bigger than Thorpe. But I cannot think on an empty stomach. I am off to the kitchen to see if Agatha has left anything edible lying around. Are you coming?'

Bartholomew walked with him. 'It is beginning to make sense. At least we know Philius was telling the truth. And Oswald, too,' he added.

'I suppose so,' said Michael. 'But things would be much clearer if your sister would allow us to talk to Thorpe. And I would certainly feel easier if I knew what had happened to Sacks's last bottle of wine.'

'I would feel easier if Thorpe were under lock and key,' said Bartholomew vehemently. He paused, his hand on the kitchen door. 'Do you think Edith and Oswald are safe? What if he tries to give the wine to them?'

'They are protecting him, Matt,' said Michael. 'He is unlikely to harm them as long as they offer sanctuary from the unwanted attentions of the big, bad Senior Proctor and his henchmen.'

He opened the door to the kitchen, and Bartholomew

headed gratefully towards the fire that roared in the hearth. The room was cosy and warm, and smelled of baking bread, stale grease and the sharper odour of burning logs. It was familiar, comfortable and went some way to dispelling the memory of being down the narrow stone chimney with the rotting corpse of Deschalers's apprentice.

Michael was in the act of stretching fat white fingers towards a plate of freshly baked cakes, that Agatha had rashly left unattended, when Cynric burst in.

'That Rob Thorpe was watching as the body was pulled from the well,' he said breathlessly. 'So I followed him after your sister took him and the others home. He was definitely anxious and left Master Stanmore's house a few moments later.'

'Oh? And where did he go this time?' asked Michael, spraying the front of his habit with cake crumbs as he spoke. 'St Mary's Church for the mystery plays? To St Botolph's Church to pray?'

Cynric shot him a mystified look. 'To the Hall of Valence Marie.'

Rain began to fall again as Michael and Bartholomew walked up the High Street towards Valence Marie. Although it was only early afternoon, the light was poor, and in one or two of the wealthier houses lamps already gleamed behind glazed windows. Tradesmen from the Market Square were already giving up for the day, and carts of all shapes and sizes were trundling towards the Trumpington Gate. There was a multitude of smells, from the warm, damp odour of trampled manure to the acidic stench of urine that trickled down the ditches at the side of the street, widening into little ponds where they were blocked with offal from the butcher's shop and rotten vegetable parings from the Brazen George.

The rain made the town seem drab and dismal. The thatches of roofs were dull and sodden, dripping brown rivulets of mould down the walls of the few houses the owners of which had bothered to paint. The others, chiefly wattle-and-daub, were scruffy with crumbling plaster, and everywhere was filth-impregnated mud. Bartholomew glanced up at the heavy grey clouds that slouched overhead and felt they matched his mood. The desire to see Thorpe confess to his crime, that he had felt so strongly when he had first recognised him, was tempered by the knowledge that Edith would hate him for it.

As they reached the junction between the High Street and Piron Lane, they met Edith herself, with her husband and one of his smaller apprentices. Bartholomew started backwards guiltily, wondering if she already knew where they were going and why.

'What are you two up to?' demanded Edith suspiciously. 'You look positively furtive.'

Michael gave one of his most winning smiles, which served to make Edith more wary than ever. 'University business, madam,' he said suavely.

'I suppose this University business involves Rob Thorpe?' asked Stanmore bluntly. Bartholomew could not meet his eyes, and even Michael was hard pressed to lie so blatantly.

'If the lad has done nothing wrong, he has nothing to fear,' said the monk eventually. 'What harm is there in our speaking with him? You can be present to ensure we treat him fairly.'

Edith was reluctant. 'But he has had nightmares!' she protested. 'He would be angry if he thought I had told you, but he wakes in the night and cries.'

Perhaps there was hope for him after all, thought Bartholomew, if he felt a degree of remorse for what he had done.

'We will handle him with care,' said Michael. 'We want only to ask him a few questions.'

Edith sighed and exchanged a glance with her husband and then gestured to the apprentice who stood between them. He was holding Edith's hand, and the dark green tunic that reached the knees of most of Stanmore's boys was almost at his ankles. He had a head of coarse ginger hair, and a smattering of orange freckles on both cheeks and across his nose. His eyes were swollen, as though he had been crying, and he clutched at Edith's fingers harder than ever when Bartholomew and Michael looked at him.

'We were actually coming to see you anyway,' said Edith miserably. 'Francis has something he would like to say.'

Francis looked as if he would like to say nothing at all, and stared uncomfortably at his feet.

'Come on,' said Stanmore, patting Francis's tousled hair encouragingly. 'They will not eat you.'

Francis glanced up at Brother Michael, uncertainly. 'Rob Thorpe has gone,' he said unhappily. 'He made us promise not to tell Master Stanmore until tomorrow.'

'Made you?' asked Michael gently.

He hooked a finger under the boy's chin, so that he looked up. Francis began to cry, and Michael drew the apprentice towards him, placing two large hands on his shoulders. Bartholomew was surprised to see the fat monk patient and gentle, but remembered Michael was popular with the youngsters in his choir, and possessed a talent for dealing with children that few who knew him would suspect he had.

'You must tell us, Francis,' said Michael, kindly but firmly. 'It is important. Your friend Rob might be in some danger.'

'Danger?' wept Francis. 'Not him! It was we who were in danger. I hate him!'

'Did he bully you?' asked Michael. 'Did he make threats?'

'All the time!' howled Francis. 'We all hated him, and we are all glad he has gone. He made us lie to you about where he was last Saturday. I do not know where he was: he was not with us. And I do not know where he is now, but I am glad it is not here.'

'No wonder you thought your apprentices were listless,' said Bartholomew in an undertone to Stanmore. 'You were worried that they were ill, but it seems as though they were subdued because they were terrified of Thorpe.'

'There is no need to belabour the point, Matt,' said Stanmore bitterly. 'It seems we were wrong and you were right. Rob has taken his belongings from our house – along with all my petty cash, a ring Cynric gave to my seamstress and the necklace of your mother's that Edith loved so much. The other apprentices were so relieved to see him gone that they were capering around their dormitory like lunatics. That is how I discovered he had left before the time they were supposed to tell me.'

'And do you know anything of a dead apprentice?' asked Michael of Francis.

Francis went silent, while Edith gazed at Michael in disbelief. 'Not this again,' she groaned. 'How many more times must we tell you? None of our lads is missing!'

'Not one of us,' said Francis, raising a white face to Edith. 'Will Harper, Rob Thorpe's cousin. He was a bully, too, and they brought that wine into our dormitory even though they knew you would be angry. Then, today, Will Harper was dragged out of the well. It *was* him, wasn't it?'

Michael nodded and Edith put a comforting arm around Francis's thin shoulders. The apprentice took a shuddering breath, and continued his story.

'The two of them – Rob Thorpe and Will Harper – took the wine to the far end of the room and started to drink it. Then Rob started yelling at Will, but he was lying on the floor in a swoon. Rob sent me for Father Philius – I wanted to get Doctor Bartholomew, but Rob told me not to. Philius said there was nothing he could do, and Rob made us carry Will to one of the storerooms. He said Will had died because the Devil had come up through the floor and snatched his soul away. He said the same would happen to us if we told anyone what had happened.'

He paused and gave a great, wet sniff, rubbing his nose on

his sleeve. Michael waited patiently while Francis composed himself.

'The next day, we looked in the storeroom, but Will had gone. Rob said he had recovered, and had gone to join a monastery to be safe from the Devil if he should come again.'

'Did you believe him?' asked Michael. 'That Will was still alive, even after Father Philius had pronounced him dead?'

Francis sniffed again and nodded. 'We all wanted him gone – whether to a monastery or the Devil we did not care. But he was in the well, yes? So he is really dead this time and will not come back to haunt us?'

'He is really dead, Francis,' said Michael softly. 'Thank you for having the courage to speak out. I promise neither Rob Thorpe nor Will Harper will be coming back to torment you.'

Francis burst into tears, his face buried in Michael's habit. Michael ruffled his hair comfortingly. 'You seem to have nursed a viper at your breast,' he said to Edith.

'This cannot be happening,' said Edith, looking from where Francis sobbed into Michael's ample girth to her husband. 'We have always been gentle with Rob. I felt sorry for him, his father being disgraced and all.'

'It may have been your very gentleness that made him bitter,' said Michael.

'Do you think his father encouraged him in this?' asked Stanmore, white faced.

Michael shook his head. 'I sincerely doubt it. Bitter and angry at his dismissal he might have been, but he would never have stooped to anything like this. And he certainly would not have encouraged his son to engage in anything so vile.'

'Are you sure?' pressed Edith.

Bartholomew put a comforting hand on her shoulder, seeing how she was clutching at straws in her desperation to shift the blame from the apprentice to someone else. It would not be easy for her to accept that the boy she had welcomed so generously into her household had repaid her kindness with such deception and wickedness.

Michael nodded. 'I am sure. I believe poor Master Thorpe will be appalled when he learns about the havoc his son has wreaked on his behalf. But enough of this wretched little ingrate. Go home, Edith. I think your other boys might need you now. They will be frightened and will need reassuring.'

Edith gave a wan smile. 'Thank you, Michael. You have been kind.' She prised the sobbing Francis from Michael and turned away to take him home. 'I still hope you are wrong,' she said in a small voice, not looking back at them.

'So do I,' said Stanmore, watching her go. 'This will break her heart, Matt. Rob was a favourite of hers. I think he reminds her of you when you were that age.'

Bartholomew, recalling Thorpe's gloating smiles of triumph and murderous inclinations, sincerely hoped he was mistaken. 'I suppose we had better see if he has fled to Valence Marie,' he said, anxious to be away from Stanmore and his distress, since he felt as though he were at least partly responsible for it.

Stanmore gave a huge sigh. 'I suppose I should come with you to help you find Rob,' he said, 'but I have no stomach for this sort of confrontation. The University is no place for honest traders.'

They left him sitting disconsolately on the low wall surrounding St Mary's churchyard.

'What do you plan to do?' Bartholomew asked of Michael as they walked along the High Street. 'Will you use Thorpe to flush out his accomplice?'

Michael stared at him and pursed his lips. 'Eligius? I think he is far too clever to be startled into a confession by us confronting Thorpe.'

'Thorpe strikes me as the sort of person who will try to

blame someone else if he sees the net closing in on him,' said Bartholomew. 'I am sure he will betray Eligius in an instant if he thinks it will work to his advantage.'

Michael nodded slowly. 'It is worth a try, I suppose.'

Bartholomew rubbed a hand through his hair. 'This is a vile business. It has led us to consider how we will bring pressure to bear on someone who is little more than a child to force him to betray his accomplices' identities.'

'He is seventeen years old, Matt. He is a man, and he is certainly old enough to commit murder,' Michael pointed out. He studied Bartholomew's face, and saw the conflicting emotions there. 'Edith cannot hold you responsible for Thorpe's crimes. Grene was foully murdered, and it does not take a genius to predict that dropping a corpse down a well might poison the water. Yet Harper's body was disposed of with a total disregard for the health of the people who live nearby.'

'Do you think he was so calculating?' asked Bartholomew doubtfully. 'It strikes me that Thorpe is more careless than malicious – he saw the well as a convenient dump and used it without considering the consequences.'

'Ask the poor people who have been drinking that tainted water whether they give a damn what Thorpe's intentions were,' snapped Michael. 'And you, of all people, should not be excusing his actions, since you have been so desperately trying to physic those who have been ill. Thorpe might be little more than a child, Matt, but he must be apprehended before he does anyone else harm. And you had better hope you are successful because, now Edith and Oswald are no longer protecting him, Thorpe might well turn on them.'

Bartholomew did not reply, but followed Michael through the Trumpington Gate. He was left behind when he recognised one of the guards as a fever victim, and stopped to enquire after his health. By the time he caught up again, Michael was engaged in a fierce altercation with the porter in the porch of the Hall of Valence Marie.

'You cannot come in. There is a formal dinner in progress.'

'I have not come to dine,' said Michael stiffly. 'I have come to look for a young man who may have committed murder, and may be planning to do so again.'

'But the Countess is here,' objected the porter. 'The Countess of Pembroke, our benefactor. She and the Fellows are having a private meal. I cannot let them be disturbed. I would lose my job.'

'Michael!' exclaimed Bartholomew. 'The Countess! Thorpe is in there with the Countess, and there is still a bottle of poisoned wine unaccounted for!'

Michael stared at him for a moment, and then shook his head. 'So? He can hardly do her harm at the dinner table.'

'Why not? He managed with Grene,' said Bartholomew, and, ignoring the protests of the porter, he forced his way through the door, across the cobbled yard and threw open the heavy wooden door to Valence Marie's spacious hall.

Acting-Master Eligius and his colleagues were just taking their places at the high table on the dais when Bartholomew charged in, Michael at his heels. Valence Marie's servants had gone to some trouble to make the Countess's visit a memorable one: the table was covered by an embroidered cloth, and all the College silver was out, polished until it shone. Delicious smells came from behind the painted screen opposite the hearth, where serving-boys waited to bring out the platters of meat that had been prepared in the kitchens. It would be cold, but very little cooked food was served hot in Cambridge Colleges, given that the kitchens were usually some distance from the refectories. Michaelhouse occasionally managed warm oatmeal, but that was about all.

At the seat of honour, in the centre of the table, the Countess was reaching for the goblet of wine set for her.

'No!' yelled Bartholomew, freezing the movements of all and sundry. 'The wine, madam! Do not touch the wine!'

There was an appalled silence, until the Countess recovered from her surprise. Bartholomew had not taken much notice of her during the installation, and noted now that she was older than he had initially thought. Money for cosmetics and fine clothes made her appear younger than her years, especially from a distance, although tell-tale wrinkles around her throat and a worldly look in her eyes betrayed her. She wore a robe of rich blue with flowing sleeves that brushed the ground. Her fingers were laden with so many rings that Bartholomew was surprised she could still use her hands, and a ruby pendant around her neck glistened like a clot of blood.

'What is the meaning of this?' she demanded imperiously, her hand arrested in the very act of lifting the goblet to her lips. 'Who are you to burst in unannounced and issue orders?'

Bartholomew walked towards her. 'I am sorry, my lady,' he said, 'but I have reason to believe that the wine you have been served might be tainted with a poison.' He pointed at Thorpe, clad in his light blue tunic and with his hair hastily darkened with soot, standing just behind her. 'He has already killed Master Grene.'

The Countess looked at her cup suspiciously, and twisted round in her chair to look at Thorpe.

'I know this man!' exclaimed Thorpe suddenly, pointing at Bartholomew. 'He is a lunatic from the hospital run by the Austin Canons. You should have him removed – he might be dangerous.'

'The boy lies,' said Michael, striding forward. 'My colleague's name is Doctor Bartholomew, and he is a Fellow of Michaelhouse. I am Brother Michael, the University's Senior Proctor. I beg you, madam, do not touch the wine.'

The Countess looked at Valence Marie's Fellows impatiently, waiting for them to explain what was happening. 'What is going on, Father Eligius? Is this man Brother Michael as he claims?'

Eligius rose, his Dominican habit hanging in untidy folds from his narrow shoulders, and opened his mouth to speak.

'He is not!' cried Thorpe desperately, before the logician could respond. 'The good Canons at the hospital must be in their cups today to let *two* madmen escape!'

'Test it,' said Michael coolly. 'Give the wine to an animal. Better still, let Thorpe try it for you. If there is nothing wrong with it, he will not mind obliging.'

'Thorpe?' asked the Countess, turning her head again to stare at the apprentice. 'But he is in York.' She looked more closely. 'You are his relative?'

Thorpe bolted, clambering over the table and sending dishes and bottles flying, only to run straight into the iron embrace of Michael. He struggled violently, but uselessly.

'It was not me!' he yelled, frightened now. 'It was him!' His flailing hand encompassed at least half the room.

'Who?' asked the Countess coldly. 'And what was not you?'

'It was him! Grene!' yelled Thorpe.

'This is nonsense,' said Eligius. 'The boy is raving. Grene is dead.'

'What is Master Grene supposed to have done?' the Countess asked impatiently, addressing the struggling Thorpe.

'Poison!' screamed Thorpe. 'It was his idea. He forced me!'

The Countess indicated that Michael should let Thorpe go. Michael hesitated, but the sudden flash of anger in the Countess's eyes convinced him that she was unused to having her orders disobeyed, and that she certainly did not like it. Thorpe shrugged himself out of Michael's relaxed grip and advanced towards her.

'You must believe me, good lady,' he sobbed, taking her hand and gazing up into her face. 'I am innocent of all this. I bought two bottles of wine from a thief in a tavern. I did not know it at the time, but they were poisoned, and one killed my cousin when he drank it. I came to Master Grene, who was my father's best friend, for help. He suggested we throw my cousin's body down the well, and told me to serve the other to him during the installation. He said it would avenge the wrong done to my father and would serve Bingham right.'

'You suggest that Master Grene encouraged you to poison him at the installation?' asked the Countess, scepticism written clear in her face.

'Yes!' said Thorpe desperately. 'He made me! It was all his idea.'

'Unlikely though it seems, he might be telling the truth,' whispered Bartholomew to Michael. 'Philius told me that Grene had been diagnosed with a fatal illness. If he was as bitter as everyone believes about Bingham's election, it is entirely possible he might have decided to exchange his last few painful months for a quick death – and at the same time, take the opportunity to strike at Bingham in a most spectacular way.'

'Suicide?' whispered Michael uncertainly. 'I do not think so. He would go straight to hell.'

'Perhaps he did not see it so,' said Bartholomew. 'Or perhaps he was so eaten up with resentment and envy that he did not care.'

'It would certainly explain his morose manner that night,' muttered Michael. 'Most people would have at least tried to be a little more gracious in defeat.'

'Why do you two whisper so?' called the Countess in aggrieved tones. 'If you have something to say, say it aloud so we can all hear.'

She sounded like a schoolmaster, thought Bartholomew. Before he could respond, Eligius had stepped forward, his dark habit swinging several inches above his thin white ankles.

'I apologise for this unseemly interruption, my lady,' he said. He looked hard at Thorpe. 'This boy has served at our high table on occasion recently, but I did not know he was a relative of Master Thorpe. We know him only as Rob. Yet I cannot believe that Brother Michael's accusations are true. I am certain Grene's death was at the hands of Bingham – as indeed I told the Sheriff when I petitioned for his arrest. I have already told you of how poor Grene voiced his fears to me the night before his death. So, I believe Rob will not mind tasting the wine, to assure you of his innocence.'

He picked up the Countess's cup and held it out to Thorpe with an encouraging smile.

'I do not like wine,' said Thorpe, licking his lips nervously. 'It makes my head swim.'

'In that case,' said Eligius, 'let us put an end to this nonsense here and now.' Before Bartholomew or Michael could stop him, he had put the cup to his lips and drained it in a single draught. There was a deathly hush in the hall. Eligius replaced the cup on the table and raised his hands. 'Well, Brother? I am still here. I am not struck down in an instant like Grene. You have clearly been mistaken in your logic.'

Michael gazed at him in disbelief. Thorpe's disbelief, however, was the greater. He looked at Eligius in horror and the blood drained from his face, leaving him an unhealthy grey-white colour.

'You seem to have made a grave mistake, Brother Michael,' said the Countess. 'You have accused a young man of a vile crime of which he appears to be wholly guiltless.'

She rested her elbows on the table and steepled her beringed fingers. Meanwhile, Eligius walked around the table to the seat next to her and sat, leaning back in his chair to fix his gaze on Michael and wait for an explanation. Michael strode forward and seized the cup, his face almost as pale as Thorpe's. For quite some time there was no sound in the hall as everyone watched Michael staring at the goblet. Bartholomew racked his brains for an answer, but he had been so convinced that Rob Thorpe had intended to harm the Countess, for some warped reason of his own, that his

mind was nothing but a blank. As far as Bartholomew was
concerned, Eligius should be gasping his last, his lips and
throat blistering from the same poison that had killed Grene,
not reclining easily in his chair with his bony hands folded in
his lap.

Eventually, when the Countess began to show signs of
impatience, and the mutters of the cook at the rear of the
hall that the food was spoiling grew embarrassingly audible,
Michael spoke.

'I am sorry,' he said, turning the cup over in his hands in
bewilderment. 'I was certain we were correct in our beliefs.
You see, we reasoned that Thorpe had killed Grene using
one of six bottles of wine sold by a thief named Sacks. An
apprentice – Thorpe's cousin – was dredged from the well
today and his body shows similar signs of poisoning as those
we observed on James Grene.'

The Countess pulled a face of disgust. 'I heard about the
body in the well. But it seems as though your reasoning
is flawed, Brother. Why should Thorpe – or anyone else
for that matter – poison me? I am no candidate for the
Mastership, and I played no part in his father's dismissal.'

Michael raised his hands in defeat and took a few steps
towards the Countess. 'What can I say? I am sorry, my
lady. My only thought was that you might be in danger,
and I acted without giving the matter sufficient thought.
But despite Father Eligius's conviction regarding Bingham's
guilt, Thorpe has admitted that he gave the poisoned wine
to Grene, and we must be allowed to question him further
on the matter. He has also stolen from his employer. If he
will come with us now, we will leave, and you will be able to
finish your meal in peace.'

He turned to Eligius, whose eyes were closed, as if in
prayer. For the third time since their dramatic entry, there
was a heavy silence as everyone waited for him to give
Michael permission to take Thorpe away. Thorpe swallowed
hard as Bartholomew looked more closely at Eligius, and

then he darted past them, aiming for the door and freedom. Bartholomew dived at him, and both went tumbling to the floor. Thorpe scratched, kicked and bit like an animal as Bartholomew fought to pin him down. The Countess leapt to her feet.

'For God's sake!' she exclaimed in angry exasperation. 'Eligius has just proved the boy's innocence: Bingham killed poor Grene and there is an end to it. Eligius? Order Brother Michael and this brawling physician to leave my presence at once. I will not be insulted in this way!'

'Eligius will not be ordering anything ever again,' gasped Bartholomew, still struggling with Thorpe. 'He is dying.'

It was not until much later that Bartholomew and Michael were able to leave Valence Marie and go to make their report to Harling. He listened to their description of events in silence.

'So,' he said, when Michael had finished. 'Thorpe maintains the whole affair was Grene's idea?'

Michael nodded, leaning back against the wall and folding his arms. 'He says he fled to Grene – his father's best friend – when Will Harper died from the poisoned wine. Apparently, Thorpe and Harper liked to drink together – Stanmore disapproves of his apprentices frequenting taverns and had forbidden Thorpe to meet his cousin on pain of dismissal from his service. When Harper died on Stanmore's premises, Thorpe was afraid he would be sacked for disobedience – or, worse, that he would be accused of his cousin's murder. Thorpe described Harper's quick, and seemingly painless, death to Grene, and Grene conceived the notion of revenge for them both.'

He rubbed his chin, and continued. 'According to Philius, Grene was dying anyway, and had very little to lose. His death at the installation was not as painless as Thorpe had probably led him to believe it would be, but the rest of the plan went perfectly. Over the previous week, Grene made claims to three other Fellows that he was in fear of his life from Bingham, including to Father Eligius on the eve of his death. The scene was set: Grene died; Bingham was arrested for his murder; Grene was avenged for his defeat; and Rob had struck a blow against the College that he felt had wronged his father over the business of the false relic.'

Harling swallowed hard. 'And this Rob Thorpe is just seventeen, you say? Yet he plotted all this murder and mayhem?'

Michael shrugged. 'With Grene's help. But perhaps he is not wholly without hope. Edith Stanmore told us he has been having nightmares over the last month or so, and all that time he spent in St Botolph's Church – such as when we thought he had fled to his accomplice – must count for something. He was clearly suffering from remorse.'

'But not enough to prevent him from attempting to murder the Countess,' remarked Bartholomew, recalling Thorpe's gloating expression when Edith and Stanmore had prevented Bartholomew from hauling him off to the Proctors' cells after he had gone to inspect Egil's mutilated corpse.

Harling was silent, shaking his head slowly and looking down at his ink-stained table. 'What bitterness,' he said at last. 'I, too, lost an election, but it never occurred to me to poison myself so that Tynkell would be blamed for my murder.'

'But you are not fatally ill,' Bartholomew pointed out.

Harling began to speak again before Bartholomew could moderate his remark so it did not sound as if he believed Harling might well have conceived such a plan given the right conditions.

'So circumstances were simply opportune,' mused the Vice-Chancellor. 'The poisoned wine coming into Thorpe's possession merely provided Grene with an opportunity for revenge that he had been considering for some time.'

'So it would seem,' said Michael, standing and walking to

the window. 'And it might have worked, had Thorpe left the town quietly after the installation as he had promised Grene he would. But Bingham's arrest was not enough for him. He decided to commit one last act of vengeance before leaving Cambridge to join his father in York.'

'The Countess?' asked Harling.

Michael nodded. 'But by this stage he had no more of Sacks's wine left: one of his bottles had killed his cousin and then been stolen by Isaac; the other he had used to kill Grene.' He gestured that Bartholomew should continue.

'Father Philius's medical notes showed that he had prescribed a powerful opiate for Grene to use should the pain of his illness become too great. Thorpe confessed to Michael that he took this from Grene's room after the installation. He then mixed all of it with the wine he planned to serve the Countess when she visited Valence Marie.'

'So this was premeditated,' said Harling sadly. 'Thorpe planned to murder the Countess as long ago as last Saturday.'

Michael nodded. 'I imagine he was encouraged by the ease with which he helped Grene to his death, and so decided to try it once again. And his reason, of course, was that by murdering Valence Marie's benefactor, he would assure the College's dissolution. His bag was already packed so that he could flee the moment he saw the Countess swallow the wine. He was appalled when Eligius drank it, and probably anticipated that he would keel over immediately.'

'And he did not?' asked Harling. 'Not like Grene?'

'No,' answered Bartholomew. 'This opiate is slower acting and less dramatic than the poison in the wine Sacks sold him. By the time we realised there was something wrong, it was too late to do anything to save Eligius. He had fallen into a deep sleep and could not be roused. His breathing grew shallower and slower until it stopped completely; he died about an hour ago.'

'So Eligius's faith in Grene's claims and his belief in

Bingham's guilt, brought about his own death?' asked
Harling.

'I suppose it might be viewed like that,' said Michael. He
sat back down on the wall bench so heavily that Bartholomew
was forced to grab the table lest he be catapulted from the
other end. 'But let us not forget the role the relic played in
all this.'

'Ah, yes. The relic,' said Harling heavily. 'I wish to God
that foul thing had never been found. It has been nothing
but trouble ever since it emerged from the foul black mud
of the King's Ditch. If I were Chancellor, I would throw it
back, where it can do no more harm.'

'Eligius was convinced that the relic was genuine – as was
Grene,' said Michael. 'Bingham, on the other hand, has the
sense to see it for what it really is – a monstrous fraud foisted
on the town by an evil man. Part of Eligius's conviction that
Bingham killed Grene stemmed from that, despite the fact
that it was an illogical conclusion to draw.'

'Even great minds like Eligius's can be confounded when
it comes to matters of faith,' said Harling. 'He told Chancellor Tynkell and me that he sensed an aura of holiness
emanating from the relic, and that its purity and goodness
touched his soul. It is difficult to argue with someone who
has convictions like that.'

Bartholomew recalled Eligius standing with him and
Michael as they inspected Grene's body, and the fleeting
expression of remorse that had crossed his face. It was not
simply faith in Grene's claims nor belief in Bingham's guilt,
nor even his total conviction that the relic was holy, that had
prompted him to drink the Countess's wine: it was his own
troubled conscience – that Grene had come to him with his
fears and he had done nothing about them. Bartholomew
was sure that Eligius held himself responsible for Grene's
death, which explained why he had initiated his own quest
to have Bingham indicted of his murder. He had even gone
to the Sheriff and made out a case for Bingham's arrest,

because he felt he could not wait for the Senior Proctor to return from dealing with the burglary at St Clement's Hostel.

Harling sighed. 'I am certain poor Master Thorpe knows nothing of his son's plans for revenge,' he said. 'There is some talk that the King has regretted his hasty decision in removing Thorpe from the Mastership, and is considering reinstating him. He will be aghast when he hears what his son has done.'

Bartholomew felt sick at the futility of it all. 'Please do not tell Edith Master Thorpe might be reinstated. All this is hard enough for her to accept without the knowledge that Rob's drive to avenge his father's unjust treatment was all for nothing.'

Harling and Michael were silent, so that Bartholomew wondered whether his request had already come too late. For all he knew, Master Thorpe was already riding south to reclaim his post as head of Valence Marie.

Michael stretched his legs out in front of him. 'So, Rob Thorpe is lodged in the Proctors' gaol, the Countess is safe, and Bingham is freed from his cell in the castle. But we still do not know how Sacks came by this poisonous wine.'

'We know it must be related to the smuggling in the Fens,' said Bartholomew. 'Hopefully, we will find out who was responsible when Tulyet arrests the contrabanders.'

'And then there is still the missing bottle,' said Michael. 'Sacks had six and we only know what happened to five of them.'

'Perhaps Thorpe had three, not two,' said Harling, patting his greased hair with both hands.

'I do not believe so,' said Michael. 'Or I imagine he would have used the last one on the Countess, instead of resorting to the unknown qualities of Grene's medicine. I think we have yet to discover the fate of the sixth bottle.'

CHAPTER 10

BEARING IN MIND HARLING'S DISAPPROVAL OF HIS working relationship with the Sheriff, Michael informed the Vice-Chancellor that they were going to advise Stanmore of Thorpe's arrest, rather than that he planned to visit the castle. Stanmore already knew about Thorpe: he had been waiting for them when they eventually emerged from Valence Marie and had gone to take the news to Edith. Some of the relief Bartholomew had felt, that Thorpe no longer represented a threat to his family, evaporated when he saw the slump in Stanmore's shoulders and his grey face.

Tulyet was sitting at a table in his room in the great keep, reading a sheaf of hastily scribbled notes. He stood as they were shown in, and offered them stools near the fire.

'What a day!' he exclaimed, sitting again with a sigh. 'I have been questioning those I have arrested since dawn, and then there was that unpleasant affair of the body in the well.'

'And?' asked Michael, stretching his feet towards the blaze. 'Are you too busy or too weary to waste time in idle conversation with scholars?'

'And nothing,' said Tulyet gloomily. 'The smugglers in my prison have told me the identities of a few other Fenmen and the locations of one or two trading routes, but I am really no further forward than I was before.'

Michael gazed at him in disbelief. 'But that is not possible!

My informant risked her life to provide you with those names I gave you. Let me question these smugglers – I will find out what you are lacking.'

'You will not, Brother,' said Tulyet. 'And you will not because I honestly believe they have already told me all they know. The names you gave me are men at the lowest possible level, and a long way from the evil minds who are controlling all this.'

'I have been thinking about this smuggling,' said Bartholomew, staring at the flames flickering over the white-hot logs in the hearth. 'There must be two independent operations.'

'Yes?' said Tulyet, regarding him intently. 'Go on. We are listening.'

'It is generally known around the town that smuggling has been taking place along the waterways for many years,' said Bartholomew slowly. 'It is a way of life for some Fenmen, and it provides a service to the town to which the authorities usually turn a blind eye. But, of late, the goods have not been trickling in surreptitiously: they have been flooding in, and anyone can buy exotic goods on the black market. You have assumed that the smugglers have suddenly become greedy and incautious, but it is their livelihood and I think they are unlikely to risk it so openly.'

'I came to the same conclusion myself,' said Tulyet, standing abruptly. 'It is encouraging to hear that you have been thinking along the same lines. I believe the unseasonably warm weather and flooded channels have attracted others to try their hand. The men I have in my cells are of the old breed – those who pilot the odd shipment of cloth, grain or spices through the Fens. The men who are bringing in these lemons and figs are using the same routes, but are doing so on a much grander scale.'

He paced back and forth in the small room, pulling at his beard.

'I am certain the men I arrested confessed everything they knew, but they were unable to tell us anything about the attacks on the travellers on our roads – including the one on you – and very little about the sudden surfeit of goods on the black market. I decided to risk all and speak to the men who are benefiting from this additional trade: I managed to frighten old Master Cheney into telling me where his extra spices had come from.'

'And they came via the Fens?' asked Michael, twisting round to look at the Sheriff. When Tulyet nodded, Michael turned back to the fire again. 'Deschalers virtually admitted as much to us when we took Julianna to him. He said he was unaware that smuggling was taking place around Denny – suggesting that he clearly knew smuggling was taking place elsewhere.'

Tulyet said nothing and Bartholomew noticed the rings of tiredness under his eyes.

'So what is wrong, Dick?' he asked. 'What is stopping you from simply arresting all these people – Cheney and Deschalers and anyone else who is profiting from this illegal trading?'

Tulyet closed his eyes and pulled at his beard again. 'While the King can be expected to overlook a little illicit trade – the odd casket of claret or consignment of wool – he cannot be expected to ignore smuggling when it has become so flagrant, and when it involves robbery and violence.'

'I agree,' said Michael comfortably. 'Arrest the lot of them – anyone who is involved at any level. Do you know who they all are?'

Tulyet scrubbed at his face. 'I am fairly certain the men in my cells gave me the names of most of the Fenmen, and once Master Cheney had started to bare his soul, it was almost impossible to stop him telling me who was flooding the black market with smuggled fruit and other goods. Then Constantine Mortimer, rather rashly, came to see why the Sheriff was taking such a long time at his neighbour's house, and I terrified him into telling me all he knew, too. Between them they named most of the people in the town who are involved in the smuggling.'

Michael raised his eyebrows. 'Well, then? Why all the gloom? You said you had learned nothing from my informant's disclosures. But it seems to me you have learned a great deal.'

Tulyet shook his head. 'Your informant's disclosures allowed me to arrest the Fenmen – the old breed of smuggler. It was the Masters Cheney and Mortimer who provided me with the names of all the people involved in the opportunistic trading that has taken place this winter.'

'But that means you have the identities of everyone involved,' persisted Michael. 'The Fenmen *and* the opportunists. It hardly matters whether the information came from Dame Pelagia or your dishonest merchants. I do not see why you are not broaching a bottle of fine wine to celebrate your victory.'

His none-too-subtle hint fell on deaf ears, and Tulyet sighed, too engrossed in his worries to think about pandering to Michael's greed. 'Although I have the Fenmen in my cells and I can arrest the opportunists at my leisure, I still do not know which of them is responsible for the burglaries in the town and the ambushing of travellers on the roads – including who organised the attack on you.'

Michael was becoming exasperated. 'But if you know who is profiting from the smuggling, arrest them all. One – or perhaps more – of them will be responsible for the burglaries and attacks. I do not see your problem, Dick. Who are these people, anyway – other than Mortimer and Cheney?'

Tulyet sat in his chair and leaned back to look up at the cracked plaster on the ceiling. 'Where shall I begin? How about with Father Paul from Michaelhouse?'

Bartholomew leapt to his feet. 'But that is not possible!' he exclaimed. 'Paul is blind!'

'So?' said Tulyet wearily. 'One does not need to be able

to see to order illegally imported goods and sell them at a profit.'

He looked pointedly at Bartholomew's grey cloak. Bartholomew's jaw dropped in astonishment. Michael laughed nervously and Tulyet continued.

'Doctor Lynton from Peterhouse; James Grene – before he died; Robin of Grantchester; John Colton of Gonville.' He looked at Bartholomew. 'Oswald Stanmore.'

Bartholomew groaned and sank back down on the stool. Poor Stanmore! First his apprentice arrested for attempting to murder the Countess of Pembroke, and now he himself was to be charged with smuggling.

Tulyet continued remorselessly. 'Michaelhouse is particularly guilty: Roger Alcote has amassed a fortune by selling silver buckles; John Runham has been importing gold leaf with which to decorate his cousin's tomb—'

Michael grimaced. 'Damn! I thought I had foiled his plans to impose that monstrosity on us by bribing the goldsmiths not to sell him any.'

Tulyet tilted his chair backwards and put his feet on the table. 'I have not finished. Father William has arranged to be sent hair shirts as a surprise gift for his students at Easter; Samuel Gray – your student, I believe, Matt – has a thriving business selling anything he can lay his hands on.'

Bartholomew closed his eyes in despair. No wonder Gray had failed his disputation if he was spending most of his time running a lucrative import business!

'What about Ralph de Langelee?' asked Michael hopefully. 'He always has money to spend on drink. He must be involved.'

'Not as far as I know,' said Tulyet. 'As far as I can tell, he and Master Kenyngham are about the only two Fellows in your College who are innocent in all this.'

'I am innocent!' protested Michael.

Tulyet eyed the heavy gold cross Michael had worn since the installation. 'Are you, Brother? Then where did that handsome bauble come from? It is not the work of any local smith.'

'That is none of your affair,' said Michael haughtily. 'But since you ask, I acquired it perfectly legally from Haralda the Dane, who occasionally works with gold.'

Tulyet smiled and Bartholomew saw he did not believe a word Michael had said. 'To continue: Jonas the Apothecary has ordered a feather bed for his wife's bad back; Constantine Mortimer has been selling fine leather gloves from France to boost the profits he makes by selling bread.' He gave Bartholomew's hands a hard look. 'But you already know that.'

'These?' asked Bartholomew, looking down at his gloves, aghast. 'Mortimer gave me smuggled goods?'

Tulyet nodded. 'Do not feign shock with me, Matt. Mortimer is a baker. How do you imagine he came by gloves to sell?'

'But I did not know,' objected Bartholomew. He sounded feeble, even to his own ears, and had clearly not convinced Tulyet. Michael simply regarded him with sceptically raised eyebrows. 'I did not buy them. Mortimer gave them to me.'

'Of course he did,' said Tulyet flatly. Michael still said nothing and the Sheriff continued. 'Do you want to hear more? There is not a merchant, and scarcely a scholar, in the town who has not taken advantage of what the mild weather has to offer – except, it would seem, Thomas Deschalers.'

'Deschalers?' asked Michael, surprised. 'He must be involved – there are lemons wherever you look in the town.'

The Sheriff gave a short bark of mirthless laughter. 'Deschalers really *has* discovered that keeping fruit in his cellars increases its lifespan. He stockpiled lemons in the summer, and is able to sell them at a profit now. Because he is doing so well at his legal trade, he has had no need to engage in illegal activities. I checked everything in his cellars and he has the proper licences for the lot.'

'Deschalers was the one who set us thinking about smuggling in the first place,' said Michael, shaking his head slowly. 'How ironic!'

'Father Yvo of Bernard's Hostel has been making money to repair a leaking roof by hawking fine quality parchment, would you believe!' Tulyet leaned forward and rested his elbows on his knees. 'He thinks the constant damp is the cause of melancholia in one of his students, and he wanted to mend it to make the young man feel better.'

'Paul gave me half the money he made from his contraband cloaks for the victims stricken with winter fever,' said Bartholomew, remembering the gold the friar had given him, 'and he sent the rest to the Leper Hospital.'

Tulyet groaned. 'It is one thing arresting half of Cambridge for committing crimes for their own gain; it is entirely another when they do it to help the sick and the poor. What in heaven's name am I going to do? Seal off the town and present the entire population to the King? What a mess!'

'Your position is not so impossible,' said Michael thoughtfully. Tulyet looked at him hopefully. 'The King will not want his prisons full of the town's leading citizens – or scholars. Go to arrest your miscreants, but do not be discreet about it. You cannot arrest anyone unless you find smuggled goods in their possession, yes?' Tulyet nodded and sat up straight. 'Inform all your sergeants what you plan to do, and make sure everyone hears what you say. Then have a leisurely meal and go about your business. Anyone who does not have the sense to take the necessary precautions within the next hour or so deserves to be arrested anyway.'

'You are right,' said Tulyet, standing abruptly. 'The King will impose new taxes on the merchants when he hears of this, and they will be too grateful that they have escaped imprisonment – or worse – to complain. It is a perfect compromise!'

Michael sat back, his arms folded and a self-satisfied smile on his face. Bartholomew looked out of the window, wondering whether the town possessed a single honest citizen other than Kenyngham, Langelee and Deschalers – who was not involved only because he was doing rather better than usual legally.

'Right,' said Tulyet, rubbing his hands together. 'After I have been home for something to eat and played a while with my young son, I will visit Constantine Mortimer. I have never liked him – he is hard on his wife Katherine and she is a kindly soul. Then I will see Oswald Stanmore and then Father Paul. Hopefully, by then the word will have spread.'

He gave the scholars an absent grin and went to make his announcement to the soldiers in the bailey. Bartholomew and Michael left him to make a conspicuous show of organising his surprise raids and began to walk back towards Michaelhouse. On the way they met Cynric and dispatched him to tell Father Paul to dispose of his smuggled cloaks, while Bartholomew went with Michael to warn Stanmore.

It was nearing dusk, and the apprentices were busy taking bales of cloth into the storerooms and tidying their tools away. Bartholomew sensed a light-heartedness that had been lacking before: Stanmore and Edith might grieve for Thorpe, but their apprentices certainly did not. Francis darted up to Michael and flashed him a grateful grin full of missing teeth, before racing off to help another boy close the storehouse doors. Stanmore emerged from his house, straining to read some jottings on a scrap of parchment. He stopped when he saw Bartholomew and Michael.

'What has he done now?' he asked with a weary sigh. 'Has he accused me of ordering him to kill the Countess? Or Edith?'

'We have not come about Rob Thorpe,' said Bartholomew. 'Tulyet is arresting people who are thought to be involved in smuggling.'

Stanmore met his eyes levelly. 'So I have heard. Are you implying I might be a smuggler?'

Bartholomew sighed. 'I am implying nothing, Oswald. I am merely passing you information. Tulyet says he can arrest offenders only if he finds evidence of smuggled goods in their possession.'

Stanmore stroked his beard and watched the high-spirited apprentices jostling and pushing at each other as they finished their chores. 'I appreciate what you are trying to do, but I assure you it is unnecessary.'

Bartholomew nodded. He had delivered his message, and if Stanmore chose to ignore it then that was his business.

'You misunderstand me,' said Stanmore, reading Bartholomew's thoughts with the ghost of a smile. 'I am not trying to tell you I am not guilty: I would have been foolish to pass up a business opportunity such as has been presented this winter – there is barely a merchant in the town who has declined the trade that has come our way, and honesty would have forced a man out of business – but I am not so unwise as to leave evidence of it lying around in my own storerooms.' He gestured with his hand. 'I can provide legal documentation for every fibre of cloth here and at my premises at Ely. And as for elsewhere, who knows where to look?'

Bartholomew was astounded. He had never entertained any doubts about his brother-in-law's ruthless efficiency in business, but he had not realised his talents extended to calm and skilful evasion of the King's taxes. Stanmore made the other merchants, whose apprentices scurried here and there carrying hastily wrapped bundles, look like amateurs.

Edith emerged from the kitchens, wiping her floury hands on her apron. Her eyes were red and Bartholomew knew she had been crying.

'Matt has been telling me that Sheriff Tulyet is rounding up all those merchants who have been acquiring illicit goods through smuggling this winter,' said Stanmore.

Edith shook her head. 'Silly men! If they are so greedy, they deserve to be arrested!'

Behind her back, Stanmore winked at Bartholomew. Edith invited them for some cakes and mulled wine and, anxious to begin to heal the rift that still yawned between them, Bartholomew accepted. They sat for some time in Stanmore's solar discussing the mild weather, the problems Michael faced in finding appropriate music for his choir, and the poor quality of the wool shipment Stanmore had recently received from Flanders – anything, in fact, except smuggling and the nasty affair of the murderous Rob Thorpe.

'We should go,' said Michael, taking the last cake and cramming it in his mouth. 'It is almost supper time.'

They made their farewells, Bartholomew relieved to escape the somewhat strained conversation. He sensed Edith was ambiguous in her feelings about his role in exposing Thorpe, but supposed she would come to accept it, given time. At least, he hoped so.

In Milne Street the scene was chaotic, with people running here and there in uncontrolled mayhem. Dogs barked, men swore and panted under heavy burdens, and furious arguments took place as merchants squabbled over buying space on the barges moored at the wharves, to secrete their ill-gotten gains away before the Sheriff found them.

The cause of all the panic was at the house of Constantine Mortimer. Indignant gibbering pursued Tulyet as he emerged from Mortimer's house carrying a box. The baker scuttled after him, his red, bellicose face outraged, while his son Edward and wife Katherine were at his heels. Mortimer saw Bartholomew, and stopped dead in his tracks.

'For God's sake, man!' he hissed, looking around him furtively. 'Take off those damned gloves or you will have us both in the Sheriff's prisons!'

'I am sure Matt will furnish me with a receipt for those – should I feel the need to ask him for one,' said Tulyet, making Mortimer jump by speaking in his ear. 'Quite unlike this wine, I imagine.'

'I had no idea that was there,' Mortimer insisted angrily. 'I never use that cellar. It is damp.'

'Of course,' said Tulyet drily. 'Someone must have slipped into your cellars and hidden it carefully behind that pile of old crates for safekeeping. It is odd how so many people seem to have found themselves in the same position today.'

'You are quite mistaken, father,' said Edward nervously. 'You bought that wine last summer. You have been keeping it to allow it to mature.'

'The King allows his wines to mature before drinking them,' put in Katherine.

'Rubbish!' said Mortimer impatiently. 'I remember purchasing no wine.'

'Of course you do, dear,' said Katherine, favouring him with an indulgent smile. 'You said we might drink it to celebrate Edward's coming of age.'

Mortimer looked taken aback, and his certainty began to waver. 'Did I?' he said, frowning.

Bartholomew went to the box Tulyet was placing on the back of a cart and looked inside. There were six bottles made of smoked glass, the wine dark red inside them. He started back. The last time he had seen such a bottle it had been smashed on the floor under Isaac's work-bench. He exchanged a glance with Michael.

'When did you purchase this wine?' asked Michael. 'And where?'

'Why?' demanded Edward, uncharacteristically aggressive. 'Father's wines are no concern of the University.'

'Really?' said Michael, fixing him with a hard stare.

'It is just good French wine,' said Katherine, smiling lightly. 'No more, no less.'

Mortimer looked from one to the other belligerently. 'All this fuss over half a crate of wine!' he snapped. 'If Katherine says I bought it, I did. I will have a receipt somewhere for it. I will hunt it out tomorrow.'

'You will not find it,' said Michael. 'Because you never

bought it.' He turned to Edward and Katherine. 'Despite the fact that your family is trying to suggest you did.'

'He did buy it,' insisted Edward. 'Just because he does not remember, it does not mean to say it did not happen.'

'You cheeky whelp!' said Mortimer, taking a step towards his son threateningly. 'Do you imply I am losing my wits? The business is not yours yet, Edward; you must wait until I die.'

Edward said nothing, although his expression indicated that Mortimer's words generated ambiguous emotions within him: while he might long to be rid of his dominating, bellicose father, he certainly did not relish the prospect of inheriting a business in which he had no interest.

'Perhaps you would care to try some,' said Katherine, leaning into the box to take a bottle and offer it to Michael. 'We have already sampled the other six bottles and found it most delicious.'

'But James Grene did not,' said Bartholomew. 'And neither did Brother Armel.'

Mortimer stared at him and then began to laugh. 'The University's poisoned wine! You think this is it! How ridiculous! Give it to me. I will prove how wrong you are.'

He snatched the wine from Katherine and raised it to his mouth to draw out the cork with his teeth. Bartholomew slapped his hand down.

'No,' he said. He took the bottle carefully from the indignant Mortimer and held it out to Edward. 'You drink it.'

Edward regarded the bottle in horror and put his hands behind his back.

'Edward does not drink wine,' said Katherine quickly. 'It makes him sick.'

'Rubbish!' said Mortimer. 'He had some last night with no ill effects. Drink the wine, Edward. Prove to these insolent scholars how they slander the name of Mortimer.'

Edward reached out a hand and slowly took the bottle from Bartholomew. Hesitantly, he began to raise it to his lips.

'No!' Katherine dashed the bottle from Edward's hand and it smashed on the ground. Everyone leapt backwards and, for a moment, all eyes were on the dark liquid that pooled in the mud of the street. Then Edward tore towards Tulyet, knocked him off his feet, and had darted up Milne Street before anyone could stop him. Tulyet's men gaped at him stupidly before the Sheriff's angry cry set them racing after him.

Mortimer looked about him in confusion. 'What is going on?' he demanded of Katherine. 'What is he doing? Stupid boy! How does he imagine he will become a Master Baker when he is given to this kind of behaviour?'

Tulyet climbed to his feet and took Katherine by the arm. 'It seems you have some explaining to do, madam. Your husband is not the only one who wants to know what you have been plotting.'

Katherine met his eyes coolly, but said nothing.

'For God's sake, Katherine!' yelled Mortimer in sudden fury. 'What is happening?'

'Nothing!' she said to Tulyet. 'Edward and I have done nothing. The wine is Constantine's.'

'It is over, Katherine,' said Tulyet quietly. 'It is clear Master Mortimer knows nothing about this wine. But it is equally clear that you and Edward do.'

'Not so,' said Katherine in the same calm voice. 'Edward is a timid boy, and he has always been frightened of his father. It was from Constantine he fled, not from you as a sign of guilt.'

'Who was the third person?' demanded Michael. 'It was you and Edward who went to Gonville to reclaim the poisoned wine from Isaac once you realised it was there. You knocked me over as you came racing out. But who else was with you? Who helped you kill Isaac?'

'We have killed no one,' said Katherine. 'I do not know what you are talking about.'

'What are you saying?' said Mortimer, bewildered as he

looked from Michael to Katherine. 'Of what are you accusing my wife?'

'Of murder,' said Michael. He pointed a soft white finger at the remaining bottles. 'Crates of wine from this part of France tend to contain a dozen bottles. So, we can assume that originally there were twelve, but that a little over a month ago six were stolen by an opportunistic thief named Sacks.'

'Sacks?' queried one of Tulyet's sergeants, as he lounged against the wall watching the exchange with interest. 'Has he been busy again?'

'Sacks sold the wine he stole from you in the Brazen George – two bottles to Rob Thorpe and three bottles to Brother Armel. One of Thorpe's bottles killed Will Harper, the boy we pulled from the well, and the other killed James Grene.' Michael's eyes never left Katherine's face. 'Harper died more than a month ago, but it was not until last Saturday that Sacks tried to sell the remaining bottles.'

'Sacks has been in the castle prison,' said Tulyet's sergeant, eager to join in. 'We kept him for three weeks for selling stolen goods. It was a petty matter and we did not think to bother you with it, Master Tulyet, knowing how all your time was taken up with hunting down the outlaws. He was released last Saturday – the morning of the installation.'

'I see,' said Michael. He turned his attention back to Katherine. 'You must have thought you were off the hook when no tales of violent death were rumoured around the town. Then last Saturday Grene died horribly and publicly at the installation. Edward was there and must have seen it – although you were absent because of your husband's illness. It was followed by rumours about the death of Armel, and you knew the wine was finally beginning to surface.'

Katherine shook her head and smiled. 'I really have no idea what you are talking about. I know nothing of stolen

wine. I have already told you we drank the six bottles you
see missing from the crate.'

Michael continued relentlessly. 'In desperation, knowing
that it might be traced back to you via Sacks, you took steps
to remove the evidence – you stole four of the bottles from
Michaelhouse, first terrifying poor Walter, our porter, out
of his wits, and then went to Gonville to see whether Matt
had been called to physic another case of poisoning. Cynric
saw you – three of you – in the shadows in St Michael's
Lane, waiting to slip unnoticed into Michaelhouse as soon
as the coast was clear. After you searched his room and
found what you wanted, you went to Gonville, where you
had heard the messenger tell Walter that Philius had been
struck down with a strange illness. You followed Isaac from
Philius's room when he went to fetch the wine he had used
in the purge, and you stunned him with a savage blow to the
head in the ensuing struggle. You could not risk leaving him
alive to identify you, so you hanged him to make certain he
would die.'

Katherine gave a short laugh of bemusement. 'How can
you think such a thing of me? How could I hang a man
from the rafters? I am only a woman, not a great brawny
ox, like you.'

'From the rafters, was it?' pounced Michael. 'But you
have not been listening. I said there were three of you,
so you did not murder Isaac alone. When you could not
find the bottle – which had been smashed by the College
cat and lay in pieces under the work-bench – one of you
stayed to look again, while the other two went to see if it
was still in Philius's room. It was while you were looking
there that Matt disturbed you, and the three of you fled,
knocking me over on the way out. But, fortunately for one
of you, Matt had found the broken bottle under the bench,
and it was an easy matter to scrape up the pieces before
you left.'

'This is all wild nonsense,' said Katherine in disbelief.

She turned to Bartholomew. 'Has the good Brother been drinking? Is he wholly in his right mind?'

'Wholly, Mistress,' said Bartholomew coldly. 'And you also killed Philius in his bed and chopped Egil's head from his neck.'

'Who is Egil?' asked Katherine with an expression of profound confusion. 'And why would I do such a foul thing? I am no warlock!'

'Because he was the smuggler who brought you this wine across the Fens,' said Bartholomew.

'But this is outrageous!' protested Katherine, laughing. 'This Egil's head was probably stolen by wild animals.'

'So that is what we were meant to believe, was it?' said Michael.

Katherine shook her head in exasperation and went to her husband. 'Constantine! Why do you stand there and allow them to insult me? Call for the Chancellor and tell him to order these University men away, because I will sue them for slander if they continue in this vein. They are trying to provoke a riot by accusing a townsperson of vile crimes!'

Mortimer looked from her to Bartholomew, bewildered. 'I do not understand how you arrived at all these conclusions. You have no evidence with which to accuse my wife, only wild guesses.'

In his heart, Bartholomew knew the baker was right. No court of law would find Katherine guilty on the evidence they had. Bartholomew was certain their reasoning was accurate, but the only clue that Katherine was involved came from her apparent attempt to implicate her bullying husband by claiming the wine was his. It was true that she had prevented Edward from drinking it, and provided him with the opportunity to flee, but it was hardly solid proof. He glanced at Michael, seeing his own frustration mirrored in the fat monk's face.

They all turned at the sound of a violent altercation

between John Cheney and another of Tulyet's men, who was attempting to inspect a large barrel.

'I will not broach it,' the spice-merchant was shouting. 'That is finest quality sea salt and the rain will spoil the contents. I have shown you all the legal documentation for it and you have no right to press me further!'

'It will take only a moment!' yelled the soldier in his turn. 'Your records show it is almost empty anyway. I just want to ensure nothing has been hidden with its legal contents.'

'But water will ruin the salt,' shouted Cheney, putting his hand palm up to emphasise his point. Rain fell steadily in fine, misty droplets.

'We could move it inside,' suggested the soldier, more quietly.

Cheney considered. 'Very well, then,' he conceded in a more reasonable tone of voice. 'As long as you put it back where you found it.'

The barrel in dispute stood just inside the gates to Cheney's yard. An idea suddenly formed in Bartholomew's mind. Katherine and her pugilistic husband forgotten, he walked over to the barrel and tapped on it. It sounded hollow.

'And what do you think you are doing?' Cheney snapped, angry again. 'Get off my property!'

Bartholomew turned to Tulyet and Michael. 'I wonder if we might . . . ?'

He stopped as he saw Katherine clutch her throat and sway dizzily. Next to her, Mortimer watched his wife in disbelief as a smoky bottle slipped from her nerveless fingers and smashed on the ground. Tulyet darted forward and caught her as she swooned, but as Bartholomew ran towards them, he could see there was nothing that could be done to save her. Her eyes rolled back in her head and she began to convulse in Tulyet's arms. Bartholomew called for water to wash the poison from her mouth, but even as he did so, he knew it would do no good. After a few moments, her desperate attempts to breathe eased and she went limp.

'My God!' breathed Tulyet in horror. He eased the body onto the ground and looked up at Bartholomew. 'She is dead already. What *is* this poison?'

Even a sudden death in one of the town's busiest thoroughfares did little to slow the frantic activity there. One or two people stopped to look at Katherine Mortimer's body as it lay in the rain, but most ignored the scene outside the baker's house, too anxious to ensure their own businesses were in order to risk interfering with someone else's. Mortimer knelt next to his wife, holding her limp hand in his with an expression of total mystification, as though he imagined she might leap to her feet at any moment and tell him it had been some kind of macabre joke. Tulyet, Michael and Bartholomew stood over him, while the sergeant shouted to one of his men to help carry the body into the house.

'Do you have any idea at all where this foul stuff came from?' asked Tulyet, poking one of the bottles in the crate on his cart with his dagger. 'Or how much of it is currently loose in the town?'

Michael shook his head. 'I made the erroneous assumption that there were only six bottles in total. Now we find there was a full case of twelve. I have no idea whether this is all of it, or whether another crate is lurking somewhere.'

Bartholomew looked down at the lifeless form of Mistress Mortimer. 'I have never seen any poison work as quickly as this before. Neither had Philius.'

'Philius was good with poisons,' said Tulyet, moving away from the crate with a shudder. 'He used to help Jonas the Apothecary prepare potions to kill lice and fleas, while his reputation for producing effective concoctions to rid granaries of rats stretched as far afield as Thetford. All the Franciscans in the Friary on Bridge Street are good with herbs and powders.'

'Well, that's Franciscans for you!' muttered Michael. 'While we Benedictines live our lives in serene contemplation and prayer, the Franciscans find themselves one of the best houses in Bridge Street and find new ways to kill things.'

Something horrible occurred to Bartholomew as he stared down at the lifeless features of Katherine Mortimer. Had he, by encouraging Philius to investigate the nature of the poison that had made him so ill and killed Will Harper, Grene and Armel, inadvertently brought about Philius's death? He spoke his thoughts aloud.

'Master Colton of Gonville Hall said he went with Philius to visit the Franciscan Friary – where Philius told me he would ask about this poison among his colleagues. It must have been the fact that he was asking questions that aroused the suspicions of Katherine and her associates, and Philius must have been killed before he could come too close to the truth.'

Michael tapped him smartly on the arm. 'You could not have prevented Philius's death, Matt. How were you – or any of us – to know that his asking questions about a kind of poison in his own Friary would make someone want to kill him?'

'We misjudged Colton, too,' said Bartholomew, facts coming together in his mind. 'I was certain his determination to suppress knowledge of Philius's murder was a sign of guilty involvement. Now I see his suspicious behaviour was nothing more than a desire to keep the Sheriff well away from his College and its activities while he was indulging himself in a little smuggling.'

'Of course,' said Michael, nodding. 'That explains why he was so nervous, and why he tried to claim his College could not be connected to the poisoned wine and the deaths of Grene and Armel – he did not want me or the Sheriff to start digging too deeply into Gonville's affairs given that the cellars are probably well stocked with all sorts of contraband.'

'But why would someone kill Philius for asking about the

poison?' asked Tulyet. 'Its nature is no secret – half the town saw Grene die.'

'It seems a curious substance to me,' said Bartholomew, kneeling to look more closely at Katherine's body. 'It killed Grene, Will Harper, Armel and now Katherine almost instantly, but it only made Philius ill. And it killed the rat, but the cat which I saw drinking it escaped unscathed.'

'You and that wretched cat!' exclaimed Michael, exasperated. 'You must have been mistaken about it. The wine has certainly killed Katherine stone dead.'

Bartholomew continued to inspect the corpse. Her husband still held one of her hands and gaped at her in stunned disbelief, while the sergeant muttered meaningless and trite words of comfort in his ear and attempted to make him stand up. On Katherine's other hand was a burn where the wine had attacked her skin as she had opened the bottle, like the ones on Isaac and the porter at Valence Marie.

The sergeant finally succeeded in prising the baker from his wife's side and led him into the house, leaving two of his men to cover Katherine with a cloak and carry her inside. The soldiers treated the body with an exaggerated care that had nothing to do with respect for the dead and a good deal to do with their respect for the poison. Bartholomew helped them, protecting his own hands with the gloves Katherine herself had given him just a few days before.

'I suppose we can assume he is innocent in all this?' asked Tulyet, watching Mortimer stumbling through the door to his house with the sergeant behind him.

'He certainly acted as though he were,' said Michael. 'His unbearable arrogance and temper must have led his wife and son to plot against him. She was quite happy for him to take the blame for owning the poisoned wine.'

'But Mortimer was right – we had no real evidence against her,' said Bartholomew. 'I am sure what we have reasoned is correct, but she must have seen we had no proof.'

'I have known Constantine Mortimer for many years,' said

Tulyet with a sigh. 'I can see he would have given his wife no peace over this – whether your accusations were unproven or not. He kept her on a short rein, and she was never allowed out unless he or Edward were with her. I am sure she knew her chances of running away from him were remote, and so she must have decided to drink the wine when she realised her future was bleak.'

'You mean just saying what we did induced her to take her own life?' asked Bartholomew, horrified. 'I sincerely hope you are wrong.'

'She killed herself because she knew we had her measure, and that it would be only a matter of time before we had the proof of it,' said Michael firmly. 'We are not responsible for her death.'

Bartholomew looked at Cheney's barrel, his scrutiny of which seemed to have tipped her to drinking the poisoned wine in the first place. Was there proof of her guilt concealed within it? 'Perhaps she has more of this wine stored there. Or perhaps . . .'

His voice trailed away as he regarded the barrel. Gradually, as realisation dawned on him, it went from being a simple container to something sinister, and he was certain that whatever it contained, it was not salt. He walked slowly towards it and borrowed a dagger from one of Tulyet's men to prise off the lid.

'What are you doing?' demanded Cheney crossly, trying to snatch the weapon away from him. 'That is finest sea salt from Hunstanton and it will be no good if it gets wet. Sheriff Tulyet! Stop this man at once!'

'Perhaps you should allow one of my soldiers to do this,' said Tulyet without conviction, leaning against the wall with his arms folded, making no attempt to prevent Bartholomew from levering at the lid, but watching with interest. 'Master Cheney does not seem to like it.'

'I most certainly do not!' shouted Cheney. 'If water spoils that salt, I shall expect you to pay for it. You have no right to force your way on to my property and take liberties with my barrels.'

The lid came off with a creaking pop and Bartholomew glanced inside. Immediately, he backed away coughing. Cheney elbowed him out of the way and looked himself. He gave a gasp of horror, hands flying to his mouth as he saw what was in it, the blood draining from his face.

Crouched in the barrel was the body of a small man wearing rough, homespun clothes, while on his lap lay Egil's decapitated head. The stench was overpowering, a sickly, sulphurous reek of decay mingled with salt and rotting wood. Cheney regained the use of his legs and backed away hurriedly, colliding with Michael as he did so.

'It is Sacks,' said Tulyet, looking down at the thief and wrinkling his nose at the smell. 'Sacks and someone else's head.'

'Egil's head,' said Michael, after a very cursory glance. 'Hacked from his shoulders after we left his body for Oswald Stanmore to collect from the Fens. We wondered what had happened to it.'

'And *we* wondered what had happened to Sacks,' said Tulyet's sergeant, emerging from Mortimer's house and peering over Michael's shoulder into the barrel. He showed no particular emotion at the grisly sight, not even surprise: he had seen a good deal worse as a soldier during the King's wars in France. 'When we realised we had not seen him for a few days, we assumed he had decided to move away from Cambridge after his spell in our prison, to try his skills where he was less well known.'

'His hands have red marks,' said Bartholomew, pointing to blisters on the thief's fingers. 'The Bernard's students said there was something wrong with his skin. He must have been burned by one of the bottles.'

He leaned in and poked around, digging into the coarse-grained salt in search of more evidence. After a moment he found it.

'Here are Egil's hands,' he said, drawing one out and holding it up. Tulyet slapped his arm down, aware that a curious crowd was beginning to gather, and that their mood was uneasy. While Katherine Mortimer dropping stone dead in Milne Street might not be cause for more than a passing glance, dismembered corpses in spice barrels were another matter entirely. Cheney gave another stifled exclamation of horror and swallowed hard.

'I suppose I will not be able to use that lovely salt now,' he said shakily. 'No one will buy it if they know where it has been.'

'You should dispose of it quickly, then,' said Bartholomew, aware that if the spice-merchant did not rid himself of the tainted salt while the vile memories were fresh in his mind, he might have second thoughts about throwing it away. Apart from one or two patches that were stained black, it certainly appeared to be clean enough, and could easily be stored until the time was right to sell it.

'My sergeant will relieve you of it now,' said Tulyet, apparently thinking along the same lines. 'He will throw it in the King's Ditch and have the barrel scoured out with boiling water for you.'

'We were right about the poison and Egil – there *are* burn marks on his hands, just like the ones on Sacks's,' said Bartholomew. 'And there are small blisters on Egil's face, too, although they have nearly healed. We must have been blind not to notice them earlier. I imagine Egil spilled the wine when he transported the bottles across the Fens. His face was probably burned when he transferred the poison to it from his hands – while Sacks's hands were burned when he touched the bottles he sold to the Bernard's students and Thorpe.'

Michael turned to Tulyet. 'Do you need more from me or can I leave this matter with you? Matt may be happy to poke about with dismembered corpses, but I have had quite enough of all this!'

Tulyet nodded assent. 'I have only one question. Matt, how did you guess Sacks's body and Egil's missing parts were in Cheney's salt? It was when you walked over to it that Katherine realised the game she was playing was over and drank the poisoned wine.'

'I did not,' said Bartholomew tiredly. 'I was going to ask Cheney if he had another of similar size that we might borrow as a water barrel for people to use while the well is drained.'

The following afternoon, Bartholomew perched on the trunk of a fallen apple tree in the orchard behind Michaelhouse and watched Tulyet. The Sheriff leaned against the wall and kicked at a rotten apple left from the previous summer and somehow missed by worms and maggots. Next to Bartholomew, Michael sat devouring the last of a fruit pie he had stolen from the kitchens. There would be hell to pay when Agatha discovered it was missing.

'I think you succeeded admirably,' Michael said to the Sheriff, ducking out of the way as pieces of apple flew from under Tulyet's boot. 'You clearly could not arrest everyone involved in this business, or the town would have lost virtually its entire population. You gave sufficient warning so that most had the opportunity to dispose of their ill-gotten gains, but yet the offenders have had enough of a fright from their narrow escape that it will be a long time before they think of cheating the King out of his taxes again.'

'I suppose so,' said Tulyet moodily. 'Although I will be saying masses for a short and very cold winter next year. All this happened because the waterways are so open.'

'Why the gloom?' asked Michael, finishing the pie and wiping his sticky fingers on his habit. 'You have done just what the King would have wished. He will raise town taxes and the merchants will be too guilt-stricken to protest. Everyone will gain from your discreet handling of the affair.'

Tulyet shook his head. 'I have the Fenmen who smuggled

the occasional barrel of brandy and I know exactly which merchants and scholars used the established routes to bring in smuggled goods since the beginning of winter. But neither of these groups is responsible for the outlaws I have been hunting. These are still at large.'

Michael raised his hands in the air, exasperated by Tulyet's continuing claims that the case was not yet fully solved. 'But the outlaws must be Fenmen hired by the merchants to bring the goods along the waterways.'

Tulyet shook his head. 'Because the Fens are flooded, it is not difficult to travel across them by boat. Anyone can do it this year, and no special knowledge of Fenland geography is needed. No new men were hired – the merchants simply used their own people to bring the goods in. For example, I know that Stanmore's steward, Hugh, was responsible for bringing cloth from the Wash to Cambridge and he has no experience of the Fens whatsoever.'

'But if you know which of the merchants' "own people" were used, arrest them,' said Michael impatiently. 'They will be your outlaws – hired louts like Stanmore's Hugh who decided to take advantage of jaunts out of town to do a little business for themselves. I do not see your problem.'

'The merchants' people are men I know,' said Tulyet. 'I cannot see the likes of Hugh committing robberies and burglaries. I may have uncovered the Fenmen's little business and unnerved the merchants and some scholars, but I still do not have the outlaws.'

'Are you sure?' asked Michael, unconvinced. 'My informant was very clear about the names of the smugglers. If you are certain the merchants and their servants are not to blame, then the culprits must be among the Fenmen.'

Tulyet sighed, and scratched his head. 'Perhaps you are right. I suppose I will have to question them all over again.'

'I offered you my services for that,' said Michael.

Tulyet nodded absently. 'Perhaps I will have to accept. But I was convinced they were being honest with me.'

'It seems honesty is not a virtue widely practised around here,' said Michael, gazing meaningfully at Bartholomew's cloak and gloves. 'I am shocked that so many people I considered principled, law-abiding citizens have gaily travelled along the paths of iniquity and turpitude.'

'Do not be so pompous, Brother,' said Bartholomew, tugging off his gloves and shoving them in his bag. He stood up and prepared to take his leave. 'I must go. I am due to lecture on Theophilus's *De Urinis* at King's Hall tomorrow, and I should prepare something if I do not want to appear totally incompetent.'

'A lecture on urine sounds almost as inviting as hearing Langelee pontificating on the creation of the world,' said Michael scathingly. 'Personally, I would rather talk to Dick's vile little smugglers in his dank and rat-infested prison.'

Tulyet smiled suddenly. 'Remember I told you that I searched Thomas Deschalers's house? His stored lemons were wholly legal as it transpired – the pomegranates, figs and nuts were imported by Cheney – but there was a woman staying with Deschalers who almost had him arrested regardless of his innocence. As I was talking to him, a lemon dropped from her sleeve, and her bedchamber was filled to the gills with them, where she had made an attempt to hide them away. She had the brazen effrontery to offer one to me as a gift!' He drew it out of his pocket and showed it to Bartholomew.

'Julianna,' said Bartholomew, in sudden understanding. 'Yes, she would.'

'She was quite a challenge,' said Tulyet, his eyes glittering with amusement as he recalled the scene. 'When I asked to inspect Deschalers's cellars, he immediately gave me permission. But this woman – Julianna – refused point blank. She overrode Deschalers as if he were her servant. Who is she? His harlot?'

Michael gave an unpleasant leer. 'His niece.'

Tulyet blew out his cheeks. 'What a harpy! She hurled

herself at my sergeant like a wild animal, and screamed that if he wanted to inspect the cellars, it would be over her dead body. He offered to arrange it and she backed off. Then, when Deschalers provided us with all the legal documentation for his stored fruit, she turned to him with such an expression of shock that I could not help but laugh. I have never seen such a performance that bespoke of her belief in his guilt in my life!'

Michael smiled. 'She was betrothed to Edward Mortimer. Perhaps he has had a lucky escape.'

Bartholomew was certain he had.

Tulyet sighed and stretched. 'I should be at home with my family – it is Sunday, after all.' He tossed the lemon in the air and caught it. 'What shall I do with this?'

'Well, do not eat it raw,' said Bartholomew. 'And do not give it to your infant son.'

Tulyet grinned. 'I heard about Mortimer's illness. Katherine probably fed him the raw lemons to see if she might kill him. You have this. I do not want to be walking around the town with bribes in my pocket!'

He threw the hard fruit to Bartholomew and departed, leaving the two scholars alone. Bartholomew put the lemon in the pocket in his shirt and shivered, reaching down for his bag.

'It is too cold to be out here,' he said. 'And there is a fire in the conclave today.'

'You would never get near it,' said Michael, leaning back comfortably. 'All the Fellows and commoners are there, and Langelee is entertaining them with some story about a journey he took to Bristol last year.'

'That does not sound appealing in the slightest,' admitted Bartholomew, sitting down again. 'I do not like that man. I was hoping he would be implicated in all this smuggling so we might be rid of him.'

'I told you that I would have a few words here and there,' said Michael, making it sound most sinister. 'I will put it about that he drinks, and that I am afraid he will spark off some incident that might cause a riot. Kenyngham will not wish to risk that, no matter who is pressuring him to employ Langelee.'

'So, Colton, Julianna and Eligius, whom I was certain were as guilty as sin, are now wholly vindicated,' said Bartholomew, his mind still running over the events of the past few days.

'Do not speak too soon,' said Michael. 'You heard Tulyet say there are still outlaws at large.'

'Colton and Julianna are hardly likely to be outlaws,' said Bartholomew. 'And Eligius is dead.'

Michael sat up straight and stretched his burly arms so hard they cracked. 'I said I would return to Valence Marie today and tell them more about what Thorpe confessed to doing in their hallowed halls.'

'And what was that exactly?' asked Bartholomew, pulling his borrowed cloak closer around him, reluctant to return to his room to start work on his lecture. 'The last I heard, he was professing his innocence and big bad Grene was entirely to blame.'

'He has stuck to his story,' said Michael. 'But we were essentially right. He turned to Grene when Will Harper died from drinking Sacks's wine, and Grene told him how and where to dispose of the body so that he would not be dismissed from Stanmore's service. He confided to Grene how he yearned to strike a blow at the College that allowed his father to be disgraced, and Grene worked out a plan that would allow him to do just that.'

'And Grene really did drink the poison knowingly?'

Michael nodded. 'I think Rob Thorpe is telling the truth – although my ability to distinguish between liars and honest men is sorely stretched these days. I am inclined to believe Grene felt sufficiently bitter to use his public suicide to destroy his hated rival, Bingham. We know from Philius that he was dying anyway, and we know from Eligius that he took some care to ensure three Fellows knew he considered himself in danger from Bingham. Even if Bingham had not been convicted of his murder, the suspicion would have hung over him like the Sword of Damocles.'

'And the Countess?'

Michael gave a nasty smile. 'That was all Thorpe's own idea, although he did try to convince me that Grene's tormented spirit appeared to him in a dream and ordered him to do it.'

'What will happen to him?'

'I imagine he will be expelled from the country,' said Michael without much interest. 'He will be stripped of his possessions and put on a ship for France – best place for him, if you ask me. The Countess wants him hanged, though. She is afraid he will try to kill her again.'

'He might,' said Bartholomew. 'Poor Eligius!'

'Yes,' agreed Michael. 'It just goes to show that you should never think good of people. If Eligius had been suspicious and cynical like the rest of us, he would never have drunk that wine. But you live and learn. Well, he did not, I suppose. Will you come with me to Valence Marie?'

'No, thank you,' said Bartholomew quickly. 'Every time I visit that College, either someone dies or someone tries to kill me. And anyway, I need to think about this lecture.'

'Walk with me to the Trumpington Gate, then,' said Michael, standing and adjusting the cowl on his cloak. 'Edith told me at church this morning that Mistress Pike is unlikely to last the day. She lives near Valence Marie, so you can keep me company and see her at the same time. You have given lectures on Theophilus a hundred times, and have no need for preparations.'

'I have seen her twice today already,' said Bartholomew. 'There is nothing more I can do.'

But he followed Michael through the orchard towards the back gate. Because it was Sunday, there were no trader's carts rattling up and down the lane, and the town was unusually peaceful. Agatha's cockerel crowed somewhere in the distance, and a blackbird sang sweetly from one of the trees in the orchard. They walked in silence, each wrapped in his own thoughts. Bartholomew's mind jumped between considering whether it was safe to visit Matilde and relieve her of Dame Pelagia, and Edith's continuing distress over Thorpe. Michael pondered how he might inveigle an invitation to dine at Valence Marie and still manage to have supper at Michaelhouse.

Above, the sky grew blacker as heavy rain clouds gathered, so that it seemed as though dusk was already approaching even though it was only mid-afternoon. A golden shaft of sunrays broke through unexpectedly, and illuminated the soft creamy stone of St Mary's Church, making it dazzle like gold in the sullen light of the clouds. As they passed, Bartholomew squinted as it reflected off the shiny ground, and stumbled from not being able to see where he was treading. But the sunlight was short-lived, and by the time they reached the Trumpington Gate, the clouds had filled in the gaps, and the first, great drops of rain began to fall, splattering into the mud.

'If this foul weather continues, we will be forced to build an ark,' grumbled Michael, glancing upwards. 'I had no idea the heavens could hold so much water!'

Still muttering complaints, he stamped inside Valence Marie, while Bartholomew continued on to the house of the ailing Mistress Pike. His journey was wasted, however, because he was told she had died a few moments earlier. Since she was well over eighty years old, Bartholomew supposed he should not be surprised, but the death of a patient always unsettled him. Her family politely insisted that he should stay until the storm passed over, but Bartholomew did not feel comfortable waiting in a house filled with grieving relatives and left as soon as he could.

The rain was coming down hard, and the cloak Paul had lent him had no hood. For an instant, he regretted his decision not to tarry at Mistress Pike's house, but then realised he would be able to take shelter in the little church of St Peter-without-Trumpington Gate. Breaking into a run as the drops fell more heavily, he dashed through the grassy graveyard and took the great brass handle in both hands to open the door. It was locked. Bartholomew swore under his breath, flinching as large, cold drips splattered on his bare head. But it made sense to keep the building secured: it was vulnerable, standing as it did outside the city gates with the outlaws' attacks drawing ever nearer to the town.

He stood under a tree in the churchyard, trying to keep out of the wet. He glanced up the High Street. The guards on the gate had abandoned their posts, and the few people who were braving the downpour passed through it unquestioned. Bartholomew did not relish the notion of walking back to Michaelhouse in weather so foul that he could barely see, and decided it might be an opportune time to visit his medical colleague Master Lynton at nearby Peterhouse. Now that Philius was dead, he and Bartholomew were the only physicians in Cambridge, and were likely to be thrown more and more into each other's company. And they could start, Bartholomew decided, by debating some of the issues in Theophilus's *De Urinis* that he was to lecture on at King's Hall the following day.

Pulling his cloak closer around him, grateful for Mortimer's smuggled gloves to protect his hands against the icy chill of the rain, he was about to leave the partial shelter of the tree and run the short distance to Peterhouse, when a sudden prod in his back made him stop. He started to turn, but was arrested by a voice hissing in his ear.

'Do not move! I have a sharp knife, Bartholomew. You do what I say, or I will kill you.' The knife jabbed again. 'Do you understand?'

Bartholomew nodded, his heart pounding. Was this one of the men who had tried to kill him and Michael in the Fens, back for a second attempt? He started to turn again, but the knife pricked at his spine, harder this time.

'Be still!'

The voice was no longer a hiss, and Bartholomew was able to recognise it.

'Harling!'

'Harling!' the voice behind him mimicked. 'Harling, indeed! Now, we are going to walk together through the churchyard and away from the road. If you shout out, or try to alert anyone, I will strike you dead. The guards are unlikely to venture from their lodge in this weather, but it pays to be cautious.'

The Vice-Chancellor took a firm hold on Bartholomew's right arm with his left hand, while his right hand pushed the knife into Bartholomew's side, just under the ribs. The physician inched away, repelled by the sickly odour of perfumed grease from Harling's slicked hair, but Harling held him tightly, and forced him back into the tangle of bushes and trees that surrounded the church.

At first, the foliage became denser, and Bartholomew wondered whether Harling meant to murder him there, where his body might not be found for days. But then the tangle thinned and he found they were at the edge of Coe Fen, an area of common land between the King's Mill and Peterhouse. The extended rains had flooded it, so it was no longer viable for grazing, and the meadows were deserted. Bartholomew moved his feet, hearing the squelch of sodden grass, and knew the chances of someone passing that way to help him were remote. Further downstream, the great King's Mill wheel pounded the water of the mill race. With a distant part of his mind, Bartholomew wondered why the miller would risk using it when the Cam was in full spate – especially considering it was a Sunday, when work was forbidden.

Harling pushed him forwards until they stood near the edge of the swollen river, close to where it swirled past in a muddy brown torrent of eddies and waves. It had ripped small trees and branches from its banks further upstream, and these bobbed and dipped in its unsteady currents. Bartholomew was suddenly reminded of his near drowning in the Fens, and hoped that was not what Harling had in mind for him.

Cursing, Harling inadvertently glanced down at the ground as his leg sank into mud to the calf, and Bartholomew seized the opportunity to attempt to break away. He hurled himself to one side and tried to scramble out of Harling's reach. But the ground was slippery with rain, and Harling's reactions were much faster than he had anticipated. Harling had pounced on him and had the knife at his throat before he could take more than two or three steps away.

'I may as well tell you now, to avoid any further efforts to escape, that I have your student Sam Gray hidden away in a safe place. If you do not want him found face-down in the King's Ditch, you will do what I say. Do you understand?'

Bartholomew gazed at him in horror, and forced himself to nod. The Vice-Chancellor moved away from him, although the knife remained in his hand. Swallowing hard, Bartholomew clambered to his feet.

'You see, I was anticipating meeting you here,' Harling continued, glancing downstream to where the waterwheel pounded the flooded river into a brown froth. 'I thought I might have to resort to trickery to entice you out of Michaelhouse in all this rain, but I underestimated your devotion to your patients – poor Mistress Pike. I could not have chosen a better place to ambush you than that jungle Peterhouse calls its churchyard.'

Bartholomew glanced down at the knife in Harling's hand, and wondered whether the Vice-Chancellor would harm him with it. Harling followed his gaze and gave a nasty smile.

'Do not fool yourself into believing that I will not use this,' he said, brandishing it. 'I fought for the King in France before I became a scholar, and killed more men than I care to remember. Run if you will, but I will get you.'

He sprang forwards suddenly and made a deft flick with his wrist. Bartholomew looked down, and saw that Harling had neatly severed the leather straps of the medical bag he always wore looped around his shoulder. As it fell to the ground, Bartholomew was left convinced that Harling's prowess with the knife was no idle boast.

'Father Philius had a more practical demonstration of my skills with sharp objects – he put up a fight when he realised my visit to his chamber was not to enquire after his health, but he died instantly once I decided he should. I was told it took you quite some time to discover what had happened to him.'

He smiled and Bartholomew felt sick. 'You murdered Philius? That poor old friar only just out of his sickbed?'

'He was asking too many questions,' said Harling dismissively.

'About the poisoned wine?' asked Bartholomew, his bewildered mind trying to make sense of Harling's revelations. 'It was yours? But then why did Katherine Mortimer kill herself? I do not understand.'

'That strong acidic poison was created in a small town in France where wolves are a particular problem. Its success has made it fairly well known to people interested in such things – I am sure one of Philius's colleagues will have heard of it. That town in France happens to be where I spent quite some time in the service of the King – as many of my colleagues will know – and I did not want that particular association to be made. Now, do you believe I am as talented with blades as I say, or would you like yet another illustration?'

'Where is Gray?' asked Bartholomew numbly, his thoughts reeling. 'What do you want from me?'

'Gray is in a safe place,' said Harling. 'And you will not find him, so do not bother to look. And in return for his life, I require something from you.'

'What?' asked Bartholomew suspiciously, when Harling paused.

'You and Brother Michael mentioned you had occasion to spirit a nun away from Denny Abbey. This nun had been asking questions of some of my colleagues in the Fens and they, foolishly, gave her some answers, thinking her to be some dim-witted ancient. I suspect she is anything but. I want to know where you have secreted her.'

'Why?'

Harling made a grimace of impatience. 'Do not act the fool with me, Bartholomew. Why do you think? I want her before she can pass this information to the Sheriff.'

'But the Sheriff already knows what she has to say,' said Bartholomew. 'Brother Michael has passed him the information already.'

'Liar!' spat Harling. 'All Michael did, after you and he went to whine to your friend the Sheriff about how you had been so viciously ambushed in the Fens, was go into All Saints' Hostel for a drink. He needed to recover from the attempt on his life that another of my employees had so badly botched. And the nun certainly is not hidden in All Saints'. I checked.'

'Michael suspected someone might be watching him, and so he left through the rear door,' said Bartholomew. 'He returned the same way, so that anyone watching would think he had been in All Saints' the whole time. So, you see, the nun will be useless to you now. Where is Gray?'

'There is no back door at All Saints',' sneered Harling. 'If Brother Michael told you that, he is not telling you the truth.'

'Michael has no cause to lie to me,' said Bartholomew firmly. 'The Sheriff knows all the nun has to tell.'

'Then why does he sit uselessly in his castle, scratching his head like some stupid schoolboy?' asked Harling. 'Why is he not out with his men looking for me and my companions?'

'He has been,' replied Bartholomew. 'He was out all of yesterday and the day before.'

His breath suddenly caught in his throat. Tulyet had said that he was still concerned that he did not have the outlaws who had been terrorising the roads around Cambridge. Was one of the outlaws Harling? Bartholomew was so confused he did not know what to think.

'Then why am I still at large?' asked Harling, smiling coldly as he read the physician's thoughts. 'And all the others who have been helping me? Why have we not been arrested? I tell you again, Bartholomew, if Brother Michael informed you that he passed Dame Pelagia's list of names to Tulyet, then he is lying.'

'Michael told Tulyet all she had to tell,' insisted Bartholomew. He watched beads of rain slide off Harling's greased hair, and the first seeds of doubt began to grow in his mind. If Dame Pelagia knew Harling to be a smuggler, then Michael most certainly had not told Tulyet: Harling was one of the few people in the town whose name was not on the list. Was Michael deliberately shielding the Vice-Chancellor in order to save the University from the embarrassment of having a criminal at its helm?

Harling raised his eyebrows, amused. 'You are loyal to your friends, which is more than can be said for Brother Michael. He has lied to you, Bartholomew – he has told the Sheriff nothing. Now, where is Dame Pelagia?'

'I do not know,' stammered Bartholomew.

'You are not good at deceit,' said Harling, unimpressed by Bartholomew's feeble attempt to lie. 'In fact, you are almost as dreadful as Michael is accomplished. I see you still do not believe me. Michael is clever and ambitious: do you think he will allow your friendship to stand between him and his goals of power and wealth? Of course he will not! And a man who passes up the offer of the Mastership of Valence Marie to wait for something better is ambitious indeed! Michael is fully aware that the smuggling ring he uncovered involves high-ranking members of the hostels and the Colleges, and that to expose it would have been an embarrassment to the University.'

'But he did expose it,' objected Bartholomew. 'Tulyet knows several heads of houses and eminent scholars who were involved.'

'Really?' asked Harling with heavy sarcasm. 'Then why do you think he suggested his clever solution – warning people to give them more time to hide the fruits of their crimes – to Tulyet? Do you think it was to save the merchants? Of course it was not! It was for the benefit of silly scholars, like the greedy opportunists from Michaelhouse – Alcote, Paul, William and Runham – not to mention Colton from Gonville and Lynton from Peterhouse.'

'But the scholars were not treated differently from the merchants,' said Bartholomew.

'That is patently untrue!' snapped Harling. 'It is the merchants who will pay the heavy taxes the King will impose when he learns of this, not the University. And while the merchants' actions will be bandied about for all to hear, the scholars' role will be downplayed. As I said, Michael will not want the University embarrassed by this affair, because what embarrasses the University will embarrass its patron, the King. Do you think Michael will risk the wrath of the King when his greedy sights are set so high? Be honest with yourself, Bartholomew! Will he?'

Bartholomew swallowed. He was uncertain. Michael *was* ambitious, and he would certainly think twice about exposing some devilish plot if he thought the King might not like it. Father Paul's warning suddenly came unbidden into his mind: Paul had told Bartholomew that Michael's ambition might bring him to harm. Would it? Bartholomew wanted to believe not, but at the back of his mind there was a nagging doubt. But why would Michael lie to Tulyet about what Dame Pelagia knew?

'Michael told Tulyet he could provide him with the names

of these smugglers,' he said, thinking quickly. 'Tulyet sent him to do it immediately. Do you think the Sheriff would have let the matter drop if Michael had failed to come up with the information he wanted?'

'I think Michael fed Tulyet false information,' said Harling with a shrug. 'I believe he sat in All Saints' Hostel, guzzling their wine, and made up a list of names that would send Tulyet on a wild-goose chase.'

'That was no wild-goose chase,' said Bartholomew. 'A good many Fenland smugglers were caught. If Michael's intelligence was false, how did Tulyet know to arrest them?'

'But Michael's so-called intelligence was all but worthless to Tulyet,' said Harling in exasperation. 'Tulyet is still seeking those he considers more dangerous than peddlers of figs, and shabby little Fenmen.'

'And you consider yourself something better, I suppose,' said Bartholomew, wearied by Harling's accusations, and with a sick feeling gnawing at the back of his mind that somewhere in the Vice-Chancellor's story there might be a grain of truth.

'Of course I am something more!' snapped Harling. 'My interests extend further than cheap gloves from France. Unlike you, it seems.' He gave Bartholomew's hands a disparaging glance.

'But why are you doing this?' cried Bartholomew suddenly, looking at the University's second-in-command as his mind failed to make any sense of what the man was telling him. 'You are the Vice-Chancellor!'

'Precisely,' spat Harling. '*Vice*-Chancellor! I have worked hard for this University, and I am *Vice*-Chancellor! The masters voted for that nonentity Tynkell over me. And Tynkell finally dragged himself from the pleasures of the Bishop's palace at Ely today, so there is no real need for me at all. Brother Michael has leached away any powers the Vice-Chancellor might have had, and it is not me Tynkell calls upon when there are important matters to discuss – it is that fat monk. So, when the opportunity came to indulge in something a little different, I decided to take advantage of it, and it has made me a wealthy man. As soon as I have Dame Pelagia, I am leaving Cambridge. And there will be an end to it. Now, where have you hidden her?'

Bartholomew gazed desperately at the swirling brown water. He guessed that as soon as Harling had what he wanted, he would show Bartholomew precisely how skilled he was with his weapon – as he had done with poor Philius. He wondered if he should jump in the river to avoid answering Harling and betraying the whereabouts of Dame Pelagia. But then what would happen to Gray? He rubbed a hand through his hair and met Harling's glittering black eyes.

'I cannot tell you,' he said unsteadily. 'She is an old lady.' And Matilde was with her, he thought. Matilde should not be exposed to any more danger just because she had been kind enough to hide Dame Pelagia at his request.

'Then Gray will die,' said Harling with a shrug. 'And I will find Dame Pelagia in the end – Brother Michael is sure to visit her at some point. Your telling me will just save us some time. Hurry up, Bartholomew. Or do you want Gray's death to be on your head – for nothing?'

'How do I know you will not kill him anyway?' asked Bartholomew. 'How can I trust you to let him go?'

'You cannot,' said Harling. 'But you are not in a position to negotiate.'

'How do I know you even have him at all?' asked Bartholomew. 'You might be bluffing.'

'I might be,' said Harling, 'but are you prepared to take that risk?'

Bartholomew thought of Matilde and her long silky hair. She was an innocent in all this, just like Gray. The only reason they were involved was because they were unfortunate enough to be acquainted with Bartholomew. He should never have suggested to Michael that they use Matilde's house to hide Dame Pelagia, and he had no doubt that once he had told Harling where to look, Matilde would be sacrificed to ensure her silence, just as would Dame Pelagia. And Gray? Harling could well be making the whole thing up: Gray would not be an easy person to take hostage because he was quick-witted, resourceful and ruthless.

'I am sorry for Gray,' said Bartholomew, coming to a decision and meeting Harling's eyes. 'But I will not tell you what you want to know.'

For a moment, Harling and Bartholomew regarded each other without moving. And then both moved suddenly. As Harling lunged at Bartholomew with the knife, Bartholomew dived under its blade, grabbed Harling around the knees and twisted to one side. The two men tumbled to the ground, spray flying high as they hit the sodden grass. Harling's dagger glinted once in the dull light of the late afternoon and then plunged downwards.

chapter 11

ARTHOLOMEW SAW HARLING'S KNIFE FLASH ABOVE his head, and twisted sideways so that it plunged harmlessly into the mud. He grabbed Harling's wrist as the Vice-Chancellor raised his arm to try again, flinching away when he saw the knife begin to descend a second time, inching inexorably towards him as Harling leaned all of his weight behind it. Bartholomew suddenly pulled downwards and to one side, so that Harling was thrown off balance and the weapon went cartwheeling away to land somewhere out of sight.

Immediately, Harling leapt at him again, hands clawing at his clothes as he tried to haul the physician towards the churning river. Startled by the ferocity of the attack, Bartholomew could do little more than fend off the blows, trying to prevent the enraged Vice-Chancellor from gaining a good hand-hold. His feet skidded in the thick, cloying mud near the water's edge as he felt himself being dragged towards it. Not far away, the great mill wheel pounded and thumped through the racing river, the hiss of the fast-flowing current almost drowned out by the creak and groan of the protesting wood. And then Bartholomew realised exactly what Harling intended to do with him.

He knew the miller would not run the wheel while the river was flooded, and could think only that Harling had managed to start it before he had captured his prey in the churchyard outside Peterhouse: even if Bartholomew were stabbed, the wheel would destroy any evidence that his death was anything other than an appalling accident.

They were at the water's edge, so close that Bartholomew could feel the breeze of it passing almost underneath his head. Another few inches and he would be under, helpless while Harling held him below the surface until he drowned. With a strength made great by fear, he struggled with all his might, succeeding in partly dislodging Harling's grip on his cloak so that he was able to rise to his feet. Harling reacted quickly, hooking a foot behind Bartholomew's legs, so that the physician fell flat on his back. Before he could move, Harling had pounced, and sat astride him, seizing two handfuls of his hair to force his head down towards the water.

Bartholomew felt icy fingers of river touch the back of his scalp and struggled for all he was worth. But Harling was strong, and Bartholomew felt himself beginning to weaken. Above him, he could see the grin of tense concentration on Harling's face as he leaned forward, intending to use the weight of his body to press Bartholomew under the water. With all his remaining strength, the physician brought both knees up as hard as he could, at the same time grabbing Harling's tabard and pulling on it. With a yelp of surprise, Harling, his balance already precarious, sailed clean over Bartholomew's head and landed with a splash in the river.

For a moment, Bartholomew could do nothing but stare up at the dirty grey clouds that gathered overhead, but then he forced himself to sit up. At first, he thought the Vice-Chancellor must have already been swept away to be crushed under the great wheel, but then he glimpsed something white, and he saw Harling gripping the long grass at the side of the river, looking up at Bartholomew in a mute appeal for help. Revolted, Bartholomew gazed back at the man who had admitted to killing poor, helpless Philius, and who had unleashed the vile substance on the town that had provoked such bitter accusations and treachery.

'For God's sake!' Harling cried piteously, his teeth chattering with cold and fear. 'Help me!'

'Where is Gray?' asked Bartholomew, edging nearer, aware that their struggles had weakened the bank, and that it might collapse at any moment and send them both away down the river towards the waterwheel and certain death.

'Help me and I will tell you,' pleaded Harling. 'Please hurry!' Terrified, he stretched one hand towards Bartholomew, clinging to the grass with the other.

Bartholomew stared at it. 'Where is Gray?' he demanded again, aware that Harling's left hand was sliding slowly, but inexorably, down the stems as the river tugged at him.

'I will tell you when I am out,' Harling shouted desperately. 'If you do not help me, you will never find him, and he will die. Hurry, for God's sake!'

Moving closer to the edge, Bartholomew crouched down and reached out until Harling could grip his outstretched hand. And then the Vice-Chancellor pulled as hard as he could. Tumbling forwards, Bartholomew snatched at the weeds on the bank, trying to tear his arm from Harling's murderous hold. He grabbed a fistful of stalks, but heard them tearing from the ground as Harling braced both feet against the bank and yanked as hard as he could on Bartholomew's hand.

And then Bartholomew's glove began to slip loose. He saw Harling's look of horror, as first one finger, and then another, came free. Then the rest flew off with a rush, and Bartholomew caught a fleeting glimpse of Harling's disbelieving face before the Vice-Chancellor was swept away by the current. Bartholomew fell backwards onto the bank, trying to shut out the sound of the thumping waterwheel, and hoping he imagined the slight change in its tempo and pitch at about the time Harling would have reached it.

Shaking almost uncontrollably, he sat up and scanned

the river for Harling, but the Vice-Chancellor was nowhere to be seen. Bartholomew did not feel able to look for the body he knew he would find squashed and battered further downstream: it would not be the first time he had seen a corpse crushed by the waterwheel, and he knew it would not be a pleasant sight. In sudden disgust, he tore off his other glove, and threw that in the river, too.

Thinking of nothing but of finding Gray, he snatched up his damaged bag, and began to run along the river path towards Michaelhouse. Dusk was falling when he reached the College, and he made straight for the student's room. He flung open the door and sagged against the wall in relief when the astonished faces of Gray and Bulbeck looked up at him. Gray leapt to his feet when he saw the dishevelled, muddy state of his teacher.

'What happened to you?' he exclaimed, drawing Bartholomew inside and closing the door. 'You look as though you have been rolling around in the mud near the river!'

Bartholomew glanced at him sharply, but Gray was already tipping some dirty clothes from a stool so that Bartholomew could sit down, and he supposed Gray's remark was a chance one. He sank down on the stool, while Bulbeck regarded him dubiously from his bed. Gray handed the physician a cup of warm milk, and Bartholomew had drunk most of it before he realised it was probably something Agatha had sent to aid Bulbeck's recovery.

'You are unharmed, Sam?' he asked Gray anxiously. 'Nothing has happened to you?'

'I am fine,' said Gray, but then exchanged an unreadable glance with Bulbeck.

'What is it?' asked Bartholomew, a cold, uneasy feeling fluttering in the pit of his stomach.

'I went out to buy a candle,' began Gray. 'Deynman stayed here to take care of Tom.' He exchanged another uncertain look with Bulbeck.

'Where is Deynman now?' said Bartholomew, sitting bolt

upright and looking around the room as though he imagined Deynman might appear from under the bed or out of the chest.

'A message came for me to attend one of the people with winter fever,' said Gray, 'but since I was out, Deynman wanted to go in my place.'

'I tried to stop him,' said Bulbeck. 'But he insisted, even though you have instructed that he is not to attend patients without you.'

Bartholomew leapt to his feet. 'Where is he? Did he not come back?'

The two students shook their heads. 'He has been gone for ages,' said Gray. 'The curfew bell will ring soon and we are worried about him.'

'Oh no!' groaned Bartholomew. He closed his eyes in despair. Gray was safe, but Harling had Deynman instead, and Harling's companions would surely kill him in retaliation for Bartholomew's refusal to reveal the whereabouts of Dame Pelagia. But, then, perhaps they would not even know where Harling had secreted him, and with Harling dead, Deynman might never be found – just as Harling had claimed. He fought to bring his appalled imaginings under control.

'Stay here,' he commanded. 'Whatever happens, do not leave Michaelhouse. If anyone asks you to run an errand, say Tom is too ill to be left. Do you promise?'

The two students nodded. 'But where is Rob?' asked Gray. 'What has happened to him?'

'I will try to find out,' said Bartholomew. 'Will you give me your word that you will stay here?'

Gray nodded impatiently. 'We have already said we will. Do not worry about us, just find Rob. He owes me three silver pennies.'

Bartholomew's only thought was to search Harling's room at Physwick Hostel first and then his office at St Mary's Church. He set off across the yard at a run, and almost collided with Michael and two beadles, returning from Valence Marie. Michael caught him by the arm as he made to rush past.

'Matt!' he exclaimed. He looked his friend up and down in horror. 'What has happened to you? We were only gone a short while. How have you managed to end up in such a mess?'

'Harling has Deynman,' said Bartholomew breathlessly, trying to tear himself free of Michael. 'I must find him.'

'What are you talking about?' said Michael. 'Harling?'

'Harling has been smuggling,' said Bartholomew impatiently, desperate to begin his search for Deynman. 'He kidnapped Rob, and said he would kill him if I did not reveal the whereabouts of Dame Pelagia.'

Michael's eyes went round with shock. 'Matt! You did not tell him?'

'Of course I did not!' snapped Bartholomew.

'Are you sure Deynman has gone with Harling, and is not just off in a tavern somewhere?' asked Cynric, emerging from some shadows where he had apparently been listening. 'It would not be the first time.'

'No, I am not sure. But he is not in his room, and Gray and Bulbeck are worried about him, so I can only assume Harling captured him.'

'Harling!' said Michael, with a glint of amusement in his green eyes. 'No wonder he discouraged me from having dealings with the Sheriff, and gave you his permission not to help me with my inquiries. Crafty old devil!'

'This is not a game!' yelled Bartholomew in frustration. 'Deynman might be in danger. He might even be dead. And meanwhile, Harling's companions are out searching for Dame Pelagia, so do not look so complacent.'

Michael regarded Bartholomew soberly. 'I apologise, Matt. Now, you cannot go out looking like that. I assume you mean to search Harling's room at Physwick Hostel or his office at the church? Well you will not get past the porters dressed like a beggar. Put on a clean tabard and wipe the filth from your face. And while you do so, you can tell me what happened.'

Bartholomew shot a despairing look at the gate, but Cynric blocked his path. 'Brother Michael is right, boy,' he said gently. 'No porter would open the gates for you while you are so covered in filth.'

Reluctantly, Bartholomew went to his room and stripped off his dirty tabard and cloak. While he scrubbed the thick, peaty mud from his face and hair, and Cynric sat cross-legged on the floor and mended his bag, Bartholomew told them what had happened. Michael immediately summoned his two beadles, drinking ale in the kitchen with Agatha, and ordered them to make a search of the river near the King's Mill for Harling's body.

'Harling could never have survived going down the mill race,' said Cynric. 'He is dead. And if he is dead, he cannot harm Deynman.'

'But he is not so foolish as to keep a student locked in his hostel or his office,' mused Michael. 'He could not possibly keep such a thing secret. We will have to look elsewhere for Deynman.'

'Such as where?' asked Bartholomew helplessly, not having the faintest idea where to begin.

'Such as one of the smugglers' haunts,' said Michael. 'But to find out where those are, we will need to question the smugglers.'

'Harling claimed you had not given Tulyet the names of the smugglers Dame Pelagia knew,' said Bartholomew, looking up at Michael as he scrubbed at his wet hair with a piece of linen.

Michael shrugged and stared out of the window. Bartholomew's stomach lurched.

'I assured him you went with Cynric out of the back door of All Saints' Hostel, so that no one would know where you were going,' he said, staring hard at Michael. 'And that you learned the names of the smugglers from Dame Pelagia, and passed them to Tulyet.'

Cynric looked uncomfortable. 'All Saints' does not have a back door, boy,' he said. 'When was this supposed to have happened?'

Bartholomew gazed at Michael accusingly. 'You said you had been to get the smugglers' names from your grandmother!' he said in a low voice.

Michael gnawed at his lower lip nervously. 'I can explain that. It is not how it appears.'

'You lied to me,' whispered Bartholomew in disbelief. 'Just like Harling said you did.'

'I was afraid for her!' shouted Michael angrily, as he leapt to his feet in Bartholomew's room, driven to rage by the physician's accusations of dishonesty. 'And for Matilde, too, if you want the truth. I knew we were being followed and so did Cynric, and I was not sure we would be able to throw them off. The last thing I wanted to do was to lead these men straight to my grandmother and your woman!'

'I am not questioning that!' Bartholomew yelled back. 'I am questioning why you lied to me. I would have understood perfectly if you had explained why you did not go to Matilde's house. Why did you feel the need to lie?'

'Because I already knew the names of some of these smugglers, and I did not want to tell you how I came by them,' said Michael, more quietly.

'I see,' said Bartholomew coldly, pulling on the tabard Cynric handed him. 'So I am good enough company when it comes to examining bodies for you and being attacked in the Fens, but I am not to be trusted with anything more sensitive!'

'That is not true, Matt,' said Michael wearily. 'I would trust you with my life and well you know it. The reason I did not tell you the truth was that . . .' His voice petered off into silence.

'Well?' demanded Bartholomew, hunting around in the semi-darkness for his boots. Cynric had fetched a candle from Michael's room and so there was a little light. 'What is this great reason?'

'That the information came from Edith,' said Michael softly.

Bartholomew's boot fell from his hands and he swung round to face Michael in amazement. 'Now I have heard everything! What would Edith know about smuggling? If you must prevaricate, Michael, at least think of something convincing to say.'

'Why do you think I have kept it from you?' snapped Michael. 'I knew your reaction would be just what it is – furious disbelief. And it was safer for Edith that only I knew. Even Oswald is ignorant of the matter. And you are right – if I were going to deceive you, I would come up with a better story than this. However, it happens to be the truth.'

Bartholomew sat on the bed and watched Michael warily. 'Tell me, then,' he said. 'How did you persuade Edith to act as your spy?'

'I did not persuade her,' said Michael huffily. 'Her involvement was her own choice, not mine.' He leaned forward and rested his arms on his knees. 'As we have said, *ad nauseam*, since all this started, smuggling has always been rife in these parts. Therefore it was no great surprise when the Fenmen grew increasingly bold and began selling their goods more openly in the town this year because the waterways have remained ice-free. At first, neither University nor town saw harm in it. Why should people not have small luxuries from time to time?'

'Most laudable, Brother,' said Bartholomew facetiously. 'It is always wise to tempt people to buy foods they have no idea how to prepare – like Constantine Mortimer and his lemons. We are lucky no one has become seriously ill. But what of Edith? And hurry up. I have to go out.'

Michael shot him an unpleasant look. 'This year, the Fen

smugglers have been especially successful. Because they have become wealthy, some of them have become brazen. A few have been exceptionally indiscreet and have been bragging about their escapades, and that is where Edith comes in.'

'Go on,' said Bartholomew, emptying the rank river water from his boots out of the window.

'From time to time, as Senior Proctor, I have to deal with students who have become lonely, homesick or love-lorn, and some of them try to take their own lives. I am no maidenly aunt as you know and I have had occasion to call upon a woman's gentle touch with some of the more difficult cases. Edith has helped me several times, the most recent example of which was Brother Xavier.'

'Xavier?' asked Bartholomew, looking up from tugging on his boots. 'Xavier from St Bernard's Hostel, who came to fetch us when Armel was poisoned?'

Michael nodded. 'I am under seal of confession, you understand, but suffice to say Xavier is a troubled soul who needed a motherly shoulder. Edith was kind and helped him immeasurably. Now, Bernard's is next to the Brazen George, and the dormitory overlooks one of its gardens. Through his window, Xavier heard some of the smugglers boasting about the profits made this year to a few of their companions and told Edith about it. Edith, acting as a good citizen, told me.'

'Why you?' demanded Bartholomew. 'Why not Oswald? Or Tulyet?'

'Partly because I was available, partly because she trusted me because I am your friend, and partly because she was afraid Oswald would prevent her from helping Xavier if he knew what the lad was telling her. You know he is overly protective.'

'And?' asked Bartholomew, unimpressed. 'This is still a long way from why you lied to me about seeing Dame Pelagia.'

Michael sighed. 'Edith, through listening to Xavier, sent

me the names of several Fenmen involved in smuggling. It was interesting to know the identities of these men, but not particularly important. Until, that is, the smugglers became more confident and brash, and we reasoned that they might be the same outlaws that Tulyet had been chasing – and even, perhaps, the same ones who hired the mercenaries to attack us near Denny. Then Edith's information became very important. I told Tulyet I could get the names he needed from my grandmother so he would not guess I had them already.'

'So you lied to protect Edith,' said Bartholomew, eyeing him with open scepticism.

'Yes,' said Michael, ignoring his friend's doubtful expression. 'As I said, when we thought we were just dealing with the Fenmen who have been running their smuggling trade for years, her information was nothing. But when smuggling developed into outlawry, and there were burglaries and attacks on travellers, her information became potentially dangerous – especially to her. And can you imagine what Oswald would say if he learns what she has been involved in? She also made me promise I would not tell you.'

'And so, when you told Tulyet you were going to see Dame Pelagia, you had no intention of visiting her,' said Bartholomew.

'Right,' said Michael. 'It was an excellent opportunity to pass along Edith's information and it did not put her, Dame Pelagia or Matilde at risk.'

'And of course Tulyet is still ignorant of who these outlaws are,' said Bartholomew, rubbing his hand through his hair in exasperation. 'Michael! How could you have been so foolish! You have assumed that the information Edith had from Xavier's eavesdropping at the Brazen George is the same that Dame Pelagia would have heard from her questions in the kitchens at Denny.'

'So?' asked Michael defensively. 'Of course it will be the same.'

'It will not!' yelled Bartholomew in frustration. 'Deschalers was surprised when you told him the smugglers were active around Denny Abbey – not that there were smugglers, but that there were smugglers in *that particular area*. Tulyet knows he does not have the men who are responsible for the attacks on the roads and the burglaries in the town. *Those* are the names Dame Pelagia has, not those of the Fenmen who have been committing petty crimes with smuggled figs, nor those of the merchants and scholars who have been taking advantage of the opportunity to make a profit from the warm weather!'

'But my grandmother told Deschalers that the men in Denny's kitchens were just the kinsmen of the lay sisters,' shouted Michael. 'You heard her!'

Bartholomew slammed his hand on the windowsill, furious with him. 'She is not stupid, Michael – unlike you it seems! What was sitting on Deschalers's table as we waited for him to come to take Julianna off our hands? Sugared almonds! An expensive commodity to leave around for casual visitors to devour, you will agree. Dame Pelagia probably suspected Deschalers was involved and did not want him to guess she knew more than she was telling.'

'But he was not involved!' Michael insisted. 'His lemons were legal.'

'But Dame Pelagia did not know that, did she!'

'Oh, Lord!' said Michael in a quieter tone, blood draining from his face. 'You are right!'

'Of course I am right!' snapped Bartholomew, rubbing a hand through his hair again and beginning to pace up and down in the small room. 'And we told Harling all about it! He came to see us here and asked what we had discovered. He even offered Dame Pelagia a safe house. Safe indeed! We should have guessed all this days ago!'

'But we had no evidence,' said Michael in a low voice. Bartholomew saw the fat monk's hands were trembling and that he was as white as snow. He swallowed his anger with difficulty, and went to the shelf near the window to pour him some wine. Michael took it gratefully and took an uncharacteristically small sip. Bartholomew imagined he must be shaken indeed.

'Well, what do we do now?' he asked, suddenly very tired, but far too agitated to sit. 'By his own admission, Harling was guilty of kidnapping, smuggling and the murder of Philius. He was also the man responsible for bringing the poisoned wine to Cambridge.'

'Just a moment,' said Michael unsteadily. 'How do you know that?'

'Because he told me he had killed Philius for asking too many questions about the nature of the poison in the wine. Which means he was probably also the third person who killed Isaac with Katherine and Edward. That whole business was well organised and no clues were left behind. It is exactly the kind of ruthless efficiency I would expect from a man like Harling.'

'But why all this death and destruction?' asked Michael, rubbing his face hard with his hands. 'None of the other smugglers has gone to such lengths to hide his crimes.'

'That is because Harling is doing this on a much grander scale than everyone else,' said Bartholomew, pacing again. 'He told me his interests extended beyond smuggling clothes and fruit. God knows what he is bringing into the country. Weapons, perhaps. Or livestock?'

'I have seen Master Harling out after curfew,' said Cynric, looking up from his sewing, 'visiting Mortimer's house.'

'The room in which I tended Mortimer when he was sick was very masculine,' pondered Bartholomew. 'I wonder whether Katherine had her own chamber, and whether Harling was visiting her as his mistress.'

Michael regarded him sceptically. 'That is something of a stab in the dark. Why could Harling not have been visiting Mortimer? We know the baker was involved in smuggling because he gave you those gloves.'

And one of the gloves was with Harling at that very moment, thought Bartholomew with a shudder, probably clutched in his dead hand. 'Because we know Harling imported the poisoned wine, and that Katherine and Edward stored it for him in Mortimer's cellars. That is the connection between them.'

'But it would be a little risky, would you not say?' said Michael, slowly drinking his wine. 'Making a cuckold of Mortimer in his own house?'

'Well, what else would Harling be doing there in the depths of the night?' asked Bartholomew.

'Counting the bottles of poisoned wine stored in the cellars?' suggested Michael. 'Discussing plans as to how they were to retrieve them after they were stolen by Sacks?'

'Well, it is irrelevant, anyway, since Katherine is dead,' said Bartholomew, looking for his cloak. He felt a twinge of guilt when he saw the clods of mud adhering to it, and determined to pay Paul for it next time they met. 'But now, we must do all we can to ensure the safety of Matilde and Dame Pelagia. As long as Harling's companions are at large, they will not be secure. And, since you say we can not help Deynman until a smuggler reveals where he is hidden, I am going to the castle to tell Dick Tulyet about Harling.'

He and Michael, with Cynric moving in and out of the shadows behind them, set off in the darkness towards the castle. Tulyet's soldiers were out in force, and they were challenged three times before they reached their goal. Cynric muttered that he thought there was someone following them, but said he could not be sure. Bartholomew peered back down the dark street, but it appeared deserted and he could see nothing amiss.

He jumped as a soft slithering sound came from behind him, anticipating an attack, but it was only an old dog scavenging in a pile of offal that was blocking the drains in a dark runnel off the main road. There were other shadows around the offal, too, beggars trying to scrape together enough to make a stew over their fire in the shelter of the Great Bridge.

For the first time since the riots of the previous summer, the portcullis was down on the castle barbican. With a good deal of clanking and rattling, the guards raised it part way so that Bartholomew, Cynric and Michael could duck under it, which they did quickly, not trusting the strength of the ancient mechanism. It was common knowledge in the town that the chains that raised the portcullis were unreliable – chains were one of many items unavailable since the plague – and that every time it was used was potentially the last. It was also well known that Tulyet was so doubtful about the safety of the mechanism that he always used the sally-port at the rear of the castle when the portcullis was down.

Bartholomew and Michael walked through the barbican towards the castle's main gate, and were challenged by two more guards whose crossbows were wound and ready. After some intense questioning, the wicket-gate was unbarred and a torch thrust into their faces so the sergeant could be certain they were who they claimed. He escorted them across the bailey to the black mass of the keep.

Lights burned in Tulyet's office and they found him deep in discussion with several of his sergeants. While the sergeants listened, grimly satisfied to hear that the University was responsible for the outlaws, Bartholomew told him about his encounter with Harling.

'Damn it, Matt!' said the Sheriff irritably. 'It would have been useful to have him alive.'

'I am sorry!' retorted Bartholomew, indignant. 'I will try to do better next time.'

With a sigh, Tulyet relented. 'My apologies. But this is a frustrating business – every time I think I have a lead, it fizzles out to nothing. But I have an idea. I will have these outlaws yet – the merchants and Fenmen are nothing. I want the third group of villains – the burglars, highwaymen and peddlers of poisoned wine. I might have known the University was behind all this!'

'And what is that supposed to mean?' demanded Michael. 'Just because Harling had turned sour, it does not prove that the rest of the University is rotten.'

'Does it not? That is not how it appears to me,' said Tulyet hotly, his frustration and exhaustion making him uncharacteristically argumentative. 'During the last few days I have seen a Fellow arranging his suicide so that his rival is blamed, using a youngster with a pathetic notion of vengeance to fulfil his plot. And I have seen supposedly upright scholars – some of them friars and monks – indulging in the evasion of the King's taxes. And now I am informed that the Vice-Chancellor himself tried to throw a colleague into the mill race. Your place of learning is a den of corruption, Brother.'

'No more so than your town,' retorted Michael angrily. 'And all the cases you mention are incidences of people acting independently of the University. Grene's fatal illness must have unbalanced his mind; Rob Thorpe was not a member of the University; the scholars indulging in smuggling – as you observed yourself – were doing so for selfless reasons and gave the money to the sick and poor or to effect much-needed repairs on crumbling buildings; and Harling . . .' He hesitated uncertainly.

'And Harling?' queried Tulyet, raising his eyebrows. 'I suppose he tried to murder Matt to protect the population from his heretical medicine? Or to save them from the unpleasant experience of being examined by his notoriously cold hands?'

'Harling was another matter,' said Michael, shaking his jowls impatiently. 'If you want lies and deceit, look to the merchants. Oswald Stanmore—'

'We have no time to waste on this,' interrupted Bartholomew quickly, before the row could develop any further in that direction. 'We need to help Deynman.'

Tulyet took a deep breath and closed his eyes to bring his temper under control. 'I can think of something we could try to move matters on a little.'

Bartholomew detected a distinct lack of conviction in his voice, and sensed that whatever Tulyet was about to suggest would be something he would not like. 'Will it help Deynman?'

'It might,' said Tulyet. 'If it works.'

'Well?' asked Michael. 'Out with it.'

'You could go to visit this informant of yours, the elderly nun,' said Tulyet. 'Harling said his companions would discover her whereabouts, so they are doubtless watching you to see where you go. So visit her. Go furtively – take Cynric, he will know what to do. When Harling's men come for the old lady, we will be waiting for them.'

'You mean use Dame Pelagia as bait?' asked Michael, shocked.

'Do you have a better idea?' asked Tulyet.

Tulyet needed time to organise his men into the correct positions, and instructed that Bartholomew and Michael should wait in his office until he gave the order that they might leave. Bartholomew paced restlessly, his thoughts leaping between fear for Deynman and concern for Matilde. Michael was silent, and Bartholomew suspected he was as anxious for his grandmother as Bartholomew was for his student and friend. While they waited, Cynric brought a message from Michael's beadles saying that Harling's body was nowhere to be found.

Bartholomew swallowed hard. 'He escaped,' he whispered in horror. 'He still roams free.'

'It is unlikely that he escaped the mill race in full flood,' said Michael reasonably. 'He is probably crushed under the wheel and his corpse has not yet surfaced.'

'I will look at first light,' said Cynric. 'If his body is there, I will find it.'

'You will not find it, Cynric,' said Bartholomew. 'He escaped – I am sure of it.'

'Well, it does not matter if he did,' said Michael practically. 'My beadles will track him down, and he is scarcely in a position to do us any more harm now that we know how he spends his spare time, and all his attention will be focused on leaving Cambridge with his ill-gotten gains.'

'I do not like this plan, Michael,' said Bartholomew yet again. 'What if something goes wrong? Matilde might come to harm.'

'So might my grandmother,' said Michael pointedly. 'But we have no choice. Dick Tulyet and his men will be on hand the instant these men make their appearance. And, as I see it, it is the only way you will get Deynman back.' He pondered. 'I cannot think why you are so keen to rescue that dimwit – he will cost the College a fortune in bribes when he takes his final examinations. What a pity Harling was involved in all this – he offered to see the boy through his disputations and thus save Michaelhouse a veritable treasure trove.'

Bartholomew did not reply and Michael let the matter drop. They waited until a soldier came to say that enough time had passed to allow Tulyet to spring his trap, and then left the castle to walk down the hill. A chill wind blew from the north, catching some dirt and swirling it around in an eddy. Bartholomew shivered, partly from the cold, but mostly from apprehension for what they were about to do.

'Someone is following us again,' whispered Cynric. 'I can hear him.'

Bartholomew felt his stomach lurch. At every step, he anticipated the searing pain of a crossbow bolt between his shoulder blades, or an attack from the shadows at the side of the road. He glanced around nervously.

'As long as the outlaws consider there is a chance that we will lead them to what we want, they will not harm us,' said Michael, noting his friend's unease.

'They tried to harm you,' Bartholomew said, referring to Michael's encounter with the knifeman.

'That was before the business with Harling,' Michael whispered back. 'They have obviously reconsidered, and realise we are more useful alive than dead as long as Dame Pelagia is at large.'

'Well that is comforting,' muttered Bartholomew. He glanced at the fat monk striding at his side. 'You seem calm. Are you not afraid?'

'Terrified,' came the answer. 'But we are nearing the end of all this, Matt. In a short while, it will all be over. My grandmother, Deynman and Matilde will be safe.'

'I hope you are right,' said Bartholomew unconvinced.

They reached the point where the High Street forked off from Bridge Street, and stopped. Cynric went on ahead and beckoned them forward, raising his hand to caution silence. Bartholomew glanced behind him, and hoped those following them would fall for their elaborate performance. He and Michael eased in and out of the shadows, allowing Cynric to decide the balance between making their precautions appear convincing, and yet ensuring the men following them did not lose them. Eventually, they reached Matilde's house, and Bartholomew knocked softly on the door, glancing around furtively. Soft yellow light was visible through the shutters on the upper window, and Bartholomew realised with a shock that Matilde might be entertaining one of her customers. He backed away, reluctant to see who it might be.

'Who is there?' came Matilde's voice through the closed door. 'What do you want?'

Bartholomew's voice stuck in his throat. Michael shot him a look of exasperation.

'It is Brother Michael,' he called softly. 'And your friend, Matthew.'

The door opened a crack to verify he was telling the truth, and then he and Bartholomew were ushered inside. Cynric was nowhere to be seen. Matilde was wearing a nightshift of soft, white linen, and her long hair flowed loose down her back. Her feet were bare, and she held a candle that shed a flickering light around the neat little room.

'What is the matter?' she asked, looking from Michael to Bartholomew and sensing their agitation. 'Have you come for Dame Pelagia? She is upstairs.'

'The Sheriff's soldiers are outside,' said Michael, pushing past her quickly and closing the door behind them. 'And we were followed here by men we believe to be the outlaws he has been hunting.'

'You mean you have deliberately led them to my house?' asked Matilde, grasping the situation quickly. 'Into an ambush where they will be caught?'

'They have Deynman,' Bartholomew blurted out. 'This seemed the best way to get him back.'

Matilde regarded him with eyes that were dark in the dim candlelight. 'I see. So what do you want to do? Are we supposed to pretend to sneak away or remain here and wait for them to come?'

'We wait,' said Michael. He looked Matilde's slender form up and down with blatant admiration. 'You should find something warmer to wear, my child.'

Matilde's face creased into merriment. 'Thank you for your concern, Brother,' she said with mock demureness. She slipped away up the stairs, leaving Michael and Bartholomew alone.

'Please do not flirt with her, Michael,' said Bartholomew primly. 'It is unbecoming behaviour for a monk.'

'You do it, then,' said Michael, unabashed by the reminder of his vows of chastity. 'That is what she really wants.'

Bartholomew shook his head in exasperation and went to peer through a slit in the window shutter. The street outside seemed to be deserted. Bartholomew felt his heart begin to thump hard against his ribs. What if Tulyet and his men had misunderstood their description of the location of Matilde's house and were somewhere else? What if Tulyet's party had themselves been ambushed as they left the castle by the sally-port? What if the outlaws did not come for Dame Pelagia at all, but shot fire arrows to burn the house down and kill them as they emerged choking into the street? He felt an unpleasant clamminess at the small of his back, and was aware that his hands were shaking.

'I will watch here,' said Michael. 'Go and see that Dame Pelagia is awake.'

'She is your grandmother,' said Bartholomew, reluctant to mount the stairs to Matilde's bedchamber. 'You go.'

'She is a nun,' said Michael, imitating the prim voice Bartholomew had used to him. 'But you are a physician. She will not mind you seeing her in a state of undress.'

'But Matilde might,' said Bartholomew.

Michael regarded him in disbelief. 'She is a prostitute, Matt! That is what they do! Hurry up. These outlaws might be here at any moment and we might have to flee.'

Bartholomew climbed the flight of wooden stairs, coughing noisily to let them know he was coming.

'Is Dame Pelagia dressed?' he asked, entering the bed-chamber and fixing his eyes steadily on the floor.

'We both are, Matt,' said Matilde. She looked at him with mischief glittering in her eyes. 'For a physician, you are very coy. You may look up. There is nothing here that might embarrass you.'

Bartholomew saw that Matilde had exchanged the nightshift for a long woollen dress and her feet were no longer bare. She had also bundled her luxuriant hair into a cap and was helping Dame Pelagia to put her shoes on.

'You have taken your time in coming to me,' said Dame Pelagia, somewhat reprovingly. 'I was beginning to think I might have to go to the Sheriff and the Bishop myself with the information I have gathered. I would have done, in fact, had I not been afraid that independent action might endanger Matilde, or that it might have interfered with some secret plan of Michael's.'

'And the Lord knows he has plenty of those,' muttered Bartholomew.

'Have you two fallen out?' asked Matilde, regarding him with concern.

'We had a misunderstanding over this information about the smugglers Dame Pelagia has,' replied Bartholomew shortly.

'I suppose he told you he had passed it to the Sheriff when he had not,' said Dame Pelagia, fixing her bright green eyes on him astutely. She gave the physician a sudden grin, revealing sharp brown teeth. 'I suspected Michael had some plot in action when he did not return immediately with Sheriff Tulyet as he said he would. This smuggling is such a sensitive business and involves such cunning people, that I simply assumed Michael needed time to spring a trap before the Sheriff was made aware of the identities of those involved. The secular law can be very crude, you know.'

'Michael told me he gave Dick Tulyet some other names – ones discovered by my sister from a student she was helping,' said Bartholomew, still not certain that Michael had been completely honest.

'That was clever of him,' said Dame Pelagia admiringly. 'In that way he could provide the Sheriff with enough information to keep him happy, but did not need to visit me to reveal my whereabouts to anyone watching him.'

'But you had plenty of time to talk on that long journey from Denny,' Matilde pointed out. 'Did you tell him nothing then?'

'Of course not!' said Dame Pelagia. 'First of all, poor Michael needed all his breath for walking – he is not fit and spry like me – and second, it would have been extremely foolish to discuss such matters on the open road. Who knows who might have overheard?'

'So you told him nothing?' asked Bartholomew.

'I was expecting him to come back to talk to me as soon as he had completed reporting the attack to the

Vice-Chancellor,' said Dame Pelagia. 'I did not think he would take days to return.'

'But you knew Harling was behind all this?' persisted Bartholomew. 'And you let Michael go to report to him, knowing that he might be signing his own death warrant? Someone tried to knife him that morning, you know.'

'I did not know,' said Dame Pelagia sharply. 'And I did not know the villain was Harling, either. I knew Katherine Mortimer was involved, along with her pathetic son, Edward. My information, for what it was worth, was simply that: that the Sheriff should devise a plot to use Edward and Katherine to uncover the identity of these outlaws. I knew the real genius behind all this was some influential official, but I had not managed to discover who. I would have stayed longer at Denny to try to find out, but Michael was insistent I left with him that night. And, to be honest, Matthew, I have grown weary of subterfuge.'

Her bright eyes and the air of suppressed anticipation about her suggested that she was anything but weary of the subterfuge she had uncovered. Matilde had been listening to the exchange with such interest that she had forgotten all about tying the old lady's shoes. Impatiently, Dame Pelagia pulled her foot away from the young prostitute, and tied the lace herself with strong, steady fingers. She stood and grinned at Bartholomew, looking far better equipped to deal with whatever the night might throw at them than was the physician.

'Matilde says we are to be the bait in a trap,' she said in a cheerful voice. 'I wondered whether you might resort to that. I wish Michael had passed word to me sooner, because then I would have arranged for Matilde to be away.'

'I lead a dull life, Pelagia,' protested Matilde, flashing the old lady a radiant smile. 'This will add a little much-needed excitement.'

Dame Pelagia laughed and patted Matilde's hand. 'Come

then, my young friend. Let us look this wolf in the jaws together!'

Together they went back down the stairs. Bartholomew looked around the neat room, wondering if he were the only person to be feeling trepidation over the events that were about to unfold. Michael was hiding any fears he might have under a veil of calm, while Dame Pelagia and Matilde seemed to be looking forward to the coming confrontation with confidence and excitement.

He went to the window shutter and peered out. Shadows glided here and there, directed by a man in a long cloak: the outlaws springing their attack. It would not be long now, he thought. Before following Matilde and Dame Pelagia downstairs, he glanced around the neat bedchamber. He had never been in the room where he supposed Matilde entertained her customers, and was curious. There was a small bed in a corner with a straw mattress at its foot, both heavily laden with blankets of fine wool. A low table stood under one window, bearing a matching water-jug and bowl, and the stools to either side of it were handsomely carved. Matilde's collection of expensive dresses hung in a line near the other window, so that the air could pass through them and keep them fresh.

He heard a voice outside, and ran down the steps to where the others stood uncertainly in the middle of the room.

'They are here,' he whispered. He drew a surgical blade from his bag, pushed Matilde and Dame Pelagia behind him, and waited.

The door was kicked open with such violence that one of the hinges was torn from the wood, and a blast of cold air gusted around the room. Then the powerful Michaelhouse philosopher, Ralph de Langelee, stood aside and gestured for Edward Mortimer to enter in front of him.

'I knew *he* had to be involved!' muttered Michael, eyeing Langelee with disdain as the philosopher followed Edward into Matilde's house. 'I have never liked him and his grasp of Plato is deplorable!'

Behind Edward were one of Tulyet's sergeants and the lay sister from Denny Abbey who had brought them their meals. Bartholomew realised that it must have been she who had been listening outside the attic door when Julianna had revealed her suspicions to Bartholomew and Dame Pelagia had pretended to sleep. She made a polite curtsey of greeting to the elderly nun, which was acknowledged, but not returned. Outside, others, whose faces Bartholomew could not see, milled around. The sergeant stepped inside and brandished his loaded crossbow, and then a fourth person stepped into the room. Harling regarded the scene with some amusement.

'So,' he said to Bartholomew. 'We meet again!'

For a moment no one spoke. Ralph de Langelee regarded Bartholomew and Michael with a gloating smile, while Edward Mortimer was clearly uncomfortable with the situation and licked his lips anxiously. The sergeant was unreadable, and stood like a statue with his crossbow aimed at Michael's chest and the lay sister at his side. But the only person Bartholomew was aware of was Vice-Chancellor Harling. He stood just inside the door, dressed in his scholar's tabard of black, and his hair, as usual, plastered into place with liberal handfuls of animal grease. There was a faint bruise on his chin, but other than that he appeared to be in perfect health.

'Do drop that ridiculous weapon,' he said, as he saw Bartholomew's surgical knife. 'If you try to use it, my friend here will be obliged to shoot Brother Michael with his crossbow.'

Bartholomew let the little blade clatter to the floor, where Langelee kicked it out of reach under a table.

'I see you did not anticipate meeting me again,' said Harling, smoothly gloating. 'At least, not in this world.'

'Then you are wrong,' said Bartholomew coldly, hating the man for his smug arrogance. 'I knew you had escaped when the beadles did not find you drowned. How did you do it?'

Harling shrugged. 'Besides my skill with knives, growing up in the Fens equipped me with skills in the water. I am an excellent swimmer, and it was an easy matter to allow myself to be swept out of sight and then strike out for the nearest river bank.'

He lost interest in Bartholomew, and his glittering black eyes took in the room's handsome furnishings, the defiant Dame Pelagia, the stunned Michael and, finally, Matilde.

'Your prostitute!' he said to Bartholomew, smiling in understanding. 'Of course! Where better to hide an elderly nun? I should have guessed.'

He nodded to Langelee, who stepped forward to grab Pelagia. Bartholomew blocked his way. Langelee made a gesture of impatience and swung at Bartholomew with one of his huge fists. Bartholomew ducked and the punch passed harmlessly over his head, but Langelee followed it immediately with another with his opposite hand that landed squarely on Bartholomew's jaw. Lights danced in front of the physician's eyes, and he fell backwards in an undignified tangle of arms and legs.

Matilde screamed and darted to his side, swearing at Langelee with words that suggested her origins might not be as gentle as her appellation of 'Lady Matilde' implied. Bartholomew rubbed his chin and tried to stand, but Langelee planted a hefty foot on his chest and pinned him to the floor, grinning when Matilde battered his thick leg with her small fists.

'Stay where you are, Bartholomew,' said Harling sharply. He nodded to Edward, who took Pelagia's arm. Michael started forward, but stopped when the sergeant cocked his crossbow. With a sudden shock that made his stomach churn Bartholomew recognised the sergeant as one of those who had been with Tulyet in his office when they discussed the plan to lay a trap for the outlaws. It became immediately clear to him that it had all gone wrong. Tulyet would not be coming to rescue them because he had been betrayed by one of his own men.

And that was it, Bartholomew thought numbly. Harling had outwitted them as easily as that. The sergeant had told him everything Tulyet had planned, and all Harling had to do was kill four people who stood in his way – the four who knew the identity of the outlaw leader and exactly what he had done. Dame Pelagia would be questioned to ensure she had shared her knowledge with no one else, while Michael, Matilde and Bartholomew would be executed where they stood. And Deynman? If he was not dead already, he would not have long to live either. Bartholomew closed his eyes in despair.

'Give yourself up, Harling,' said Michael with a boldness Bartholomew was sure he could not feel. 'You cannot escape. Tulyet knows your part in this affair.'

'Tulyet knows nothing!' said Harling in disgust. 'He did not even know that some of his trusted sergeants have been persuaded to join us in our business. I thought it would not be long before he became suspicious of his lack of success in hunting us down, and started to look towards his own soldiers when his attempts to catch us were repeatedly foiled. But he did not. He continued to chase around in the Fens, not realising that each time he missed catching my men at their camps, it was because they had been forewarned. The Sheriff is a fool. Do not look to him for deliverance.'

'He is waiting nearby with an armed detachment,' said Michael, with admirable cool.

'Of course he is,' sneered Harling. He gestured to the sergeant. 'And this is one of them. Far from ambushing me, Tulyet has been drawn away to where he will fall into a trap himself.'

Edward Mortimer shifted nervously, casting a quick glance towards the street. 'He speaks the truth. The Sheriff has been enticed to the river, where our men in his ranks will turn on him.' He looked at Harling. 'But nevertheless we should not stay here longer than necessary. Kill them now and let us be away.'

'You are monsters!' whispered Matilde, gazing from Edward to Harling. 'Why are you doing this?'

'The usual reason, madam,' said Harling. 'I am weary of giving. It is time to take.'

'You will not get far,' said Michael. 'Cheating the King of his taxes will be regarded as treason. You will never be safe from him.'

'Rubbish!' said Harling. 'I have purchased a pleasant manor in the north country – under a different name of course – and will spend the rest of my days enjoying the proceeds of this most lucrative winter. I had hoped that Katherine Mortimer might be able to enjoy it with me, but, unfortunately, circumstances dictated otherwise.'

'How can you have accrued such wealth in so short a time?' said Michael in disbelief. 'A few figs and the odd pomegranate cannot make a man's fortune.'

'Foolish monk!' said Harling, his eyes glinting silvery black in the candlelight. 'Do you think I would waste my time with fruit? That is for the poor devils who lurk about in the marshes with their pathetic little punts and their sacks of ancient oranges. And, anyway, I have been engaged in this business since last September – the day after half-wits like you voted for Tynkell instead of me.'

'What about poisoned wine?' asked Michael. 'There is probably a lucrative market for that.'

'I daresay there is,' said Harling. 'But I do not peddle poisoned wine. I merely had a dozen bottles – specially prepared with a strong French poison – delivered to present to a few of my acquaintances before I left. Among others, I planned to give one to Chancellor Tynkell; one to you, Brother, for leaching away my power as Vice-Chancellor; one to Master Bingham of Valence Marie who spoke out against

me so unfairly when I stood for election – although Rob
Thorpe almost saved me the trouble by having him indicted
of Grene's murder. Unfortunately, neither Physwick Hostel
nor St Mary's Church are places I could hide such gifts, and
so I was forced to store them with the Mortimers. Half were
promptly stolen, and I had to go to extraordinary lengths to
get them back, so they would not be traced to me before I
was ready to leave. You must admit I was thorough.'

'Oh, very,' said Michael heavily. 'You arranged for Armel
to be buried early to prevent too close an examination of his
body; you, Katherine and Edward stole the four bottles from
Matt's room at Michaelhouse, then you went to Gonville,
where you retrieved the fifth one and killed Isaac; you killed
Philius when he began asking questions about poisons at his
Friary; and you killed Sacks.'

'I most certainly did not kill Isaac,' said Harling indignantly. 'That was Katherine and Edward. As Bartholomew
observed earlier today, I have some skill with knives, and
I would not have resorted to hitting the man on the head.
While they were doing that, I was innocently searching
the kitchens for the wine, unaware that murder had been
done.'

'But you helped us hang him once I had knocked him
senseless,' said Edward wearily. 'You were not as entirely
innocent of the affair as you would have them believe.'

'And it was you who attacked Matt in Philius's room,' said
Michael. 'Why did you not stab him then – and Philius, for
that matter – to save yourself the trouble later?'

'Would that I had,' said Harling, not without bitterness.
'But I was interested only in retrieving the wine at that point,
and thought I was being merciful in sparing your lives. I knew
if I started a fire in Philius's room, Bartholomew would feel
obliged to stay to ensure his patient was not burned to a
cinder, thus allowing me the opportunity to escape.'

'Sacks stole six bottles from you, but we found only five,'
said Bartholomew. He shifted uncomfortably, trying to ease

the pressure of Langelee's weight from his chest, but the sergeant swung his crossbow in his direction, and Langelee's foot pushed down harder still. 'Where is the last one?'

'It was with Sacks when I killed him,' said Harling dismissively. 'Unfortunately, it was smashed in the fight we had, before he expressed a curious desire to see the inside of Master Cheney's salt barrel. I had planned to dump that barrel in the marshes, but that is no longer necessary now you have discovered its secrets.' He brushed imaginary specks of dust from his gown.

'Did you desecrate Egil's body to hide the fact that it was he who brought you the wine?' asked Michael. 'Because his hands and face were blistered from touching it?'

'At last!' said Harling. 'You have been uncommonly slow in dealing with the few facts that have trickled your way. Perhaps the rain has rotted your minds. When Cynric so kindly informed me where you had left Egil's corpse, I went to claim it, knowing that you would notice the blisters on his hands and face in the cold light of day. Unfortunately, he was very heavy. I hauled him as far as I could, and then settled for the easier option of removing the incriminating parts – the burns from where he had touched the bottles as he brought them across the Fens from France. You were supposed to think he was savaged by a wild animal.'

'Very selective wild animal,' muttered Bartholomew. 'Taking only hands and head.'

Michael moved restlessly, and the candlelight glittered on the ornate crucifix he had worn since the installation. Bartholomew saw it had caught Harling's eye, too, and suddenly the Vice-Chancellor's business in the Fens became crystal clear. He had said, quite clearly, that he was not interested in clothes and fruit, and that he considered himself in a league far beyond all the other casual opportunists. And, when Bartholomew saw him looking at Michael's cross, Bartholomew knew exactly what the Vice-Chancellor's trade had been.

'Treasure,' he exclaimed. 'You are smuggling treasure!'

'Good again,' said Harling appraisingly. 'Gold and silver is indeed what my companions and I have been smuggling. It was astonishingly easy: boats were available; pilots were ready to be hired to take the cargo through the Fens; and officials had been bribed so many times before that they had not the slightest qualm about being bought into silence again.'

'But where does it come from?' asked Bartholomew. He tried to rise, but Langelee's foot was immovable.

'It comes from Brittany,' said Michael in sudden understanding. 'Oswald Stanmore and I were telling you only the other day how hostilities between England and France might have died down, but that the war is still very much in progress in Brittany: there have been many reports of bands of the King's men roaming the country to attack villages and religious houses.'

'And you are buying the treasures from these sacked religious houses and smuggling them into England?' asked Bartholomew of Harling. He answered his own question. 'Items like Philius's collection of crucifixes, the handsome chalices at Valence Marie and the gold plate at Denny are all objects monasteries and convents would own – and that would be easy for looters to carry away.'

'I had surmised as much,' said Dame Pelagia casually. 'When I saw that gold plate on which the Abbess served us cakes, I knew it was nothing the Countess had donated. It was Italian and the Countess is not an admirer of Italian craftsmanship.'

'It is really very simple,' said Harling. 'There is no market for plundered church plate in Brittany, and so, unless the soldiers doing the ransacking do not mind donating their treasure to the King's bottomless coffers, the only way they can profit from their hard work is by selling it to me – cheaply, of course. I then bring it to England where I can sell it at a suitably inflated price. You bought something of mine, I see, Brother.'

Harling eyed Michael's gold cross again. Michael looked shifty, but did not offer to return it. Harling went on.

'Philius bought some, too, which I later reclaimed. But I know when to stop, and I have more than enough wealth to keep me and my companions comfortable for the rest of our lives. Of late, I have been unable to control the soldiers I hired to bring the treasure through the Fens. They began to attack travellers on the roads and then even places in the town – like the Round Church and St Clement's Hostel. It would have been unfortunate to have them recognised as the perpetrators of these crimes while they were visiting me on business.'

'So it was you who sent them to kill us in the Fens?' asked Michael.

'You are tenacious when it comes to mysteries,' said Harling smoothly. 'I knew it would be only a matter of time before your investigation of the poisoned wine led you to me – or to one of my companions who would not have had the nerve to brazen it out. When you did not accept that Bingham had murdered Grene – as Eligius very conveniently believed – I decided to take action before you had time to begin an inquiry. I sent my best man, Alan of Norwich, to deal with you, but he failed miserably. On my orders, Egil returned to look for you, but he met with his unfortunate accident.' He turned to Edward. 'You are lucky to escape that marriage, my friend!'

Bartholomew saw Langelee tense and shoot Edward a nasty glance.

'And was it you Julianna heard talking at the abbey, and who later set fire to the guesthall?' asked Michael, oblivious to the exchange between Julianna's suitors.

Harling sighed. 'Of course not. Had that been me, we would not be having this conversation now – you would have died in the fire. Those were a couple of clerks who work at St Mary's Church, and who have let me down badly with their bungled attempt on your lives.'

'And another attempt was made when that puny little fellow tried to knife me,' said Michael. 'And, simultaneously, someone else was waiting to shoot Matt with a crossbow outside Gonville Hall.'

'The man with the crossbow was me,' said Harling. 'When John came running out as though the Devil himself was after him, I guessed he had revealed something he should not have done and so I shot him instead. Bartholomew was not an immediate threat at that point, and I knew I could come back for him at a later date.'

'But how did you know I would visit Gonville?' asked Bartholomew, easing himself up slightly when Langelee's attentions seemed to be more on considering Edward's association with Julianna than on Harling's revelations, 'Did Colton tell you he had summoned me?'

Harling sighed. 'Think, man! I had just killed Philius. Who was Master Colton going to call to help him under such circumstances? All I had to do was wait, because I knew either you or Michael would come. And I was right.'

'I see why the Abbess did not object when I suggested we might stay longer at Denny,' said Michael. 'She, of course, knows all about what you are doing and was perfectly happy to see us roasted alive in her guesthall. She even used Julianna's wiles to keep us there instead of reprimanding her lewd behavior as any good Abbess would have done. I was very wrong about her – I thought she was noble and saintly.'

'What lewd behaviour?' demanded Langelee, removing his hefty foot from Bartholomew and moving towards Michael. Bartholomew scrambled to his feet. 'You slander that fine woman's name, Brother.'

Michael stood his ground. 'She offered to perform "little services" if we remained at Denny. It is possible that her intentions were innocent, but they certainly would not sound so to a worldly ear.'

'But you are a monk!' exploded Langelee. 'You are not supposed to possess a worldly ear!'

'I was referring to the Abbess,' said Michael primly. 'Master Harling's partner in crime. She was your accomplice, I assume.'

'Naturally,' said Harling. 'I needed someone of intelligence and integrity whom I could trust in all this. She has proved herself superb. Who would ever guess she was involved? You did not – until now, and now it is too late to do anything about it.'

'And where is Deynman?' demanded Bartholomew, suddenly weary of Harling's boasting.

'Deynman? You mean Gray? I never had him. You were right when you said I was bluffing – he is probably in some tavern. But enough of this. Langelee, you volunteered to dispatch them for me. Do so, and then return to Michaelhouse to await payment. You will forgive me if I do not stay. But do not take long over it – all this must be completed before any more of the night is lost.'

He turned and strode out of the room, followed by Edward and the lay sister who held Dame Pelagia by her arm. Langelee drew a long hunting knife and turned towards Bartholomew.

CHAPTER 12

THE ROOM WAS SILENT EXCEPT FOR LANGELEE'S HEAVY breathing and the receding footsteps of Harling and his associates as they made their way up the dark street with Dame Pelagia. Bartholomew glanced at Matilde, who was trying not to look frightened, and wished with all his heart that he had never had the idea of secreting the elderly nun with the woman he regarded as one of his most dear friends. Langelee kicked the door closed with one foot and tightened his grip on the long hunting knife.

'Watch him,' Langelee ordered the sergeant, gesturing with a flick of his head at Michael, who was clearly poised to lunge. Langelee's attentions were fixed on Bartholomew.

In a movement that was lightning quick, Langelee had crossed the room and struck the sergeant a heavy blow on the side of the neck. The sergeant crumpled into a heap. Bartholomew gazed from the unconscious sergeant to Langelee in bewilderment, an expression mirrored in the faces of Michael and Matilde.

'We do not have much time,' said Langelee urgently. 'We must help Tulyet. Then we must try to save Dame Pelagia.'

'But what—?' began Michael.

Langelee opened the door and peered out into the darkness. 'No time for that,' he said. 'Suffice to say I am loyal to the King.' He turned to Matilde. 'Bind this man securely and lock your door when we have gone. Open it to no one but the Sheriff.' He leaned down, kissed her fully on the lips and was gone, leaving Bartholomew and Michael in utter confusion. Matilde scrubbed at her mouth in distaste. 'Hurry!' came Langelee's voice from the street.

Dazed, they followed him outside. Cynric emerged from the darkness, his face anxious.

'What is happening?' he whispered. 'The Vice-Chancellor has escaped and the Sheriff is chasing shadows by the river.'

'Bartholomew?' called Langelee. 'Follow Harling with Cynric. Michael, you go to the castle for reinforcements. I will head down to the river and see what might be done to help Tulyet.'

With serious misgivings about leaving Matilde alone with the unconscious sergeant, and even greater ones about pursuing Harling, Bartholomew followed Cynric to Bridge Street, Michael panting along behind. Ahead of them, moving shadows in the darkness showed where Harling and his accomplices were hurrying Dame Pelagia towards the Barnwell Gate, presumably aiming for the open Fens to the north of the town.

'Matt, we will never find them if they escape that way,' groaned Michael. 'The Fens are a labyrinth of hidden channels and secret causeways. My grandmother!'

'Go to the castle,' said Bartholomew, giving the monk a shove to get him moving. 'Tell Tulyet's deputy to send someone after us before we all get lost in the marshes.'

'How do we know we can trust Langelee?' asked Michael, grabbing Bartholomew's sleeve. 'He might be leading us into another trap.'

'We have no choice,' said Bartholomew, watching the dwindling shadows in the distance. 'Had he meant us harm, we would be dead by now. And you had better ask Tulyet's deputy to relieve him – assuming of course that the deputy is not one of these traitors among Tulyet's garrison.'

He pushed Michael in the direction of the castle, and slipped away after Cynric towards the town gate. Distantly, there came the sound of men fighting, and Bartholomew hoped Michael's message to the deputy would be in time to relieve the beleaguered Sheriff.

The Barnwell Gate was deserted, and Bartholomew assumed the guards were in Harling's pay until he saw the dark outline of a body lying on the floor inside the hut. His physician's instincts urged him to tend to the man, but Cynric dragged him on and out through the gate and into the open country beyond the town.

It was a cold night, with heavy clouds piling up against each other in readiness for yet another downpour. Here and there, however, patches of clear sky could be seen, with stars flickering against the blackness of space. At times, the moon was visible, sliding out to bathe the countryside is a soft, silvery light. The pathway was treacherous with thick mud from the rains of the afternoon, and Bartholomew skidded and slipped like a drunk, his fear of losing sight of the moving shadows ahead making him clumsy and incautious.

Near the town, small homesteads were scattered along the road, frail, vulnerable shacks with reed-thatched roofs and wattle-and-daub walls. Beyond them stretched their strips of fields, carefully hoed and lined with rows of winter vegetables. Doors opened slightly as they went past, and shadows could be seen moving behind the boarded windows as their occupants prepared to defend their kingdoms against those who would steal their meagre produce under cover of darkness.

Gradually, the houses became fewer, and then they died out altogether as the arable land gave way to the alder and willow tangle that marked the edge of the Fens. Once there were small trees to slink behind, and bushes that threw confused shadows across the pathway, Cynric increased the pace, attempting to close the gap between pursuer and pursued. The ground underfoot became waterlogged, rather than simply muddy, and the causeway rose above the surrounding land to cross the first of a series of bogs.

'How many of them are there?' Bartholomew asked Cynric as he trotted breathlessly behind.

'Shh. Four and Dame Pelagia. We can take them.' Cynric eased back into the shadows as one of the men ahead glanced back.

'We cannot!' said Bartholomew in alarm. 'There is more to Harling than you think.'

'But we will lose him once he reaches the marshes proper – and Dame Pelagia too,' hissed Cynric. 'Even if we manage to follow him, what do you imagine we can do? Which one of us will return for help? And how will he find his way to the other again?'

'Then what do you suggest we do?' asked Bartholomew, feeling his heart thudding painfully against his ribs. 'I have no weapon, and even if I could manage Harling – which I do not think I could – that would still leave you with three others.'

'You are too crude in your thinking, boy,' said Cynric, drawing his long Welsh dagger. 'We will slip up behind them and pick them off one by one.'

'Will we now?'

Bartholomew and Cynric spun round at the sound of Harling's voice so close to them.

'This is becoming tiresome,' said the Vice-Chancellor. He had drawn a knife from his belt, and Bartholomew saw it glint in the moonlight as it flicked towards him. The physician jerked backwards, skidding on the slippery ground as the weapon flashed past his face. There was a blur of movement and he saw Cynric dart forward with his own dagger drawn, but Harling's reactions were too quick, even for Cynric, and he had leapt out of the range of the hunting knife before it could do more than catch his sleeve. While Harling was occupied with Cynric, Bartholomew rushed at him, snatching at the hand that held the weapon, but Harling simply stepped to one side, and a well-placed foot sent the physician sprawling to the ground, legs and arms becoming hopelessly entangled in his long cloak as he fell.

Harling, meanwhile, had seized a stout stick from the ground, and wielded it in his left hand. He feinted at Cynric with the dagger, and then hit out with his branch, sending the Welshman tumbling into the bushes. Harling turned his attention to Bartholomew. The physician struggled to free himself from the cloth as Harling advanced, but the more he squirmed, the tighter the folds seemed to envelop him. He managed to release one arm and shot out a hand to grasp Harling around the ankle, pulling hard so that the Vice-Chancellor fell heavily and his knife skittered from his hand.

'I am here, boy!' cried Cynric, emerging dishevelled from the undergrowth, as Harling took a firm hold on the stick and prepared to strike Bartholomew with it.

Cursing, Harling abandoned the branch, scrambled to his feet and raced forward, bowling into Cynric so that they both fell over the edge of the causeway and disappeared from view. Bartholomew crawled cautiously towards it, and peered down. At that moment, the moon came out from behind a cloud, bathing the Fens in an eerie light and illuminating the spot where Harling was trying to force Cynric's head into a marshy puddle. Cynric was struggling valiantly, but Harling was bigger, stronger and had both knees pressed into Cynric's back, making it difficult for the Welshman to move to defend himself.

With a yell of fury, Bartholomew launched himself at the Vice-Chancellor, who abandoned his attempt to drown Cynric and backed away quickly.

'Your friend will die unless you help him out of the bog,' said Harling, gesturing to where Cynric was trying to extricate himself from the clinging mud. He took a step towards the causeway.

'I will not!' yelled Cynric, floundering helplessly in the marsh.

'Keep still, Cynric,' called Bartholomew urgently. 'You will sink faster if you struggle.'

'Fight him, boy!' the Welshman howled. 'You can do it! He is a coward when he has no weapons.'

'He will slip below the surface, and you will never see him again,' said Harling. He reached the bottom of the causeway bank and began to inch up it. 'He will be sucked down to the bowels of the Earth – to the very mouth of hell.'

'I can get out of this,' gasped Cynric, his voice carrying less conviction than a few moments before. He fell to one side, so that not only were both his legs caught to knee-height in the thick, cloying mud, but one arm, too. 'Watch him or he will escape!'

'Cynric, lie still!' Bartholomew's gaze went from the trapped book-bearer to Harling as he began to climb the bank.

'Look at him,' said the Vice-Chancellor, eyeing Cynric pityingly. 'Help him now, Bartholomew, or say your farewells while he can still hear you.'

Bartholomew did not answer and began to move towards Harling, determined that he should not evade justice yet again. An involuntary gasp from Cynric, as mud oozed into his mouth, made him falter and he glanced quickly at the Welshman. When he looked back to Harling, the Vice-Chancellor had clambered over the edge of the causeway and was lost from sight.

'After him, boy!' shouted Cynric furiously, pointing to where he had disappeared 'Do not let him escape!'

But by the time Bartholomew had scrambled onto the causeway, the road was deserted and he could see nothing moving in either direction. He ran a few steps one way and then the other, peering desperately into the darkness, and trying to detect the slightest of movements that might tell him which way Harling had gone. There was nothing. He stopped and closed his eyes, listening intently for footsteps or the crack of a twig, but all he could hear was Cynric's agitated flapping as he fought to free himself from the marsh. It was hopeless! Bartholomew knew he could never hope to track Harling without Cynric's help, and, reluctantly, he slithered back down the bank and picked his way towards his book-bearer.

'Give me your hand,' said Bartholomew, reaching towards him. Immediately, his own feet began to sink. He stepped backwards to the relative safety of a mat of dead reeds.

'Throw me your cloak!' said Cynric. He gave an exasperated sigh. 'Not the whole thing, boy! Keep hold of one end so you can tug me free.'

Bartholomew heaved as hard as he could, his feet sliding in the slick mud, but he felt himself being dragged towards Cynric, rather than the other way round. After several abortive attempts, it occurred to him to wrap the cloak round a tree trunk and use it as a kind of pulley.

'It is working!' called Cynric triumphantly, as one knee emerged from the sucking slime. 'Pull, boy! I have no wish to enter hell through a bog.'

'Harling was lying,' gasped Bartholomew, hauling with all his might. 'The marshes near the town are not bottomless. Those are further north. He was just trying to distract me to give himself time to escape.'

'Well, he succeeded,' muttered Cynric, not without disapproval. 'He used me to prevent you from following him. You should not have listened to his treacherous words.'

Cynric's feet came free of the mud with a foul plopping sound, and he was able to reach Bartholomew's hand. Together, they stumbled from the bog, and climbed the slippery bank to the causeway.

'Where did he go?' Cynric demanded urgently, looking one way and then the other. 'Which direction did he take? We might catch him yet!'

'You are soaked,' said Bartholomew. 'You should return to the town before you take a chill.'

'And leave you here alone?' asked Cynric, in the tone of

voice that suggested it was not an option worth considering. 'I am fine, boy. But what of Harling? Did he head east or west?'

Bartholomew was forced to admit that he did not know. Cynric gave him a look of appalled disgust, and wordlessly began to search for clues. In desperation, Bartholomew ran up the road until he was forced to stop and catch his breath, but, apart from the sound of his own laboured gasps, the marshes were as silent as the grave. He doubled back again, panting heavily, and hating to think he had allowed Harling to outwit him so easily.

'It is too dark,' muttered Cynric, slashing viciously at the undergrowth with his dagger. 'I cannot see well enough to track him, even when the moon is out.'

'Please try, Cynric!' cried Bartholomew, crashing around uncertainly in the dense shrubs at the side of the causeway, searching for some hidden path that Harling might have taken. 'He will kill Dame Pelagia for certain if you lose him!'

Cynric's shoulders slumped in defeat. 'I cannot, boy,' he said softly. 'He has given us the slip and I can do nothing about it until daylight.'

'Daylight?' echoed Bartholomew in horror. 'But that may be too late! Dame Pelagia might be dead by then!'

Cynric nodded slowly, but turned his attention back to the task he knew was hopeless.

While Cynric continued to hunt in vain for some clue as to the direction Harling might have taken, Bartholomew lumbered about in the bushes near where Harling had attacked them. The task was impossible, but they continued relentlessly until the first threads of dawn began to lighten the sky in the east. Out of the semi-darkness, they heard the thud of hooves, and Cynric dragged Bartholomew into the bushes until he recognised the horsemen: Michael, Langelee, and Tulyet with some of his men. Bartholomew could not meet Michael's eyes when he told him how they had lost Harling and Dame Pelagia, and turned away when Michael sank down at the side of the road and put his head in his hands.

Tulyet had sustained a cut over one eye in the skirmish near the river, and he told Bartholomew that reinforcements from his deputy had arrived in the nick of time. Langelee had apparently fought like the Devil, and it was only with his help that Tulyet and those soldiers who had remained loyal had managed to hold off the ambushers. The deputy's force had tipped the balance, and those of Harling's men who had not been killed in the fighting were now safely in the castle prison – among them Alan of Norwich and his mercenaries.

As Tulyet gave Bartholomew and Cynric this information, one of the soldiers said he knew where there was a track that led to the village of Fen Ditton through the marshes. He led the way a short distance to the north, and gestured at the undergrowth, but Bartholomew could see nothing that remotely resembled a path. Nevertheless, he followed the soldier through the tangle of vegetation with the others trailing behind, Cynric pointing out broken leaves and footprints that indicated someone had passed that way, although whether it was Harling and Dame Pelagia was impossible to tell.

'So who *are* you?' asked Bartholomew of Langelee as they walked together. The big philosopher looked pleased with himself, basking in the glory of having saved the Sheriff and his garrison from certain annihilation. 'An agent of the King?'

'Of sorts,' said Langelee. 'I work for the Archbishop of York. There is a grammar school master there by the name of Thorpe, who passed the Archbishop some disturbing information.'

'Thorpe?' asked Bartholomew, startled. 'Robert Thorpe, the disgraced Master of Valence Marie? What could he know about this? He had gone from Cambridge long before winter started.'

'He left in October. But do not interrupt if you want your questions answered,' said Langelee importantly. 'While Thorpe was travelling from Cambridge to take up his new position in York, he had occasion to seek refuge at Denny Abbey during a sudden storm. As he waited for it to pass, a nun told him of a conversation she had overheard between the Abbess and some unidentified University man, during which they discussed plans to bring treasure from sacked Brittany abbeys and convents into England.'

'And I suppose this nun was Dame Pelagia,' said Bartholomew heavily. 'Michael said she was spying there.'

'This nun charged Thorpe to report the matter to the Archbishop when he reached York,' continued Langelee, ignoring him. 'Thorpe was only too pleased to oblige – thinking it might go some way to placing him more favourably in the King's eyes after the mess he made of the Mastership of Valence Marie. He passed the message to the Archbishop as soon as he arrived in York. The Archbishop informed the King, and it was arranged that I should take a position within the University, so that I could work myself into this scholar's confidences to uncover the identities of all his accomplices and recover this treasure.'

'Yet another spy,' sighed Bartholomew. 'Sometimes I wonder whether I am the only person at the University whose purpose is to teach.'

'I have rather enjoyed teaching,' said Langelee. 'Perhaps I will leave the Archbishop's service and stay at Michaelhouse. It is far more interesting – and exciting – than life as an agent.'

This Bartholomew could well believe. 'But how did you know it was Harling that Thorpe overheard plotting with the Abbess? He was very careful to leave no such clues behind him.'

'He told me himself,' said Langelee with a casual shrug.

'I arrived at the University, and put it about that I was not above being asked to perform certain duties in addition to my scholarly ones. Within weeks Harling asked me if I would be interested in a little extra-curricular activity involving trips into the Fens.'

'How fortunate for you,' said Michael coldly. 'And what would you have done if Harling had not been recruiting for his smuggling operation?'

Langelee gave a superior smile. 'Since he was, that question is an irrelevancy. He has a number of clerks from St Mary's Church, and even a couple of Fellows, in his pay. Including the outlaws he has hired, he probably has about fifty people working for him.'

'Fifty!' gasped Michael. 'My God! His operation is vast.'

Langelee nodded. 'And so are his profits, believe me. In fact, the whole organisation is remarkable. He only started this after you lot failed to elect him as Chancellor last year, and he has been extraordinarily successful. You scholars made a grave mistake by not using his talents to further the interests of the University. By now, Cambridge might have been rich beyond its wildest dreams – and even been in a position to take steps to suppress your rival University at Oxford!'

'Most of us would rather not have a contrabander as Chancellor,' said Bartholomew stiffly. 'We generally prefer academics.'

'Then you are bigger fools that I thought,' said Langelee earnestly. 'Harling is a brilliant man. Not only did he have this huge operation up and running within a few weeks, but he knew when to stop. Had I not wormed my way into his confidences, he would never have been caught.'

'And I suppose our little roles in all this count for nothing?' asked Michael scathingly.

'Precisely!' said Langelee, with a superior grin. 'And you would not even be alive now, if it were not for me.' He beamed at them, oblivious of Michael's indignation.

The air was still, damp and cold, and Bartholomew was painfully reminded of the last time they had ventured into the secret, mysterious world of the Fens. Somewhere a bird pipped and hooted and was answered by another in the distance, but otherwise the only sounds were their feet trampling through the undergrowth. A low mist was rising in the early dawn, sending ghostly fingers of white to ooze across brackish water and around the squat trunks of stunted alder trees.

Bartholomew shivered, realising for the first time that he had left his cloak wrapped around the branch of the tree where Cynric had been caught in the mud. Within the space of a day, he had managed to lose his new cloak and new gloves, and facing the rest of the winter without them was a bleak prospect. He felt drained, cold and miserable, acutely aware that Harling had bested him at every turn. His boots were full of icy water, his tabard was filthy with black mud and he was so tired he could barely walk. No such discomfort seemed to assail Langelee, who strode along buoyantly, as though he were on some pleasant countryside jaunt, thoroughly enjoying relating his tale to the dejected scholars who trailed beside him.

'So, after Harling recruited me into his service, I made myself indispensable to him. Then, when you two started investigating the poisoned wine, Harling realised he needed to prevent you from looking into it any further, and so he arranged for you to be ambushed in the Fens. When that failed, he decided he had made enough money and that it was time to stop before he was caught. Obviously, I wanted to get *all* of Harling's accomplices before he sent them to all four corners of the country, so I decided it was time to reveal my part in the affair and acquire Tulyet's help.'

'Did Tulyet know of your role in all this from the beginning?' asked Bartholomew faintly, hoping that the Sheriff could not be numbered in the list of people who had lied to him or deceived him over the past few weeks.

'No one knew except Master Kenyngham,' said Langelee airily. 'And he had been sworn to secrecy by the King himself. What I was doing was potentially very dangerous, and I did not want anyone to be aware of my real business at the University except the Master of my College.'

So Kenyngham had been instructed to hire Langelee as Master of Philosophy by no less than the King himself, thought Bartholomew. Michael had been right in his supposition that Langelee had a powerful sponsor. Smiling complacently at their surprise, Langelee continued.

'I was on the brink of telling Tulyet all I knew, when events started to take on a momentum all of their own. I was in my room, in the very process of writing a report on my findings to present to him, when Harling himself paid me a visit. He said he needed my help to round up his men and to load the last of the smuggled treasure onto a cart.'

He swore as, not paying attention to where he was going, he trod in a puddle that was deeper than he anticipated and black mud bubbled up around his knees. He held out his hand to Michael to be helped out. Hands on hips, Bartholomew watched the fat monk haul and tug, while Langelee became muddier, wetter and increasingly frustrated at Michael's incompetence. It did not cross the philosopher's mind that Michael might well be pulling so inefficiently on purpose – although it was perfectly apparent to Bartholomew. Eventually, and entirely as a result of his own struggles and not Michael's assistance, Langelee was free. He brushed himself down and continued with his story, unaware of Michael's spiteful smile of gratification.

'Before I left Michaelhouse to do Harling's bidding, I charged Bartholomew's student – that stupid Rob Deynman – with handing my report to Master Kenyngham. He tried to refuse, claiming he was off on some errand of mercy to save a patient's life. I impressed on him the importance of my report and the dire consequences that would occur should it fall into the wrong hands. I must have impressed a little too firmly, because finding Kenyngham out, Deynman was too afraid to go to look for him. He simply settled himself in Kenyngham's room to await his return. He was there most of yesterday.'

'So he was not kidnapped by Harling at all?' asked Bartholomew.

Langelee shook his head. 'Gray told me you thought Deynman might be in some danger and, knowing Harling, I guessed he had told you he had the lad secreted away somewhere. Deynman spent most of yesterday asleep on Kenyngham's bed, but had handed him my report with all solemnity when Kenyngham returned. Deynman never left the College, and your patient with winter fever was never tended.'

Bartholomew rubbed his eyes, uncertain whether to be relieved that Deynman was unharmed or angry that he had been so single-minded. He could at least have told his friends what he was doing.

'So why have you been so antagonistic to your Michaelhouse colleagues?' he asked Langelee. 'Why did you try to start a fight with me the other day? Surely that was not necessary?'

'Sorry,' said Langelee, with an unrepentant smile. 'You see, Harling was becoming paranoid about the poisoned wine, and ordered me to search your rooms to see if you were withholding information from him. I had just finished searching Michael's chamber, and was about to look in yours, when you returned to College clearly ready to go to sleep.'

Bartholomew recalled Langelee perched on his table, going through his scrolls and looking around at his few belongings with interest.

'Surely there were easier ways of getting what you wanted than picking a fight?'

'I needed the information quickly and you were about to go to bed. I did a preliminary search with you there, but I needed a closer look. It would have appeared suspicious had I knocked you senseless for no reason, and so I tried to goad you into a brawl. You showed admirable restraint, but then Kenyngham caught us.'

They walked in silence for a while, their feet squelching in the wet grass. The day was growing much lighter, a sensation enhanced by the pale mist that rose all around them. It was like walking in a great white bubble, the fog seeming to accentuate even more the deathly silence of the Fens. Cynric moved from side to side, absorbed in broken twigs and crushed blades of grass that no one else noticed. The soldier led them deeper and deeper into the marshes and Bartholomew found himself walking ever more slowly, alert to the possibility that they were being drawn into yet another of Harling's complicated traps.

'It was not easy, worming my way into Harling's confidence,' said Langelee after a while, wanting to ensure that the two scholars fully appreciated the magnitude of his achievement. 'He drinks, you know, and often insisted I should join him, even early in the morning. I did not wish to arouse his suspicions and so complied. I can barely remember some days.'

Bartholomew remembered them, however, when Langelee had reeled belligerently around Michaelhouse, yelling at the servants and frightening the students. He also remembered the alcoholic fumes that had wafted into his face when Langelee had tried to force him to fight. Langelee may have been on the right side in the end, but Bartholomew strongly suspected much of his loutish behaviour was no act.

'And you cultivated Julianna's friendship because you imagined her betrothal to Edward might bring you information?' asked Bartholomew.

Langelee stopped dead in his tracks and his brows beetled together. For a moment, Bartholomew thought the powerful philosopher was going to strike him, but the moment passed. Langelee began to walk again.

'I knew nothing of this betrothal,' he said shortly. 'I

"cultivated Julianna's friendship", as you so unpleasantly put it, because I find her company charming.'

Bartholomew shuddered.

'Her uncle sent her away to Denny when he found out I had been paying her court,' Langelee went on. 'But she managed to find her way back.' The admiration in his voice was crystal clear. Bartholomew dreaded to think what a meeting between this violent, aggressive, self-confident pair would involve: Langelee would probably find Julianna's belligerence attractive while Julianna would consider Langelee's pugilism manly.

The soldier ahead of them stopped sharply, gave a horrified yell and backed away, colliding with Bartholomew who walked behind him. Bartholomew edged forward nervously, wondering what could have caused the soldier's sudden distress. Langelee shoved him, trying to squeeze past on the narrow path, but stopped abruptly.

In front of them was a bog, an evil morass of sloppy mud topped by a still layer of water. Protruding just above the surface was a smooth cap of black hair, the grease of which had kept it shiny and water-free. To one side of the cap was a pale, cold hand, its fingers still clenched around the branch of the tree with which it had attempted to haul its owner free. But it was the other hand that caught Bartholomew's attention. It held the clean, white veil that Dame Pelagia had worn.

He twisted round, intending to prevent Michael from seeing it, but was too late. Michael's green eyes became round with shock and he let out a great wail of grief.

'No! Oh, no!'

Michael's cry echoed around the Fens, causing some ducks to take to the air noisily, the panicky flapping of wings in the undergrowth loud in the ensuing silence. Langelee, Tulyet and his soldiers, Cynric, Michael and Bartholomew stood in a circle, looking down in horror at the dead hand and what it held. Harling might be dead, but he had taken Dame Pelagia with him. Bartholomew recalled Harling trying to throw him in the mill race and then attempting to force Cynric's head under water just a short time before – Harling had been determined to drown someone.

'Come on,' said Tulyet, quickly coming to his senses, and clapping his hands to marshal his soldiers' attention. 'The others cannot be far away and I do not want them to escape. Cynric, take Master Langelee and search over to the south. I will look to the west with Justin, while the rest of my men can cover the ground to the north. Matt, you had better stay here with Brother Michael.'

'Damn!' shouted Langelee in frustration, kicking a rotten tree stump. 'I wanted to take Harling alive to present to the King. All my hard work and it ends like this. It is not fair!'

'It was not fair that Dame Pelagia died at Harling's hands in a desolate marsh either,' said Bartholomew quietly.

Langelee glanced at Michael's stricken face, and relented slightly. He stamped off through the undergrowth after Cynric, leaving Bartholomew and Michael alone with the grisly spectre of the drowned Vice-Chancellor.

'Get it back from him, Matt,' whispered Michael unsteadily, his eyes huge in his white face. 'I do not want her veil in his filthy hand.'

Holding Michael's arm for balance, Bartholomew leaned towards the bog, and grabbed the piece of white material. Harling's grip on it was vice-like, and, as Bartholomew pulled, he felt the body moving with it. With a shudder, he let it go, so that the veil trailed in the mud, the crisp linen quickly becoming wet and brown. He was turning to suggest that they leave it until there was someone else to help, when the veil suddenly disappeared under the black surface of the water. Puzzled, Bartholomew stared at it. And then Harling exploded from the water with a sword in his hand and an evil smile on his face. Droplets and spray scattered everywhere, drenching the two scholars, who stood rooted to the spot with shock at the edge of the marsh.

Aghast, Bartholomew watched as the Vice-Chancellor landed on the dry land beside him, dashing the water from his eyes and drawing in great gulps of fresh air. Michael gave a howl of anger, and launched himself at him, murder written all over his face. Calmly, Harling seized Bartholomew, touching the tip of his sword against the physician's throat.

'Think again, Brother,' he said softly. 'Or you will be mourning more than your old nun.'

By the time Bartholomew's numbed brain could make any sense out of what was happening, it was far too late to act, and all he could hear was the sound of Harling breathing heavily and hotly against his ear. He struggled, but felt the cold touch of metal on his neck.

'Be still! I will not be so gentle with you this time, Bartholomew!'

'But how could you hold your breath all that time?' stammered Bartholomew, still not sure he believed what was happening, and half expecting to wake in his own bed at Michaelhouse and find it was all some dreadful nightmare.

Harling made an impatient sound. 'Reeds, of course!' he snapped. 'This place is full of them, and I told you I had good water skills. Surely you did that as a child, used one as a pipe to breathe through while you stayed under the surface?'

'I cannot say that I did,' said Michael coldly. 'What have you done with my grandmother?'

'Your grandmother is it?' asked Harling. 'Well, that explains your uncharacteristic selflessness in protecting her – not that she needed anything from you, Brother. That woman had a mind cunning and devious enough to delight any scholar. It was she who led Edward and that dim-witted lay sister into this part of the Fens – where she knew they would flounder and make slow progress. How they allowed themselves to listen to her advice when she was their captive I cannot imagine.'

'Where is she?' demanded Michael unsteadily. The use of the past tense to refer to her had not escaped his attention.

Harling gestured carelessly to the marsh, where the very tip of the veil could be seen just under the brown surface of the water, disappearing into the blackness below. At that moment, Langelee and Cynric burst into the little clearing, alerted by Michael's yell of fury. Bartholomew watched the bushes for signs that Tulyet might be close, but the Sheriff had left some moments before Langelee, and had probably been too far away to hear Michael's shout.

'Drop your weapons!' Harling ordered Langelee and Cynric, tightening his grip on Bartholomew's neck. 'Throw them in the bog or I will kill him right now.'

'Go on, kill him, then,' said Langelee, drawing his own sword. 'He is expendable. There are far higher stakes in this game than the life of an anonymous scholar.'

'Put it down, Langelee,' said Michael, taking a menacing step forward. 'Do as he says.'

Cynric hurled his dagger into the pool of water with a splash that distracted Langelee, and then relieved the philosopher of his sword while his attention strayed. A hunting knife followed it, leaving Langelee spitting with impotent rage.

'Fool!' he spat at Cynric. 'Now he will kill us all!'

'There,' said Cynric, raising his empty hands and ignoring Langelee's enraged spluttering. 'Now let him go.'

Harling gave a mirthless smile, and pressed the point of his sword to Bartholomew's chin. 'I am not stupid, Cynric. You can also dispense of the knife you carry in your boot, and the one you have in your sleeve.'

Cynric blanched, but did as Harling ordered. When the weapons were no more than a trail of bubbles in the water, Harling suddenly shoved Bartholomew away from him so that he crashed into Langelee. Langelee stood like a rock, and one of his ham-like hands stopped the physician from falling, while Harling moved a safe distance away from them, wiping droplets of water from his eyes and dispensing with his sodden cloak. Bartholomew backed up against a tree, his legs shaking from shock and fatigue.

'What do you mean to do?' demanded Langelee, rather more petulantly than was wise given who was holding the weapon.

'I want you, Langelee,' said Harling with his nasty smile. 'You have betrayed me for months, worming your way into my confidence, while all the time you were an agent for the King. I would never have left Cambridge without settling my score with you, and now you have played right into my hands – I knew you would follow me here.'

He selected a knife from a collection in his belt that he seemed to have acquired since he had attacked Bartholomew and Cynric on the causeway, and balanced it in his palm, still holding the sword in his left hand. Bartholomew's fingers closed around a piece of loose bark that he had tugged from the tree against which he leaned. Harling raised one arm, and took aim.

Without stopping to consider the consequences, Bartholomew hurled the bark at the Vice-Chancellor as hard as he could, causing him to falter just as the knife left his hand. The weapon skimmed past the philosopher's head and thumped into the trunk of a tree, where it quivered from the force with which it was thrown. Harling cursed angrily, while Langelee took advantage of the opportunity to scramble away into the bushes. Michael and Cynric were not long in following his example.

'Damn you, Bartholomew!' screamed Harling, seeing his quarry gone. 'Why do you persist in foiling me at every step?'

He grabbed another knife from the collection in his belt and held it like a spear, narrowing his eyes as he aimed.

Bartholomew dived away from the tree, and twisted to one side as Harling's arm dropped. The knife embedded itself in Bartholomew's medicine bag, spinning him round and smashing phials that immediately began dripping.

There was a shout from the undergrowth, not far away. Tulyet must have heard Michael's yell after all, and was making his way towards them. If Harling intended to kill them all, he did not have much time.

Bartholomew scrambled away, desperately looking for somewhere to hide. Harling followed, his eyes filled with a grim purpose, and the others seemingly forgotten. He drew yet another knife, and Bartholomew's foot slipped in mud so that he fell to his knees. He tried to duck around a thick willow tree, but Harling followed him and was standing so close that Bartholomew could hear his agitated breathing. There would be no escape this time. He turned to face Harling, and saw the glitter of triumph in the Vice-Chancellor's face as he raised his arm to throw the dagger that could not miss. Bartholomew closed his eyes tightly, waiting for the searing pain that would end his life.

'Matt!' came Michael's anguished yell.

Bartholomew forced himself to open his eyes. Harling's expression of hatred turned to one of surprise, and he lowered the knife to waist level. Bartholomew waited, confused. Did Harling mean to stab him, rather than simply to throw the knife? The Vice-Chancellor looked down at him oddly, and then pitched forwards, the knife still in his hand. Bartholomew saw the weapon aimed at his chest as Harling landed on him, knocking him flat on his back.

For a few terrifying moments, he was unable to move, and was uncertain whether he had been stabbed or not: he had been told many times by dying patients that their mortal injuries were painless. But then Langelee and Michael ran forward and heaved the inert Vice-Chancellor away from him, and he found himself unharmed. Protruding from Harling's back was a long, thin blade, embedded so deeply

that Bartholomew wondered if it had skewered him clean
through. Behind them stood Dame Pelagia, poised to move
quickly should Harling show further signs of life.

Dame Pelagia stepped out of the undergrowth and came
towards them, smiling beatifically. Michael elbowed
Bartholomew and Langelee out of the way and tore towards
her, taking her up in a bear-like hug that Bartholomew was
afraid might crack her ribs.

'Grandmother!'

'She is *his* grandmother?' asked Langelee, turning an
astonished face towards Bartholomew. 'Dame Pelagia?'

Bartholomew nodded, while Langelee watched the reunion
with fascination. There was a rustle in the undergrowth
and Tulyet emerged, flanked by his men. He saw Harling
motionless on the ground and gaped at him.

'We saw him drowned!' he exclaimed. 'Is he some kind of
demon to defy death and rise from his grave to persecute us
all?' He crossed himself vigorously.

'Dame Pelagia made an end of him,' said Langelee,
nodding to where Michael still held the old lady in a
protective hug.

'Are you sure he is not still alive?' asked Tulyet, prodding
the Vice-Chancellor cautiously with his foot, as though he
imagined Harling might still leap to his feet and attack
them all. 'Check him, will you, Matt? We should be certain
this time.'

Reluctantly, Bartholomew knelt next to the body and felt
for a life-beat in the great vessels of the neck. There was
nothing, and Harling's eyes were wide open and staring. The
knife was perfectly positioned to penetrate his heart, and
was embedded almost to the hilt. Dame Pelagia possessed
a powerful throwing arm, it seemed.

'He is dead,' he said, standing and backing away from
the body.

'Well, wrap him in his cloak and make sure you bind him

tightly,' said Tulyet to one of his men, taking no chances. 'And then continue the search for his companions. They cannot have gone far.'

'Edward Mortimer is trapped in a bog over there, while his accomplices fled in that direction,' said Dame Pelagia, pointing with a soft, wrinkled finger. She disengaged herself from Michael and walked towards them. 'They will not get far. The silly fools did not take the rains into account when they allowed me to convince them to take a short cut. At any other time of year it would be perfectly safe, but the water level is far too high at the moment.'

'Is Edward Mortimer alive?' asked Tulyet, dispatching his men away in the directions she had indicated.

Dame Pelagia smiled sweetly. 'Oh yes. Just trapped. I have been keeping up his spirits with a few tales.' Her smile widened into a grin, revealing her small, pointed teeth.

Bartholomew was certain he would not like to hear any tales Dame Pelagia might tell.

'I am sorry to have taken so long to come to your rescue,' she went on. 'I could not get a clear shot and too many innocents have already died in this ungodly mess without me adding another.'

Michael seemed surprised. 'That would not have prevented you trying ten years ago.'

Dame Pelagia sighed and then patted her grandson affectionately on the cheek. 'You know me too well,' she said with the grin that seemed to Bartholomew to be rather wolfish. 'The truth is that I only managed to grab one of Harling's knives when I escaped from him. I could not afford to miss him and hit one of you instead, because that would have been the end of us all.'

'How did you escape?' asked Bartholomew. 'It looked to me as though Edward and that lay sister had you held firmly between them.'

'They are amateurs and hardly worth mentioning,' said Dame Pelagia with patent indifference. 'I bided my time, slowing them down whenever I could, because I wanted to ensure Harling did not escape and I knew you would be tracking our progress. Reinforcements were, however, a little later in arriving than I had anticipated.' She looked accusingly at the Sheriff and then at Bartholomew.

'That is what happens when you work with normal people instead of cunning and experienced agents,' retorted Bartholomew, irritated at the criticism after all the trouble they had taken to help her. 'But Harling said that you were in the bog and that he had killed you.'

Dame Pelagia waved a dismissive hand, much as Michael often did when Bartholomew suggested something he did not consider worth discussing. 'Harling fell in the water and then tried to drag me in with him. I simply allowed my veil to slip off and then shoved that ridiculous lay sister in after him. One nun in a wet habit looks much like another and he drowned her not me. It just goes to show that – as all we agents are taught – it is dangerous to allow your attention to stray, even for a moment, or you may end up killing someone who was on your side.'

Bartholomew gaped at her. The hem of her cloak and her shoes were wet and muddy, but other than that she was spotless, a marked contrast to everyone else with their sodden cloaks and filthy, dirt-splattered clothes and faces. If she had engaged in some kind of struggle with Harling and the lay sister, then she had managed to do so with minimum effort and absolutely no disturbance to her immaculate appearance.

She chuckled, amused by his shock, and turned her attention back to Michael, clucking over a small scratch on his hand and setting his gold cross straight against his habit.

'Is she really his grandmother?' asked Langelee yet again, staring at them as they walked away together.

'Yes. She really is,' said Bartholomew, finally recovering himself, and taking the philosopher by the arm so Michael and Dame Pelagia might have some privacy. He failed to see why their relationship should be any concern of Langelee's – or the Archbishop of York's.

'But that is Dame Pelagia?' said Langelee in awe.

'I know,' said Bartholomew drily. He doubted he would ever forget it. Langelee continued to gaze at Michael and the old nun, resisting Bartholomew's attempts to pull him away.

'You have not heard of her, have you?' said Langelee, shaking his head slowly. 'Dame Pelagia is one of the greatest and most respected of all the King's agents, and it is said that she is one of the few people who knows all the details of the mystery surrounding the death of Edward the Second – he was our current King's father.'

'Was he really?' asked Bartholomew innocently. 'I had no idea.'

'You scholars!' said Langelee, condescendingly chiding. 'How can you expect to teach when you know so little of the world? But I was telling you about Dame Pelagia. It is not mere chance that Queen Isabella, whom we all know played a role in her husband's murder, spends her days at Castle Rising near a Franciscan nunnery – a house of Poor Clares, which is Dame Pelagia's Order. It is common knowledge at Westminster that the King would entrust the wardenship of his murderous mother to no one but Dame Pelagia.'

Bartholomew looked at the old lady with renewed suspicion. No wonder Michael was unwilling to take a post as a mere head of a University College with those kind of family connections!

'A year or so ago,' Langelee went on, 'the King relieved her of that charge, and allowed her to retire into the less arduous service of the Bishop of Ely by living at Denny – she was supposed to keep an eye on the Countess of Pembroke when she visited. But it was not long before Dame Pelagia routed out trouble on the King's behalf. As you concluded earlier, it was she who passed the message to Thorpe to give to my Archbishop.'

'But why did she send this message with Thorpe to the Archbishop of York?' asked Bartholomew. 'Why did she not tell Michael? He told me she meets him on occasion to pass the Countess of Pembroke's secrets to the Bishop.'

'I imagine because it was quicker to send a message with Thorpe. Denny is very isolated and it might have been some time before she could waylay anyone trustworthy enough to carry a message to tell Michael to meet her.'

'But she did not inform Michael that she knew a scholar was behind all this,' said Bartholomew, still confused, 'or that she had sent a message to the King via Thorpe and the Archbishop of York.'

'I have already told you,' said Langelee impatiently. 'No one knew about my mission except Master Kenyngham and the King. Dame Pelagia doubtless guessed that someone like me was infiltrating the University, but she was not officially informed. And she is too professional to have risked endangering another agent and his duties by gossiping about what she had overheard to the Bishop of Ely – who did not need to know about it. She knows how to keep a secret.'

'I am sure she does,' said Bartholomew. 'But what about when all this started to come together – when she came with us back to Cambridge to pass the information she had gathered more recently to the Sheriff? Why did she not tell Michael then?'

'I imagine she did not have the chance,' said Langelee. 'She was hidden away most of the time that she was in Cambridge, and I know Michael did not visit her because Harling had him followed constantly. And she certainly would not have discussed the matter on the open road – she is too experienced an operator to make a silly error like that.'

'But why, if she knew about this operation in October, did she wait until now to act?'

'She *did* act in October,' said Langelee impatiently. 'She was responsible for me being put in position. But recently she must have sensed that Harling was about to fold up his business, and decided to take precautions – by telling Michael she had information for the Bishop and the Sheriff – in case I failed. Do not forget that she was at Denny, cut off from outside news, and had no way of knowing whether I was even alive. I am sure she considered very carefully what course of action to take, and how best she might serve the interests of the King.'

'But why did the King bother with you at all?' pressed Bartholomew. 'Michael is a good and loyal agent, and the University is under the jurisdiction of the Bishop of Ely, not the Archbishop of York. Michael would have been well placed to expose Harling.'

Langelee shrugged. 'When I was first given this mission, the identity of the mastermind behind all this was not known. It was better that an outsider looked into it. In fact, it was what Dame Pelagia recommended in the report that Thorpe carried to York – she suspected that the scholar she overheard plotting with the Abbess was a high-ranking University official, and considered it prudent to charge some stranger with the task of unveiling him.'

Bartholomew regarded the elderly nun with a new respect. No wonder spying and subterfuge were so deeply ingrained in Michael – not only was it in his blood, but he had probably been given some expert tuition. Bartholomew felt uncomfortable when he thought of how he had inflicted such a wily old character on Matilde and hoped his friend had not learned any bad habits.

Dame Pelagia looked as serene and unruffled as she had been when she had pretended to be asleep so she could overhear what the silly Julianna had to say. He studied her intently, watching the secretive glint in her green eyes, and suddenly felt sorry for the likes of Edward Mortimer and the lay sister for attempting to take on such a formidable opponent. She saw him staring at her and gazed back so that he felt as though she were reading his very soul. She gave him the slightest of smiles before allowing Michael to lead her back to the causeway.

'Well, that is that,' said Michael late the following afternoon, stretching his long, fat legs in front of the fire and selfishly stealing the warmth from Cynric. Cynric sighed and moved his stool to the other side of the hearth. Bartholomew sat between them, leaning forward with his arms on his knees and staring into the flames.

Agatha brought another plate of the cakes with the strange, crunchy texture, and Michael began to wolf them down. Bartholomew bit one cautiously, and realised it was pomegranate seeds that lent the cakes their peculiar taste and grittiness. Since Michael seldom chewed anything, the disconcerting cracking as the seeds splintered under the teeth did not deter him from eating them as it did most of the other scholars.

They were sitting in the conclave, the small, pleasant room off the hall in Michaelhouse. The weather had turned from wet to cold, and Master Kenyngham had at last given permission for fires to be lit nightly. The Fellows were in the conclave and the students were in the hall, singing some disgraceful song that had Father William pursing his lips in prim disapproval. He would have gone to silence them, but Langelee was relating the story of Harling and his monumental wickedness to Master and Fellows, and William was reluctant to miss out on such rare entertainment.

Bartholomew listened to the philosopher with half an ear, but, with the exception of some vivid details that seemed to have more to do with amusing his audience than truth, Langelee said nothing Bartholomew did not already know. Michael watched the philosopher and his increasingly sceptical audience, his baggy green eyes alive with sardonic relish, and Bartholomew was reminded of his terrifying grandmother.

'We are heroes,' said the monk drily. 'Or, rather, Langelee is and we played a minor role in defeating one of the most evil minds the world has yet known. But it is all over, so there is no need for you to look so glum. You were even back in Cambridge in time to give your lecture at King's Hall.'

Bartholomew winced. 'But not early enough to change. I gave the best and most inspired lecture of my life, and all the audience could do was stare at the state of my tabard. What a waste!'

Michael chuckled. 'I shall remember that the next time I am asked to speak on metaphysics. You know how I hate that subject! I shall roll around on the river bank so that my appearance distracts the class from my words, and I will be able to tell them anything I like. Have another cake, Matt. You look as though you need a little feeding up. Just like me.'

Bartholomew flexed his aching shoulders and took one of the cakes, wondering why he and Michael felt so battered by their experiences, but why Dame Pelagia had not seemed affected in the slightest. When they had arrived, exhausted, back in the town, the old lady announced pertly that she was going to visit Matilde, and asked Bartholomew to escort her. Warily, he accompanied her through the streets, certain that she would have been a good deal more effective at repelling cutpurses and thieves than he could ever hope to be, and found Matilde waiting in a state of high agitation.

'At last!' she cried, flinging herself into his arms. 'I have been worried to death!'

'Dame Pelagia is well following her unpleasant experience in the marshes,' he said formally, startled by the intensity of her reaction. 'Although we bungled our attempt to rescue her.'

Matilde waved her hand in dismissal, still with one arm looped around his neck. 'Pelagia knows how to look after herself. It was you I was worried about.'

After Dame Pelagia had related their story in clear and unembellished phrases – so free of exaggeration that Bartholomew later wondered whether she and Langelee had even shared the same adventure – and Matilde had satisfied herself that he was unharmed, Bartholomew had taken the old lady to the Chancellor's lodgings. Tulyet was to escort her back to the peace of Denny Abbey after a few days' rest, when he would take the opportunity to arrest the Abbess for her role in smuggling the stolen treasure. Edward had confessed his part in the affair in a wailing voice all the way back to the town and, once again, Bartholomew wondered what Dame Pelagia had done or said to induce his almost frantic desire to confess.

Absently he took a bite out of the cake, and the loud crack of a seed between his teeth wrenched his thoughts back to the present.

'So Denny Abbey provided a storage place for Harling's treasure,' Michael was saying. 'It was a perfect choice. Who would have thought of looking for stolen treasure in the cellars of a nunnery?'

'Who would have thought of looking for treasure at all is more to the point,' said Bartholomew. 'If your grandmother had not overheard Harling's conversation with the Abbess that prompted the King to place Langelee undercover here, we might never have guessed what the Vice-Chancellor was doing. We still would have been looking for pedlars of pomegranates and figs.'

'I do not think so,' said Michael, somewhat indignantly. 'Do not try to give Langelee more credit than he deserves. You started to unravel the mystery when Harling tried to throw you in the mill race, and we both guessed about the treasure when we put all the clues – my new cross, the chalices at Valence Marie and the gold cake-plate at

Denny Abbey – together. Neither Harling nor Langelee told us about that – we worked it out on our own.'

'I suppose so,' said Bartholomew. 'It all happened so quickly, though. We had too little time to discuss it. We should have spent less time charging around and more time thinking.'

Michael gave him a playful poke with his foot. 'Enjoy your victory, and do not dwell on what might have been,' he preached. 'As far as King and Bishop are concerned, it is another job well done on our part.' He looked distastefully to where Langelee still entertained the Fellows with his tale of daring and danger, the exploits becoming increasingly outrageous as the level of wine in his goblet fell, and sniffed. 'It is a pity Langelee was not implicated in all this. I still do not like him.'

'He is going to ask the Archbishop to release him from his service so that he can stay here to teach philosophy,' said Bartholomew. 'He finds a scholar's life exciting compared to that of a mere agent. Perhaps we should exchange posts. I have had enough of spies and intrigue.'

'You always say that,' said Michael.

As they had been speaking, the volume of the students' singing had been gradually rising, and Bartholomew saw that Alcote and Father William would not countenance their vulgarity much longer. He left his fireside stool and went to warn them to keep the noise down. Gray stood on the high table with a rug shoved up his tabard and a piece of rolled up parchment in his hand, leading his friends in a grotesque parody of Michael conducting his choir. Bartholomew hid his amusement and watched Gray jump from the table somewhat sheepishly.

'He looks just like Brother Michael, do you not think?' piped Deynman, brightly. The other students groaned and Gray gave him a withering look. Bartholomew raised his eyes heavenward and went back to the conclave, closing the door behind him.

'Langelee has just offered us a repeat performance of his adventures in the Fens,' said Michael with a grin, watching the burly philosopher taking a break from his labours as he crammed one of Agatha's cakes into his mouth.

'What, again?' asked Bartholomew without enthusiasm. 'He has only just finished enthralling us the first time.'

'He is not a man for false modesty, apparently,' said Michael. 'And so he will relate once more the tale of how he single-handedly saved the kingdom, starting as soon as Cynric has replenished the wine in his audience's goblets.'

'That is rash of him,' remarked Bartholomew. 'There will be discrepancies between the story he just told, and the one he will tell again. He will never recall all the lies he has already spoken. Father William will be on him in an instant, and will expose him as a fraud.'

'I thought as much when I persuaded him to accede to the Master's request for the tale to be repeated,' said Michael smugly, stretching his hands to the fire.

Bartholomew laughed. 'Dame Pelagia would approve of that.'

'No,' said Michael, musing for a moment. 'She would consider it too unsubtle.'

Bartholomew laughed again, and looked back to where Langelee was raising a wine bottle to his lips – a bottle of smoked glass, just like the ones that had killed Armel, Grene, Will Harper and Katherine Mortimer, and had dragged Bartholomew and Michael into investigating the poisoned wine with such dire consequences.

Bartholomew's stomach began to churn as he realised, with absolute certainty, that Harling had been a good deal more clever than they had supposed. Michael was wrong: the horrible events of the past few days were not over! Harling had not been fooled for an instant by Langelee's duplicity and had not been surprised in the least that he had been followed into the Fens – he had known Langelee would not kill Bartholomew and Michael! He had told Langelee to return to Michaelhouse to await payment. Part of the payment must have been a bottle of wine – in a smoked glass bottle – the last of the six that Sacks had stolen! Harling had lied, and it had not been smashed in the fight with Sacks at all. It was his insurance that Langelee would die, even if he escaped the final confrontation in the Fens.

The students' singing in the hall raised to a crescendo once more, drowning out Bartholomew's warning shout. Langelee paused to listen to something Kenyngham was saying, and then brought the bottle to his mouth again to remove the cork with his teeth. The cork! Suddenly, the whole issue of the poison became horrifyingly clear. Grene and Armel had died instantly, yet Philius had merely become ill. The poison was not in the wine – it was soaked into the stopper! While Philius had ingested some of the poison washed from the neck of the bottle as it had been poured, Armel and Grene had either drawn the stopper from the bottle with their teeth, or had put their lips to the neck of the bottle to drink.

Just as Langelee was about to do.

'No!' he yelled, leaping to his feet.

Langelee paused again, but it was nothing to do with Bartholomew. He was paying attention to Kenyngham, and the physician's voice was drowned out by the students laughing and cheering in the room next door. Michael watched curiously as Bartholomew tried to push past Father Paul to reach Langelee. The blind friar Paul stumbled, and grabbed at Bartholomew to steady himself. The bottle was inches away from Langelee's mouth, and Bartholomew could not extricate himself from Paul's grip.

As he struggled to push Paul away, he felt something hard in his shirt pocket. Tulyet's lemon! He drew it out and hurled it with all his might, aiming to strike the bottle from Langelee's hand.

The throw went appallingly wide and smashed through one of Michaelhouse's newly installed, and much admired windows. The other Fellows leapt to their feet in shock, while Langelee dropped the bottle as he ducked away from the missile that sailed past his head. He gazed at Bartholomew in bewilderment, his mouth hanging open. Master Kenyngham turned to Bartholomew in horror.

'Matthew!' he cried. 'Our lovely glass!'

'Well done, Matt,' muttered Michael, sardonically, from his chair near the fire. 'Our one chance to rid ourselves of the appalling Langelee, and you go and save his life!'

The following day Bartholomew threw himself into his teaching to take his mind off the events of the previous week. He and Michael had successfully resolved the deaths of Armel, Grene, Philius and Isaac; removed any suspicion that the town was trying to kill the University's scholars with poisoned wine; Harling was dead and his accomplices either killed or in Tulyet's care; Rob Thorpe was under lock and key; and the merchant smugglers were suitably subdued. Yet Bartholomew felt anything but satisfaction. He fretted over Edith's grief over Rob Thorpe, and was disturbed that a man like Harling, who had given the University his loyalty and energies for so many years, should suddenly turn on it with such bitterness.

When the bell rang to bring an end to the day's lectures, Bartholomew felt drained, and trailed apathetically after his students to the hall for dinner. Kenyngham was spending the day with Chancellor Tynkell and Langelee at St Mary's Church, writing the official report about Harling that would be sent to the King, and Father William was due to preside over the midday meal. Bartholomew's spirits sank at the prospect of food eaten in silence, and long graces, during which each of the Franciscans would take it in turns to say more than a few words. When he saw the friars carrying various books and scrolls with them from which to read, his appetite began to wane, and he decided to risk their displeasure and miss the meal altogether.

He skulked in his room until all the scholars were in the hall, and then began to walk across the yard to the gate, intending to buy one of Mortimer's pies and take it to eat in the deserted water meadows behind Peterhouse. He was startled to hear his name hissed urgently from Michael's room on the floor above. He looked up, and saw Michael leaning out of his window, beckoning frantically to him.

He climbed the wooden stairs to the room that Michael shared with three Benedictine undergraduates, and pushed open the door.

Michael sat on his bed with a small strongbox open on his knees. 'Is anyone about?'

Bartholomew shook his head. 'They are all in the hall. What are you doing?'

'I had to pack up Eligius's possessions this morning,' said Michael. 'They need to be returned to the Dominicans at Blackfriars in London. While I was in his room I came across this box. No one knows I have it, but I need a witness to what I have found.'

'No!' said Bartholomew vehemently, beginning to back away. 'I have had enough of University politics! Choose someone else as your witness.'

'Matt!' exclaimed Michael in exasperation. 'Look!' He held up a handful of small scraps of parchment, each bearing a few words of writing. Bartholomew regarded them blankly. 'The voting slips from the chancellorial election,' Michael explained. 'And almost every one of them bearing Harling's name. Here is yours.'

Curious, despite his reservations, Bartholomew stepped forward and saw that Michael was right. In the box on the monk's lap were dozens of the small scraps of parchment that had been used by the University Fellows to vote for their favoured candidate as Chancellor. Bartholomew leaned down and took a handful of them, leafing through them quickly. He exchanged a glance of puzzlement with

Michael, and then inspected the piece that bore his name and Harling's.

'So?' he asked, nonplussed. 'You said Eligius and Kenyngham counted the votes. Why should they not be in Eligius's room?'

'Because the ballot slips from chancellorial elections are stored in the University chest in St Mary's Church tower,' said Michael. 'When you expressed doubts last week about the validity of the election, I went to look at them. Or I thought I did. I confess I was surprised when mine showed I had voted for Tynkell, when I distinctly remember writing Harling's name. It crossed my mind that you might have changed it, since you took my vote to St Mary's Church because I was ill. But of all the people I know, you are the last one to do something so dishonest. And you have always said you preferred Harling to Tynkell.'

Bartholomew let the parchments fall from his fingers. 'Eligius and Kenyngham falsified the election?' he asked, stunned. He looked at the slips scattered on the floor. 'You are saying that these are the originals, and that there is a second set – a forged set – in the chest at St Mary's Church?'

Michael nodded. 'That is exactly what I am saying. And this subterfuge was no spontaneous act, either – writing out a new set of election slips must have taken considerable foreplanning. You remember I had a fever on the day of the election that you said was caused by overeating? The reason I had overeaten was because I had been sent three large apple pies the day before. By Father Eligius.'

'You think Eligius doctored them somehow to make you ill?'

Michael nodded. 'With hindsight, yes, I think he did. Not with something very terrible, but with some potion to put me out of action for the day.'

'I wondered why you were prepared to continue to consider him a suspect when all the evidence pointed to Bingham,' said Bartholomew. 'But why would Eligius want to cheat on the election results? And what of Master Kenyngham? Surely he would suspect something was wrong?'

'Not necessarily,' said Michael. 'Usually, one person reads out the names, while the other keeps a tally. Eligius must have done the reading, while Kenyngham did the adding. If Kenyngham had expressed surprise at any of the votes, Eligius could simply have shown him the slip he himself had written out prior to the election. Kenyngham is far too much a man of integrity ever to have asked anyone why he voted in a certain way. He would have been the perfect partner for Eligius's cheating.'

'But why?' asked Bartholomew again. 'Did Eligius admire Tynkell so much?'

'I imagine it was more a case that he disapproved of Harling,' said Michael. 'Harling was among those of us who exposed that business of the false relic at Valence Marie. Eligius believed that relic to be genuine right up to his death.' He held up a scroll. 'Here is Eligius's diary. He bemoans the wrong done to his College by the discrediting of the relic only the day before he died. He even mentions that he proposed to discuss the possibility of its reinstatement with the Countess when she visited the following day. And here, in an entry made last autumn – just before the election that Harling lost – he records a discussion with Tynkell, in which Tynkell agreed to allow Valence Marie to display the relic if he were elected Chancellor. Essentially, Eligius arranged to have Tynkell elected so that the relic would be returned to Valence Marie.'

Bartholomew sat on one of the beds in the cramped room and rubbed his eyes. 'This is terrible, Brother! It means that just for the sake of those wretched bones – that we proved beyond a shadow of a doubt did not belong to a martyr – Harling was cheated out of a position that was rightfully his, and was led to all this murder and crime.'

Michael nodded. 'Poor Harling thought he did not have

the support of the scholars. The reality is that he had a vast majority of votes. People liked him, and knew he would make us a good Chancellor.'

Bartholomew sighed. 'So what shall we do now? Harling is dead; we can hardly reinstate him.'

'There is nothing we can do,' said Michael. 'Can you imagine what kind of scandal would ensue if it were known that our Chancellor of the past several months was fraudulently appointed? All the writs and charters issued by him would be rendered invalid, and the University would lose a fortune in property. And the students whose degrees were conferred by the Chancellor would have them deemed null and void. Chaos would ensue. All we can do is hope that either Tynkell makes a good Chancellor, or that he is so disastrous we can easily rid ourselves of him.'

'But he obtained his office by cheating,' said Bartholomew. 'We cannot allow him to retain it.'

'There is nothing to suggest that anyone other than Eligius knew of the deception,' said Michael. 'I feel certain that Tynkell is unaware of it. When it was declared that he had won, I am told he looked more startled than anyone else in the church. He had agreed to stand only because it was necessary for there to be two candidates for an election. He had no real hopes for success and all he really wanted was the name of his poor hostel to become better known among the University community.'

Bartholomew recalled Tynkell's reaction as Kenyngham announced the result of the election, and was certain Michael was right. Tynkell's face had registered a strange combination of horror and shock when he had been pronounced the winner. It was an expression that had been mirrored in the faces of many other scholars in the church, including Harling's. 'So are you suggesting that we should forget all this?'

Michael nodded and closed the lid on the box, securing it with a large lock. 'Only you and I know, so I think it best that we keep the knowledge to ourselves. Unless it serves our purpose to reveal it at some point in the future,' he said with a conspiratorial grin.

'Your grandmother is quite a lady,' said Matilde to Michael, as he sat in her house with Bartholomew that evening drinking spiced wine.

'I know,' said Michael with pride. 'Her aim was as true and strong as it was when she won a knife-throwing contest at the Tower of London – against some of the finest knights in the country – when she was only seventeen.'

Bartholomew suppressed a shudder, and decided he would not want to make an enemy of a nun like Dame Pelagia.

'Are you certain Harling is dead, Matthew?' asked Matilde. 'I would not like to think of him returning to wreak revenge on us all.'

'I am certain,' said Bartholomew. 'The blade pierced his heart. And, anyway, I saw him buried today in St Michael's churchyard. Of course, if he is the Devil Langelee claims him to be, that will not be much of an obstacle to him.'

Matilde and Michael gazed at him in horror.

'Matthew!' breathed Matilde fearfully, glancing towards the door as though she imagined Harling might crash through it at any moment. 'Do you think he will come back?'

'No!' said Bartholomew, astonished that they should take him seriously. 'Of course not. It was a joke.'

'Not a very funny one,' said Michael disapprovingly. 'I have known many stranger things to happen in this town than dead men rising from their graves, and so have you.' He shuddered, and sketched a blessing in the air, as if to ward off Harling's evil spirit.

'So all is well again?' asked Matilde uncertainly, sipping her wine as her eyes went once more to the door.

Michael pursed his lips. 'I would not go as far as that –

we still have Langelee in our midst.' He gave Bartholomew an unpleasant look. 'Thanks to you.'

Bartholomew grimaced and wondered how long Michael would remind him of the fact. They sat in silence for a while, watching the flames creep slowly over a damp log.

'Let us go back to when you snatched Langelee from the jaws of death,' said Michael to Bartholomew eventually. 'There is something I do not understand. How did you work out it was the stopper, and not the wine, that was poisoned?'

'The Gonville cat,' said Bartholomew. 'It smashed the bottle and drank the wine with no ill effects, yet the rat died. That detail had been bothering me for some time. When I saw Langelee tip the bottle to draw the stopper with his teeth, I realised that I had made the assumption that both cat and rat had drunk the wine. They had not. The rat had gnawed at the cork stopper. Mortimer had been about to pull the stopper from the bottle with his teeth, too, and Armel, the apprentice down the well, and Grene did the same – or drank from the bottle itself. That was why Philius did not die: he drank wine that had been poured and diluted with other ingredients for the weekly purge that Isaac made for him.'

'It was lucky you happened to have a lemon in your pocket,' remarked Michael. 'A fig or a handful of currants would not have worked nearly as well.'

'But a handful of currants would not have smashed Master Kenyngham's beloved window,' said Bartholomew ruefully. 'And I would not have to pay for its repair.'

'True,' said Michael archly. 'So next time perhaps you will be a little more selective before you attempt to save someone's life so selflessly. Langelee is a lout. Harling did right to leave him a gift of his wine. But I still cannot believe Langelee was so stupid, or so greedy, as to have attempted to drink it after all that had gone on.'

'Did Langelee not offer to pay for the window?' asked

Matilde, surprised. 'It would have been the least he could do.'

'He did not,' said Bartholomew. 'He will not even agree to re-examine Bulbeck on account of his being ill when he took his disputation.'

Michael's eyes gleamed with humour. 'Just before we left to come here, he asked me if I would persuade you to let him borrow your copy of Aristotle's *De Caelo* for his debate.'

'I hope you told him to go and buy his own,' said Matilde indignantly.

'I said its hire for a week would cost him the price of a window,' said Michael, leaning forward to refill his cup with spiced wine. 'He said he would seek another copy.'

Bartholomew sighed. 'What a nasty business! And what has been gained from it? The town is in disgrace for smuggling; Edward Mortimer and Rob Thorpe are awaiting trial; I have lost my cloak and gloves; and we are stuck with Langelee – unless Julianna can come up with a plan to spirit him away. Perhaps I should have a word with her and see what we can devise.'

Matilde stood and presented him with a neatly wrapped package. 'Edith gave me some cloth to sew this for you.'

Bartholomew looked at the warm, dark cloak with surprised pleasure, but then tried to pass it back.

'I cannot take such a fine thing from you,' he said reluctantly.

Her face fell. 'Why not? Can you not accept a gift from a friend?'

'That is not what I meant,' said Bartholomew quickly when he saw he had offended her. 'I am not good at looking after clothes – you heard what happened to the cloak Paul lent me. I would be afraid to wear it lest I damaged it.'

She smiled. 'If you tear it, you will just have to come to me to have it mended. And at least it is long enough to hide that dreadful red patch on your leggings.'

Later, as they walked down the High Street on their

way back to Michaelhouse, Michael poked Bartholomew in the ribs.

'She likes you,' he said.

'She likes you, too,' replied Bartholomew.

Michael shook his head impatiently. 'You know what I mean.'

'Michael, she is a prostitute,' said Bartholomew quietly. 'There could be no future in such a relationship. An occasional indiscretion might be overlooked, but a long-standing affair with one will do more than raise a few scholarly eyebrows.'

'Where is your evidence of her harlotry recently?' asked Michael. 'She is said to be particular in her customers, but I have discovered no one who has secured her favours for a long time now. Edith believes Matilde allows the rumours to persist because she finds them amusing, but that there is no truth in them any longer.'

'But what about all the other prostitutes she mingles with?' asked Bartholomew. 'How would she know them if she were not in the same business?'

'I imagine they come to her for advice,' said Michael. 'They trust her: she is a sensible woman. My grandmother has a great respect for her. You might do a lot worse, Matt.'

Bartholomew stopped and looked back up the road to Matilde's small house. On the upper floor, lamplight gleamed yellow through the shutters before it was doused. He turned away and walked back to Michaelhouse.

epilogue

AS THE DAYS PASSED, THE MEMORIES OF THE UN-
pleasant events with Harling and his smuggling
empire began to fade in Bartholomew's mind.
He immersed himself in his teaching, determined that his
students would pass their next disputations – even Deynman,
if that were humanly possible. He taught each morning,
visited his patients in the afternoons, while evenings were
taken up with writing his treatise on fevers by the light of
some cheap candles John Runham sold him – probably the
remnants of his brush with the smuggling trade.

The mild weather ended abruptly and winter staked its
claim with a vengeance. The river froze, and children made
skates from sheep leg-bones to skid across a surface that was
pitted and uneven from the rubbish that had been trapped
in the ice. And then the snow came – tearing blizzards that
turned the countryside from brown to white in the course of
a day, and buried whole houses beneath drifts so deep that
they were like rolling white hills. The country was paying
dearly for the mild start to the year.

One afternoon, as the light was beginning to fade and
cosy glows could be seen through the gaps in the window
shutters of the houses in the High Street, Bartholomew
finished setting the broken arm of an old man – who had
been sufficiently drunk to believe he could still skate like
a child across the King's Ditch – and made his way back
towards the College. The smells of stews and baking bread

followed him as he walked, because the frigid temperatures suppressed the stench of sewage and rotting rubbish that usually pervaded the town.

The first flurry of snow, heralding yet another storm, tickled his face, and he drew his cloak more tightly around him, grateful to Edith and Matilde for their thoughtfulness. The wind stung his ears and blew his hood back, making his eyes water. He hurried down St Michael's Lane, into Foul Lane and ducked through the wicket-gate into Michaelhouse. As he strode across the yard to his room, he was intercepted by Cynric, who gave him a message that Thomas Deschalers was ill and needed to see him immediately.

Since Philius's death Bartholomew had received a number of calls from the wealthy merchants who had been under the care of the Franciscan physician. He anticipated, with some relief, that they would not retain his services for long when they realised he had no time for malingerers and refused to leech his patients on demand or indulge them in time-consuming astrological consultations.

By the time he arrived at Deschaler's house, it was snowing in earnest, great penny-sized flakes that drifted into his eyes and mouth as he walked, and that promised to settle and cover once again the filthy slush that lay thick across the town's streets. Shivering, he knocked on the door, and waited a long time before it was opened the merest crack.

'There you are!' said Julianna, opening the door a little further. 'I sent for you ages ago. Where have you been? I might have died waiting for you!'

'I have other patients to attend,' said Bartholomew shortly. 'And you do not appear to be at death's door to me.'

'How would you know that?' she demanded. 'You have not consulted my stars. Anyway, do not keep me out here in the cold with your idle chatter. Come in before you let all the heat escape.'

She gave him a predatory grin and stood back so that he could enter the house. He hesitated, backing away from her.

'Oh, Doctor Bartholomew!' she said, the grin fading as she gave an impatient stamp of her foot. 'Do not start all this side-stepping and dancing around again. Come inside, man! I do not bite.'

Unconvinced, Bartholomew stepped across the threshold and stood uncertainly in the hallway. His reticence to be there with her increased a hundredfold when he saw her look furtively up and down the street before closing the door.

'Is Master Deschalers ill?' he asked nervously. 'Because if not, I am very busy . . .'

'We are all busy,' retorted Julianna. 'No one is ill, but I have something to ask of you. You heard what my uncle said: that you owe me a favour for saving your life. And do not try to claim otherwise because my uncle tells me that this Egil of yours was deeply involved with Vice-Chancellor Harling, and that he was trailing you across the Fens in order to kill us all.'

'What do you want from me?' he asked suspiciously. 'Have you had enough of life in the town, and want me to spirit you back to Denny Abbey in the dead of night?'

Julianna laughed. 'Oh no! Life here is infinitely preferable to the drudgery at Denny. Since I have returned I have seen bodies dredged from wells, had soldiers searching our house for stolen goods, and witnessed a dramatic fight on the river bank between Tulyet and some outlaws.'

'And what were you doing out at that time of night?' asked Bartholomew. 'Looking for someone to kill with a heavy stone?'

Julianna's eyes narrowed. 'That is none of your business,' she said coldly. 'But we are wasting time. My uncle will be back soon, and he will think you are attempting to seduce me if he finds us here alone.'

'Then I am leaving right now,' said Bartholomew with determination, starting to push past her towards the door.

Julianna stopped him. 'I want you to take a message to Ralph de Langelee,' she said.

Bartholomew regarded her doubtfully. 'Is that all? Then you will consider your favour repaid and will leave me alone?'

She nodded.

Bartholomew shrugged. 'Give it to me, then. I will put it under his door as soon as I get back.'

Julianna sighed heavily. 'I cannot entrust what I have to say to parchment. And, anyway, I do not write. You must memorise the message and repeat it to him.'

Bartholomew shrugged again, noting that there was a very distinct difference between 'cannot write' and 'do not write'. 'Very well. What is it?'

Julianna regarded him appraisingly for a moment. 'You must promise not to tell.'

Bartholomew strongly suspected he was about to be drawn into something of which he would disapprove, or, worse still, which might lead him into trouble.

'I hope this is nothing illegal . . .'

Julianna dismissed his objections with a wave of her hand. 'Do not be ridiculous! What do you think I am?' Bartholomew refrained from answering and Julianna continued. 'You must tell Ralph to be prepared to admit me to his chambers at midnight tonight. He should have a priest at the ready and we will exchange our marriage vows in St Michael's Church.'

Bartholomew regarded her dubiously and wondered, not for the first time, whether she was totally in control of her faculties. 'How do you plan to get past the porter?'

She gave a snort of disdain. 'Your porter sleeps all night. That will be no problem.'

'Not since he was attacked,' said Bartholomew. 'Although I am sure his vigilance will not last for much longer.'

'Damn!' said Julianna, chewing her lip. She brightened suddenly. 'No matter. I will meet Ralph at the church instead. That will be better anyway – it is not so far to walk.'

'And where is Langelee supposed to find a priest who will marry you in a dark church in the depths of the night?'

Julianna shrugged. 'Ralph says Michaelhouse is full of priests.'

'Not ones who will agree to perform that sort of ceremony,' said Bartholomew. 'And what do you plan to do afterwards? Go back to his chamber and ask his room-mate John Runham to turn a blind eye while you consummate your union?'

'Ralph is to have horses ready and we will flee into the night.' She twirled around happily, her eyes glittering with excitement.

'Flee where?' persisted Bartholomew. 'And what of Langelee's position as Master of Philosophy? Is he to abandon it?'

Julianna gave another impatient sigh. 'Of course he is. But that is none of your affair. You owe me a favour and I charge you to deliver this message to him.'

Bartholomew raised his hands. 'All right, I will tell him of your plan. But have you considered that he might prefer a more conventional form of courtship? I see no reason why your uncle should refuse him permission to marry you now that your betrothal to Edward Mortimer is dissolved.'

Julianna pouted. 'Uncle does not like Ralph.' Bartholomew could see why. 'He would not accept him willingly into our family. And, anyway, I am with child.'

'Langelee's child?' asked Bartholomew tactlessly.

Julianna gave him a nasty look. 'Of course,' she said sharply. 'And I will not be able to conceal it much longer. Look.'

Bartholomew glanced down to where she pulled her loose dress tight around her middle, and saw that she was right. It was fortunate that the novice's habits at Denny had been loose-fitting, or her aunt might have noticed some weeks before. No wonder Julianna was prepared to go to such desperate lengths to leave Denny and to return to the arms of her paramour. He rubbed a hand through his hair and shrugged yet again.

'I will pass your message to Langelee, but will return to inform you if he cannot make it at such short notice.' He could not imagine that Langelee would agree to a midnight flight with Julianna, and did not like to think of her wandering the streets after dark alone – although, he reminded himself, she was more than able to look after herself if there were large stones to hand.

Julianna opened the door and ushered him out into the snow. She stood on the front step, her hands on her hips, and winked at him in a conspiratorial way that made several passers-by nudge each other and point at him. He wondered how she had succeeded in avoiding learning even a modicum of the decorous behaviour usually expected in the female relatives of wealthy merchants. He walked back to Michaelhouse in low spirits, and knocked at the door of the comfortable chamber Langelee shared with the smug Runham.

The philosopher was sitting at a table, scowling in concentration over Aristotle's *De Caelo* in preparation for his forthcoming public debate. He had one of the largest lamps Bartholomew had ever seen, and the brightness that filled the room was eye-watering.

'What do you want?' he growled when Bartholomew put his head round the door. 'I am busy.'

Bartholomew repeated Julianna's message and watched Langelee's eyes grow wide in his red face. When Bartholomew had finished, declining to mention Julianna's advanced pregnancy, Langelee expelled his breath in a whistle and sat down on his bed.

'She certainly knows her mind,' he said admiringly. 'Do you think Brother Michael will do the honours?'

'You mean to go through with this?' asked Bartholomew, astounded.

Langelee looked surprised. 'Well, of course I do! Deschalers will never permit me to marry her otherwise. He thinks I want his money. I would not mind it, actually, and perhaps he will change his mind when presented with a *fait-accompli*.'

'Perhaps he will disown the both of you,' said Bartholomew. 'Perhaps he will claim you took Julianna by force and apply to have the marriage annulled.'

'He will do nothing so petty!' said Langelee confidently. 'Now, let me think. I must arrange for horses. Meanwhile, you ask Brother Michael whether he will marry us. He is more likely to agree if you put it to him.'

He bustled out of the room leaving Bartholomew to follow. Speechless, the physician walked into the courtyard, staring at Langelee's broad back as he strode purposefully across the yard, humming to himself. And then he started to laugh. Michael, emerging from the kitchen after devouring a large plate of honey cakes – originally intended for Alcote who had paid for the ingredients – saw him, and picked his way mincingly across the slippery snow.

'What were you doing in Langelee's room? And what is so funny?'

Bartholomew told him, and Michael narrowed his eyes in thought. Bartholomew's jaw dropped in horror, feeling the humour of the situation evaporating like the Fen mist in the sun.

'Do not tell me you are going to oblige! This is madness, Brother. Deschalers would never let the matter rest: Julianna is all he has in the way of an heir for his business, and he will not let her go to someone he does not approve of.'

'This was not your idea?' asked Michael, surprised. 'You suggested to Matilde that you would see if you could persuade Julianna to spirit Langelee away so that we could be rid of him. I simply assumed all this was your doing.'

'It most certainly was not my idea. I want nothing to do with it.'

'But it might be an excellent opportunity for us to lose Langelee. He can hardly remain a Fellow of Michaelhouse if he has eloped with a merchant's niece. Fellows are not permitted to marry.'

'But how can you consider implicating yourself in all this?' protested Bartholomew. 'You are always stressing how important it is to maintain good relations with the merchants. Deschalers will be outraged if you marry Julianna to that brute of a man.'

'We must weigh up the pros and cons,' said Michael smoothly. 'And being free of Langelee is a pro not to be lightly dismissed.' He thought for a moment. 'I think I will accede to their request. I can always claim later I did not know the arrangement was anything but legitimate.'

'In the middle of the night? In a dark church?'

Michael rubbed his chin. 'You have a point. But my grandmother tells me Julianna is pregnant, so I can always claim I thought the secrecy was because of that. Speaking of which, I must tell her about this. It will amuse her no end!'

He strolled away, whistling, leaving Bartholomew speechless for a second time. He determined to put the whole unsavoury business from his mind and went to bed early that night so that Michael might not be tempted to ask him to help. He was overtired, and thoughts of his sister and her continuing distress over Rob Thorpe tumbled through his mind in an uncontrolled fashion. His room was freezing and flakes of snow found their way through the cracks in the window shutters to form damp little piles on the table: he did not know whether to be grateful or irritated that his teeming, unpleasant dreams were so often interrupted because he woke from the cold. When Michael shook his shoulder to wake him for mass early the following morning, he felt exhausted.

Swearing under his breath, he hopped from bare foot to

bare foot across the flagstone floor to the water in the jug Cynric left each night, while Michael waited for him, eating some nuts given by a patient in lieu of payment.

'It has frozen solid again,' said Bartholomew tiredly, shaking the solid mass in the jug to see if he could hear water slopping about underneath. There was nothing. 'I will have to fetch some from the kitchen.'

'You washed yesterday,' said Michael impatiently. 'Is there no end to this cleanliness nonsense? Just get dressed and let us be off before we are late for the third time this week.'

'Did you marry Langelee and Julianna last night?' asked Bartholomew, fumbling around in the dark for his shirt.

'Not so loud, Matt! You will wake the others,' warned Michael. 'Just because we have to be at the church early does not mean that the entire College needs to be up with us.'

Bartholomew hauled the cold, damp garment over his head. 'Sorry. But what of this nocturnal wedding? What happened?'

'We will speak of the matter after mass,' said Michael. 'I will meet you by the gate. Hurry or you can pay my fine for being late as well as your own.'

Bartholomew finished dressing and, hauling his tabard over his head, ran across the snowy yard to where Michael had pulled the bar from the wicket gate. There was no sign of Walter, but the weather was foul – sleet being driven almost horizontally by a bitter wind – and Bartholomew imagined very little would extract him from his cosy room to open the gate for scholars off to early morning mass.

'It is dark this morning,' mumbled Bartholomew, glancing up at a black sky laden with heavy clouds. He shivered as icy flakes flew into his face. 'And cold.'

Michael was walking up the lane towards the High Street with uncharacteristic speed, but Bartholomew was grateful because it stirred the blood in his veins and he felt some warmth begin to creep through his body. He followed Michael through the knee-deep drifts of snow in St Michael's graveyard to the porch. Someone already waited there and Bartholomew froze in his tracks.

'Julianna!'

She came towards him, surprised. 'I did not expect you to be here,' she said. 'I thought you were against my marriage to Ralph.'

Bartholomew spun round to Michael, realising exactly why the night seemed to black and why he felt so tired. It was not nearing dawn at all: it was midnight!

Michael raised his hands in a gesture of innocence. 'I did not lie to you. I only said we would speak of the matter after mass. Which we will do I am sure. If the marriage is to be legal, I need a witness and you are the only one I can trust to do it discreetly.'

'You trust me?' said Bartholomew harshly. 'When I cannot trust you?'

Michael laughed softly in the darkness. 'You can trust me for important things, and that is what matters. This is a trifling business.'

'Not to me,' proclaimed Julianna huffily.

'Nor to me,' growled Langelee from behind them.

Bartholomew heaved a huge sigh of resignation and followed them into the church. He struggled to light the temperamental lamp while the others waited impatiently.

'Hurry it up, Bartholomew,' ordered Langelee imperiously. 'We do not have all night.'

Bartholomew was about to suggest that Langelee should light the lamp himself – knowing that the philosopher's thick, clumsy fingers would never be able to perform the intricate operation required – when it coughed into life. Langelee snatched it from his hand and led the way inside. Michael had apparently made some preparations the night before, because the Bible was opened to the relevant page and the altar was draped with a white cloth. Something glittery to one side caught his eye. It was Wilson's black marble tomb, now topped with a grotesque effigy of a man in a scholar's gown, partly faced in gold.

'That monstrosity will have to go,' muttered Michael, seeing Bartholomew staring at it with loathing. 'It would be bad enough if it were all one colour, but now the smuggling is over Runham cannot lay his hands on sufficient gold leaf to finish covering the thing. We have Wilson with a golden stomach and a face of cheap limestone.'

'At least it does not look like him,' said Bartholomew, helping Michael to lay out the regalia for the mass. 'I suppose we should be grateful for small mercies.'

While Michael ripped through the Latin wedding ceremony at an impressive rate, Bartholomew sat at the base of one of the pillars and watched moodily. He wondered what the offspring of such an alliance would be like and hoped they did not move back to Cambridge so he would find out. There was a sudden draught of wind and the lamp fluttered dangerously. Michael looked up from his reading and Bartholomew went to close the door that the fierce wind had blown open.

He heaved it closed, his feet skidding on the wet tiles as he fought against the blizzard, and went back to his place at the base of the pillar. Moments later, the same thing happened again. Michael scowled at the interruption.

'The latch must be faulty, Matt. Shut it properly. If the lamp goes out I will have to pronounce them man and wife in the dark and I do not want to end up kissing Langelee instead of the bride.'

'I thought the groom was supposed to kiss the bride,' said Langelee. 'Not the priest.'

'And who is the expert on religious matters here, you or me?' demanded Michael. 'Go and check the door, Matt, or we will all freeze to death before I kiss anyone!'

Bartholomew hauled himself to his feet a second time and went to the door. And stopped abruptly when he saw

Master Kenyngham struggling to close it. He closed his eyes, disgusted at himself for forgetting that it was the feast day of St Gilbert of Sempringham and that Kenyngham, a Gilbertine friar, would certainly keep a midnight vigil in the church in honour of the occasion.

Kenyngham turned to put his back to the door to force it closed, and smiled happily when he saw Bartholomew standing in the shadows.

'Matthew!' he exclaimed in genuine pleasure. 'What a lovely surprise! I assume you are here to keep me company while I say matins for the feast of St Gilbert of Sempringham?'

'Not exactly,' said Bartholomew, moving forward to help latch the door.

'Who is there?' called Michael. Bartholomew heard the slap of his sandals as he huffed his way up the nave to find out what was happening.

'Brother Michael!' cried Kenyngham in delight, taking his weight from the door so that it blew open again. Bartholomew caught it as it flew backwards, and leaned into it, making the others jump when the wind dropped and it slammed with a crash that sent echoes reverberating around the dark church. 'And Master Langelee, too! All here to pray with me and celebrate the feast day of Gilbert of Sempringham, the saintly founder of my Order! And you have brought a friend, I see.'

He reached forward and placed a hand on Julianna's head in blessing, muttering a prayer as he did so. Bartholomew and Michael exchanged a glance of bemusement, not at all certain what would happen next.

'I am to be married,' announced Julianna proudly. 'And then I am going to live in France, where the sun shines all the time.'

'Do not go to Paris, then,' said Bartholomew.

'France?' asked Langelee doubtfully. 'You have not mentioned France before.'

'Congratulations, my child,' said Kenyngham, still smiling beatifically. 'I shall pray for you. Who is to be the lucky man?'

Only an innocent like Kenyngham could have failed to notice the way Langelee's arm was wrapped indecorously around Julianna's waist and the way in which the lovers looked at each other. Bartholomew and Michael exchanged yet another mystified look.

'Ralph de Langelee,' said Julianna loudly, as though she were talking to someone either very old or very deaf. 'I am to marry Ralph de Langelee, Master Kenyngham.'

Kenyngham's smile faded slightly. 'Ralph de Langelee? But he is a Fellow of Michaelhouse; you cannot marry him!'

'Why not?' demanded Julianna indignantly. 'He is a man, is he not?'

'Not all men are available for marriage,' said Kenyngham gently. 'And if Ralph de Langelee married you, he would have to resign his Fellowship and he would lose the opportunity to make a name for himself by teaching philosophy – and perhaps even to be the Master of the College himself one day.'

'God forbid!' muttered Michael under his breath. 'And the name he would make for himself by teaching philosophy would not be one I would repeat in a church!'

'Why should I resign?' asked Langelee, startled. 'Why can I not marry Julianna and keep my Fellowship as well?'

'It is against the rules,' said Kenyngham. 'No Fellows are allowed to marry. But the choice is yours: marry and have a happy and fulfilled life with children and a wife who loves you, or stay at Michaelhouse and take part in the shaping of young minds or perhaps tread in the footsteps of others before you and become an emissary to the King or the Pope.'

'Really?' asked Langelee, intrigued. 'Scholars from Michaelhouse have become emissaries to popes and kings?'

'Not very many,' said Michael quickly. 'And the opportunities are few and far between, and very competitive.'

'We would have such fun,' whispered Julianna, leaning against him seductively. 'We could set up business together and become rich beyond our wildest dreams.'

Langelee was silent, thinking. All Bartholomew could hear in the dark church was the splattering of sleet against the window shutters and the sound of Langelee's heavy breathing as he pondered his dilemma.

'Well,' said the philosopher eventually. 'Now, let me see . . .'

bISTORICAL NOTE

BEFORE THE DRAINAGE OF PARTS OF EAST ANGLIA IN the seventeenth century, the Fens were an area of wilderness, a myriad of channels, ditches and lakes winding round innumerable small islands that were heavily wooded with tangles of willow and alder. Routes through the marshes were treacherous, and most were known only to the Fenlanders who lived there. For boats, there were winding reed- and sedge-choked waterways, and for horses and pedestrians there were unstable causeways comprising paths that led from one islet to another. The Fens saw England's only serious rebellion against the Norman Conquest: Hereward the Wake used his knowledge of the area to lead William's troops a merry dance until a proper causeway was built between Cambridge and Ely.

Smuggling was not uncommon in medieval England, and there was a brisk trade between there and France in the fourteenth century, despite the fact that for most of Edward III's reign the two countries were officially at war. The Fens were almost impossible to police and were widely acknowledged as an area where contraband could be hidden and then transported to the surrounding towns and villages.

The Black Death evinced many social and economic changes. There was an increase in the popularity of shrines containing the relics of saints. It also influenced the course of the Hundred Years War, with hostilities virtually ceasing between France and England until they received a new lease of life when the Black Prince arrived in Languedoc in 1355, and spent two months happily slaughtering whoever he could catch (unless they were likely to be worth a ransom) and burning crops and villages. Skirmishing, however, continued in Brittany right through the 1350s, and there is some evidence that the King was well aware that his soldiers were ransacking religious houses, but was inclined to turn a blind eye. The chronicler Edward Walsingham recorded that, even in 1348, the country was flooded with French plunder, some of it from the religious houses of Brittany.

Michaelhouse was founded as a College at the University of Cambridge in 1324, and continued as such until it was merged with King's Hall, Physwick Hostel and several smaller institutions to form Trinity College in 1546. Thomas Kenyngham was Michaelhouse's Master in the early 1350s, and other members of the Fellowship at this time included John Runham and Ralph de Langelee.

The Hall of Valence Marie was founded in 1347 by Mary de Pol, the Countess of Pembroke. She called her new institution the Hall of Valence Marie, although it was called Pembroke Hall until the 1830s, when it became known as Pembroke College. The Countess of Pembroke was born in about 1304 and married the heroic Aymer de Valence, although she was a widow by the time she was twenty years old. Aymer's death left her immensely rich and she was able to found the College, as well as endow a community of Franciscan nuns – Poor Clares – at the little convent at Denny to the north of Cambridge. Robert de Thorpe and Thomas Bingham were its first two Masters.

Gonville Hall, otherwise known as the Hall of the Annunciation of the Blessed Virgin, was founded by Edmund Gonville by a licence from the Crown in 1348, and on 4 June 1349 John Colton of Terrington was appointed as its first Master. Another College, founded just three years later, was Corpus Christi, but it was unusual in that it was established by donations from two of the town's guilds – the Guild of St Mary and the Guild of Corpus Christi. Because of its proximity to St Bene't's Church, it was often called St Bene't's College.

Richard de Wetherset was Chancellor of the University from 1349 to 1351, Richard Harling took over in 1352 and William Tynkell held the office from 1352 to 1359. Although de Wetherset returned for another term of office in the 1360s, Richard Harling disappears from the records.

In the town, John Cheney, Constantine Mortimer and Thomas Deschalers were all merchants who were also burgesses in fourteenth-century Cambridge. The Deschalerses were a powerful family in East Anglia, although their fortunes had begun to wane by the 1350s. The Tulyets or Tuillets were also a powerful family. A Richard Tulyet was mayor from 1337 to 1340, and also in 1345 and 1346. He was also a bailiff, and was among a group of townsmen accused of instigating riots against the University in 1322.

Fragments of the Cambridge of the fourteenth century can still be seen. Some stone coursing in a building on the southern side of Trinity Great Court shows where one of Michaelhouse's buildings stood, while the name 'King's Hostel' and a lovely range of gothic arches to the north of the Great Court are remnants of King's Hall, along with the splendid gatehouse that was moved from its original location after Trinity College was founded. Meanwhile, nine miles to the north, the lovely, tranquil ruins of Denny Abbey are in the care of English Heritage and can be visited from April to September. The abbey has been subject to so many building phases that it is difficult to interpret, but the great pillars of the Clares' church and fragments of the Countess of Pembroke's sumptuous apartments can still be seen.

Finally, King Edward II was murdered in Berkeley Castle in 1327, and was succeeded by his fourteen-year-old son, Edward III. It was no secret that Queen Isabella was complicit in her husband's death, and when Edward III was old enough to dispense with her services as Regent in 1331, she retired from his court to Castle Rising in Norfolk. She spent the rest of her life enjoying the pleasures of the country – hawking, hunting and travelling around her estates – and giving generous gifts to a nearby community of Franciscan nuns. She died in 1358, having entered the Order of Poor Clares.